MADOC—The bastard prince who fled his cruel oppressors and led a mighty fleet to the shores of North America. There he would risk his life—and heart—in an unknown, savage wilderness. . . .

TUMKIS—The bewitching Natchez princess born to a tribe of strange and mystical pagans, she was both ·feared and desired by Madoc's men. Yet she alone had the power to save the brave Welshman she burned to love. . . .

SNORRISON—The powerful Norseman had sailed with Madoc to the New World to make a better life for his family. Until he found himself enchanted by a primitive, raven-haired beauty. . . .

YNGVILD—Snorrison's proud Icelandic wife, she would fight for her husband's love—and never share him with another woman—even if the other woman was carrying his child. . . .

RHYS—The Welsh poet who married into the fierce Shawnee tribe, he was Madoc's most loyal follower—and would do anything for the man the natives had hailed as the Great White Chief. . . .

GWEN—Madoc's lovely daughter, born in the New World, she would struggle to survive in a wild and untamed land—and follow her father in his perilous quest for freedom. . . .

Bantam Books by Pat Winter

MADOC

MADOC'S HUNDRED

MADOC'S HUNDRED

Book II in the
Madoc Saga

Pat Winter

BANTAM BOOKS
NEW YORK • TORONTO • LONDON • SYDNEY • AUCKLAND

For Miss Floreta Skinner

MADOC'S HUNDRED
A Bantam Domain Book / March 1991

ISBN 0-553-28521-1

Published simultaneously in the United States and Canada

PRINTED IN THE UNITED STATES OF AMERICA

OPM   0 9 8 7 6 5 4 3 2 1

The White People

Agnes = (dead in Book I) wife of Huw
Andrew (Brother) (Swimming Upstream)
Ari Al Ghazal O'Daliagh
Bjorn = father and son of Yngvild
Brian (Father)
Caradoc the Mediciner
Cari = daughter of Rhiannon
David ab Owen = brother of Madoc & Rhiannon
David Iron = Eagle Ring Man's white name
Dewi = son of Ffiona & Edwin
Edwin
Einion = son of Owen & Teleri
Evan ab Powys
Fair Beard Snorrison = husband of Yngvild
Ffagan (Brother)
Ffiona = wife to Edwin (dead in Book I)
Gurd = Norse sailor
Gwalchmai ab Melir = poet to Owen
Gwen (Gwyneth) = daughter to Madoc (Moon Fire)
Hannah = Snorrison daughter
Huw ab Tewdr
John = Father
Lev = a Norseman
Llywellyn (Llyw)
Lludd = Wil and Mary's son
Madoc ab Owen = son of Owen & Brenda
Mary = wife of Wil (ab Hennin)
Matthew and Mark = Brian's sons w/Hayati (Running Cloud)
Math = Wil and Mary's son
Owen Gwynedd = king of Gwynedd
Pawl ab Powys = (dead in Book I) brother to Evan
Rhiannon = daughter of Owen & Cristen
Rhys ab Meredydd (Sun Eyes)
Simon (Father) (dead in Book I)
Teleri = (dead in Book I) wife of Madoc
Ulf = Norse sailor
Weather Eyes = Madoc's Yuchi name
Wil ab Hennin = husband to Mary
Tegan = (dead in Book I) wife of Llywellyn
William the Saxon

Wyn (Brother)
Yngvild = wife of Snorrison

The Red People

Arrow Always Red
Ahoskas = Tumkis's servant
Buffalo Eagle = Oldtown bonesetter and councilor
Burning Rose = Turtle's aunt
Butterfly Man = Turtle's tattoo artist
Eagle Ring Man = David Iron's Yuchi name
Father Folded Hands = Wyn's yred name
Fire Wolf = a daykeeper at Ixtulan
Firefly = a Natchez woman
Five-Tens-and-Two = Turtle's 52nd son
Fox = chief of the Cherokee
Lily = Winnowed Rice's sister-in-law
Laughing Dog = a Yuchi tracker (Brother Paul)
Green Woman = Tumkis's servant
Hannah = Fair Beard's child w/Tumkis
Hard Walker = a noble from Ixtulan
Hayati = Brian's Muskogean wife
Heartless Singer = master of protocol at Ixtulan
Imala'ko = a Chickasaw warrior
Istepapa = Panther
Mickanac M'kin Mah'kina = Turtle-in-the-Sun
One Reed = Turtle's gardener
Onwa' Pahta = Gwen's red name
Panther = high priest of Ixtulan
Simple Greenbrier = one of Turtle's servants
Sky = A shawnee woman
Sun Eyes = Rhys's nickname
Morning Owl = one of Turtle's servants
Sun Caller = chief of the Yuchi
Swimming Upstream = Bro. Andrew's red name
Tumkis = a Natchez woman (Sunshine Woman) (Lady Sun)
   (Sun Child) (Tumbling Water)
Weather Eyes = Madoc's red name
Winnowed Rice = Rhy's Shawnee wife

GLOSSARY

ab = son of
atlatl = weapon
ayat = from now on
blamen = Norse for dark skinned man
bloom = molten iron
bloomery = ancient iron foundry
Bright Snake = Morning and Evening Star
chunkee = game
coracle = Welsh leather boat
curragh = Irish leather boat
Durendal = Madoc's sword
ell = unit of measure, @ 45 inches
fathom = unit of measure, six feet
furlong = unit of measure, @ 220 yards
gihli-gasi = dog pull (sing. & pl.)
hatki ahaka = invisible
the *Horn* = a ship
Iceland eye = crystal for seeing sun through fog
larboard = left side of a ship looking forward
league = unit of measure, @ 15 miles
kanegmati = blue eyed snake
kanskak = cane
the Kisser = Fair Beard's sword
knaar = Norse longboat
Llais Mel = the harp (Honeyvoice)
the Mabinogi = Welsh stories
Magh Mel = legendary land of honey
mam = Welsh for mama
nipowoc = tobacco
nocturnal = star sighting instrument
Odin's nosehair = an anchor
O Florida = Medieval reference to Paradise
potechas = merchant priests
pulque = Mexican liquor
raptor = predatory bird
the *St. Ann* = a ship
the *St. Brendan* = a ship
starboard = right side of a ship looking forward
stinkard = low caste Natchez
tad = Welsh for daddy
tangletongue = red name for the Norse
Te Deum = hymn

tsalu = corn
tun = container
u'yu'gi = Cherokee for disease
vealh' = stranger
yn y cwch = into the boat (Welsh)

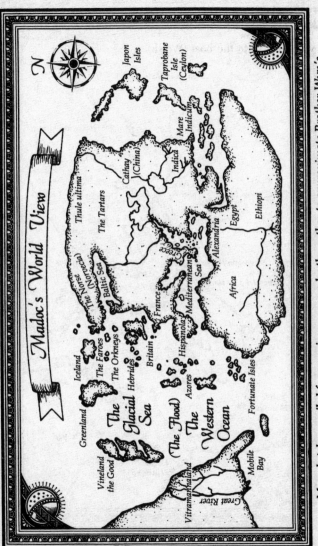

Map sketch compiled from various sources by the author to approximate Brother Wyn's gold map, which would represent Madoc's World View.

Sketch of routes used by Madoc's Hundred into the Mississippi
Valley by way of the Gulf of Mexico (Chechimec Sea) and
Brother Wyn's westwards journey to Jerusalem.

PART ONE

I was in many shapes before I was released:
I was a slender magic sword.
I was rain drops in the air, I was star shine;
I was a word in letters, I was a book in origin;
I was lanterns of light for a year and a half;
I was a bridge that stretched over sixty rivers;
I was a path, I was an eagle, I was a coracle in seas;
I was a bubble in beer, I was a drop in a shower;
I was a sword in hand, I was a shield in battle.
I was a string in a harp enchanted nine years, like foam;
I was a spark in fire, I was wood in a bonfire;

I am not one who does not sing; I have sung since I was small.
I sang in the army of the trees before Britain's ruler . . .
I wounded a great scaly animal, and beguiled the crested snake
*   in whose skin a hundred souls are punished.*

—from *The Army of the Trees*
by Taliesin
Welsh, c.a.d. 500

Chapter 1

The river was. The river is. The river always will be as long as there is sky and earth and sun. It is waters separating waters, the fourth thing made, the next-to-the-last magic that salted the sea and so finished creation.

"Waters separating waters," Rhys thought out loud as the rattling water of the wide Tennessee rolled beneath him, its current carrying the fleet of coracles and the ship on north. He let his right hand drop from the sleeping baby's head in a sling on his chest. Her fine hair smelled yeastly like new mead. Through his tunic, her head vibrated warmth he could feel as a small red spot on his chest.

After her heat it was a pleasant shock to plunge his hand into the cold blue silk river purring like a great cat, close enough to put a fine spray on his face when he stiffened his fingers against the flow.

The water sang, it opened up its loose flesh around his intrusion and rushed to accommodate him, nibbling, sniffing, tasting. Beneath its torn, compliant surface he imagined that he touched the being of the river as alive as himself under the warm sun he could feel on his face and chest.

"Did you say something?" Winnowed Rice asked, her voice coming from behind him as she guided them downstream in their oblong canoe, her spine strong against his as they sat back-to-back. It was pleasant labor; she used the paddle only to keep them away from the shallows and among, but not so near as to tangle with others of their flotilla. Rhys knew she was enjoying herself because she was singing a low, soft song in husky Shawnee.

He could faintly hear someone calling from up ahead—it did not sound like Madoc's voice, but it was too far away over the

3

muttering current to make out words or the answer that another in their hide-and-wicker armada called back.

The river darkly colored Rhys's fingertips. The cool tint moved up his wrist, arm, and elbow and spread across his chest to the baby's warm spot that lay like a ruby in a black setting of his mind's eye. This was the way the red people saw their rivers. *I am thinking as they do,* he realized as he felt the river touching him, tasting his being and recognizing the sun on his flesh and listening with curiosity to the hot color of life in the child against him, wondering what little sun this was in the firmament of the man's senses. *So,* he thought, *the river is blind, too.*

"I cannot hear you," Winnowed Rice called behind him.

"I said the river has a peaceful sound," Rhys answered dreamily, "as though it has been rolling on forever."

"Hmmmff," she replied.

"What?" he asked, his misty, river-induced trance dispelled by Winnowed Rice's voice.

"The Uktena knows we are here," she said in Shawnee over her shoulder. Like the Natchez and Muskogeans, Winnowed Rice called the river the name for a mythical serpent-being that tradition said looked much like Madoc's Norse ship ahead. "Too many boats wake it up."

Rhys knew Winnowed Rice meant the Natchez canoes he could hear gaining on them at the left. The six men in the dugout rowed in unison with a vibrating chant to set their beat. Even now their three-noted song moved closer.

Winnowed Rice had explained that this was the canoe of Arrow Always Red, the stern dark-skinned Natchez warrior who sported a collection of tattoo bracelets on every surface of his legs and arms, who even now sat the prow of the sleek boat carved from a single huge log, keeping the beat with the song and a rhythmic thonk-slap of his baton against the dugout's resounding wooden edge. This one canoe would rush ahead of the other small craft and the big ship; then, the rowers having proved their prowess, they would backpaddle and let the big ship and the other small craft overtake them again. Then the Natchez would repeat their dramatic rush, pass up everyone else to the feminine cheers and whistles coming from the big ship, then fall far back to bring up the rear of the flotilla. They had been at this since the flotilla left Muscle Shoals under the watchful eyes of the Cherokees and their thousand allies at dawn this morning.

"But no Chickasaw?" he replied, and felt her winsome shrug against his back. It was a gesture he was learning to hear in her voice as he grew to know this woman who had come into his life so recently but had become such a big part of it.

"No Chickasaw that I can see," she answered drolly, turning her keen gaze toward the western bank. "But then, it is not Chickasaw I can see who worry me."

It was a brilliant day after several under fog. She saw sliding sleekly into her leftward glance the big Natchez war canoe, a brightly painted and carved log that could accommodate two dozen armed warriors. The men, the paddles, the tuffed water falling beneath their perfect strokes moving crew and craft as one long swift creature, were beautiful to behold, and she admired their skill but frowned under the dazzling sunlight.

The west bank, about three arrow shots beyond the Natchez canoe, was exclusive territory of the Chickasaw, who had the most terrible reputation for brutality of any nation known by the wandering Shawnee—even more brutal than the Leni Lenape, who were fierce but would absorb an enemy who put up a good fight.

The Chickasaw, it was widely reported, were cannibals.

"Luck was with the white-hair tangletongue," Winnowed Rice continued, meaning Madoc's pilot and partner Fair Beard Snorrison.

Now as Madoc kept his promise to the Cherokee and rode the lazy Uktena into northern Shawnee territory, the Natchez outriders freed the whites from fear of the people-eaters.

But still, Winnowed Rice frowned when she scanned that far western bank where there seemed to be no sign of Chickasaw but where there were surely Chickasaw hiding.

"No Chickasaw," she mumbled.

"Ah," said Rhys after a thoughtful silence, "but now we have the Natchez."

It made her laugh, but grimly, as she nodded. She had grown fond of this white man for many reasons, not the least of which was his understanding of the situation, any situation he seemed to be in despite the fact that he had no eyes—a condition that would mean death among her nomadic people, where only the most able-bodied survived.

"The Natchez, yes," she said. When Madoc asked her what

could be worse than the Chickasaw, she had warned him about the Natchez. They did not eat human flesh, but they had another kind of unsavory but better-founded reputation for shrewd, extremely tricky bargaining. They were also rumored to have unnatural sexual practices. They picked the bones of their dead and kept them neatly organized in bonehouses, which they replaced every few years atop immense pyramids.

The white chief had listened to her advice, but honored his friend Fair Beard's alliance, which had already proved to be so valuable against the Cherokee.

Among themselves, Winnowed Rice and her nomadic sisters called the Natchez and other settled tribes the men with roots, which had the connotation of a dirty joke.

Rhys knew all this and was intrigued to know more. In so small but diverse a company of men and women as Madoc's Hundred, gossip was an ongoing entertainment.

"Is she as beautiful as the men say?"

Without breaking her stroke Winnowed Rice brought her elbow back in a playful jab in Rhys's ticklish ribs. She knew very well the *she* he meant.

He caught her elbow under his own so that Winnowed Rice was unable to paddle; he could feel the current gently tug them askew as she growled back at him and jerked free. He pressed against her back. She responded with a sensual rippling movement up the muscles of her spine that made him wonder what it would be like to take her right here in the skimming boat under the knowing sun. *What would the old river-snake make of that?*

"The Natchez sun is truly as beautiful as the men say," she replied in a different tone of voice, knowing he meant the Natchez noblewoman on board the larger ship.

Winnowed Rice was a fairly tall Shawnee woman of about forty years with work-hardened hands, stringy and strong from a lifetime of walking. Among her own people or strangers, she would not be called beautiful except for the warmth that sparked her glance. The fire of her inflamed men's desire as though she had been a beauty. She had keen eyesight, could handle a shortened hunting bow as well as any man, and indulged her curiosity more than most red women, who were traditionally shy.

Rhys whispered a sensual Shawnee word she taught him, and she responded by putting her weight against him without interrupting her paddling. "We would surely shock the Natchez," she replied dryly, an incongruous thought to shock a nation known for brazenness. "Besides, what would Father Folded Hands say if he saw the feet of our four-legged beast kicking over the edge of this boat?"

Rhys sighed and reached his arms around behind himself to embrace her. "Is Wyn aboard the *Horn*?"

"I see the sachem robes from here—he must be one of them. I see many faces all looking out. So many people—even the big canoe sinks down under all those people."

She could see the great ship not an arrow-shot ahead, red and white people lining the rails and crowding the decks, sitting or standing in groups while the crew of white men controlled the single square sail made of many great leather patches sewn together in three bands.

The *Horn* was immense by red standards—sixty feet long with a twelve-foot draught at the keel, her prow and stern raised high. At the tip of the forty-foot mast snapped a dark flag with a rampant dragon stylized in red. This was the heraldic designator for the house of Gwynedd, of which Madoc was one of two dozen sons, legitimate and bastard, he being of the latter inheritance back home in the place called Wales by the English but not so long ago the sovereign Celtic nation of Cymru. While this ship was essentially a Norse knaar, its builders had forgone the traditional dragon head that was associated with bandits. Still, it had the high-necked and high-tailed look of a long, graceful creature, a snake or bird, especially with the sail unfurled and full of wind like a great wing. This is what it looked like to Winnowed Rice, who never ceased to marvel, along with all the red people, that such a man-made craft could be. It looked like traditional descriptions of the Uktena, or water serpent said to have lived in local rivers in the old days, before the world had set into its present condition.

At the tiller starboard aft was Fair Beard, recognized by his long, loose yellow hair, who would sing out from time to time a monotone command as he deftly guided the ship downstream and reaching into the sou'westerly breeze. As the men answered his commands, the rigging creaked with their tacking adjustments to get the maximum push from the wind coming from behind them.

Not far from Fair Beard, Winnowed Rice saw the big blond

woman Yngvild, who stood with her fat, pink-cheeked toddler. This was Fair Beard's wife, who had been faithful to him during the long time that he was thought dead. She and her husband were talking quietly but intently together as he casually steered the ship, leaning against the top strake on a folding bench built into the railing.

The baby, an enormous boy Rhys said was named Bear in the tangletongue, was trying to squirm toward his father and away from his mother, who held him back by his chubby waist. There was no indication of what the man and woman were discussing, but from where Winnowed Rice sat, it looked like an argument between two people who had no privacy and were trying to keep it to themselves. Complicating things was the strong, willful child between them.

"And Snorrison's Natchez sun?" Rhys asked.

"Under a pavilion of palm leaves."

Rhys laughed when he imagined what that must look like, Fair Beard's dusky Natchez sun ensconced on her cloud of pillows with her three serving women feeding her mussels from the shell. That was the report this morning, which scandalized the Shawnee and had everyone talking. The fancy war canoe made its dashes on her side of the ship—it was she and her serving women who continued to cheer every time the warriors whisked by, even though by the fifth dash forward, everyone else was trying to ignore the boastful Natchez headman, who was sworn to insure Tumkis's safety.

Rhys was more curious about Fair Beard. He wondered how Yngvild was taking the news that her long-lost husband had taken this remarkable new wife while absent from her bed—not just a mistress, but a stunning dark-eyed, raven-haired, royally tattooed little princess in a finely beaded mulberry-bark dress and red feathers on copper rings in her ears, who knew her ancestors for ten generations back; who had a war canoe with six warriors for protection, and who, with noble and noticeable bearing, carried Bjorn's half brother or sister into the sixth month of life.

"But," Winnowed Rice added, "she is near the yellow-hair and watches him closely while pretending not to."

"Hmmm." Rhys, always listening for interesting gossip, wondered how Madoc was faring. The lord of this tattered company had been wounded in the fight that took the life of his wife and several others at Muscle Shoals. Rhys hoped Madoc was belowdeck under enough of Caradoc's medicine to keep him down. Otherwise the man would ignore his injuries and climb into the rigging like one of his seamen.

"Anyone on lookout?" Rhys asked, because that was where Madoc liked to stay, aloft on the mast as the eyes of the great dragon-headed ship.

"No, but something is happening over there," she said, and did some maneuver with the paddle that flung droplets like cool stars onto Rhys's face. Rhys took his hand from the water and held on to the leather-bound rim of the canoe, trusting her completely, as he must, but taking a cue from the roughening water that felt as though they had reached bumpy shallows.

He could hear a call coming down the line.

"Beach them!" a male voice rang, now close enough to hear, and Rhys relayed the order to those behind him: "Beach the coracles," he called through cupped hands to those who followed, then said to Winnowed Rice, "The sun has not reached noon—wonder why he wants to pull in so early?"

She made a noise that said she wondered, too, but was busy with maneuvering.

Rhys heard the brittle saw of reeds scraping the boat's leather hull as Winnowed Rice brought their little craft to shore while the large ship nodded well out in deep water, booming sounds of wood on water-soaked wood echoing off the river.

The cane overhung the coracle and brushed Rhys's face with toothy dry spears. He felt cattail fluff burst against his cheek and lightly touch him here and there. Without thinking he cupped his palm protectively across the baby's face.

From the right he heard a bird shriek, no doubt furious at the troop of more than a hundred human intruders storming into its territory.

As Rhys waited for the Shawnee woman's callused hand to guide him from the canoe, he could not shake the palpable feeling that the river was alive. He had been dreaming that the river was alive and cunning but also curious about its riders.

Suddenly from behind he thought he heard a shout from the river itself calling him back. It was a barking sound, a sharp crack that uttered his own name. The impression gave him a chill, even under the broiling sunlight.

But then he thought it must have been someone else pulling in a coracle, someone shouting in Shawnee. People were splashing all around him, mothers calling children, the men hauling in the heavy cargo canoes, cursing in a half-dozen languages as they tied them down. Behind these local noises the splash of the anchors, the grindings of the ship, announced her berthing; the rigging creaked, and oak thudded on the deck Rhys knew was crowded because he could hear the murmur of many voices from that direction downriver.

He was glad to feel Winnowed Rice's hand on his shoulder, and her other hand waiting, open and palm up, when he slapped his own into it and stood with their bodies touching momentarily at the hip before he followed her out of the lapping water and up onto a crunching beach.

"We have landed on another long island," she volunteered, handing him his worn staff, which she retrieved from one of two cargo canoes tied behind their own. "This beach is about twenty paces wide, backed by thick underbrush and pines. A hundred paces in either direction, and you will be swimming."

He took the staff but did not let go of her hand around it.

He felt her squeeze back, and he started to embrace her, somewhat awkwardly with the sleeping baby slung between them, when Madoc called, "Rhys—Rhys ab Meredydd!"

Rhys reluctantly released the warm pine-scented woman and turned toward his duty, for it seemed that all his life Gwynedd's princes had been calling him, and he had been turning to answer.

"Come here—I need you!" Madoc called.

No different this time, Rhys thought, and took from his belt a tattered silk sash, which he proceeded to wind around his face.

"You smear the paint," Winnowed Rice said. She had carefully applied charcoal, ocher, and yellow clay mixed with oil in sunburst designs to his empty eye sockets.

"No, love, Weather Eyes does not like to see me painted," Rhys said, his Shawnee improving. He used the name Madoc favored among her people, who were impressed with his gray eyes, something they had never seen before.

"But—"

"Weather Eyes is chief."

After she helped him tie the sash, he turned and waded through the shallows toward the commotion coming from the direction of the *Horn*.

Behind him Winnowed Rice watched Rhys walk toward the

ship where the dark-haired, bearded chief himself was hanging over the rail-strake urging Rhys to hurry. Winnowed Rice still was not used to seeing men with hairy faces and was glad her white man kept his lip and chin smooth; in fact, she had learned to shave him just to keep it that way.

Madoc released another of the round boats lashed to the rail-strake; then, still holding onto the line, he sailed the wicker-and-hide craft out and across the water to skip in front of Rhys. Madoc's aim was perfect, and the poet had only to bend forward where he heard the craft splash to feel his way into the bouncing boat. Little Cari still slept in the sling on his chest despite the splash that sprinkled her and soaked the man's soft moccasins, breeches, and tunic. Rhys held his staff across his lap and turned his face toward the chief as Madoc used the line to haul the coracle closer to the huge mothership.

Winnowed Rice could hear the two men joking across the water as the coracle drew closer. Their water-echoed discussion had awakened the baby, who was now fussing.

Winnowed Rice could pick out only a word here and there—she was learning this man's language, but it was difficult. When the coracle bumped the mothership, he reached out to grasp the hempen sidelines and began to climb aboard, helped over the rail by the chief, who clapped him on the back and continued in mild harangue as he led Rhys away from the rail.

"You must travel with me aboard the *Horn*," Madoc was saying, continuing as they walked away, speaking faster than Winnowed Rice could follow. She saw Rhys stop, politely arguing in his fine singer's voice, turning slightly back to indicate herself.

Madoc peered around his counselor and motioned to Winnowed Rice. "Help her up here—" he barked to one of his men.

She saw now that their chief was not well. Stripped to the waist of his usual light woven tunic, Weather Eyes was bound by a white cloth stained with blood on the right side. His forehead was tied with another bandage. His flushed face glistened with sweat that was from fever as well as from the sun, and his strange gray eyes were round with ordeal, sunk more deeply into his angular cheekbones. He seemed to have more silver in his hair since they left the mountain; he was as thin as a lance. They should make the man go to sleep for a couple of days, Winnowed Rice mused, thinking about which medicines in her baggage could assist him.

"Yngvild!" Madoc called, pressing Rhys toward the captain's makeshift cabin set up forward on the open deck. He could quickly have a tent thrown over his little command post—the rest of the ship was bulkhead to bulkhead with people, far too crowded for safety, not to mention comfort. The crew had to step around passengers for every maneuver. Even the Natchez princess was forced against the stack of great long oars, racked longwise on both sides of the mast in raw new tending blocks of Alabama cypress, sharing her shaded pallet with all her women.

"You must talk to Gwen, make her understand," Madoc was saying in a hoarse, agitated voice as he guided Rhys through the throng that parted for them, toward a spot as far forward as there was decking. There, Madoc's red-haired daughter was sitting straight and still with her back to the rest of the company.

The wind gusted pleasantly off the great flat expanse of the river. On the beach someone already had a fire going; the wood was aromatic on the breeze. This would be their noon break.

"Yngvild, take the baby, please," Madoc was saying as he helped his counselor disencumber himself of Madoc's infant niece, Cari, who was making ever more insistent noises around Rhys's finger, which was fast losing its charm as a pacifier. In another moment she would erupt into cries.

The Norsewoman left her own Bjorn climbing up his father's chest, his fat little fists clinging to the beard, and moved to obey Madoc. Since Cari's mother suicided, Yngvild had been wet nurse to Bjorn and this little girl conceived on the far northwest shore of Britain but born in the Tennessee highlands.

Behind Yngvild, the Natchez woman approached Fair Beard and with light laughter and a charming toss of her loose blue black hair, relieved him of Bjorn.

The little boy was startled by the tiny Natchez woman leaning back for balance, the cascade of her sable hair swaying below her knees. She looked like a child herself despite her swollen belly that announced yet another Snorrison on the way.

Bjorn leaned back on her arm and stared down at Tumkis, who made funny noises for him before he started to cry. Fair Beard spoke to her and then to the child, who looked back mournfully and lifted his arms for his father's rescue from this stranger.

Tumkis bounced him and cooed, stealing his fear from him with her charm and with the trilling sound of tongue on teeth so much like the sound of water.

Fair Beard reached for her when he heard this sound because it was the same vibrato she used on his ear and other parts when she took him down into her fleshy gardens. That sound was an old Natchez magic for taming wild babies, animals, and men. Deftly the Natchez woman, whose name meant Dancing Water, spun on her diminutive heel so that the stout little boy was between them, squealing his delight at her game.

Yes, thought Winnowed Rice. *The Natchez sun is very beautiful as only a witch can be*.

Yngvild had just turned with Cari at her breast so that she saw this exchange with her babe and with her husband, but Winnowed Rice was too far away to read anything in the Norsewoman's face that showed feelings as she strolled slowly around the wide hold opening and intercepted Fair Beard, who seemed intent on following Tumkis still playing with the baby on her pile of cushions. Her women were making much over the little fellow, feeding him sweetmeats, tickling the bottom of his feet, and dangling a toy on a string so that he looked cross-eyed.

Yngvild did not speak a word to Fair Beard, but she gave him a piercing look. She was only a head shorter than he, who towered over everyone in the company including Madoc. He finally broke the stare, exasperation on his features. He turned back to her, and they exchanged words too soft to hear.

Winnowed Rice in the shallows was the only one to catch the miniature drama of the man between the two women as it flickered by amid the crowded, noisy company shoulder to shoulder on the deck. People—monks, half-naked crewmen, and several women—were moving up from the hold to board coracles. The crew simply jumped into the river and swam to the near shore.

At the temporary camp, children—red and white boys from about five to twelve years—chased each other across the gravel while a woman yelled at them to gather firewood. They ran off screaming toward the little stand of dogwood and thorn-trees, where tangled deadwood promised easy pickings.

Back aboard the *Horn*, Madoc with Rhys in tow had not broken his stride toward the forward crates and coils of rope that delineated his command territory. "Explain to Gwen why we cannot stop," Madoc was saying, and Winnowed Rice overheard enough to follow what they said.

By now the two men were within the captain's nook, where Madoc's daughter, Gwen, sat with her back to the rest of the ship. The Shawnee woman could not hear what the two white men were saying now as they approached the red-haired young woman, but she knew as did everyone else that there was trouble up there.

The set of the white woman's back beneath the long coppery coils said much. The tone of the chief's voice said the rest.

Winnowed Rice tied up her several little boats and waded toward a spot where yet another coracle had been dispatched with one of the yellowed-haired Norsemen hauling at the paddle. He helped Winnowed Rice board the craft behind him and began rowing them back to the *Horn*, where everyone avoided the forward area of the ship as they went about the business of disembarking.

The last of the coracles that had been on the river were pulled up onto the sand. People were stretching, talking, passing around water gourds.

Everyone aboard this ship wanted out of these cramped quarters. They pressed aft, where coracles were peeling off, leaving the Natchez women to one side, still tickling the baby; Yngvild and Fair Beard unmoved and still whispering; and Madoc, Rhys, and the red-haired young woman in their intense conversation behind the privacy of a barrel.

Suddenly Bjorn saw his mother standing across the deck nursing the other baby and launched himself in a fast-paced crawl in her direction. Tumkis, no less quickly, was behind him, bending to catch him. But instead of stopping him, she caught his fists and let him hold onto her fingers. Slowly she lifted his hands until the child was off his knees and standing. He giggled as he took one, then another, and a third tottering, shaky step, still hanging onto Tumkis's fingers. Then he boldly let go of one, then the other finger, and pointed himself head-first toward Yngvild, who by now had turned at the sound of her child's gurgle.

Fair Beard peered past her, witnessing his son's first steps—a dozen at least as he careened across the bleached decking toward his mother's skirt. Tumkis was right behind him so that when he tottered too far in the last plunge and would have fallen against the splintered boards, she caught him up bubbling with joy and hugged him safely to her. Then she lifted her lovely black eyes and smiled sweetly to Yngvild reaching for the baby, who threw himself at her across the gap between the little Natchez and the towering Norsewoman.

"Good boy," Fair Beard exclaimed, ruffling the baby's blond curls.

"Your fine son walks early, mother," Tumkis said shyly in her lilting singsong language and using the word *mother* as a title of honor. "He will surely be a great warrior."

Yngvild hugged the squirming baby and looked down at her rival with icy lack of response.

Fair Beard translated for her. "You see," he added, "I told you she loves children. She wishes only to be your sister, wife. She is content to be second to you, for that is the custom among these people." He was perhaps too enthusiastic because of his pride in his son and because he wanted to thaw Yngvild so badly and thereby keep the two of them rather than choose.

Yngvild eyed him but did not respond.

"Honored sister . . ." said Tumkis, bowing her head a little, holding her hands together as if offering something on her palms. Behind her, her serving women stood still like a bosomed wall, their hands neatly folded together.

"She is saying that she wishes only to serve you, to ease the labor in your lodge."

Yngvild's eyebrow arched above a withering glance at him, and she still withheld any comment.

He gently urged her forward, but she resisted, hugging the baby tighter in one arm while not disturbing little black-haired Cari, who had fallen asleep on her other arm but had not let go of the teat, which she continued to noisily suck from her dreams.

Bjorn turned to stare down at Tumkis, his weight almost too much for his robust mother.

He reached out and patted Tumkis's shining black hair,

uttering a baby word, then held his arms out so that his weight dropped him toward her waiting arms. She kissed him while Yngvild looked down, still holding onto Bjorn, who was making this almost impossible, her arms too full of babies and ready to let the boy go to keep hold of the nursling.

Fair Beard patted her shoulders and winked down at Tumkis; she made that sound again that Bjorn and Fair Beard understood and Yngvild could only guess at.

"I will love him as my own," Tumkis said in her language like small silver bells ringing.

Fair Beard translated, then boldly, arms like the branches of a blond and furry tree, he embraced both his women.

Only Tumkis laughed.

Things had gotten quieter up forward where Rhys now sat head-to-head with Gwen. She shook her head slowly side to side—no, no, she was saying, no, and leaned her brow on his shoulder as he spoke so that only she could hear. She turned once, tears glistening on her cheeks, her lip a fine trembling line, staring miserably at her father, who stood to one side while Rhys continued to reason softly with her.

Madoc had to look away from that stare, it put such a hole in him.

"Please, tad," she begged. "Please wait for him."

Rhys lifted his face toward Madoc and found her hand to hold.

"You know we cannot, Gwen, and you must see that it is so," Madoc said.

"No." She looked down. "No. I promised my husband I would wait for him at the Duck, and that is what I intend to do."

"I have given my word against our lives, Gwyneth." Madoc was furious with David Iron, the Yuchi who had taken white ways and religion with his bride but who had disappeared last night without a word to anyone save her.

Gwen persisted: "I said I will stay. He will be along very soon, a day or two at the most, and I will be at the Duck waiting for him. The rest of you go along, and we will follow."

Madoc made a gesture of complete frustration—palms out as though he were tossing this obstacle aside—and looked away, arms akimbo. She was suggesting that he abandon her alone here in the wilderness to wait for her husband, who might or might not ever return to her.

Her stubbornness turned him aside, where he stared for a long, lip-biting moment at the wide river that rolled on by without regard for the small affairs of men.

"Then," he said quietly, frustration hardening to a cold species of anger as he turned to speak to her again, "we will not stop at the Duck."

"Then I will wait here," she said, suddenly picking up three small bundles and a draped wicker cage.

Madoc watched her awkward progress toward the sidelines, where several people still waited to disembark. He reached out as she passed him to catch her arm, but the movement threw off the cage covering, where a large golden eagle shrieked when he saw Madoc. The creature beat at him through the bars, and though there was no danger of its escape from the latched cage, its rancor was startling. Madoc stepped back and called to Fair Beard across the length of the ship, "You talk to her, Snorrison—she used to listen to reason!"

Fair Beard intercepted Gwen near the rail, but she shook him off and would not look at him as he tried to put an arm around her shoulders and begin a reasoned argument.

Rhys stood, reaching out to hold Madoc's arm, alarmed at how fevered he was.

"Winnowed Rice?" Rhys called; she was there immediately at his elbow. He spoke softly in Shawnee, "Get your kit, love. We must slow our chief down before he falls over."

She had her satchel over her shoulder and was already pawing around inside it for the item that would do the trick.

Chapter 2

A glow lingered behind the western horizon, where the almost-full moon had set.

The silhouette of the big ship nested close to the eastern bank of the languid Tennessee, shrouded in darkness, while near it on the eastern shore several campfires crackled, illuminating loose knots of red and white people settling down for the night. In one group near the ship but well back from the bank, where small flies buzzed, Tumkis sat amidst her women. The Natchez warriors could not be seen but formed a perimeter around this bevy of females, one of whom brushed Tumkis's hair while the Natchez sun held onto an elm sapling, bracing herself against the motion that pulled her blackbird hair out more than an arm span between herself and the old woman brushing it.

"Harder, Ahoskas," Tumkis murmured, her voice inaudible above their circle and the incessant murmur of the river close by. "Hard enough to make the blue sparks fly."

Her lipless mouth a drawn thin line of determination, the dry, lean red woman holding the slab of hair pulled it tightly enough to draw back Tumkis's eyes, making of them even more elongated ovals.

"Harder," the young Natchez woman insisted, tears forming in her eyes as she gripped the sapling to steady herself.

The other two women of the circle watched as they went about their handwork. The young one beading was named Firefly. The other, a plump middle-aged wife called Green Woman, sewed feathers to a leather jerkin she was making for her son, Arrow Always Red. He was somewhere out in the shadows in eternal vigilance over Tumkis according to his vow of allegiance to her uncle, the high miko of the Natchez. With a low whistle Tumkis could call the warrior now to do her

18

bidding, whatever she wished. It had occurred to her but fleetingly that she could summon him and his men to prepare the war canoe that would take her home, by a long but sure route away from this patchwork red-and-white tribe and the loss of face that might await her as a woman scorned.

"Harder, I say."

"My arm, Sunshine Woman, my arm is cramping," Ahoskas replied as she raked the hair with another pull, breaking teeth from the halved-thistle brush.

Tumkis steadied her forehead against the tree and braced herself with her right arm hooked at the elbow while letting go her other hand, which she flipped back to catch Ahoskas on the cheek, producing more of a noisy slap than actual pain. "Do not stop now, Old Dog, not when you have the magic going." The old woman, whose name meant The Survivor, did not cringe but let the impact rattle her flesh, her eyes shut only for an instant. She did not miss a stroke as she watched light spots float in her vision.

"My lady," said Green Woman, dropping her featherwork and offering her head to be slapped since Ahoskas outranked her. "This one humbly reminds my Lady Sun that it is Green Woman's honor to take any punishment."

A little flustered at being corrected on matters of protocol, Tumkis slapped impotently at Green Woman's bent neck, playfully pushing her away. "Very well, Green Woman, set aside your beautiful work and take over for our sister," said the gentled sun.

Satisfied with her duty done, Green Woman took the wad of hair in one hand, leaving the next stroke to the other woman, then relieving her of the brush so that the rhythm was saved.

Soon static electricity crackled over the bristling mane.

Very softly Green Woman crooned a chant, though she did not slow down the brushing.

Tumkis smiled as more sparks crackled through the blue-black tresses while Ahoskas slumped to one side, rubbing the muscles in her wiry arm. The old woman, lounging back on her own bedroll, joined the low, mournful chant that sounded half lullaby, half dirge.

"Rest now, Auntie, and I forgive you," Tumkis said too sweetly to Ahoskas.

"My lady."

Green Woman smiled to herself and put her chant up higher

in the spaces behind her nose and eyes, causing a double-voiced trill to vibrate from the orifices of her face.

"Green Woman, Green Woman, everything you do is impeccable," Tumkis said, closing her eyes with the pleasure of the pain in her scalp.

Green Woman's mouth thinned with the determination of workmanship, and she made a subtle sound that was part of the chant and also a wry snort, minutely ruffling the tattooed flesh beneath her eyes as she bore down on the task.

Soon the sun's hair was fairly humming with blue sparks dancing like a halo from under the brush.

"Now, my dear friends Green Woman, Firefly, and Ahoskas," Tumkis said, the order of the names an insult to Ahoskas, who took it with stifled dignity. Sparse, emotionless tears ran down Tumkis's cheeks from pressure against her eyelids as the currying drew back the skin of her face. "Now it is time to think right thoughts in my direction."

All three attendants took up the chant, and those two who were unoccupied let their eyes roll back, bodies swaying slightly on the ridgepole of the spine.

Tumkis's lips moved, but she spoke no word anyone could hear as she watched the ship out there in the sooty darkness. She was repeating a phrase to insure power as she peered into the well of distance between here and there, focusing her vision and energy to the far point of faint red light that illuminated the deck aft where Fair Beard rested near Yngvild. The white couple were conversing without much space between them. The ship rail was not pierced but was a solid carved strake, so only their heads were visible above it.

Yngvild had finished serving him a cup and now moved slightly away to look down—Tumkis knew she was looking at the robust blond baby who was in a makeshift pen on pillows between crates and wooden fixtures.

"Look at them, sisters," Tumkis instructed, but the three servants did not shift their eyes lest it break their concentrated chant as she continued in a tone of address. "I did not understand the white men until I saw this. They do not use the cradleboard, and therein lies their fatal flaw—they do not learn when very young that there are limitations to all human action."

The chant poured on from the three women, Green Woman still dredging the sun's hair for blue sparks.

Out on the ship the Norsewoman leaned over out of Tumkis's line of sight and stood straight again after a moment, still observing something that caused her to look downward momentarily before she turned back to Fair Beard, her large face clearly illuminated like a long pink gourd from the Natchez woman's point of view.

She must have picked up the child.

Tumkis narrowed her gaze on Yngvild, concentrating as she repeated a soft formula, her women crooning for her, her hair standing on end as Green Woman put aside the mutilated brush. The hair expressed itself in a floating charged cloud, clinging to Green Woman's fingers as she smoothed it down again and again. She oiled her palms from a shell set out for that purpose and began to polish the hair, which gradually allowed itself to be tamed, longer than the girl's torso and flowing like an obsidian waterfall onto the blanket where they sat.

Tumkis, back as straight as a war-lance, kept her eye on the ship and her man there. She had known Fair Beard had another wife among his own people. He had told her so when he first came to live in her village on the Great River Road. He had picked Tumkis immediately out of the town's eligible females, since he came as an honored guest with powerful weapons her uncle prized enough to make the outlander his war-chief. Together they had won many battles since then, from their enemies on this and the west side of the Great River Road. Now, watching him with the woman from his own people, Tumkis was repeating a strong old formula guaranteed to keep a man's soul ensnared. But she bit her lip when she saw him reach out and pull the yellow-haired woman toward him.

Round-eyed, she waited to see what would happen next, but the couple on board continued speaking with their heads close together, apparently sitting on crates so that their silhouettes could be clearly seen in front of the glow from the hold behind them, where the white chief lay incoherent with fever.

"Thank all of you for right-thinking in my direction," Tumkis said formally, silencing their hum. She sighed mightily and leaned back, relaxing a little, her glance caught by Green Woman, who said, "Sunshine Woman. This man is lost to you, I think."

Tumkis stared at the ship where Yngvild had knelt below

Tumkis's line of sight, perhaps preparing a bed, so that only the top of her golden hair was visible.

"What does it matter to your noble self?" Green Woman asked. "Divorce him, I say. Get rid of him now before he sets you aside."

Ahoskas inserted a comment. "That buffalo-cow will never accept you, not even as second wife."

It was Tumkis's right as a noble, a sun, among her people to choose any husband she wanted as long as he was of an inferior social ranking based on direct descent from certain ancestors. It was a strange custom, that nobles could marry only beneath themselves, and nobody, least of all the Natchez, knew why it was so. She, as a noble, could divorce him at any time, unlike common women who had to have a reason.

"He is a commoner who sometimes smells unbathed," Ahoskas added to one side, completely ignored.

Tumkis saw Fair Beard standing now, looking over his shoulder toward the unseen peg stair that led into the bowels of the ship. She tightened her lips. "He is going to see Weather Eyes."

"Ah, that one," Green Woman said. "That one will follow the sun tonight, I think."

Ahoskas nodded agreement, leaning her head back upon her bedroll.

"That one is a true king, a miko. Did you see it on him?" Tumkis asked coolly. "It shines like a fire in his eyes."

"Hmmmh," from Green Woman.

"He might be saved."

Green Woman shrugged. "He has the Chickasaw arrow poison in him."

Ahoskas offered, "His lips will turn purple, and his fingernails will rot. From the wound outward until his whole body is consumed, he will turn black and begin to stink even before he is dead. I have seen it happen before."

"Green Woman knows the antidotes to Chickasaw poison."

"It is meant to be, even if he is a grand miko," Green Woman said seriously. "Kings must die like ordinary men."

"Still . . ."

"What are you thinking, my Sun Child? That you will save Weather Eyes for yourself?" Green Woman asked softly.

"He is a fitting spouse for me. Even more than my big golden man."

"Her big golden man," Green Woman reminded her.

Ahoskas said, "Why do you want these filthy, hairy white men anyway?"

Firefly, who had been silent except for the chant, suppressed a small giggle behind her hand.

"I am merely treading the path I find beneath my feet, Auntie, as you and Green Woman have taught me."

"Well . . ." said Green Woman in a professional tone of voice.

"Well, with the help of the little uncharmers from the swampy backpools over there, and the stuff in your kit, we might help him." The black powder was not a single medicine, but a compound made up of the flowers, roots, and leaves of more than a dozen plants called in other languages sage, calamus, baneberry, sarsaparilla, mugwort, pea, gormwell, dogbane, and ginseng, plus several species of ground insects.

"Too late, I fear, my child."

Tumkis pressed her argument. "He has powerful allies, and he is a strong, healthy warrior with a fair chance if he gets the right help." The Natchez sun was thinking of the blind man with the painted face who was down in the ship with the chief now, he and his Shawnee dog-woman. Tumkis's well-formed upper lip curled in disgust at the wandering unclean Shawnee, who tradition said lay with their half-wolf dogs from whom they acquired their legendary magic and stories.

"But in his own household, his ignorant daughter keeps an eagle imprisoned." Ahoskas shook her head. "What chance does that give him?" she asked rhetorically.

Tumkis bit her lip lightly; it was true what they said. "Perhaps I can convince her that it is helping to kill her father."

Green Woman shrugged noncommittally.

"And," Tumkis said like a final piece of convincing evidence, "strong life is still in him."

Green Woman shook her head. "Not without the formulas, not without a medicine man to plant the beads for his soul. We might heal his body, but who is there here to remove the magic some worm-eating Chickasaw magician has planted in his soul?"

Ahoskas leaned closer to Tumkis to ask, "Would you really want a man with no soul? What if an evil being has inhabited him while he is sick? Would you lay down your precious body of the sun's own blood with a demon?"

"Please, Auntie," Tumkis said with a tone of condescending patience.

Green Woman said thoughtfully, "Perhaps his own shaman knows formulas."

Ahoskas shook her head and turned away, piqued by Tumkis's patronizing voice. "I outrank Green Woman," she said petulantly. "*I* should be your chief counselor."

"Enough of this negative talk!" Tumkis flared, and in a single swift movement grabbed the crushed thistle pod and stabbed one of its thorns into the pad of her left index finger.

Ahoskas shut up and dropped her gaze, murmuring a liturgy, "Blood of the sun, blood of the sun."

"I am going to *do* something," Tumkis said meaningfully as she squeezed her perforated finger, picked up a small downy feather from Green Woman's work sack, and used it to absorb the shimmering drop of blood, glancing up as she did so at the women who sat transfixed at the sight of her bleeding. "It would be good of you to continue right-thinking in my direction for a little while longer."

Firefly and Green Woman both nodded as though on the same string and narrowed their eyes at her to prove their duty done while their mistress dropped the stained feather into the coals, which flared minutely blue, continuing her whispered formula as she stared needles at the long-necked ship and its foreign inhabitants.

Tumkis would have been disturbed by the Norse couple's conversation.

"You must not cause her to lose face," Fair Beard was saying low in his throat, almost a croak.

Yngvild broke the suction of the boybabe; a pale bubble popped at his lips, and he sighed from the depth of his slumber. "Why must I be concerned for this woman's feelings?" she asked, nesting Bjorn beside Cari, blissfully sleeping under a shawl below the crate where she sat.

When Snorrison looked at Yngvild, his wife of ten sailing seasons who had borne him three other sons, all of whom had died, and now held this new one pink and perfect at her swollen breast. She had endured more than most wives, even Icelanders honed to hardship. Yngvild had suffered being a sea-widow alone thrice as much as husbanded, providing for herself with her weaving skills, faithful to him beyond what he had imagined before now to be the limit of female endurance—when he looked at this woman, he was surprised to see her eyes rimmed with tears. She had never cried in his presence before, though he had heard her several times through closed doors (and once through a hatch when she bore their first child aboard ship, confined to his cabin while they got a load of timber back from a western place that had no name).

"And what about my feelings, son of Snorri?" She lisped now, because she was missing two upper front teeth—the old wives' explanation being a tooth for every baby. Caradoc had pulled them finally for her only recently, and her mouth was still tender. She tended to protect her gums by chewing with the side teeth, and when she spoke, she would look down so the gap did not show. Often she would lift a hand so that fingers lay across her lips. This she did without realizing it, and the gesture, to her husband, was something new and strange in this familiar woman.

"It is not feelings, wife, but her rank. If you abuse this woman's pride, her uncle's men will be bound by duty to vindicate her."

"They will not counter you, Snorri, and you know it."

He shrugged modestly, his pale lashes downcast, his big lips and hollow cheekbones in harsh contrast in the clam-shell lamplight.

"You are a god to them because of the steel."

"I had to magic the bastards, or they would have slit my throat in sacrifice," he said, shivering a chill of remembrance of the first time among the Natchez when they were measuring him for it sure enough. What stopped them was his singing battle-ax, filigreed with minute holes that whistled ominously when he spun it above his head. He cast a glance up at her from his slouch, a plea. "I will get rid of them, the whole mess of them, canoe and all, love. The trick is to do it without stirring them up."

"You want to get rid of all of them?" This woman's voice was normally powerful, but here she lowered it. The effect was further muted as she let her forefinger stroke her upper lip. But he could still see the bald red gums behind it and without thinking compared this to Tumkis's sweet young mouth full of sharp teeth that provided incredible sensations upon the parts of his body most responsive to touch.

He would not let Yngvild break his stare; not for the life of him would he let any woman do that, not even this one, stubborn daughter of the rough Faroes and willing to wrestle with him if necessary. "I cannot lie to you, Yngvild. I want her, surely, but if I have to choose . . ."

She narrowed her fjord blue eyes like a pinch on his tenderest spot; say it, her gaze demanded. In her home country she came from a proud family who owned land and cattle; she had come to Snorrison a fresh thirteen with a handsome dowry that helped to outfit his first ship. She had never taken his name, though she allowed his sons to it, but her claim on him was ironclad.

". . . I would always choose you, love," he said because he knew he must, smelling on his beard a whiff of the Natchez princess. He buried the telltale whiskers in Yngvild's loose dark blond hair, shot through already with silver here and there. She had aged since they last embraced, but the yeasty, cheesy aroma of her nape intoxicated him as it always had while it blurred the red woman's signature, and his erection revealed no secret inspiration.

He was about to extinguish their clam-shell lamp when someone shuffled toward them from the darkness. Its small glow caught the intruder, Caradoc the mediciner, a rotund, pinkish fellow who always seemed to be sweating, glistening as he was now with a sheen from the close quarters down below.

"Well?" Snorrison demanded sharply, not wishing to leave Yngvild but knowing by the look on the physician's face that he must. The man did not have to speak and did not, being thoroughly intimidated by the Norseman.

Fair Beard got to his feet after touching his wife's shoulder.

Used to waiting for her husband, Yngvild settled back among the cushions with the sleeping child laid beside little Cari, watching him as he crossed the deck behind Caradoc to the reddish glow from belowdeck, where their chief lay sunken into a cot built into the sidestrakes.

Even as he descended the peg stair, Fair Beard could see Madoc's unconscious face like a pale lamp, no color, a bad sign, he thought as he moved closer.

There was Rhys in the shadows behind Madoc's bed, and Brother Wyn. The monk's cassock sleeves were rolled up, exposing his sunburned arms, well muscled by his other profession, that of smith and armourer to the house of Gwynedd, whose representative lay unconscious beneath the

whispered Latin prayers. Wyn's head was bent. Fair Beard did
not understand the language, but he knew the situation was
grave. He had heard this mournful prayer before over dying
and dead Christians.

Madoc was the color of ash except for the tips of his bluish
fingers. There were minute X-shaped gashes of dried blood
here and there on his pale arm. Caradoc, lacking leeches,
which as yet he had not found in this strange land, had done
what he could to draw blood, his best battlefield treatment for
curing just about anything.

Fair Beard's nostrils flared; he knew this smell for more than
mere sour habitation and did not want to know more. His
attention was caught by Rhys, who looked up at him from the
Shawnee sunbursts painted in place of eyes.

The Norseman sighed as though kicked, unable to avoid
looking at the man on the cot. He had known Madoc for all the
latter's manhood, had taught him the craft of the sea since
before the Welshman started to shave, owed him his life three
times over, and was indebted to him for two ships. Fair Beard
had always supposed it would be himself who would go first,
being the elder of the partnership they had formed early on
and had kept in honor to this day. Despite himself the big
Norseman felt his eyes water, felt his heart clutch; his old
friend would not be around to finish this enterprise they had
begun together a year ago when Madoc's father, king of
Gwynedd, had exiled him to save his life from vengeful
brothers and invading Englishmen.

Rhys was unlocking a highly polished old harp from a case,
his nimble fingers as fine as eyes at this task he so often
performed. He touched the strings as he found the tuning and
began to play a melody that would accompany an ancient style
of versifying the genealogy of Gwynedd's sovereigns. But he
put off singing. His gradually strengthening notes rattled
through the dank air of the hold, where the smells of many
crowded people still lingered over that of the unmentionable
coming from their unconscious chief.

Fair Beard knew it was customary for a Welsh poet to play
the royal family history when a king lay on his deathbed. He
knew that out on the island nearby, all the people who had
come with this man would know by this music what was
transpiring below the ship's boards. Rhys would play for as
long as it took. Madoc was a strong and healthy man in his

prime. He might last for days like this, Fair Beard mused morosely as he brought himself to touch his commander as chill as a reptile now and damp in the shroud of buffalo-hide robes donated by his Shawnee orphans.

Overhead on deck there suddenly rang the footsteps of several men, mustered from their stations, Fair Beard imagined. They trod toward the port side.

Someone was boarding by the sidelines. Soon their tread crossed to the hold, where Fair Beard went to meet them.

Over the rim of the hold, two of Madoc's men just in from the watch looked down into the gloom.

"Well?" Fair Beard whispered.

The two men tried to look past him at their commander, but the Norseman stood between them on a peg, hiding the deathbed from view.

"Definitely Chickasaw directly across the river," said Evan Powys, a light-haired fellow from a kingdom neighboring Gwynedd who had sworn loyalty to Madoc's father before him.

"How many?"

"They light no fires. Hard to tell," Evan said, resting back on his heels.

The Cherokee whom Madoc had fought yesterday had spared him on the vow that his people would leave this territory immediately, take this river north, downriver, until they were out of Cherokee domains. Part of the agreement was that Madoc's Hundred would not stop along the way and would never come back on pain of death.

The Chickasaw were allies to the Cherokee in this, perhaps for the first time in generations between traditional enemies.

Evan watched the huge Norseman, who had taken command from Madoc, knowing that Fair Beard was familiar with the reputations of the Chickasaw and the other river nations who shared a common culture and language with the tattooed warriors. He also knew that Madoc trusted this man more than any other to assume command in his absence. Yet Evan did not like it, that he must obey this one, a stranger who spoke his language with a thick Scandinavian accent—no wonder, Evan reflected, that the red women called them tangletongues.

Fair Beard finally nodded to dismiss Evan and the others who had been on that shift of the watch.

Evan lingered, his eyes speaking concern for his lord. He heard Rhys's harp down there, playing a special music that would accompany royal genealogy, and he tried to see past the Norseman to determine what it meant. He and everyone else in the company knew that Madoc had not been mortally wounded in his recent battle. All had seen the wound, a miraculous puncture that apparently missed vital organs on its passage through him.

"You are Evan ab Powys, are you not?" Fair Beard said, surprising Evan that he was known; despite Madoc's association with the Norseman, Evan had never served with him.

"I knew your brother."

Evan's lip twitched; his twin had served aboard a ship commanded by Fair Beard just before they left Britain.

"He died a hero, son."

"Sir," Evan said, dropping his gaze because of the painful emotion he knew it betrayed.

"Who follows you on watch?"

Evan looked up with new respect for the Norseman and rattled off a couple of men's names. "And Ari, sir."

"Not my blamen!" Fair Beard exclaimed, and took another peg up the stair. "Is my black man still alive—how can it be that the devil survived?"

"As well as any of us, sir."

"I swear, Ari is my good luck—I would sooner part with my own right hand than lose him," Snorrison said, thinking that Ari was overdue payment on the contract Snorrison had with the black man's family. "We are long past the time of his bride-journey," he added, meaning the sea voyage Snorrison's grandfather had promised the Ethiopian's grandfather from time to time to bring them wives from Africa by way of the slave market of Constantinople. It was a contract the old Norsemen had made to the black warriors defeated by vikings several generations back; brides for their sons' sons' sons to thereby preserve their families in northern regions.

"He married a red woman from Mabila who carries his child," said Evan, who understood the complicated liege contract between the old Norsemen and their vassals.

"Red and black—now that will be a combination, will it not? Especially if the right side gets his mother's skin, and the left his father's!"

The image drew a grudging grin from Evan, who took it for dismissal when Fair Beard stepped back down the stair, shaking his head in wonder at the games that fate played with men's lives.

Another sound from above took his attention, stopping him in his tracks. Someone in moccasins was daintily treading the deck above his head. By the time he returned to the peg stair, he knew when he looked up whose eyes he would be looking into, though he did not know what informed the hunch.

She stood where Evan had crouched at the edge of the hold, looking down at him with those luminous dark eyes, bewitching him even now with his legal wife no doubt staring from her territory out among the crates and children.

Tumkis bent down, he thought to whisper at him in her lilting musical voice and language like perpetual song to the Norseman used to the more guttural Scandinavian. But she did not speak, hardly acknowledged him at all as she swung one tiny moccasined foot over and deftly descended the peg stair before Fair Beard could stop her.

She looked up defiantly at him, still wordless, but he knew she knew. Her nearness filled him with heat, even so, even knowing that he would have to lose her. She knew that he was going to put her down—that is what passed between them in that moment; still she did not bend under what should have been loss of face to a woman of his or her nation. He thought this was what she had come for, to defy him with her sensual presence, to torment him as long as she might even under his wife's disdaining eyes, but he immediately saw this was not her business at all.

Tumkis had a satchel over one small sculpted shoulder, whose grace was evident even through the beaded dress she wore. Glow from the dim lamp beside the sick man's bed reflected off the copper spools in her ears and made blue shadows on her long, fine hair, usually braided, but undone now as it was before they made love. Sparks snapped between them, causing her hair to flare out like a thing of independent life as he reached out to touch her.

She stepped back, demurely lowering her glance to her rounding belly, where their child grew. She denied him the touch of her now that he had made his choice. How did she know, he wondered, not having spoken to her or even looked into the twin wells of her eyes since reuniting with Yngvild.

"I will save your miko," she said in her song-language. He had picked up the Natchez language quickly while living with them these past few months, but he did not quite understand what she said because she distracted him so. Beneath his jerkin, he felt his body respond.

She flicked her gaze upon him in that vulnerable moment. She knew, damn her. A subtle play across her lips revealed that she knew how she aroused him. Witch, he thought, wanting to throw her down right here within the sound of his lord's death rattle, all else be cursed, and take her.

"What?" he stammered.

She patted the bag slung over her shoulder. "Right here, tangletongue, right here is what he needs."

Without further remark she turned away from the golden man.

Though no word had been spoken, Fair Beard ground his teeth, felt pain in his incipient erection, and knew in his bones that he had lost her forever.

Chapter 3

Rhys missed the beat when he heard Fair Beard's conversation with Tumkis, and his nostrils flared when she moved closer to his position at the head of Madoc's cot. The woman's aroma was musky, entirely sensual, blended with things in her loosened medicine bag that he was unable to distinguish, but which presented their combined scents to his sensitive nose.

Gwen, pale in the shadows, her sleeves rolled up past her elbows, held a damp cloth; she had just sponged her father's vacant face and rinsed the cloth again in a basin on the boards. The stirring water made a crystalline sound in the heavy air of the hold. She turned with the dripping rag to cool his brow as Tumkis approached.

"What—?" said Caradoc, his sharpened lancet poised ready to draw more of Madoc's blood when he saw the diminutive Natchez woman, no taller than a girl, approaching his master with determination in her eyes, her hand in the stiff bag, and complete indifference to anyone but the unconscious white man on the buffalo robe sweating away his life in the pale lamplight.

She whipped out a thick bladder of her simples; the smell was stronger as she opened the drawstrings.

Caradoc reached out to touch her, to stop her from meddling, but Fair Beard's voice stayed the mediciner's hand.

"Let her try," Snorrison said as he joined the group around the chief's bedside. He was so tall in the low-ceilinged hold, he had to stoop slightly to avoid bumping his head on the timbers above. "What can it hurt?"

Caradoc hesitated with another glance at the unconscious man breathing so shallowly that he did not seem to breathe at all, then caught Fair Beard's warning, a narrowed glance, and drew back.

32

"I am against more bloodletting, myself," Gwen said, wiping Madoc's face again, leaning close to his ear and whispering "Tad, Tad," which in her language was the word for *daddy*.

"My authority is no less than the great Aristotle himself, who prescribed bloodletting for any venomous condition," Caradoc protested.

Rhys plucked a few more notes of the dirge he had begun on the old harp named Llais Mel, Honeyvoice in the Cymraeg language. Behind him, Winnowed Rice stood up from the short stool where she had been sitting, her nostrils flaring with recognition of most of the compound aromas coming from Tumkis's bag. Softly—in trade Muskogean, which all nations hereabout spoke—she said, "I have already tried this remedy."

Tumkis did not look up from her busy hands as she threw off the buffalo robe, exposing Madoc's bare chest and abdomen where a stained rough cloth, someone's torn hem no doubt, was tied over the puncture wound.

"Here now," said Brother Wyn, who had stopped his silent prayer when the red woman entered the hold.

"Remove it," Tumkis ordered directly to Caradoc, herself disdaining to touch the filthy rag.

Fair Beard translated her order as he stepped beside the monk, this having the same effect as an admonition. "The Shawnee woman has done her best; likewise our fine physician. Let Tumbling Water have a go at him." Himself, he had said farewell to his old friend, counting Madoc hopeless in his present condition.

Reluctance weighing every move, Caradoc untied the bandage and with Gwen's help slipped it from beneath Madoc, who might have been a slab of meat for all his response.

Tumkis speared the Norseman with a meaningful glance. He had watched her work before and moved in to assist with a secret pang in his gut to see her talented fingers touch the flesh of another man—especially this man, who owned the Norseman's devotion and loyalty—even to minister to fatal illness.

Tumkis sprinkled half the contents of the bag onto Madoc's damp, pale stomach, careful not to get any on the puckered bluish wound, where glistened a fleck of blood at the spot where the bandage had adhered to flesh when Caradoc pulled it away.

"Boiling water," she said officiously, and handed the half-empty bag behind her without looking to see who might catch it, while Fair Beard translated.

"Mix this into the water to make a thin paste. Bring it back to me still hot."

Caradoc caught the pouch falling and left them to go up on deck, where supper's charcoal was still hot on its bed of sand.

Rhys let the notes slip from his instrument and fade with a twang in the dank air, but Tumkis said to Winnowed Rice in trade jargon, "Tell your shaman we need the song, Dog-Woman."

Winnowed Rice bristled at the insult, though she knew this was what other nations commonly named the Shawnee because of their use of dog-pulls. She said to Rhys in his language, "It is good to continue playing, husband."

Tumkis looked up at her with a sly smile. "So, you too have learned to love them, eh, sister?" It was so direct and personal a comment on the heels of insult, Winnowed Rice was taken aback. She did not respond in words.

Tumkis added, "They do have certain . . . attractions which are of interest to a woman," and continued her work, spitting onto the powder on Madoc's flesh.

"Now wait just a minute—" Wyn started to protest as the Natchez woman smeared her spittle into the foul stuff, slipping her fingers over the sunken abdomen and near the man's groin.

Fair Beard flung out an arm to stop the monk from interfering, pierced by the irony that he, too, was in conflict over her ministrations upon the body of his friend.

Still thoroughly massaging the pasty mixture over the abdomen except for the spot circling the wound, she looked up at Fair Beard and said, "All of you can leave now."

Fair Beard's narrowed eyes rounded, and his lip rippled, while Winnowed Rice leaned backward with an exclamatory sound.

"What did she say?" Wyn demanded, handling the cross tied to his rope cincture.

Gwen needed no translation; though she did not speak Natchez, she comprehended through that language's similarity to Muskogean, and by tone and gesture.

Snorrison commanded, "All of you, leave."

Rhys abruptly stopped playing the harp; notes rang thinly and faded.

"You—" Tumkis said sharply in her language, looking at the blind man's face painted with stylized suns in place of eyes. "Continue to play near the hold, all night long, until I tell you to stop."

He had no doubt she was speaking to him because the tip of her finger tapped the leather jerkin on his chest, beaded exquisitely with dyed porcupine quills by the hand of Winnowed Rice. He intuitively knew what the Natchez was saying, but lest there be any misunderstanding, she meaningfully twanged a harp string.

Winnowed Rice translated softly, anyway, and pulled at his elbow. Rhys made a stubborn sound, but she pulled harder, and he finally complied as Tumkis announced over her shoulder, "Shawnee woman, we will need a sweatlodge before dawn."

She observed that Winnowed Rice hesitated. Thinking she was loath to say she was in her moonblood, Tumkis signed that it was understood. Red women from all the nations were horrified that whites did not practice isolation, but those red sisters who chose to stay among the whites had accepted their looser custom. Such scruples would be impossible under the Hundred's exile circumstances; still, it meant a wife did not cook or sleep in her husband's bedroll because of her own more disciplined customs. To build a medicinal sweatlodge was likewise taboo during menstruation.

Tumkis said, "Tell my servants I said to build the sweatlodge for him." She regarded her unmoving patient. "We will need much cedar to burn for this one."

"I will not leave him," Wyn protested, but was ignored. Twice he had started last rites for Madoc, but Gwen's penetrating stare had stopped him, and she said, "It is only the medicine that makes him sleep, Domme; do not be so gloomy." But he had kept around his shoulders his prayer shawl, the one woven on Mona Isle of the finest wool in relief tapestry of the stations of the cross, and held a breviary in his hand as he prayed while their earthly lord slipped farther and farther away.

"Snorrison, you cannot mean to leave him with this . . . this witchery," Wyn protested, but the Norseman only looked up at him with an affirmative nod.

"Tell the physician to bring the medicine as soon as possible," Tumkis said to Fair Beard, who turned and said to the

monk, "The bloodletter must be hurried with that potion."
Wyn angled his big head morosely upon his stout neck and
continued toward the peg stair, where Rhys preceded Winnowed Rice up to the deck.

"You, too," Tumkis said to the Norseman without looking
up.

He was silent as she worked another few rounds on Madoc's
abdomen, then stopped and wiped her hands on a square of
mulberry cloth from her satchel. She took out a thin stick
frayed into a brush, and two clam shells sealed with pitch.
From the first she applied charcoal-and-oil paint in a neat
circle a handwidth around the bare wound.

She spit on the brush and wiped it against the stained cloth.
She painted inside the black circle with red ocher paint mixed
with powdered pine pitch from the other shell, all the way up
to the swollen lips of the wound.

"What are you going to do?" Fair Beard demanded as she
threw off the corners of the robe to expose all of Madoc's pale,
hairy body and began to massage the compound into the skin
of his chest and upper arms, where many old battle wounds
had healed into puckered scars and ridges.

Fair Beard watched her diligent labor as she slowly coated
Madoc with the blackish paste, from time to time spitting to
spread it more evenly, before he repeated the question in her
language.

He waited a full minute as she began to work on the sailor's
strong thighs, well muscled and toned despite his condition.
"Answer me, woman—what are you going to do?"

She startled him when she stood up straight from her bent
posture, so close he felt the rounding of her abdomen where
their child grew, her hands held away from her sides so that
she did not touch him with the sticky medicine. "I am going to
draw the Chickasaw poison from him. I am going to draw it out
and battle the evil that has been placed in him. I am going to
do this with my own body, which is a fragment of the sun itself,
and it will be dangerous to him and me and to our son, Man
Whose Weapon Sings." This was Snorrison's Natchez name,
and an erotic pun to boot because the word for *weapon* was
also anatomical. "Dangerous to anyone who is near, especially
to another man who has felt my body as close as you have so
that we were once one."

Her implication stung him into a step backward.

"What do you expect me to do, Tumbling Water?" he begged of her in her language, an uncharacteristic whine in so big a man as himself. "I told you I had another wife, and you accepted."

"I accept her," Tumkis answered in a softened voice, but still standing before him with her hands flung out and fire in her eye. "You must make her accept me. I am of higher rank among my people than she is among yours. It is for her to realize what an honor it is that I, niece of the high miko, offer to be her little sister."

That was the euphemism for a second wife among the Natchez.

It was as if she had smacked him the way she had earlier struck her servant. She looked at her stained hands and then at the patient between them.

"You cannot save him," Fair Beard spat. "You are just doing this to twist the knife in me, making me watch you touch another man's sex." Actually she had scrupulously avoided that part of the chief's anatomy with her paint.

At that moment, Caradoc returned with the mixture she ordered, sucking a scandalized breath at the lord's nakedness in front of his daughter and the immodest red woman. He lingered after he handed the paste in a wooden cup to Gwen, loath as he was to participate directly with the savage female.

Tumkis took it, not glancing up as the physician, ignored, departed again, but slowly, shaking his head at what he considered the shame of the situation, muttering something to Gwen no one else was able to hear, watching the Natchez woman as he stepped upon the bottom peg.

Tumkis held the cup of thick dark brew in both hands between herself and the Norseman but made no further motion.

"I will not leave you alone with him to do some Natchez trick," he sputtered, imagination rampant with knowledge of some of her techniques.

Gwen said softly, "She will not be alone with him, Uncle Snorri," but he seemed not to hear anything in a European language so furied was he at Tumkis's stubborn determination. Still she did not move, as if to say by stillness that she would not continue until her conditions were met.

Fair Beard swore loudly and kicked the stool where Winnowed Rice had been sitting. It rattled across the boards and hit the straking with a crack that startled Gwen, who had never seen the man like this before except in battle.

Tumkis did not move, as though turned to stone with the cup in her hands.

"Damn you, bitch," he said in Scandinavian, his lips the merest slit of a line, and chewed in fury at the inside of his mouth.

Eyes downcast, she sighed loudly with her next breath, but made no further move.

"This is only to torment me," he hissed just above a whisper. "You know he does not have a chance."

Just then, as though to confound his old friend, the man on the cot moaned in his dark sleep and twisted from something specific that only he could see behind closed eyes. This was the first movement, other than shallow breathing, that he had made since falling into unconsciousness. Gwen dropped to her knees to touch his temple with a cool hand. He turned toward her, but without opening his eyes, his bruised-looking fingers clutching at the bedding. He seemed to be saying something, though not even his daughter heard what it might be.

Tumkis looked at him and then gave Fair Beard an I-told-you-so. "The poultice is already working," she said, and took a step even closer to the Norseman. "But the poultice alone will not save him. It will only make his death more painful without the formulas."

Out on deck beneath the stars, Rhys began another tune, something different from what he played earlier, in a lighter key.

"Admit you are trying to punish me, and I will do as you say," Fair Beard said hoarsely as, up on deck, Winnowed Rice called out to the Natchez women on shore, "Your sun says to build a sweathouse—"

Again Tumkis demurely dropped her glance, staring into the thick stuff in the cup. "You must influence your other woman."

Above, muted by the ship's timbers and echoing across the water, Ahoskas replied a water-echoed affirmative to Winnowed Rice.

Gwen, who had stepped toward the Norseman, laid a calming hand on his muscle-knotted arm, evilly bruised from recent battle. He blinked once as though realizing for the first time she was there. "Do not worry, Uncle Snorri—look at him—I think she has already helped him."

Fair Beard stared at her, then glared at Tumkis, muttered a filthy but limp curse beneath his breath, and stamped from the presence of his Natchez wife, leaving the two young women alone with Madoc, whose lips moved silently as he argued with demons tearing him apart from the inside out.

Up on deck all eyes were on Fair Beard as he climbed from the glowing hold. Rhys was playing a lilting soft Celtic song, sitting near Yngvild and Winnowed Rice over by the crates where the two babies were cradled, one of them beginning to fuss. The sailors near the brazier were standing, the better to see the Norseman stride across the deck, but they turned away upon his approach so as not to seem curious. Two others had been hanging in the rigging near the yawning hold, though no tasks needed doing up there this late on a dark night. Quietly they scurried down, both handling a coil of rope to look purposeful. Fair Beard saw that neither was on duty, though, and snarled as they passed him on their way to their bedrolls aft.

Between himself and the hot sassafras tea he smelled brewing on the coals, there stepped the Natchez warrior Arrow Always Red, spectral in his many tattoo rings on arm and leg and all the way up his chest and neck. Most of his skin was bare, though the night grew chilly; it was October according to Madoc's calculations, and though this was a much more southerly clime than the isles of Britain, not to mention Fair Beard's homeland of Iceland, winter was still on the way.

But the Natchez brave showed more tattooed skin than leather clothing, though he did wear a long decorated loincloth and a sort of turban of beaten mulberry bark around his wide head. His hair was cropped in various twists and hanks tied off and banded with leather thongs and feathers. The single bit of metal on his person was a copper nose ring, the puncture wound of which had turned the flesh of his septum slightly green.

The two men nodded at each other, in the wordless Natchez manner that said much, and stood to one side with their backs to the rest of the company, who tried not to appear too interested in what they were saying. Fair Beard, as nominal chief during Madoc's incapacity, was naturally the focus of everyone's interest, though gossip had spread through them like a flash fire that the captain still lived down below.

"How stands the west bank?" Snorrison asked in fluent

Natchez, himself fully three heads taller than the stockily built warrior, who was all thighs and shoulders with a stout neck and triangular face accentuated by his tonsure.

"Thick with Chickasaw, Man Whose Weapon Sings."

"Ready for blood?"

"They mumble among themselves. They say your Weather Eyes broke his vow."

Fair Beard nodded. Among Madoc's own people, a vow was as sacred as it was to the red people. He could not explain exactly why the white chieftain had broken his against his own conscience, especially since a royal vow was more inviolate than a commoner's; but personally Fair Beard Snorrison would have done exactly as Madoc ab Gwynedd had done to save his ship, this ship now steadily anchored beneath his own bare feet. Madoc was a man who made quick decisions, often on instinct, and more often than not, correct ones.

Still, among some men a vow is a vow. Among the red nations, Madoc's new vow to head downriver on the Tennessee was under suspicion.

"What action will they take?"

"For now they wait and see. But," said Arrow Always Red, "they will come across the river if we are here after dawn."

"You will explain to them that Weather Eyes cannot be moved until he regains his health."

The warrior nodded. He did not smile, but the lower portion of his jaw relaxed, and he tilted his head in the direction of the hold. "My lady Tumbling Water will have him up on his feet in two sunrises."

Fair Beard almost snarled, then caught himself lest he give his feelings away to one who would judge them unmanly.

"A minor wager, Man Whose Weapon Sings?" The warrior's tar eyes flickered with disturbing mirth. Among the lowest-caste men of his nation, the only men a noblewoman like Tumkis was permitted to take for a husband, there was a saying: "Do not complain of heat if you take the sun to bed."

Fair Beard involuntarily glanced toward his yellow-haired wife, whose attention was somewhere else, involved with one of the babies—the little girl from the sound of it, who had not resumed sleep, though her father continued to play music that usually lulled her. From where Fair Beard stood in the soft illumination coming from aft his position, Yngvild was the beauty he had married, no wrinkles about the eyes, no naked gums beneath her lips. A tall, handsome woman, he thought. He forced himself to stare at her so he would not think of the dark female with magic hands on another man's body below his feet under the boards.

The ship groaned slightly with the current and a little breeze, which had come up suddenly from the west on an otherwise calm night.

Arrow Always Red knew Fair Beard would not bet against his friend's recovery, no matter how much he shared the Natchez's love of gambling on any and every chance, and man to man. But it gave secret satisfaction to the gritty red fighter that neither this outlander's strength, his size, his wit, nor his terrible iron weapon with the voice of the deathbird could defend him against the woman who would have her way down there.

"My lady Tumkis is a powerful sorcerer. She loses a patient only when she means to."

Fair Beard glared at the man, hating him and Tumkis and their entire nation for giving such power to a woman. He cursed them all in his and their own languages, plus Cymraeg. Then he swore in Irish and threw in a Moorish and a Hebrew curse, gleanings from his youthful travels.

The Natchez grinned hugely as the tangletongue exhausted his vast store of profanity.

Arrow Always Red thought about several curses he might give him at some other time to add to his impressive collection. The Natchez were known for three things—their shrewd deal making, their women suns, and their curses. For now, there passed between him and Snorrison an unspoken agreement—Arrow Always Red would meet the Chickasaw should they appear in the morning—and neither spoke of any bet they might have made.

Across the ringing water, the Natchez women hailed red sisters among the Hundred. "Come help us prepare a sweatlodge for Chief Weather Eyes." And Mabilan and Shawnee voices returned inquiries about his condition and about what the Natchez sun was going to do.

"She is going to save your miko, cousin," sang Green Woman, and others took up the chant, adding Madoc's red name, Weather Eyes, Weather Eyes, Weather Eyes, to the song.

Rhys retrieved Cari from the Norsewoman's care and

stowed her, fussing, in the cradleboard on his back, where she began to coo as she found the beat irresistible. Honeyvoice sprang to the rhythm, which was close enough to a spirited hymn for the monks to join in with Latin affirmation—all this music swelled above the wide, slow river like a mist wafting westward to the shadowed places where Chickasaw warriors crouched gnawing cold jerky, listening to the foreign sounds coming from the strangers and their red allies.

One of the old Shawnee men died that night, and the next morning the Shawnee women and children of Madoc's Hundred were getting ready to say good-bye with a traditional round dance and keening circle.

Tumkis appeared on deck and approached Fair Beard in Yngvild's arms. They lay beneath the blanket where the baby Bjorn sat in a puddle of pee, clapping his hands and mumbling in baby talk.

The child saw the Natchez woman and cried out a note of joy; she clucked her sound at him and swooped him up, arching her back to balance the huge child on her hip. She spoke a nonsense chant that pulled a loud squeal from him, waking his father, who came awake as if kicked, naked and squinting at the bright morning light and the sounds of red ceremonial coming from the beach.

Yngvild more lazily groaned and rolled over to touch the baby who was not there. She started and looked up with the brightness of the sky in her eyes.

"Greeting to our father the sun and another day of life," Tumkis said formally, reciting the phrase that began each Natchez dawn.

Fair Beard snorted and growled; Yngvild beside him got quickly to her knees and reached for Bjorn, who did not see his mother for the dark smiling woman who held him.

Tumkis did not look as though she had spent a night without sleep. Her eyes were clean and her hair unruffled, though her hands were still filmed with residue of the black poultice. The astringent aroma lingered around her as she bent to deposit Yngvild's son in his mother's arms.

"You must tell your men to bring Weather Eyes to the sweatlodge, husband," Tumkis said in Natchez, which Yngvild did not understand.

Fair Beard got clumsily to his feet, the bedclothes wrapped about his waist as he reached for his jerkin, which hung on a handy part of the ship's equipment. "How is he?" he asked, squinting at her over his shoulder as he drew on his trews and leaned to find his boots.

"Da-ma-wah!" Bjorn insisted, trying to free himself from Yngvild's grasp as she found her breast and offered the nipple to what should be a hungry babe. He pulled in Tumkis's direction, where she clucked at him softly until Yngvild gave her a scathing look. A fleck of milk oozed from the swollen nipple she would as soon have emptied.

Tumkis sank to her knees to touch the child's hand and turn his face to his mother's teat. Yngvild, squinting in the new light and at the nearness of the woman in her veil of strong, strange aromas, stared at Tumkis. Bjorn latched onto the breast like a limpet, drawing a gasp from her—she plucked at his fat cheek to get him to loosen his toothless bite. He twisted, still holding painfully onto the nipple with pink naked gums, to giggle in Tumkis's direction.

Rhys and Winnowed Rice approached from their own nest amidships, with Cari wriggling in the sling and beginning to call out for breakfast. Rough-cheeked and gravel-voiced from a long night of singing, Rhys leaned to hand her over to Yngvild, who bared her other breast.

Tumkis scowled at this man who insisted on caring for a baby, something no red man of any nation or status would have done, and said to Winnowed Rice, "Tell your man he should let Yellow Flowers care for the baby girl, and I will watch Little Bear, because all this day he must play the magic songs."

Winnowed Rice nodded, and Tumkis added, "Why does he insist on doing women's work with the child?"

"Her mother was a suicide," Winnowed Rice replied, "and he thinks he must make up for her loss."

"What did she say?" Rhys asked.

"She wants you to continue making music for Weather Eyes."

"Well," he replied.

"For the magic, you see," Winnowed Rice said to him in the Shawnee language. "She says she will watch Little Bear so Yellow Flowers does not have too many babies to care for."

"She has a good idea, Yngvild," Rhys said, and translated for the Norsewoman, who asked, "What was it she called me?"

Tumkis leaned over with her childlike face and smiled sweetly as she patted the Norsewoman's long thigh, repeating the nickname while Rhys explained. Yngvild was momentarily abashed at the unexpected gesture and covered her empty breast while securing Cari in the crook of her other arm.

"Like my own child, Yellow Flowers," Tumkis said softly, mother to mother with the thick blond baby's head between them.

By then the strongest back in the crew, Fair Beard's, was engaged in hauling the captain from the hold, assisted by several sailors who darted here and there to wait at the sidelines for the Norseman to reach the rail.

"You tell her not to make him cross-eyed," Yngvild instructed Fair Beard, and he, nodding, translated.

Tumkis tightened her full lips, but nodded in return. Her servants had been training the baby's eyes in the noble stare, considered important for his rank as the son of the chief.

"And no cradleboard."

"Oh, it is too late for that now, Man Whose Weapon Sings," Tumkis replied when he told her the added condition. "Too bad, because your son should have the noble brow."

When Snorrison told his white wife that his Natchez wife would abide by her wishes, Yngvild seemed to darken but found no argument against it. She grudgingly nodded, and Tumkis sprang to her feet, arching her back to balance the child as she padded across the deck, all eyes on her as they lowered Madoc in the buffalo robe into the round boat bobbing in the shadows against the mossy side of the vessel. She said something privately to Fair Beard, who took Bjorn as she scuttled as quick as a crab down the network of sidelines and settled into the coracle in front of Madoc, who was dazed and uncoordinated, blinking under the assault of sunlight.

When she saw his hand trailing in the water, she leaned forward to retrieve it—no alligators lived in these colder waters, but such precautions were an ingrained habit to the lowlander woman. Just as she tucked the chief's hand on his lap, he opened his smoky eyes in a burst of lucidity and said something to her in his rolling language.

"All is well, white man," she assured him the way she might speak to a frightened child.

From above her in the sidelines, one of the sailors handed down Bjorn. Behind him stood Yngvild at the rail, staring down and unmoving. Tumkis accepted the wiggling child and couched him with a soothing cluck betwixt her thighs, took the paddle in her hand, and began to maneuver the coracle across the short water to shore.

All on deck stood watching with amazed eyes. Madoc lay back in the little boat, shielding his eyes from the brilliant sun, which exploded upon the river suddenly as it soared above the low mist hugging the water's surface. He was still as gray as clay and appeared not to have strength in his arms and legs, but he was alive and moving, was awake and not complaining as the small woman with the straight spine and long hair that flashed like a bird's wing in the light pulled them closer to the shore. There her women waited for her and her patient with robes of trimmed buffalo hides, which they flung over the shoulders of the two as they disembarked the trembling craft at the water's edge and were whisked off to the new sweatlodge made from trimmed and notched saplings. The fire was banked with red-glowing stones from the Tennessee, and when they cracked the hide flap to admit the red woman and the shaking white man, great warm billows of pure hissing steam rose up to join the river mist, which the sun was quickly burning off.

And all day long Gwen sat near the river's edge, the empty eagle cage tumbled at her feet, looking upstream between sudden naps, waiting for David Iron to meet them as he promised he would do. Tumkis had talked to her as they massaged her father back to life in those dark hours; the Natchez princess had told the Cymreig princess that she must undo the bad luck she and she alone had brought on the company by keeping an eagle in a cage. Tumkis repeated several stories of serious ill fortune that descended upon those who tampered with the freedom of eagles.

Once, she said, an old Natchez woman decided to raise eaglets to sell the feathers to young warriors. She was turned into an alligator by her greed and beset upon by an eagle who tore out her eyes and feasted on her brain while she lived.

Tumkis promised Gwen that if she immediately released the eagle, her husband would appear. He would come canoeing downstream, she was sure, with a fleet of Yuchi canoes behind him, leading his father and those of his Yuchi band out of Cherokee lands to reunite with their white allies.

Depressed by events and physical exhaustion, and burdened by guilt that she might have added to her father's illness, Gwen finally opened the weir and let the bird soar out on its feeding run. She kicked the cage and smashed it underfoot, and when the young bird tried to land on her arm, she shrieked at it, threw river sand up, and called the Shawnee dogs to bark until it flew off, confused, to the higher trees in the center of the island.

While Madoc steamed in the earthen lodge, which the Natchez and Mabilan women kept supplied with driftwood and deadfall from the island's small heartland grove, the Shawnee, in mourning clay paint, pulled their hair, slashed their arms, and laid their circular patterns on the sandy beach. They danced to quickened drums and whistles, little boys smeared with river mud stamping out steps their dead fathers and older brothers had taught them were the proper farewell to an old warrior.

And everyone thought—some even said aloud—that the old Shawnee man had died in Madoc's place. Nobody argued, because this seemed to be the truth of it in the Tennessee morning sunlight quickly burning away dew and the river's nighttime sweat. Every leaf, blade, and branch looked polished. The slow old river itself murmured optimism and reasons for hope, even against the arrival at dawn of the Chickasaw in sleek painted boats, their eyes shifting with suspicion just as Arrow Always Red had predicted.

Chapter 4

A t firstlight they came in, silently inscribing a circle around the big ship anchored in its calm little backwater bay. They came in half a hundred sleek canoes riding so low in the water, that the three or four hundred naked, plucked, blue-tattooed rowers seemed to be walking along the bottom, up to their waists in the flow.

Fair Beard and all his twenty or so men, fully armed and armoured and ready for battle, stood nervously down on the western beach, milling about and muttering while Arrow Always Red waded ankle-deep to formally address the Chickasaw headman.

Bowmen on deck had arrows nocked; all the red women stood behind the shore contingent, which included the mixed bag of children, the white women, a few off-duty seamen, and Caradoc, and in a southerly knot gathered the clergy enrobed for Mass.

Only five of the crowd were not visible, though they certainly were present. Tumkis and her women tended Weather Eyes in the sweatlodge, despite great mumblings from those who stood through the night, the off-duty seamen and the monks. Nearby were scattered several Natchez warriors under the command of Tumkis through her champion, Arrow Always Red, who stood before the Chickasaw host.

"Tell your warriors to loosen their strings, brother," said the tattooed chieftain, looking over the shoulder of Arrow Always Red at the tense fighting force. He was an honored warrior among his swamp clan, his hair tied off in various hanks and braids, some burnt short, some tied with cord, a distant cousin to Arrow Always Red on his mother's side. They had confronted with red-painted war sticks between them several times, and each had drawn blood.

47

"My honored opponent, Imala'ko." Arrow Always Red started to explain that the white chief almost took the westward journey last night.

Imala'ko, whose name was a pun that meant both Man Who Whips Up Many, and Man Whom Many Whip, held up one hand, which was tattooed so completely that even his fingertips held indelible blue dots that connected him with the most venerable ancestors. "My honorable opponent, I do not come here for conflict."

Arrow Always Red held a long stare with the other, then turned and said something to Fair Beard, who shouted for all the whites to relax.

From three canoes stepped three Chickasaw bonepickers, elaborately black-feathered and mud-smeared and stark naked otherwise, save for tattoo bracelets up and down every limb and neck.

This trio of birdish and beaded witchery approached Brother Wyn and Father John. Behind the two monks the handful of brothers, including Father Brian, crossed themselves and began to recite the Lord's Prayer in unison to counter the glaring Chickasaw medicine men.

Laymen joined in. Rhys touched Llais Mel, and the Shawnee women stamped their feet in time to the monks' chant while the river underscored them with its constant murmur.

"Why do you come in red paint this morning if not for conflict?" the Natchez politely asked the Chickasaw.

"To bid you wait here. Continue your journey after the moon is full."

"But by doing this I will break Fox's directive."

"This is his new directive. You are to wait here for the Yuchi." He held out a bundle of slender carved sticks, one for each of the days in the extension granted Madoc's Hundred.

The word he used left no doubt that he was not speaking of a single Yuchi person, perhaps David Iron returning from his mission. He meant the plural, the nation, or at least part of it.

"The From-Far-Aways have taken up the trail?" The Yuchi nation had been sedentary corn growers for untold generations, with only a vague oral history about a former migration to their upcountry between the Mabilans and the Cherokee in the headwaters of the Tennessee River. Their name meant Children of the Sun from Far Away. But for short, and in derision, their neighbors called them the From-Far-Aways.

"They follow their headman, Sun Caller, and his council and three Yuchi villages. Leading them all is Eagle Ring Man."

"This is wonderful," Gwen said as she stumbled down to the water's edge. She had enough trade Muskogean to understand that she was hearing affirmation of Tumkis's prophecy—she said all this would happen if the eagle was freed. Behind Gwen the red women who understood Chickasaw rippled with excitement; the people-eaters were not going to attack.

Gwen started the women clapping and calling out their joy.

The tension broke after that, and people began to drift away from the center as the Chickasaw and Natchez warriors stepped up out of the water and sat down to have a smoke. Arrow Always Red mentioned to the Chickasaw chief that the whites wanted to trade for more corn now that it appeared they would be delayed.

Fair Beard joined them, and they held a council that lasted until firstlight broke through thick clouds in the east, with the end result that the Chickasaw bartered forty bushels of corn and ten bags of meal for three glass beads, two iron kitchen knives, and a bent hoe-head.

The women had the fires stoked. There was plenty of deadfall on this island, which had snagged much debris from the river's last crest. Breakfast bread was soon frying on hot stones kept buried in overnight coals as birdcalls echoed from the eastern bank blotted out by river fog.

The light on the tops of the tallest trees was like butter melting down as the sun climbed higher.

Butter, Brother Wyn thought sitting on a log beside his monks' smoldering campfire, his meditations on Celtic saints born in the month of October interrupted with associations churned up by the golden light. The few monks under his shepherding as head of a monastery that no longer existed halfway around the world, were off with Father John selecting a site to celebrate a Mass for continued deliverance from their enemies and for Madoc's recovery, leaving their abbot alone to hagiologic meditations calculated to provoke a sermon to cover both a funeral and a thanksgiving.

Saints Colman, Kenneth, Coman, Donatus, beloved Bee of Cumberland and her magic bracelet, escaping a forced marriage to flee eastward across the Irish Sea to the rugged coast of exile to wed the Christ; and, of course, Wyn's own namesake, missionary to the Germans celebrated October 21.

The buttery light melted down the muffin trees.

How long since I last tasted butter? He tried to remember—was it at Owen ab Gwynedd's house on Mona Isle, or before, the night of the raid on the monastery where Wyn had served most of his adult life as blacksmith forging chain links, plowshares, and horseshoes. The taste of butter mingled in his recall with the smell of burning oak. He tried to imagine the monastery changed into a Saxon minster, the oak trees chopped down because the English always punished the oaks for their association with the ancient Druids who held them sacred, though the old pagan religion descended from the ancient Greeks had been wiped out by the Romans more than a thousand years ago.

The night of the raid he had stashed away a cold biscuit in his cassock pocket and eaten it secretly on the road to Owen ab Gwynedd's estate, where the community was given sanctuary. There, Wyn had met Madoc and joined the exile that led to this moment. The butter had hardened between the flaky layers of bread. His last taste of butter was in the commission of that little sin of hoarding, because he did not share the buttery morsel with any of his brothers that night on the trail, but munched away in the darkness. It took him seven hours to eat it all, and he shared only those crumbs he turned out of his greasy pockets to be found by ants or birds in his wake.

Far behind him the bells, drums, and voices of these other pagans, the Shawnee, braided with the murmur of the Tennessee River as they went about their burial rituals. They had lost several of their tribe during the past few days, and the old man's death last night was their good-bye to them all. This was the first chance since leaving Cherokee country to perform the dances that would send the departed on their way westward to follow the sun—not so different from the Celtic idea of the west as God's Paradise, Wyn mused, missionary zeal deflated by circumstances. He found himself deeply moved by Shawnee devotion to their grandfather, who had been the eldest of their once-prosperous tribe, reputed to have achieved one hundred or more years.

Their mourning was dramatic and authentic, wrenching to the heart to hear all the women and children moan together, hair smeared with mud and their own blood, and he longed to comfort them with Christian assurances.

He despaired that they would ever accept Christian services, further burdening himself with his failures as a missionary. At any moment he could feel the spot on his back where during the Battle of Muscle Shoals his golden map had stopped an arrow right in the middle of the Holy Land, which he interpreted as a clear sign from the Lord that his duty lay in that direction. If Madoc was right and this was Cathay, then the Holy Land in the hands of the Infidel was over there in the direction of the gone sun that had left a smear of red light like a last ember in the charcoal sky. That had been last night.

But today, the Shawnee music that sounded so much like wind and running water was oddly comforting and appropriate as his thoughts wandered to mundanities of his lost nation of Cymru (Wales to the English invaders), to the little luxuries and homey comforts missed only because he would never taste them again in this beautiful wild country bereft of sheep, pigs, and cows.

Butter.

God forgive me, Wyn thought, closing his eyes. He remembered the fat, thick taste, the rich transparent golden oil coating lips and fingers, lactary perfume steaming up from the soft broken heart of a flat circular oat loaf crusty on the outside, the bottom slightly singed just off the hearth.

He wondered if the furry cattle-like creatures they encountered back on the mountain might yield milk, butter, and cheese. What did the red women call them. Te. That was it, but he recalled the te were belligerent and unlikely to domesticate. Surely there was some sort of dairy animal here. For there not to exist in this region animals mentioned in scripture was to place it in some kind of perdition, some border country between God's and Satan's domains.

These thoughts led him to speculate upon alternatives to what he was used to in the way of farm animals. Perhaps deer, he mused, recalling a story that the Countess of Chester in his home cantref kept tame deer from whose milk she had cheeses made that she donated to the archbishop. Himself, Wyn was a lowly monk who was too far down the ecclesiastical line to collect so much as dropped crumbs of deer cheese, but he was ready to experiment with the abundant local beasts.

"Butter . . . " someone said nearby, startling the abbot out of his reverie. He blinked and turned where he sat on a fallen log near his monks' smoldering campfire separated by laurel from the closest women. He saw Rhys ab Meredydd on the arm of his Shawnee consort.

"I say, Domme," the blind man repeated, not butter at all, while Winnowed Rice dropped modestly back to leave them alone. "May I sit with you?"

The poet was newly shaved—Brother Wyn could smell the soaproot Winnowed Rice had used to lubricate his cheek—and wore a clean sash over his empty eye sockets; but Wyn could see the red woman's artwork just beneath the cloth, which was slightly stained ocher by her bear-grease paint and lightly tinged with pine scent.

"Of course, my son," Wyn replied, nodding pleasantly to Winnowed Rice, who looked back briefly. He made room on the makeshift bench.

Rhys sighed as he seated himself, laid his staff against his shoulder, and stretched his arms before him while taking a long sniff at the warming air. "I have interrupted your prayers, Domme."

"Not at all. I was reminiscing, actually, about home."

The sun's rays had reached the lower branches of the oak trees, already turning dusty brown with the season. Behind them laurel leaves rattled in the warm breeze that belied the month; it might be June but for the telltale turning of the foliage to golds and reds all around them on this island in the Tennessee stream.

"What do you miss most?"

"Food," Wyn confessed without shame.

"The smell of roasting pork," Rhys reminisced, salivating at the mere thought.

"Buttered bread."

"Mead. I miss the golden mead."

"And the honey that makes it. Can you imagine that we would land in a country without honeybees?" They had brought their own bees from home but left them behind on the mountain, where the hive quickly went wild and thrived. *Well*, Wyn thought, *at least this will no longer be a land without honeybees.*

"But the corn is good," Rhys said. "We are all well fed, at least."

Wyn watched as Winnowed Rice moved farther away toward the circle of her dancing sisters, thinking that Rhys must have satisfied other needs besides hunger. "By the grace of

God, we are generally blessed," he agreed and crossed himself. "Thank Jesus that our lord abides." He referred to his temporal lord, Madoc ab Gwynedd. His duty and that of his defunct order that Gwynedd founded was to pray for the souls of Madoc's family in perpetuity, and wherever else they found themselves. And there his charge was now, still in the sweathouse with the Natchez woman who, Wyn had to admit, had brought Madoc around, though he disdained speculating on what sorcery she used to accomplish it.

Rhys seemed reluctant to speak his mind.

Brother Wyn watched the blind man, who rarely sought him out; what did he want to say that brought him to share privacy with the abbot? Wyn would wait without urging, but he suspected what it was that troubled the poet as he stamped the worn butt of his staff on the gravel underneath his buskins.

"Domme," he finally said, placing strong, callused hands together, his elbows braced on his knees. He was dressed completely as a Shawnee brave, in soft golden deerskin fringed and beaded, his light brown hair in multiple braids, though he did not use feathers or other decorations except for the face paint that he often covered. "Domme, I come to ask you to annul my marriage so that I can marry Winnowed Rice."

Brother Wyn shifted position but did not immediately reply.

"You know Princess Rhiannon married me under duress."

"And she is now most likely dead, my son."

"True, but we will never know, will we, without a body?"

It was blunt. The poet was gifted for eloquent statement and was by nature a man who did not abjure blunt truth. "She will never come back to us, Brother Wyn."

Wyn felt an ache he did not express for this man who had married Owen's daughter out of duty to Madoc, beautiful as she had been, knowing that she did not love or choose him. This man more than most needed a wife to care for him, to guide him and keep him well tuned like any fine instrument; and now the man had taken personally the care of the little orphaned babe upon himself. There was something of the saint about him, Wyn considered, though he would never have spoken it. Everyone knew Cari was not Rhys's natural child. Most likely she was born of rape, because her mother would never name the baby's father, though it must have been someone significant back home because she came here advanced in pregnancy. Some cynics had darkly hinted Cari was the get of the princess and her own randy father, though Wyn doubted that calumny.

Brother Wyn considered Rhiannon a secret, mysterious woman, who, because of her icy beauty, had provoked lust in men, not the least of whom was Madoc himself, saved from incest only by his putting her off on this loyal servant. Wyn was proud to have influenced the captain in that direction.

"And," Rhys continued with a catch in his throat, "I believe she is alive after all. Winnowed Rice hinted that she saw Rhiannon among the Cherokee at the Battle of Muscle Shoals."

Wyn thought for a time about the complications of the situation. "Our lord Madoc does not need to hear this," he murmured, and fell into another blue silence that Rhys did not offend with response. After a while, when the sunlight had almost reached them, Brother Wyn remarked, "Your Shawnee lady will never accept Christianity, Rhys, and you know it."

Some of the red people seemed to be genuinely converted, as had Gwen's Yuchi warrior David Iron, but not the beloved woman of the Shawnee Whippoorwills. She could not hide her disdain for the white shamans who held no congress with the wind, and who considered Old Red to be evil incarnate. She had asked many questions of Rhys and found no satisfaction in any of his answers except when he told her that it did not matter to him how she regarded the monks or their philosophies.

Wyn finally said, "Wait a while as a widower and see what happens. Perhaps she will be more compliant. A few months do not matter."

"It matters to me."

Wyn sighed. Annulment after consummation was unusual.

"Winnowed Rice is pregnant with my son, Domme."

Ah, so that was it.

"You are that sure, eh? A son?"

"We have both had identical dreams." Rhys grew suddenly reticent because it sounded as though he were forming Shawnee superstitions.

"Well," Wyn said, seeing that the man's stubbornness was born of such strong experience as a mutual dream with the woman he had chosen. "I will speak to Father John about this matter."

This seemed to satisfy Rhys, who nodded his gratitude without further comment.

"Walk with me to see how our captain fares," Wyn said as he stood.

Rhys stood with him, cupping the abbot's elbow in one palm as he stepped over the log and aimed them toward the sweatlodge the Natchez women had built farther up the rise near a stand of low trees they used even now for fuel. As the two white men approached, the three red women watched them, Yngvild's child Bjorn in the arms of one, he bright amid their dark skin and hair. The eldest woman stood to prevent Wyn from opening the flap to enter the lodge half-buried in the slope.

"Hold it right there," the woman said in the singsong Natchez tongue, with no trace of humility, not the slightest deference to the abbot.

Although he did not speak that language, Brother Wyn knew exactly what she was saying and bristled at her interruption of his intention.

"Step aside, woman, so that I may see my master—my miko," Wyn ordered, using the only word he knew in her language while hitting his own chest possessively.

Ahoskas said nothing further, but she did not move, either, though she was two heads shorter than the abbot.

Rhys gently pulled Wyn back, but he persisted, elbowing Ahoskas aside as though she were a hinged door.

Inside, the sweatlodge, half-buried in the sandy ridge of the island, was dim, with a low, hot fire banked and crudely chimneyed with flat stones.

Through smoke and steam Wyn was unable to see distinctly, but saw enough to make out the naked sweat-glistened bodies of the Natchez woman and Madoc on a pile of furs, vessels of pungent oils and herbs warming near the fire. She was on her knees leaning over Madoc, who appeared to be sleeping, his breathing regular and his color improved.

Tumkis looked up, startled at the interruption and the swift blast of light and cool air that momentarily invaded her medicinal gloom.

Wyn was taken completely aback by the topography of her brazen skin, her bare toes curled as she crouched on the fur, her nipples like dim eyes staring back at him, the rounded globes of her thigh and gravid abdomen in the pinkish light, which disclosed only the most timid scattering of pubic hair in stark contrast to the woolly Welshman reclining under her hands.

Outside he could hear Ahoskas and Rhys speaking trade Muskogean, sharply, as though batting a ball back and forth between themselves.

Wyn had begun to sweat beneath his woven buffalo-wool cassock, but he continued staring, unable to stop himself. "What are you doing to him?"

"Go on—get out of here—and do not lose my steam—" she snarled back.

He grabbed for her hand, which seemed to be handling Madoc in some secret way beyond his view. His movement upset a shallow clay pan she had been holding close beside the puncture wound. Wyn saw something writhing there and looked further, despite the nearness of the Natchez, who was saturated with what seemed to the monk to be evil perfumes. He was revolted to see that the pan held the slimy bodies of several leeches of an unhealthy plumpness and color. Even as he stared, another dropped off the wound, contorted several times in what must be agony, and moved no more.

Tumkis reached into a bell-shaped pottery beaker and put something in her hand against the wound. When she took her hand away, a thin pink leech was already embedding itself in the raw lip of the puncture. Several others of the creatures in various stages of discoloration clung to the wound.

"The little uncharmers are sucking the poison," she remarked when she saw the look of astonishment on the white sachem's face. She thought he might become violent for a breath or two, but he relaxed a little when he saw what was happening, though his lip was still curled with more than revulsion at a treatment not unheard of in his home country.

She playfully pulled at his cincture, the ropy woven band with designs that told a story from scripture, and caught the hem of his cassock, flipping it up to expose his pale, hairy, sweating shins. "Take this off and join us, sachem," she invited lightly, freezing him like a hare under her hawk's eye. But he flung his glance away at the last moment, averting her bewitchment as he snatched at his habit and scrambled from the low dark hole as fast as possible.

He burst from the sweatlodge with a cry, a little puff of

steam billowing behind him as Tumkis pulled the flap securely closed.

"Well?" Rhys inquired as the abbot got to his feet, straightened his clothing while bestowing upon himself a sign of the cross hidden in his grooming movements, and wiped his forehead without speaking, in a huff palpable enough for the blind man to read. "Brother Wyn?"

"He is still alive," Wyn remarked sharply, blinking in the sunlight with sweat salting his eyes.

"Is that all?" Rhys persisted.

Wyn pawed at his eyelids and began walking directly away from the red camp, back toward his own, where he could see Father John and the monks returning from their junket through the veil of laurel foliage.

"What happened, then?" Rhys demanded near Wyn's ear, walking faster to keep up with him.

"Nothing, poet. All is well." With that he pointedly shrugged the poet's hand from his shoulder and stamped away, leaving Rhys standing alone on the beach.

Winnowed Rice was there when he turned back toward the aroma of cedar coming from the sweatlodge.

"Let us join our chief," he said to her, and they returned to the old woman feeding the fire beneath the bank of stones.

Winnowed Rice said something to Ahoskas, who nodded as the Shawnee woman and her white man crawled behind the flap. Presently Winnowed Rice threw out their clothing and snapped shut the hide covering, and there they stayed into late morning while outside around them the various hues and tones of the Hundred waited.

Later the couple emerged wrapped in buffalo hides to stagger down to the cool river and plunge into the water. Then, modestly wrapped in the drenched hides, they carried water in tightly woven baskets back up the slope to the lean-to the Natchez women had constructed, and where Tumkis helped Madoc to sleep peacefully for the rest of the afternoon. The pavilion was only hours old yet was already draped with strings of drying leaves from various plants the industrious Natchez servants had hung up under the cane rafters; the garlands of wild onions, bouquets of sage, and brooms of chamomile and mint swayed in a breeze off the river.

Fair Beard and some of the men, the abbot, and finally Gwen all came to speak softly to the chief during the stretched-out hours of that day, which grew warm enough to draw small insects out along the waterline. Madoc seemed to comprehend, when told about the Chickasaw announcement, that a Yuchi contingent was on its way, but he made no comment except to Gwen, who did not repeat what he said.

Signs of Chickasaw occupation increased across the river; smoke from many fires curled up like another mist so that both riverbanks looked gauzy in noon light. But they came no closer and sent no other delegations to the east bank, but only watched from their own side of the river.

The tension of waiting under such circumstances droned out into a kind of tense boredom throughout the lazy afternoon under a sun that could only be called summer.

Several others came to take a steam in the little grounded lodge that Ahoskas and Green Woman kept hot all day, while the children gathered deadfall from farther away on the long, narrow island. Later, after the red women had taken their turn and the whites who wished to partake had done so, including Brian with his Mabilan wife Hayati, Tumkis helped Madoc to reenter the den for another long steaming. Outside and not too far away the monks sang a hymn of thanksgiving. Father John held his Mass, during which he prayed for the soul of the departed Shawnee grandfather, attended by all the red women and most of the whites, even Fair Beard's Norsemen, who stood to the sides, wordless but watching what had become an all-too-familiar ritual, for whatever comfort there was in it.

Everyone who saw Madoc agreed he was looking well. Green Woman brewed up a stew of mushrooms, corn, and mashed nuts, said to be appropriate fare after a poisoning, and the sun drew long shadows as the children splashed in the shallows, a bevy of red and tan bodies gleaming in the late-afternoon light.

Even Yngvild loosened her moccasins and waded in the cool water, singing to Cari in her arms. The baby accepted the splashes of water on her fair toes, and the Norsewoman sat on a low platform of rock that jutted out into the steam and playfully touched the little girl here and there with drops of Tennessee water. Ahoskas ventured out with Bjorn in her arms, crouching in the shallows where the water came only to her ankles, the little boy snared between her legs while he splashed and laughed completely unafraid with his toy boat, his mother watching nearby.

Toward dusk hunters who had set out for the eastern mainland returned with turkeys, rabbits, and a good-sized deer, which the red women set about roasting over coals prepared for that purpose. Others washed and stacked the abundant tubers that grew well back from the waterline. These they nested among the coals, and soon smells of dinner wafted on the air. Fishermen among the sailors brought in a string of drumfish from a sheltered inlet upriver, away from the bustle of the camp. These, broiled with wild onions, plus boiled greens from a mainland meadow and thin flaky corncakes fried on hot stones, made a feast where everyone could come back for seconds.

Tumkis let Madoc eat a little broth, then hurried him back into a rebanked sweatlodge for a final baking through the night. Near the turn of the watch, which Fair Beard kept on and off the ship, Tumkis was awakened by a single choking cry from her women's fire outside. Before the cry was repeated, the Natchez sun was covered and emerging from the lodge, walking purposefully into the lowering glow of the fire, a deep red now with two long logs feeding the blaze under the rocks of the sweatlodge.

Ahoskas sat on her knees as though grinding corn, her hands cupped over her thighs, her head bowed. Beside her stood Arrow Always Red, pierced by his lady's entry into the circle, his face stricken with some drawn-out emotion that announced better than further cry that something dire was wrong.

Tumkis glanced briefly around at her contingent, the three women and a couple of the warriors under command of Arrow Always Red, but nothing appeared immediately amiss.

"What?" she demanded of Ahoskas, who did not look up but threw herself full-length on the dust, begging forgiveness, grasping for Tumkis's bare feet on the mat the old woman had woven from fresh cattails for her mistress.

"What?" she insisted, grabbing at the old woman's braids and yanking her head back so that her eyes could not evade scrutiny. They were glazed with terror; she was babbling incoherently.

Tumkis dropped her like a hot stone and lanced Arrow Always Red with unspoken demand.

"My lady, we tried to find him, but the river—"

Tumkis shot her glance around the group, looking for the white baby.

She took a step toward Arrow Always Red, who saw her coming and blurted out, dreading the consequences of bearing such bad news:

"Little Bear is gone, Lady Sun." The big warrior stood before her totally humbled, bent by shame so that he fell to his tattooed knees before her, and still he was taller than she.

She struck out at him so swiftly he could not duck the blow; it could not hurt him, but he cringed beneath her abuse.

Green Woman slipped between them without a word, inserting her own bare shoulder for Tumkis to strike.

Arrow Always Red stepped back, his face twisted with mixed emotions, and let his mother offer herself in his place, as was her duty.

Tumkis hesitated a moment, caught herself, and reined in her fury, the protocol of the surrogate whipping having its restraining effect upon her actions. The Natchez princess seemed to simmer in cloaked wrath, knotting her fists but dropping them at her side, while ordering Arrow Always Red through clenched teeth, barely above a whisper, "Go out and find him. Do not come back without his body."

Arrow Always Red stumbled off backwards, nearly tripping.

"You stopped thinking right thoughts in my direction," Tumkis said with eerie softness as she turned on Ahoskas, whose duty it had been to take care of the Yngvild's child.

She did not lift a hand or raise her voice, but Ahoskas cringed farther against the solid ground, sobbing, wiping her wet face against the dirt, covering the back of her head, expecting and even praying for the blow that would finally dispense punishment.

And Green Woman stepped between Tumkis and the flattened old woman, calmly holding her hands before her, eyes downcast.

Tumkis stayed her hand a second time, restraining herself against the correct behavior of her servant. She stared at Green Woman as though trying to penetrate her flesh and reach the one on the ground beyond.

Whatever Tumkis might have done next was interrupted by a masculine voice from the shadows, followed by a woman's question in trade Muskogean, "What is the trouble here?"

Rhys intimidated all the red people, even Tumkis, who could not escape the powerful symbolism he was audacious enough to allow the Shawnee woman to paint upon his face.

Now, when she saw the twin suns peering at her from the shadows beyond the fire, she shivered and lingered over the prone body of her servant.

The younger Natchez woman, Firefly, the only one of Tumkis's servants not in the line of the current crisis, whispered to Winnowed Rice, who groaned and swallowed hard before repeating to Rhys that Yngvild's baby had been lost, most likely in the river where he had been playing earlier that afternoon.

"Is there any proof he drowned?" Rhys queried, and when they answered there was none, that the child was simply gone, he continued, "Well, then, he may just be curled up under a bush out here somewhere."

"There is enough moonlight, sister—we will search for him," Winnowed Rice said before the Natchez could answer, and all she could politely do was accept the Shawnee offer of help; privately she knew it was futile.

Winnowed Rice aroused the Shawnee women, exhausted from their dancing and deep in slumber, but not so much that they could not be revived for this task. Soon the upstream end of the island winked with clam-shell lamps in many red hands.

While they searched, Rhys entered the sweatlodge to tell Madoc, but found the fire gone out and the captain chilled and fevered under the buffalo robes. Winnowed Rice got the fire hot again and sat with Rhys, explaining the intricacies of Natchez social protocol and rank behavior. She decided not to sweat Madoc further, thinking it best to let him sleep over in the corner of the warm hut. He seemed to need rest more than anything, though he called in delirium throughout the night for Tumkis, who ignored him as she sat beside the river impervious to any plea, waiting for Arrow Always Red to return, ready to begin mourning.

The moon was bright enough to cast shadows that night and pick out colors for the sharper eye. The searchers beat the bushes for Little Bear, combing all the ground clear to the eastern beach and downstream to a pileup of debris that held no trace of human passage.

Tumkis began her rituals, her women sobbing behind her.

Long after moonset, just before firstlight, when the searchers were dragging home to their campfires with only deadwood the reward of their nightlong search, footweary and solemn because not the slightest footprint had been found to indicate what happened to the child, Arrow Always Red pulled in from his sorrowful hunt downriver. All were pained to see he did not return empty-handed.

A little later Fair Beard, aroused on board the ship where Yngvild stood behind him wrapped in their bedding, called over the echoing water to Rhys, wondering what was wrong. The sound in the poet's voice drew the Norseman and his wife to take a coracle to shore where the Natchez warrior had brought in his canoe.

Chapter 5

When she saw the baby's toy boat, Yngvild let out a long negative moan of denial, translatable into any language and understood by all.

She stumbled in the shallows, almost overturning Fair Beard still in the boat, grabbing the toy from the hands of Arrow Always Red, who was unfortunate enough to have twice been the bringer of the worst news a man or woman can hear, that a child is lost and here is some common reminder that survived, a scrap of clothing still imprinted with his scent, or something as innocent as this crude white bow-wood carving that David Iron had sculpted with the first iron knife Brother Wyn taught him how to forge, hammer, and sharpen.

Arrow Always Red had found the toy a league downstream. Its pale wood glowed in bright moonlight, wedged into a rocky point around which the seasonally calm river scattered briefly before flattening out again on its long, lazy approach to another mighty river flowing from the northeast, the Ohio, just joined with the Shawnee, the resulting trinity of streams shortly thereafter joining the Great River Road flowing forever southward, dividing this land of the east from the land of the west.

The toy canoe was all the evidence he was able to find of the boy, and though he did not dare express his true feelings, he was certain the great river spirit had claimed another occasional victim.

Fair Beard saw in the early light that this was likely true and held his wife back as the awful realization dawned on her.

"Skraeling bitch!" she screamed as she fell on Tumkis like a blond shadow or an ax of light, while he prevented her from smashing in the Natchez woman's face with fists thickened by fury, screaming all the while, using the derogatory word vikings of a hundred years ago called red people they fought in a western place like this one.

Tumkis did not lift a finger to protect herself. Had Fair Beard not intervened, Arrow Always Red would have done so, even to the point of killing the white woman. But he hesitated on the Natchez sun's command.

"Do not move against her," Tumkis ordered under her breath.

Arrow Always Red bit his lip but stepped back. He saw that two white men held the maddened white woman securely, though she continued to struggle against them, spitting and baring her teeth with utmost disrespect in the direction of the Lady Tumbling Water.

While her three women sobbed, keening for the living and the dead, Tumkis stood barefoot with her head bowed. Her clothing was torn. Her long, shining blue-black tresses were hacked as raggedly as a hearth broom and as full of ashes. This hair was her badge of rank, for only the most noble suns wore it loose and unbarbered.

Apparently she would have let Yngvild do her worst.

Lifting a tearless face, Tumkis offered her own unborn as a replacement for the lost child, clutching her swollen belly in an obvious gesture while pleading in her musical language. Dark red parallel lines, already drying brown, were cut precisely into her wrist, like bloody bracelets. Tumkis concluded softly in a formal Natchez phrase, "Yellow Flowers *must* accept this humble offer."

Fair Beard with his arms full of Yngvild was stirred deeply by the dark stains that ran down Tumkis's hand. Knowing the significance of such dramatic tattooing, which would leave designs of permanent mourning on this exquisite woman's arm, he thought hers a generous offer, which he freely translated.

But Yngvild only bit his ear until his own blood ran. She might have done worse if she had had all her front teeth.

One of her husband's men, a brown-haired Norseman named Dag, pressed his hand over her nose to force her to let go.

Another sailor took her husband's place with a hammerlock on her from behind that kept her from doing further damage.

"If she refuses, Tumkis will suicide," Gwen said to Fair Beard. Perhaps only he of all the whites knew this was true.

"And I will gladly help her, you filthy bilge scum ratshit," Yngvild roared in her own language, not at Tumkis but at Snorrison. He pulled back, clutching his savaged ear, while she, imprisoned in the two men's arms, raged on.

Frothing, blood and saliva flecking her lips, she snatched one hand free and flung the little wooden ship at her husband so hard that it struck his left eye and bounced away to be caught by a red hand before it was swept back into the water.

"The river always wins," muttered Winnowed Rice, who splashed her fingers in it briefly, a small sacrifice to compensate for rescuing the toy a second time.

Ahoskas, meanwhile, ghostly under dust, had gained her feet and witnessed the attack on her mistress, the terrible loss of face she suffered at the hands of the white woman. Unable to watch any more, the old woman ran into the low woods, where she let the branches catch her face, and did not cut away the greenbriers that snagged her skin and clothing.

The sky at that moment chose to break into two halves, a misty opalescent one below and, just beyond the treeline across the river, the overturned bowl of sudden dawn.

Green Woman stood in silence before Tumkis for a long, tense moment while the two women arrived at some wordless understanding after a protracted silent argument.

Finally Tumkis broke the tension by nodding a private assent to Green Woman, who turned without further hesitation and stiff-backed, head proudly high, followed Ahoskas into the bush.

After that Tumkis utterly ignored everyone, took abortifacients from Green Woman's collection, then found a place of vigilance near the water's edge, hugging herself and rocking back and forth as she mumbled an old formula that prepared for the worst.

Her remaining woman, the girl Firefly, smelled the strong aroma of a potent variety of mint and other herbs. She interrupted her own prolonged mourning keens to rail at Tumkis, imploring her mistress to consider that she was too many moons into pregnancy for such medications.

But Tumkis turned a deaf ear to all advice, huddling in her star-robe on the rocky point, drinking sad tea, and staring out across the wide river toward an overcast west, while behind the veil a spot of sun crawled toward noon.

As the day wore on, the southern horizon fuzzed out

entirely, and its darkness began to grow into a cloud front stitched here and there with lightning too far away to hear report of, but inexorably moving closer.

Arrow Always Red stood to one side looking big and helpless. The things the women said were taboo for him, and spoken in old, secret words of women's grammar, just as the warriors spoke among themselves a special dialect never uttered within a woman's hearing.

Standing in the shallow water, pacing sometimes or just shifting his weight from foot to foot, he stared into the underbrush where his mother had gone, then called mournfully to Tumkis once or twice, imploring her with some formal necessity.

"I want you to stop her," Tumkis snarled, "not make it easier for her to deprive me of her service."

Arrow Always Red gave his mistress back a steady eye. "You know you cannot stop this," he said.

"This is very displeasing to me," she said, lips drawn even tighter.

"And to me, lady," he replied with a crack in his voice. He took out his own flint knife and let the firelight catch its translucent edge. "All she has is a dull cooking knife. . . ."

Tumkis's lips almost disappeared with her fury that she could not defy tradition with her will. She hissed back at him, forbidding him to help his mother die, but he replied in formal words of apology and ran off under the darkening sky, leaving her hunched farther into her robe.

The other red women, the Shawnee and Mabilans, understood but were shamed that such a thing was being undertaken so publicly. No man of their tribes would wait upon the word of a young woman in the matter of his mother's well-being. And certainly men in their tribes would not know what to answer if asked about herbs and procedures that would eliminate unwanted babies. Women's modesty in such circumstances was protection. Men must never be allowed to make such decisions, and for that reason such matters should be whispered about only among members of the women's lodges in isolation huts on the far edges of communities. Only the Natchez had inscrutable customs that violated these precepts, which embarrassed and disgusted the other red people in the company.

Ominous rolling thunder was heard from the south the rest

of that day, which Wyn calculated to be a Sunday, so the clergy celebrated a Mass. Father John prayed for guidance, and Wyn as pastor preached a sermon on the need for each Christian to witness to the unbelievers so they would be spared the results of savage behavior.

The white people did not try to figure out the red people's behavior—it all looked sordid and savage and off the point from their perspective. The children, red and white, seemed somehow to pick up the disjointed, confused thoughts of the adults. They ran around screaming at each other, throwing sand and rocks until Fair Beard shouted for some of the crew to go herd them in. They separated the elders from the youngest—about ten or so red boys, a couple of red girls, and three white boys, including Mary and Wil's twins and Einion, Madoc's stepson.

But they continued to squabble even when the seamen found chores for the oldest to do, and the youngest were put to work gathering watercress from a branch trickling over a gravel bank on the lee shore of the island.

Yngvild hissed in the direction of Tumkis's vigil and would not be calmed by Fair Beard or Gwen, who tried to say soothing things to her.

And Cari cried because Yngvild in her hysteria refused to let the baby nurse. Winnowed Rice, after consulting with the elder women, improvised with cornmeal and mashed hickory nuts, abundant on the mainland. But still the baby cried, and Rhys in distress would not put her down, so Winnowed Rice called in her yellow bitch lurking on the perimeters of the camp, herself with sagging teats abused by her spring litter—about two dozen Shawnee dogs had followed the Whippoorwills along the river and sometimes swam in it.

"I want you to help us, here," Winnowed Rice spoke to the dog, stroking her ears while Rhys stood nearby shifting his weight from one foot to the other in a useless attempt to placate the whimpering infant.

"This little girl will die if someone does not feed her."

The dog nuzzled her hand while Winnowed Rice continued as she groomed the dog's pelt, finding a late tick embedded in her ear. She pincered it with her nails, twisting it without pulling until the tick let go.

Winnowed Rice offered the pest to the dog, who licked it off her finger, groaned in pleasure, and lay down, exposing her belly to be rubbed.

"Your babies are fat and ready to wean, anyway, so will you help us?" She took the baby from Rhys and laid her close to the flank of the bitch who had no name—the Shawnee loved their dogs, but never named them because sometimes when food was short in the long, lean winter months on the nomad's trail, they had to perform the ultimate service for their masters.

The big yellow creature licked Cari's black hair while she fussed, plastering it down across one delicate pink ear, then stretched out with a low sigh, surrendering herself to gravity and the baby with her long little fingers entwined in the bristly mane, quiet for the first time that afternoon.

Everyone breathed easier after that except for Mary, who stood to one side looking askance that a princess of Gwynedd should be fed whelp's milk.

"But think of Romulus and Remus, the first kings of Rome suckled by the wolf bitch," Rhys said as he unleashed the harp and began a song by Taliesin, which could be sung in any mode, about a shape-changer. This time he chose to make lullaby music around the words:

> I have been a blue salmon.
> I have been a dog, a stag,
> A roebuck on the mountain.
> A stock, a spade, an ax in the hand,
> A stallion, a bull, a brick,
> A grain which grew on a hill.

Snorrison ordered several of the crew to take coracles out to make another search downriver. They grimly set off in twos on the stronger current, while Yngvild continued to fill the air with vile invective.

Finally, just for the peace, her husband ordered her bound and transported in a coracle to the ship, quieted with a potion of hemp and other simples Caradoc mixed and administered while they held her down, with someone to watch lest she tear her skin where she was bound. Still she raged mad and screaming on and off the rest of that day, their second on the island.

The sky looked threatening to everyone, but the women began preparing the evening meal anyway because of the old habits of their days. They still had much Chickasaw corn, and both white and Natchez hunters continued bagging plenty of fowl on the mainland, so as the sky darkened more quickly than mere sunset, they had plenty of food prepared.

But it was a gloomy feast. Some of the women who were not cooking set the coracles upside down to make instant tents against certain rain. While cutting cane to support these quick little beehive huts, one of the Shawnee found Green Woman dead in the brambles, her wrists cut parallel to the artery as was the ritual custom. Arrow Always Red prowled nearby, forbidding them to touch the body, scaring them off with menacing advance.

This sad report further deadened the evening, grown damp with a chill not even the fires or a warm supper could dispel. Everyone avoided the crazy Natchez woman, whose behavior ordained such serious punishment on herself and all around her. Only Firefly stayed near her, and later, under a red-streaked sunset, Ahoskas returned, wordlessly wrapped in her own buffalo robe, her face and arms scratched and dried bloody from the greenbriers, but river-washed and calm and apparently reconciled with her mistress as though nothing had happened. She swabbed the gashes where thorns had torn her.

Tumkis saw her smearing medicine on her shoulders, unable to reach her shoulder blade, and took the salve in her own hand to rub into her auntie's wounds.

Then Ahoskas swabbed the new tattoo scars on her mistress's wrist with the same medicine, with the succinct comment that the lines were well cut and would heal quite nicely into delicate, distinctive scarification, a lifelong testimony to a most honorable sorrow. "You do have a sure hand, my lady."

"Because you taught me so well, Auntie," Tumkis replied.

This mutual grooming made the whites uncomfortable and curious with questions the other red women found too unsettling to answer, even in a familiar language among themselves.

The Natchez group thus isolated, everyone else red and white was drawn to a single fire near the river that sent sparks high up into the night and reflected incandescent ripples on the black surface between the shore and the mossy side of the *Horn*, anchored but restless in the growing current like a beast held too long under rein.

Gossip made the rounds in several languages—where was

Chief Weather Eyes? Had someone seen him being carried onto the ship by the Chief Tangletongue?

There was an argument in progress—had the Natchez sun cursed Weather Eyes? Would he now, without her magic, die from what poison remained in him? Each red woman gave Winnowed Rice advice, since she was closest to their chiefs, but those who had white men offered similar advice, so that all thoughts were pointed in his direction.

With distant thunder rumbling under a moon past full and dim behind the mist, people still munched on the last tidbits of dinner as Fair Beard held informal conference with Brother Wyn, Father John, Rhys, and the eldest of the seamen, Wil and Dag, while all the others, even the red people who could speak no Cymraeg, and the smallest child, lingered listening near the rosy campfire.

Holding a damp press to his ear, the Fair Beard said, "We are in the worst sort of position," to start off on the common ground of the situation's gravity, leaving as obvious the fact that he must separate his two women before there was further bloodshed. "Our chief is sicker than before, and we are quickly losing our only allies in enemy territory with winter coming and more dependents on their way to be fed and defended by only a handful of men among us—maybe forty if Brother Wyn's monks take up arms."

Wyn nodded solemnly, and his few religious behind him. They had fought in the old country. They would fight again if they had to; this was greeted with cheers by the crewmen under both Madoc and Fair Beard.

"Still, it would be better if we did not have to fight," Rhys said quietly, and Fair Beard, who usually loved to fight as much as any man, surprised everyone by agreeing without any argument.

"We are so outnumbered, I hate to think of going against that force across the river," he admitted. "Think of what would happen to the women and children after they killed all of us."

"So?" Wyn asked, speaking for all of them. Fear showed in their faces, seeing Snorrison afraid.

"I would sail immediately downriver," said the Norseman, leaning back with his arms crossed over his metal-covered chest. "We could outrun this slow storm if we break camp immediately."

"What about the Yuchi?" Rhys countered.

"Let them join us later. David Iron is leading them, and he knows we are headed with the Shawnee to their homeland. All he has to do is follow the river."

The Shawnee had confirmed that their homeland was at most two days northward.

"And we get going before winter sets in," Father John commented, eyeing the sky.

"And Gwen ab Gwyneth?" Wyn inquired, looking around for her.

"Gwen David Iron waits for her husband," she said, stepping into their circle.

"You defy your father," Wyn reminded her.

"Scripture tells me to be true as Ruth was to her husband's people," said Gwen, torn beyond Wyn's understanding. "Besides, someone should stay with the message for our allies."

"You, unprotected in the wilderness?" Wyn said directly to her. "Your father will kill me if I let this happen."

"It is not such a gamble—we have the Chickasaw word that the Yuchi are on their way with my husband leading them," she replied to Wyn, who was as corrugated and bent by concern as Madoc would have been, and more so. "Tumkis and her people will stay with me until my husband arrives."

"You would trust that baby-murdering witch?"

"She did not purposefully hurt Yngvild's baby, Domme."

"No, she had her servant do the dirty work."

"What would be her motive?"

Shaking his head, but speechless against the monk's uninformed opinion, Fair Beard snorted to himself and folded the wet rag stained with blood over and over upon itself, neatly, as though he were stacking line.

"The wicked wrath of a woman put aside—"

"Brother Wyn," she said patiently, "these people have a venerable tradition of second and third wives, and they do not have inheritance through patrimony such as we Britons do—"

He might have rebutted her, but her passion was running high and she would not be shouted down.

"—and they value every child who survives, not one child over another just because of who its father was."

Fair Beard made a sound of positive witness off to one side, but was ignored by Wyn, who had earlier rebuked him severely for bringing such trouble into their midst.

"Do you blaspheme against the word of God, Gwen ab Gwyneth?"

"Patrimony is not scripture, Domme; besides, we are few among their many and cannot assume our own legalities out here in their country. When in Rome, eh, Domme?" She tried to soften him, but he would not let her touch his hand, so she said, "Tumkis is innocent of wrong and stands unjustly accused."

"The witch ordered the brave to commit murder on his own mother just to have someone to blame." Wyn turned on her and bared his teeth with recitation of unspeakable evil she seemed intent on ignoring. "And he *obeyed*—"

"Arrow Always Red did not kill Green Woman."

"By all reports he slit her throat."

"No—he risked the fury of his mistress by providing Green Woman a sharpened knife when Tumkis ordered him to stop his mother."

"Then the witch ordered her servant to commit suicide in the place of a higher-ranking servant—murder, suicide, which sin is the worse?" demanded Brother Andrew, one of the brothers behind his abbot.

Gwen shook her head. "She did not order anyone to do anything. Green Woman took Ahoskas's place according to an ancient tradition—I am not calling it right or wrong, but it is the way they have worked out to treat transgression. If Yngvild had accepted Tumkis's baby, this would have been prevented."

"Barbarians," Wyn sneered.

"When she would not accept, Tumkis was left with no way to make restitution except by suicide. Ahoskas would have taken her place. By their tradition Green Woman took the place of Ahoskas."

"If this absurd logic is correct," young Andrew continued, righteously caught up in the debate, "then why did the still lower-ranking Firefly not take the place of Green Woman in turn?"

"Because she is still of childbearing age—it is no use—you will not understand because you condemn them before you ask these questions." She turned to Wyn, who had stepped back to let his younger man carry on the debate, but the abbot's strong smithy arms were crossed on his chest in adamant opposition to whatever this misguided girl of his own congregation was saying. "We may not understand it, Brother, but we have to respect their scruples in attending to duty."

"The witch has bewitched you, m'lady, and I will pray for your soul wandering so close to perdition."

"My soul is doing quite well, thank you, and will wait here with my body for my husband."

"Tumkis will keep her word," said Fair Beard, focusing the eye Yngvild blacked with the thrown toy upon Gwen, who did not need reassuring, and to Wyn remarked, "I could not better protect her myself—do your own words not prove Arrow Always Red will obey his mistress against any obstacle?"

"You should leave immediately," Gwen said quickly before Wyn could pose other arguments.

"I will not leave the captain's daughter," Wyn pronounced, stepping between them, with his back to Gwen.

"If it is someone's children you are worried about, why not take those unruly boys in hand, Domme?" Gwen challenged.

"The tides are always ready here," Snorrison replied, indicating the river, which did seem a little swollen, a little thicker with sediment, just as the southeastern quarter of the sky had been darkening with storms beyond that horizon where the river fattened.

Wyn squeezed a note of despair from his throat and strode off, fists clenched, followed by Father John and the other religious, who were muttering support for their abbot.

When it was clear they had removed themselves from the discussion, Rhys asked, "And the red women?"

"In the coracles, of course. They are our little sisters." The Norseman, with one arm thrown across Gwen's shoulder, laughed because it was true; without the Shawnee they might not encounter a warm welcome in the Land Between Two Rivers.

He clapped his hands together and called out to them a phrase in Cymraeg that Madoc during the past year had often yelled, "Yn y cwch—into the boat!"

A sharp-eyed lookout reported to Snorrison that the Chickasaw across the river were also holding a meeting with all the war chiefs in attendance, and equally sharp-eyed Chickasaw were watching the eastern bank of their river to see what was happening among the crazy white people and their red allies.

The Chickasaw war chief Imala'ko sat amid his counselors, the elders of five tribes under the Chickasaw grand miko, uncle to Imala'ko, listening to their advice concerning the whites, and the meanings for their filling up the forest with lights the night before. After all the old men had their say, the consensus of which was that the whites were practicing formidable magic, and perhaps it was not in the best of Chickasaw interests for them to remain, the eldest among them turned and requested some speech from the young war chief.

Imala'ko did not immediately talk, but lit the ceremonial pipe, took a long, thoughtful pull on its tube of sacred red stone, and handed it over to the old gentleman, who had requested he speak his mind.

The young war chief stood taller than the average of his nation. He was deeply bronzed by the sun, and heavily tattooed. His face was long, made more so by the cradleboard flattening of his forehead, which marked him as a noble among his rank-conscious people. As was the fashion among Chickasaw warriors, he plucked every hair he could find from his face and head, except for significant hanks tied off and permanently glued into stiff bolts of thick black hair, blunt cut and tied with clan and rank-marking ribbons of colored string. He was the youngest among his people to wear the buffalo horns, an honor usually reserved for elderly men-at-arms who had a lifetime of proved wisdom. He was not wearing the ceremonial buffalo headdress at the moment, but he held himself regally, as though the bonnet of horns and eagle feathers rested on his head, while he watched with bright, intelligent eyes as the toothless old man sucked on the pipe.

Only after the grandfather finished his draw on the tobacco and handed it farther down the line did Imala'ko begin to speak of the meaning of the signs they had witnessed. He emphasized the big canoe across the river, which fulfilled so many legends of the red people living along the river. He spoke with eloquence of these legends, of the bones of such dragons that hunters had found all along the exposed cliffs of the rivers, and the significance of ancient rock paintings depicting other similar serpent-bird creatures memorialized in song and dance among all the red nations.

Then he recalled old stories of long-dead ancestors who came from places far away, who brought great gifts and then departed, saying they would come again from the land of the sun. But he countered these stories, told for ten generations among his grandfathers, with other more sinister legends of another kind of visitor, demons, who arrived from the under-world. These had brought pestilence and drought so that the corn did not grow with its usual abundance in Chickasaw river-bottom fields, the richest in all the country.

"I confess, my learned grandfathers," for such was the proper way for one as young as he with so much at his command to speak to the august council, "I confess I do not know what to make of these kanegmati—that is what they are called, because the Yuchi headman had a dream about them a moon before they arrived in that nation. I agree with the Cherokee that they should either be killed or sent on their way with a promise never to return to these parts."

The old men buzzed around him.

"We do not even know if they are human beings," Imala'ko continued.

The eldest nodded. "Some of us think they are spirits."

Others mumbled behind him.

"Evil spirits."

Imala'ko glanced at the circle of wrinkled, squinting faces around him, then asked the elder, "What about the baby your men snatched?"

The old man shrugged. "He eats. He cries. He shits like any ordinary baby. I sent him to Red Village for my own wife to examine."

"No," the young war chief said after some deliberation, which the old men respected. "Take the baby to my mother."

The old man nodded, jangling the shells around his neck and dangling from stretched earlobes. His tattoos verified he was a war-planner of the second-highest degree, and the grandfather of ten and two grandsons and nine granddaughters.

Imala'ko, young enough to be the old warrior's grandson, wore his war trophies on his mussel-shell belt as small scalp tassels painted and braided with eagle feathers denoting reknown as a knife-wielder and hunter. He still wore his paint from the battle at Muscle Shoals, renewed to display that he had accomplished seven touches on an enemy, with a special starburst to indicate that one of his own arrows had hit the Uktena-canoe. "Take great care of him on the way and let your own eyes see to it that he is hidden and protected from just anyone. My mother will know how to nurture him and observe if he is remarkable in any dangerous way." He was disappointed that the men had not been able to secure an older child with whom he could speak and learn quickly more about these strangers.

But the old warrior was his favorite uncle, and he did not want to scold him, so he nodded to him and gave him a small bag of powder with significant beading on the flap. "My mother's brother has once again performed valued service to this one."

The old man beamed and accepted the honorarium, reputed to be a special formula for curing the old-bone, traded through many hands from western places across the Great River Road. The beads were of silver and sky blue stones reputed by traders to have come from the western land that bordered the underworld.

The pipe had made its way around the circle and now returned to Imala'ko's hands. He took it and drew a last inhalation from its long stem, held the smoke, and released it, veiling himself in a thick blue cloud from which he said, "We have to protect our people from evil spirits and evil men— both are enemies. But I have to think of those into whose land we are sending these blue-eyed snakes, our friends and cousins of Ixtulan."

The counselors fell silent, all of them in awe of the nation that lived farther down this river and then up the Great River Road.

"I think we should alert the grand miko of Ixtulan," he said finally, pronouncing the antique word softly, "It-sheee-tulan . . ." because the people of that place were the most ancient ancestors of all the people of the sun in these parts, and their name was sacred. Then he volunteered to be the messenger to do it.

Hoarse-whispered like that, the name had an eerie sound to it, and none envied the task the young man had set for himself. That place of many high temples had a reputation for mystery, for ancient rituals, and for heavy tribute when her grand mikos once claimed more than their own territory a couple of generations back. Now it was even more isolated than before; all surrounding native clans had dispersed south or allowed themselves to be absorbed by the nation of Ixtulan while they kept their secrets in the high places, storied about by travelers and traders who still visited their upriver precincts.

The mysterious northerners were hot for arrowheads and raw chert, for which the Chickasaw were middlemen between them and the Sioux-speakers of the mountains that would someday be called Ozarks. They bartered feathers from their own swamps and from those farther south on the delta of the Great River Road, for the people of Ixtulan liked to dress their grand miko in the finest, brightest feathers of any tribe around.

They would also trade huge amounts of their fine corn, parched and crushed, but never seed corn, though the Chickasaw had stolen some and bought some on the sly; it never grew as richly as in the muddy-bottom fields of Ixtulan because, as everyone knew, the miko of Ixtulan had more powerful medicine. The people of the city traded for hard minerals, raw crystals, copper and gold nuggets, rocks of unusual shapes or colorations, and oddities among the animals like two-headed snakes and birds with extra beaks, or doe kids born with five legs and no tail. They would always pay the highest trade for alligator and snakeskins, and were in the market year-round for hides of any beast. They especially favored the black bear and buffalo, which their hunters did not like hunting because of traditions concerning their own foundation and these animals, and because they were farmers and traders almost to the exclusion of any other form of subsistence.

For all these things the grand miko would pay great baskets of corn, and his priests would also buy children in hard times from all the tribes along the rivers that joined the Great River Road. His merchants were known for cunning and for canny trade. Rumors lingered around them. They were whispered about and left alone by other riverine peoples, even taboo to some like the Shawnee up in the Kantuck.

"Why do you personally want to go into those serious places, Imala'ko?" asked one of the counselors, a relative of the war chief who did not want to lose him because of the honor he brought to his family by such high position at such a young age. "Everyone knows there are evil magicians up there who make secret rituals away from the eyes of the people."

"I have always wanted to see the fabled ballfield of Ixtulan," replied Imala'ko, himself more interested in the traditional games than even warfare. "Perhaps I will play there and beat the ballplayers of Ixtulan and bring even more honor to our nation."

"In the past," the elder said with a sour face, "some of our best ballplayers have never returned from that place, that Ixtulan." There were dark stories about a skull rack beside the ballground and the price of defeat.

"I have defeated many enemies and have always returned to my own fireside," the warrior replied, and several of his men ranged behind him showed their support for him by shaking their atlatls, jangling the pottery weights against the cane rods.

"The Cherokee best-beloved did not order you to do this thing."

"The Cherokee best-beloved is not related to the miko of Ixtulan as is my own family and our nation, grandchildren to the Ixtulan, and he does not have to maintain an alliance with such a powerful neighbor; otherwise, he would not have neglected to warn them about what he is sending into their territory." He gave that a moment to sink in. "After all, did he not warn us?"

A lookout came dashing into the circle of elders, breathless with news that the migrants had the big canoe moving out on the river surrounded by all the little round canoes—already and without any warning they had doused their fires, climbed aboard their vessels, and were paddling out to catch the river's mainstream.

It was close to dawn of a heavily overcast day, but there was enough light to see across the river.

Imala'ko and his counselors ran to the water's edge, trailing their buffalo robes painted with symbols of daring exploits. They arrived at the bank just in time to see the big canoe move toward the island's northerly headland and its tangle of debris. They could see many people on the deck, and the men swarming around the deck and up into the rigging, singing the monosyllabic tunes that communicated their maneuvers to each other.

The great sail in three perpendicular bands billowed out with the prevailing breeze that smelled of rain from the south, tilting the great craft away from the beachhead toward her destination downriver.

Behind her like ducklings around a goose swarmed the round coracles, each with its one or two red women, white monks, and various children and baggage. They were all moving quickly now as they found the main channel. They called in several languages and song, and the breeze coming up behind the Chickasaw took the strangers' voices with the vessels downriver.

The Chickasaw were too far away to hear a couple of people yelling from the great vessel. But back on the island from where Gwen stood watching the flotilla depart, Madoc could clearly be seen and heard in thick-tongued confusion beseeching his daughter from the rail of the ship where Rhys and others tried to draw him back.

Among the dozens of small craft attending the big canoe, Winnowed Rice paddled her own coracle, rafted with two cargo vessels, close enough to see Weather Eyes pale and wild-haired in the wind, yelling at the rail, "Turn back, damn you, Snorrison."

The chief swore again at the Norseman farther aft and would not let even Rhys pull him below.

On the island's long west shore, Gwen was waving, calling something he could not hear.

Still calling, she started trotting downriver. She picked up speed as the ship accelerated, so that soon she was running along the pale sand and behind the rock where sat one dejected red person. He could not see if it was a woman or a man, though from the ragged hair Madoc judged it to be a warrior huddled in heavy robes.

Gwen ignored the gloomy figure on the rock and kept running, jumping rivulets and leaping driftwood logs and tangles of river-grass as wide as a barrel. She almost lost her red kerchief but saved it in hand, and that loosened the flag of her extraordinary red hair.

He was sure she would leap too far and miss, tangled in fringed suede hems. But she lifted her skirts, gracefully, he thought, though worried for her pregnancy, and ran on until she ran out of land and stood ankle-deep in the water beside mossy logs and tangled branches.

Madoc followed the rail aft, where Fair Beard was in his favorite place, the small pull-down sternman's bench well oiled with his sweat. He lounged against the straking, eyes sunk to slits under the shadow of his brow, his arm steady against the tiller. The current was pulling stronger now, he thought, because of the upriver rain they had seen on the southern horizon. He was thinking about oars and all these passengers in his way and in the way of the crew.

"Do not leave her out here to die all alone," Madoc growled and struck at the Norseman, but weakly, as much from the interrupted cure as from what had ailed him.

Fair Beard called out one long note followed by a hoot that was a secret signal to clear the decks. The men fell to immediately, herding the people down into the hold.

Down on the water Winnowed Rice saw Rhys just behind the chief, imploring him as Madoc worked his way to the stern to watch Gwen for as long as possible. The shaman Wyn, whom Winnowed Rice thought of as Father Folded Hands, stood at Madoc's right hand gripping the thickly beaded top strake.

He clung to the rail to remain upright as he watched the island grow smaller with their quickening passage, and Gwen standing there waving the scarf, dwindling back into a smaller and smaller red-haired girl, shrinking to the size of a child, then an infant, then a doll, blurring to a faint red spot against the greenery and brownery and watery sweep of color.

"Have no fear, captain," Fair Beard said. "Tumkis is with her."

"Tumkis?" Madoc said, seeing double and unsteady on his feet, the hand that had driven attack against the Norseman now resting for support upon his shoulder.

"How could you forget Tumkis?"

Madoc squinted into the glare of morning behind the diffused sky; the island was too far away to see anyone now.

Meanwhile, from below, Yngvild railed at her husband, calling him filthy names from notorious northern docks. Her imprecations burned Snorrison's already abused ear while she cried to Madoc, who sank against a bale of hides, his aching head tilted against the bulkhead vibrating with increased flow against the hull that was sending them more swiftly along.

"They steal our children, Captain, they steal them and kill them and tie us up so we cannot even avenge our own flesh and blood—"

The Chickasaw on the west bank heard only strident calls echoing over the water as though from argumentative birds. Overhead they saw an eagle circling the island, and took that as further sign of significant happening over there where only one fire remained.

Tumkis saw the bird, too; it made Arrow Always Red uncomfortable, but they did not speak about it at the time.

Later, when they had eaten a quiet meal, Firefly and Ahoskas sat near the fire binding the body of Green Woman in Tumkis's own fine robe, not the one marked with starry constellations, but another, even finer, of beaded quill and fox-trimmed mulberry cloth, which was more supple than the highest grade of mouseleather.

They chatted softly, amiably, an older woman teaching a young woman the intricate preparations of the dead for burial. They had lovingly washed and dressed her in Tumkis's own white deerskin ceremonials encrusted with seed pearls.

Tumkis also contributed her supply of red ocher and the rarest of compound scents and crushed blossoms of wildflowers to sprinkle with cedar boughs around the body, which would be transported with great honor back to the Natchez homeland in a special canoe even now being hacked from a cedar log down on the beach.

Ahoskas and Firefly worked away, binding up the shroud with sturdy stitches of dried gut line—every animal cleaned was a contributor to their constant store of line, bone implements, fur and leather oddities; even the tail was used, as Madoc found it amusing to observe, even the whiskers.

Behind their musical voices thumped the flint adzes on the heart of the cedar in one-two rhythm. Faintly on the breeze wafted the scent of smoldering cedar because the canoe-makers were using fire to burn out the hollow where Green Woman would lie on her final journey home.

Arrow Always Red was not among the carvers but crouched on his heels near the coals, poking with a stick at the glowing heart of the fire.

He said something low in his throat, without emotion.

Tumkis replied as flatly; Gwen recognized only one word, yes, a command that said too much.

As the warrior stood and stretched, adjusting his weapons and a slim kit on his back, Gwen watched him, startled by his evidently purposeful movement.

"No—" she said when she saw the eagle's swift coursing shape swoop above the tree line, not an arrow-shot away. She turned on Tumkis and placed five fingers firmly against the Natchez woman's clavicles. "Tell him no, Tumbling Water."

The Natchez looked at her sharply and said in trade

Muskogean so that the white woman could not possibly misunderstand, "Shut up and sit down."

The warrior had paused in the outer perimeter of fireglow. Tumkis glanced his way and dismissed him with a subtle movement, then stared deliberately into Gwen's eyes and said very gently, "Too much power when the world of the birds mixes with the world of humans. Too dangerous. You have spoiled this creature, and now what you have done must be undone. This warrior is very brave to take care of this important matter for you, and you will be indebted to him for the favor."

Gwen, unable to hold back tears, ran, flapping her fleecy robe at the eagle, who was lowering to the head of the laurel thicket, mewing for his usual treat of innards from the day's hunt.

Startled by the trusted woman's attack, he failed to land on a branch and swooped over the clearing, through the smoke of the campfire, screeching back at her.

She ran below, whirling the robe around her head, making a strange whooshing sound that Arrow Always Red felt impelled to counteract with a magical sound of his own, on a two-noted flute carved and painstakingly fire-bored in deer antler.

The bird started to circle, but Gwen flung rocks at him silhouetted against the deep blue of the sky and screamed to him that he should go away.

The eagle rolled off beyond the island's ridge, leaving Gwen breathing hard from exertion and far from the comfort of the fire.

With exquisite gentleness, Tumkis approached behind her and took her hand, leading the shaking white woman back to the pavilion while making soft, soothing musical sounds: "I know, I know it is painful, but the sun will shine again, it will, it will."

Gwen let herself be led, in fact, laid her head against the red woman's shoulder for the genuine comfort she found there.

Big raindrops splatted the dust at the women's feet.

Later a Natchez scout met a Chickasaw scout on the mainland trail that skirted the river. After each recovered from the surprise of looking up to see another armed warrior whom unusual circumstances made neither enemy nor ally, they shared a smoke while the Natchez related recent events on Bear Island.

That Chickasaw returned to his side of the river and repeated the story. He also reported that the copper-haired white woman and the small band of Natchez conducted somber funeral rituals under a cane pavilion all night long in the drumming rain over there on what would be called Bear Island for generations afterwards until the river meandered in a big flood and washed it away.

Chapter 6

Madoc awoke with the feel and smell of warm sun on his closed eyelids.

Before he opened his eyes and broke his dream, he savored the sensations on the flesh of his cheekbones, thinking still in halls of sleep that this must be something like what Rhys saw when he looked at the sun.

He let himself wake minutely, stealing back to consciousness, cheered by the sound of wind against the sail and the occasional voices of crewmen about their duties. The ship was trembling in a satisfactory manner beneath the—what was this under his fingers, lamb's wool or chest feathers from a fine goose? Clipped buffalo fleece, his fingers told him.

He further tested himself; what time of day was it? With the ship below him moving in what he remembered was north all the way, and the sun there glowing through his eyelids in the sky, so it was nearly noon.

Perhaps, he thought, she is near. Perhaps if he laid quietly, she would come as she had come when he thought he was dead and there might be something to the stories of heaven. He waited to get a whiff of her pine-scent aroma, or the perfume of her blue-black hair glistening with sweat in the steamy little house buried in the ground, where they traveled together through the underworld to see the Unknown Woman to get the magic stone. That was what the red people called their Earth Mother, a kind of gross red St. Brigit who was responsible for teaching human beings about corn, similar to the old Celtic earth goddess. The black-haired woman led him there to the ancient hag, who lived deep inside a Natchez burial mound. The dark angel haggled with the old woman for the life of Madoc—he had stood to one side in the warm earth-smelling lodge while they negotiated and finally settled on a price for his life. Then, the stone in her medicine bag, the dark angel led him back to return to the land of the living. He did not know how he knew her language, but when the dark angel spoke, he understood every nuance of her speech.

Madoc knew it was a dream. But it was so real in his memory, he clung to the possibility that at least the dark angel would prove to be part of reality, too.

He wanted to ask her what she paid to save his life.

He waited for her for some time, anticipating her voice, her scent, or touch. Moments passed or hours with his only comfort the movement of the ship beneath him. The dark angel did not come back, and he fell asleep again without opening his eyes.

Madoc woke the next time in soft darkness and the cool dew of evening, with the sounds of people mumbling over supper around him but not so close as to enable him to hear what they said. Beneath his head was well-packed fleece that felt as though it had held his shape a long time.

In the air was the smell of burning hickory, and baked fish and mussels in the shell, and under all, the pervading aroma of corn crisping on hot rocks. Children laughed somewhere off in the near distance, then wet wood bumped against something else wooden—echoes off water.

"Fair Beard?" he asked, eyes springing open to a hazy night sky where star-glimmers and a pale moon declining toward the last quarter showed through the overcast. Immediately above was the silhouette of the ship's naked mast with line rubbing the wood, the sail reefed and tied off. Not far from his head were the butt ends of several newly pecked oars stacked like huge bones in cradles carved on the other side of the world.

Someone unseen, perhaps Ari, bid him good evening and remarked that it was fine to see him awake. Was he hungry, did he need anything?

"Snorrison."

The dark shape hurried away and soon was replaced by two, Ari trailing behind with a glowing lamp, a flame in a clam shell. What a rough illumination, Madoc thought. For an instant he had not crossed the Western Ocean at all but was still at home on Mona Isle in his father's great smoky hall, wakened by a servant with a candle, shaking him as he slumped over the trestle with the fire dying on the great hearth where a lazy greyhound lounged on the warm slate.

It was a sweet memory, but fleeting, gone with the shine of the shell lamp, a crude object that identified this wilderness journey without amenities such as candles and thrust him firmly into the present, halfway around the world, awakening with vague, persistent aches under strange southern constellations.

"Welcome back." It was Snorrison, smelling of wild onions and sweat, bright gems of water dripping from his wet beard just washed in the river.

"Where are we?" Madoc tried to get up, but Fair Beard discouraged him from doing so by sitting down cross-legged on the deck just beyond the bale of hides.

Red people were singing off in the distance over water that made short lapping sounds against the ship; their music was celebratory, sung in several languages, but keeping common time. He gradually heard his own language and, among the copper bells and tom-toms, old Honeyvoice rang under Rhys's hands in a tune that suited the red women's beat.

Strange brew, those sounds, but they made pleasing music.

A sailor's hornpipe joined the ruffled song, kept up for a while, then faded out as Madoc heard Fair Beard saying slowly and with new sadness, his big shoulders hunched as he toyed with a length of line, ". . . a good day's downriver sail from Bear Island, but then you probably do not remember."

"I dreamed a woman." Madoc watched his friend outlined in the darkness.

"You did that all right." Fair Beard chuckled without a trace of amusement.

"She was real then, one of the red women?" Madoc propped himself on an elbow and looked around, but the music told him all the red women were on shore.

"You remember nothing?"

"Just this woman." He sat up farther in the makeshift bed.

"Swamp poison kills you with dreams," Fair Beard quoted one of the Natchez who taught him about such things.

"But she was real. Is real, is here now?" His eyes, still a little wild, darted in the direction of the mainland, where on yet another beach the Hundred had survived to pull out their few remaining skillets and cook yet another evening meal.

So, whispering there in the shadows, Fair Beard made himself comfortable, wishing he had some beer to drink while he gave brooding account of the last few days to his old friend, who had grown silent and sullen, recalling before Snorrison said it, that Gwen stayed behind.

The red people called him Weather Eyes because his gray gaze could change so suddenly with a mood, even when he gave no other evidence. Now it darkened like the sky this afternoon over the ship racing north down the wide Tennessee River.

He held up his hand to stop Fair Beard in the recitation of what he already knew.

Fair Beard paused, handling the line, pulling through and tying off a series of successively perfect ring-in-hand or sheepshank knots, loosening one, knotting another, watching his fingers flying faster and faster amid the weave instead of looking at Madoc.

"You abandoned my Gwen."

Ari, his eyes reflecting the light of the clam-shell lamp he held behind the Norseman, looked aside, embarrassed that Madoc was chastising his pilot and friend. Fair Beard had gone through much lately and deserved a little consolation.

But Fair Beard took it, finally hitting his limit with the knot and losing the loop; he chose that moment to meet Madoc's gaze. "Let go, my friend," he said, as deft as a conjurer at a fair, spiriting the string around his fingers in a quick, elegant cat's cradle; then, with a casual flip, he unleashed it and laid the limp string across the hand Madoc had raised against him. "We do not own our children."

Madoc was moved by Fair Beard's indirect reference to the child he had lost, nay, two children and a woman, this dark-haired, exotically scented woman who lurked just behind his own dreams and seemed to be with himself and Fair Beard even now, though she, like his own sweet Gwen, had been left far behind.

Embarrassed, Madoc looked down, feeling the tug of the river around the ship, smelling rain in the breeze.

Someone approached with a tray from the sailors' charcoal rack. Caradoc leaned into the lampglow, offering Madoc soup in a turtle shell, and crispbread curled like fried parchment as delicate as thin, hot ice on the tongue. Madoc took the food gratefully, and Caradoc handed him a cupped crescent apparently made of antler or bone—no doubt a Shawnee artifact. It took Madoc a moment to realize it was a spoon, carved from a natural form as translucent as a jewel.

The soup was some kind of red meat basted with onions, and the corn with its unique taste and texture was sprinkled with a surprise.

"Salt!" Madoc explained, licking his lips. "Where did you get salt, man?"

"The Chickasaw, along with bushels of parched corn," Fair Beard answered. "Cost us a kitchen knife, a bent hoe-head, a couple of trinkets."

"Strange what one misses most from home," Madoc said, sucking another corn chip for the startling flavor of salt so long absent from his palate, then crunching into one of the delights of this country, maize, unknown back home. He especially liked the way the red women would smear a dab of cornmeal paste upon the face of a hot rock, instantly crisping the paste lightly, thin enough to see through. He was amazed the women did this trick so often and never singed a fingertip.

"I dream about beer almost every night," Fair Beard confessed with solemnity, the quality that suited him most comfortably. He continued detailing the situation that had impelled their leaving Bear Island. This led them to talk about all manner of things ending with Madoc's comment that he wanted to plot how far north they had come.

"When did you last take the sun?" he inquired, meaning when had the pilot taken a reading on the sun's relative position to determine high noon.

Fair Beard had to admit that in the press of events he had gotten slack.

"We will take Polaris tonight."

Fair Beard calculated that he had not taken a sighting on the pole star since just prior to the Battle of Muscle Shoals.

"And," Madoc added, more dependent on charts than the Norsemen, "every night hereafter."

Though the storm was coming in from the south, they took a reading with Madoc's sunboard on the North Star, it and its guard stars faintly discernible through the overcast. As they moved up the nearly straight river, Polaris would continue to appear higher and higher in the sky at midnight. They were definitely moving back up into the home latitudes. They argued softly for a long time afterwards about just how far north they had come, a clam-shell lamp illuminating Madoc's charts unrolled on deck, everyone but the watch sleeping around them.

"I tell you we are at least as far north as Spain," Madoc insisted as he placed a pin representing tonight's sighting. But Fair Beard, who disdained charts and relied in the Norse tradition on memory, thought they could not be above the latitude of Northern Africa, perhaps at about the Fortunate Isles, where they made west for open ocean upon the great current that brought them to the shores of this unknown country not so long ago.

The next day they plowed on, the ship fairly skimming directly leeward with the fleet of slower coracles fanning out behind her, driven by the current in league with the strong sou'westerly smelling of rain that dogged their heels but never dampened their backs.

Wil and a couple of men kept themselves busy sounding, but the depth of the main channel remained well below their keel. Though they spied occasional shallows, the river was wide enough to give them a berth around these reedy zones, and never once did Fair Beard have to call out the oars. Finally he allowed the men to recradle them and let people come out for air on deck to silence their complaints.

Madoc wished he was steady enough the next day to climb to the top of the mast and watch the land go by. He found his personal things—his knife and cinch purse plus the small tools he usually wore at his belt with his own blue knife. Rummaging around in his sea chest, he growled at Ari that he could not find his sword.

"But, sir, you do not remember?" Ari was stopped in the middle of a task he had set himself, clearing a single below-decks spot for Madoc's personal belongings, gear and bedding, all of which had been separated and pushed into various nooks and crannies with the increased population of the ship in the dash away from Muscle Shoals.

Madoc dreaded the implication in the black man's voice. "Durendal is gone?"

It was a special weapon, given to him by the king of France during one of the diplomatic errands he had run a few years back for his father. The story was that it belonged to the great French hero Roland, but it was dear to Madoc because the sword was meant for his father. Owen had given it to Madoc, saying that such a blade should not hang on an old man's wall, but at a young man's side.

"As part of the terms, Fox demanded you surrender it."

Madoc groaned with sudden recall.

"It is a terrible injustice," Ari said, but Madoc shook his head.

"No, he outfought me. I remember that much."

"You gave him a good fight."

"I suppose he deserves to keep it since he took it from me."

Ari could not dispute that, and handed Madoc the small astrolabe the master usually wore at his belt.

Madoc took it, seeing that all his things had been put away in a permanent manner.

"You did not expect me to make it, did you Ari?"

"You were very sick, sir." He looked up earnestly. "As long as you live, we all live."

"The king's luck, eh?" Madoc said, aware of the tradition back home that the people were the king's personal spiritual responsibility. He slapped himself here and there, as though to playfully test his body, and found it sound: "I think we have a chance," he said, having long given in to the burden of that tradition.

"With the help of God," Ari said, and crossed himself.

Madoc watched him as he continued to rearrange a small section aft, walling it off with crates and scraped buffalo hides so that the captain could have privacy. Married life seemed to be sitting well on Ari Al Ghazal O'Daliagh. On their way up to the mountain last year, Ari had found himself a Mabilan wife who came attached to her mam and little sister. Now he looked for all the world like a well-kept brave of that nation, decked out in a finely beaded mulberry-bark tunic with fringed leather leggings, tall moccasins, a snakeskin belt, his curly black hair neatly braided.

Madoc had always been curious about this fellow. But he had never had the opportunity to question him about his life back in Dublin. His people had been brought to the Norse city in Ireland as slaves a few generations back by the same vikings who raped Madoc's own grandmother and infused Scandinavian blood into the native Celtic stock.

He might have taken this opportunity to learn how Ari, a descendant of black men, had retained his grandfather's complexion among a white population, but the crew was yelling up on deck at some sighted obstacle—a huge tree trunk, from the sound of it.

Now that he had his tools, Madoc thought he might climb

the mast and have a look around, but Ari discouraged him. "We want to take good care of you," he said with a grin.

Madoc scratched his full beard.

"Let Caradoc shave you."

"I fear I have grown sloppy without you to help, my friend."

"It is true that a man cannot serve two masters," Ari said.

"I forgive you for returning to Fair Beard, who after all owns your allegiance."

"He owns *me*, sir."

It was a poignant moment, which Madoc found acutely discomforting, for he hated the idea that one man could own another.

Ari, aware of the other's scruples, diverted him with a silver mirror he found in the sea chest.

"I look like a bear," Madoc said, pulling at the scraggly beard.

Ari shrugged, reluctant to criticize the captain.

Madoc normally wore the long mustaches affected by his father and other men of his country, with a clean chin. Ari had opted to be clean shaven, as had most of the men in Madoc's and Fair Beard's crews.

He had to admit he still felt too light-headed to climb the forty-foot mast and stay up there swaying and battered by the wind; and he did keep thinking it would feel grand to have a clean face again. So he took Ari's advice and called Caradoc, who set about the task on deck.

Winnowed Rice was close by as Fair Beard piloted them on down the stream, the oarsmen standing ready beside the white pine oars lying crossdeck, ready in their sockets, because upon approaching the Ohio they expected the current to roughen. Snorrison wanted to take that river east back to its confluence with the Shawnee. It would be a tricky bit of navigating, though the Shawnee woman had given fair report of the marriage of wide, slow streams in flat country. During this season, as long as it was approached before the winter rains began, the current was traversable by a strong canoe team.

But she flatly stated that she did not think the coracles could make the journey up the stream and had doubts that they should put the ship against the current even with its strong sail and with the guidance of the wind, which she said blew from the northwest in those regions. Windward sailing was out of her experience. Though this was river travel, and on a stream he had never traveled before, Snorrison believed his ship could handle a spunky river as it had done before, especially if local canoe teams commonly made such runs. Between sails and oars he was sure he could make it, even if he had to dance around currents or sandbars.

Finally he said to Winnowed Rice, "Please, if you do not wish to stay aboard for this journey, join your sisters in the coracles."

Her eyes full of bright glints of understanding, Winnowed Rice thought over his offer.

"Go ahead, Shawnee Woman," he said. "You do not wound me."

But she knew it was a test of loyalty if not courage, so she declined to take one of the smaller vessels, which would put in at a Shawnee camp ahead, she being the only one of the Shawnee to ride the ship.

Fair Beard shot an inquiring glance at Madoc, nominally still master although since Fair Beard's reappearance with the ship, neither had had the time or inclination to discuss captaincy. Now that Madoc, who owned the ship and her command, was feeling better, they were falling back into the old comfortable, familiar pattern he and Fair Beard had shared on many voyages with himself as commander and the other as pilot. Madoc shrugged and asked Winnowed Rice about the shorelines on approach to the junction. He was gratified to hear there were several good bays where canoemen often put in to portage across the narrow northernmost point of the Land Between Two Rivers.

"The home village is off this water, anyway," she said to Rhys, who translated the name of the place as Meadows-of-Mint.

"How far?" Fair Beard wanted to know, and she described a foot journey that would take the company nearly another day's travel over an ancient trace to the big village on the other river, which was called the Shawnee.

"The ship will make that in a twinkling," Fair Beard said, hungry for action with the restless crew behind him.

Madoc, newly shaved and lounging at the rail, was silent, almost dreamy in his detachment, which Fair Beard ascribed to this recovery. When pressed by the Norseman for an opinion, he said he would opt for a sail over walking any day of the week.

It failed to rain—the storm never made it this far north, but it chilled and dámpened the air, and as the banks slid by on either side, the country took on more appropriately October colors. Traveling Moon, as the red people called it.

The wind swung more from the northwest with a bite to it, so everyone broke out woolen clothing and put it on beneath their leather clothes. Now Madoc's Hundred looked Shawnee by dress if not by decoration. Every deer taken had been transformed by busy red hands into someone's new shirt. The white people had stopped weaving their wonderful cloth while traveling; and as things wore out on the move more rapidly than when settled, replacements were from the trail and drying on improvised cane racks just behind the stewpots.

Before quitting the mountain, the white women of the Hundred had knitted socks, heavy woolen tubes that fascinated the red women used to wearing double moccasins lined with cattail fluff against the cold. Now every red woman wanted a pair of socks for herself and her children and worked at making them each night when the men pulled the ship up to make camp.

The Shawnee dogs slunk closer to the fire that night as Wil's wife Mary and the clergy were teaching the red women how to knit the amazingly soft and supple buffalo twine with long bone needles made from the legs of herons and kingfishers. Half the red contingent worked on spindles to make the yarn, while the other half happily clacked away, exclaiming over their first crude but quickly improved cabling.

Yngvild, who might have helped with this because she had a fair hand at weaving, stayed belowdecks aboard the *Horn*, though she no longer had to be tied. But she would not endure the presence of any red woman, and of the whites only Mary ab Hennin, who would talk, and she would listen.

Morose and drawn into his blankets against the gathering chill, Madoc watched Mary instructing the red women, making them undo imperfect stitches. She was a narrow plank of a woman in contrast to her strong, stout husband, who had been Madoc's quartermaster for as long as he could remember. Her gray-streaked hair was always neatly pulled into the braided bun worn by the women of her home country, the rugged coast of Cumberland, a part of western Britain between Cambria and Scotland.

Mary was wearing mostly leather, as were all of them these

days, woven goods having been bartered away. But though the only woven cloth she wore was her shift, plus a crocheted shawl she brought from home, all of her leather clothing was cut in the style she knew from home. She disdained the one-piece dress of the red women and wore a fully gathered apron, though it bulked out her waist. She had cut off all fringes, which the red people liked trimming their clothing. She wore no beads, and in fact, the only decoration on her was a slim thong around her neck with a punched gold coin strung upon it—a gift from his father's treasure that Madoc had given to all the Hundred some time ago to mark their passage over the ocean. She used Shawnee words sparingly, but for the most part she spoke to the red women in Cymraeg and corrected their usage whenever they did not pronounce something correctly. Still, her twin seven-year-old sons ran with the pack of Shawnee boys and usually could be distinguished from them only by their brown hair, which the sun lightened as it reddened their bodies.

They could be heard at their games off to one side even now, playing the Shawnee version of chunkee with a smooth round stone one of them had found in the gravel this afternoon. Madoc mused that he had never learned the fine points of any version of the noisy, boisterous game, in which it seemed the idea was to throw sticks at the rolling stone, the goal being to change its trajectory or stop it with a direct hit.

The knitters ignored the yells stirred up along with dust by the boys between this spot and the laurels that shielded the monks' camp as Mary leaned over to yank at a stitch made by Lily, sister of Winnowed Rice. As she went about the instruction, Mary had a trenchant, tactless way about her of tapping a finger at the offending stitch, which the red student pulled out and attempted again. She perused the handiwork with the posture of the farsighted. As he watched, Madoc was seized with a strange fondness for the parchment-pale woman, whom he hardly knew despite their shared adventure of the past year plus the years her husband had served him.

He realized with a piquant bite of nostalgia that now that Gwen was gone, the tight-lipped Cumberlander was the last woman of his own country left among the Hundred. She and poor mad Yngvild hiding in the ship's belly were the last two white women who had survived.

With Wil as the one exception, the men of his crew who had

either come here wed or married countrywomen since landing were all widowers: Huw had lost Agnes, Llywellyn lost Tegan, and Edwin still mourned his wife and baby lost in bondage to the first red tribe the Hundred had encountered.

And then there was Rhiannon, he thought, blinking as sparks flew up from the bonfire. On the other side of the blaze, Rhys tuned up Llais Mel and began to sing a long ballad about a hero who must win his love from a giant.

He and Rhys both had lost Rhiannon.

And Teleri; Teleri was lost because he thought he might have a chance to return home and so broke his vow to the Cherokee.

Now Gwen was gone again and without much chance for her admittedly incredible luck to save her a second time.

And here were the survivors, two middle-aged mothers in the huge, wild land of so many red women. Realization was like a slap in the face. He knew there was no chance now, in fact there had been no chance for a long time, for his company to retain the life-style and language of home. The red ways would surely win.

The fire flickered on the painted face of the poet in the middle of his song, half Shawnee, half Celt.

And if that were not enough, there was Fair Beard smoking a long, thin pipe, a beautiful thing and no doubt about it made by clever Natchez hands of blood red stone in the shape of a kingfisher, the stem being the tail feathers. Nipowoc was a red habit. The Norseman passed the pipe to one of his seamen. They coughed and laughed softly together, barely audible under the music that many voices now joined.

Madoc sat rubbing his wrist. He had broken it building a ship a couple of years ago, and now he knew from twinges there when rain was likely. His impressions weighed on him, still absorbing the cold equation that only two white women had survived. It struck him as strange and sadly ironic until he remembered little Cari, Rhys's adopted child and surely a white female and Madoc's own little half-sister by way of events that occurred back home before this journey was undertaken. But whatever her bloodline, he was sure the little girl would grow into womanhood more red than white.

He could not shake these melancholy ruminations. As he stared at the people around him, red women and white men, his thoughts wandered toward home and what must be happening there now, a year after his departure. Had his father, Owen ab Gwynedd, made peace with Henry of the English, or were they still at each other's throats? Or had his brother David's alliances changed the board entirely?

Madoc's plans for going back had cost much and had gotten him no farther in that direction. But inside his exhausted and still-healing self there smoldered a small spark of hope that it was still possible to return, gather allies, and come back to this place with as many of his countrymen as wanted to depart the broken homeland. Leave it to the English, after all, he thought. The sheer size of this new country offered shelter to all Britons who might be dispossessed by English dreams of empire.

He felt a clutch in the gut because he loved his homeland, her green hills, ragged coastline, and the fields of grain bent under the sea wind rolling over Mona Isle. But, he thought, leave that wretched, blood-soaked piece of sod behind, for all its untamed beauty; just give it to them and let them eat the rocks, and make a new Cymru over here. That was as fine a triumph over the English as Madoc could imagine—it was sweet enough to make him chuckle to himself and dispel his gloom.

One among the company was aware of the mood change in their chief and approached him to remark it.

"They said we must be very quiet because you were sick," Einion said as he inched closer.

Madoc held out a hand to the boy, Teleri's brown-haired orphan, who gratefully leaned against him so that Madoc had to turn to protect his still-tender side where the puncture wound was rapidly healing. He had never seen such a wound close so quickly—it already looked a fortnight old.

"You hurt your hand," Madoc said, rubbing the child's scraped palm.

"I fell on the gravel."

Traces of the colored clays the red children rubbed on themselves clung to his straight, lusterless hair, roughly braided in the Shawnee manner. His leather tunic was filthy, and his knuckles and knees were scabbed with layers of scrapes.

"Brother Andrew made us pick watercress all day."

Madoc could feel the child shivering as he instinctively leaned closer to adult warmth; he opened the wings of his buffalo robe and enclosed the boy in it with him, feeling the cold skin riddled with gooseflesh.

"I hate watercress, how about you?"

"Winnowed Rice says I must eat it to get well," Madoc said, and confessed in a whisper. "But I would sooner eat dirt."

Einion wrenched a giggle from himself. "Running Cloud says a warrior does not eat rabbit food." The boy kicked at the sand with his bare foot, starkly clean up to the ankle, past which it was sooty.

"Rabbit food—yes," Madoc agreed. "Running Cloud is one of the Shawnee boys?"

"He says I cannot play chunkee with them." Einion glanced at the boys settling down after their wild play on the other side of the fire. Though he was tall for his age, he was a frail boy; probably, Madoc thought, the butt of the bigger, rougher boys' teasing.

"Which one is Running Cloud?" Madoc asked, expecting Einion to point to one of the leathery Shawnee lads.

"There," Einion replied "with Mam Mary."

"But that is one of Mary's boys." Madoc tried to remember the names of the twins, who looked enough alike to get a second look, but they eluded his recall.

Einion pointed to a lad who was burly like his father, with his mother's pursed lips, but everything else about him was Shawnee—from braided hair with the feathers of small birds woven into the coils, to a leather breechclout. He stood among the other boys and, unless one knew what to look for, was indistinguishable from the pack. His eyes were quick as he watched the company of adults engaged in sock knitting, his glance grazing among them all but stopping on no particular action. He wore the breechclout like the Shawnee boys, along with a light leather vest quilled and beaded with whatever scraps he could find.

He must have claimed some rank among the red pack because of the knife in a crude scabbard at his cinch—it looked like one of Mary's cast-off kitchen knives, sharpened so many times that the blade was only a ghost of its original edge, a thin, chipped blunt sliver of iron and almost useless with a broken point. But in the society of the boys, it set him apart and allowed him to be called Running Cloud, who stood otherwise like the others with his arms crossed over his chest, his feet bare despite the chill, and pinkly clean from his day of collecting cress from a trickling stream.

Madoc shivered to see them all so naked. Then he remembered. "Math," he said. "That boy's name is Math, and his brother is . . ." He looked around for Wil's other son.

"Lludd," said Einion. "But they all took Shawnee names. Math said he would break my arm if I did not call him Running Cloud."

Madoc leaned back with a sigh of comprehension. "Einion, what happened to your golden penny?"

Einion glanced at Math before he looked shyly up.

"Did they take it from you?"

Einion nodded, and Madoc fished in his cinch-purse. "This was your mam's."

Einion took the thumbnail-sized coin in his smudged fingertips, his eyes wide. It was a gold copy of a Roman penny that dated from the time of the vikings more than two hundred years before, awl-punched with a hole Madoc had put into it with his own hands.

"I took it off her hem just before we buried her back at Muscle Shoals. I have been keeping it, waiting for just the right use for it." It had been only a few days since this boy's mam had died, pierced with the same arrow that had punctured Madoc's side.

The boy's eyes were brimming as he held the coin up to the firelight. It had been less than a week since he watched them put her into the ground, and he was not much more than seven years old.

"Have you something to tie it on?" Madoc asked, searching his own person for something that would do. Finding nothing, he remembered he had used Fair Beard's cat's-cradle string to hold his collar flap closed. He unthreaded it now and gave it to Einion, who quickly threaded the coin upon it.

"Give it an anchor knot," Madoc suggested, and took the line to show the boy how to tie it to secure the coin. "To keep from cutting the line."

Madoc gestured, and the boy leaned over so the thong could be tied around his neck, eyes glistening when he looked up again.

"Let nobody take this one from you."

Einion put his fist protectively around the coin and shoved it under his tunic, slowly shaking his head, then like any youngster who senses he has adult sympathy, suddenly asked Madoc, "Can I stay with you on the ship? Just tonight, and I will be very quiet, I promise."

"Actually, I could use some help, Einion."

"You mean me?"

"All my servants have left me for their wives. Ari has returned to Fair Beard, and I need someone to help care for my sunboard."

The boy nodded eagerly, all cold and discomfort forgotten, and Madoc instructed him to fetch a crewman drinking from a clay water jug. When he did, Madoc asked the sailor to fetch the wooden device and navigational charts from his personal sea chest back on the *Horn*.

"Why do you need a sunboard at night?" the boy asked, settling in beside Madoc while they waited.

"A nocturnal is a better name for it, but the truth is that with it we can take a reading on the sun even at night." Madoc searched the sky, which was muted with high overcast but full of stars. "See that bright star there near the center of things?"

Einion leaned back and stared up.

"There."

"Yes."

"Well, it is the center, and everything else in the sky makes a circle around it."

Einion looked intently at the vast reaches above their heads. "Nothing is moving now."

"Slowly. Very slowly."

Together they watched the sky for a while, then Madoc said, "You know the Little Dipper?"

Einion, a child raised inside gloomy, windowless halls and stone fortresses, shook his head, no, he did not know the Little Dipper.

"There—see why they call it a dipper?"

"Yes—" the boy exclaimed in genuine delight at seeing this for the first time. Madoc was secretly ashamed that nobody had taken the boy's vital education in hand, and he blamed his father for so casually dropping sons in his later years and leaving them to be instructed by capricious chance.

By this boy's age Madoc had known all the major constellations. He made several cruises as a cabin boy to one of his father's allies, an Irishman who eventually took Madoc in as a foster son for his later education as a sailor. Such was the tradition in Celtic countries, so that alliances were formed with genuine affection between foster children and parents, sometimes even greater than that between children and their natural parents.

"The Little Dipper swings around Polaris once every twenty-four hours. When those two big stars, the Guards, there and there, the ones in the Dipper farthest from the North Star, line up so that a straight line can be drawn from the Star through the two guards to the ground, then it is midnight. If you know midnight or noon, you can figure out your directions with—"

The sailor hunkered down to offer Madoc's nocturnal in its leather case with brass corners.

"With this." Madoc took the octagonal case and flipped it open dexterously, then removed from a cushion of silk a round inlaid board in a protective leather bag. "Thank you, Huw."

While Huw and Einion watched, Madoc lovingly slipped the device from the leather bag. It was a skillet-sized circle about the thickness of a knuckle, made of rosewood inlaid with walrus ivory, pearls and gold wire in the form of Celtic spirals, a masterwork from some ancient craftsman's hand and one of the few material objects Madoc had kept throughout a sailor's traveling life.

A band of brass encircled the wood on its edge, extending from this above the surface at one point in a sighting hole as finely engraved with Celtic coils as a king's seal ring.

Various colors of wood and inlay formed the geometric pattern of a sliced pie—the airts, or cardinal directions, North, South, East, and West, with four quarters further subdivided. Near was a five-pointed star cut of brass, enameled with the likeness of a stylized human figure with his limbs marking off equal wedges of the circle. The little man wore a pointed cap that could be aimed at north, and the entire figure could be rotated around his navel, where the figure was pinned to the center point of the marked circle.

Madoc tested the movable figure and blew what felt like sand grains from its pin. He pulled at the tattered hem of his tunic, the last piece of woven clothing he owned, made by Rhiannon's hand from the softest buffalo fleece back on the mountain, and wiped at the glowing oiled surface that was at least a hundred years old.

He raised it so that he could look through the sighting piece.

Dampness had crusted the hole with verdigris; he found a slim stick and reamed it through the aperture a couple of times and looked again, then handed the sunboard over to the boy to see for himself.

"Huw, do you think we could use the services of a cabin boy aboard the *Horn*?"

"Have you anyone in particular in mind, now, Captain?" the sailor inquired, sitting on his haunches admiring the beautiful sunboard.

"Should be a lad of, oh, say, seven or eight."

Huw nodded gravely, a ragged hank of sandy-colored hair bobbing, while he studied the tips of his fingers. A seaman since before this boy's age and a member of Madoc's crew for more than a dozen years, Huw ab Tewdr had lost his wife a year ago in a fight with the Alabamans, the first red people the Hundred encountered. He was a quiet, private fellow, made more so by that loss, which he had not sought to make up for with any of the available red women despite Madoc's urging. "Perhaps this boy will do, sir."

Einion beamed.

"I do not know, Huw—he is quite green."

"Someone would have to take him in hand, then."

"Teach him the ropes," Madoc said, groaning when Einion grabbed him and hugged him, inadvertently irritating his tender side.

There were eyes in the woods that watched them, Chickasaw eyes full of wonder. Imala'ko the Chickasaw had paused in his northward journey and stealthily crossed the river to observe these amazing whites who would parallel his own path until they arrived at the Kantuck. The Chickasaw nation owned the southern bank, so he would part with them where this river met the next, his destination being farther north toward the great city of Ixtulan on the Great River Road just south of its confluence with the river they called the Great Muddy, and which someday would go by the name Missouri.

Later, when the past-full moon leaned far over the western horizon like a lidded eye, and the guard stars almost pointed their straight line to the earth below Polaris, Madoc walked with Einion and Huw to a low rocky point on the river. There, where they had an uninterrupted view of the vault of sky, they took the sun at midnight.

Chapter 7

Though north is definitely its tendency after the Great Bend, the Tennessee River is not quite a straight line. It kinks and curls like any liquid stream that by nature meanders around obstacles, forever seeking the lowest way.

Just before it is drawn into the Ohio on the way to the Great River Road, the Tennessee River whips west. At that point, where it changes direction for the last time, lies a bight, determined by underlying geology, where there had been a settlement as long as people lived in the region for a long time. It was called the Land Between Two Rivers.

If the Tennessee were seen as a long bent arm, the shoulder would be back in the eastern mountains, called Unakas by the Cherokee; the elbow would be in Muskogean territory down at the Great Bend, and this smaller turn west would be the wrist. In November of that year, 1172 by Madoc's reckoning, the Shawnee maintained a local camp at the wrist of the Tennessee where clans met, traded, or traveled on to the buffalo plains or an ancient regional trading center that came to be called Paducah at the junction of the Tennessee with the Ohio. Many nations traded there, but this lower camp was in Shawnee territory.

The lower camp was the northern terminus for the wide arc of the migration route traversed by several Shawnee bands, including Winnowed Rice's Whippoorwills; it was on an east-west path between the Tennessee River and the Shawnee main village, Meadows-of-Mint, located to the east on the banks of the other river, which would someday be renamed for Wil and Mary's native country of Cumberland. At this time it was named for the Shawnee, whose ancestors had occupied that vast, fruitful country between the Ohio and the Tennessee rivers for as long as anyone could remember.

The camp at the wrist of the Tennessee was a permanent village by this time because of its strategic location and was used mainly to gather goods that would be taken farther on to the larger center downriver. The people who lived there most of the year were used to seeing odd things float by. They knew what foreigners looked like, mainly the people from the west and southwest beyond the Great River Road. Yet they had never seen anything like the great canoe that came floating down their river that afternoon with the sun behind it firing up the clouds, the sail loose and luffing as she angled directly into the wind.

The weather was bright and cool, with a lingering autumn dryness before the first real winter weather. The air sparkled. Scrapping breezes worried at the last leaves on the oaks and sumacs along the river.

The big ship was dazzling in the crisp sunlight. Along either side of her sprang the long oars, a dozen in all. They dipped into the silvery water and splashed dripping, bell-like notes when the oarsmen pulled back, used by the pilot at this point to control the ship's direction with the compliant current.

Fair Beard was taking no chances. He already had men hauling up the sail, ready for what he expected farther on down the stream, according to Winnowed Rice.

As the *Horn* moved along, red men paused above teeming fish nets all along the wide, swampy shore, staring in awe at the great uncommon snake incarnate in the common afternoon sunlight. This was harvest season, so there were an unusually large number of Shawnee laboring in the lowlands along the leagues of the river. In addition to the fishermen who worked in teams hauling in drumfish northeast of the camp, there were long canoes of rice-harvesting female teams from many clans who shared the homeland on a semipermanent basis.

A band of children variously attached to the laboring adults ran ahead along the path that followed the bank approaching camp, yelling with excitement, "The Uktena is coming!"

At their heels camp dogs set to barking.

Old men came out of their smoking lodges, squinting in the golden autumn light full of dust motes and humidity that had begun to settle on the area as a pearly haze. Women at their corn mortars looked up. Four traders from northern places left the market plaza in the center of town and strolled, with one visiting and three resident shamans, to the water's edge to peer seriously riverward. Behind them was a growing crowd of women and braves who had been agitated by the reports of the children and were curious to see what they could be talking about.

One group of Shawnee traders from Meadows-of-Mint was organizing a dozen dog-pulls and tying down baskets of corn traded for buffalo hides and did not have time to stop and join the curious. But when they heard the exclamations of those nearer the water, they left their harnessed hounds and followed the others just in time to see the great canoe heave into sight around a shallow tideland.

Its approach was long and slow, since the wind had dropped somewhat, shivering what sail was up and causing the crew to scramble around among the oarsmen. Ringing song rippled through their ranks as their pilot skillfully angled the ship around the little bay where outlander canoes had been pulled in and overturned for safekeeping.

A few of the women on shore cried out when they saw the thing out on the water grow larger from the hazy distance. One shrieked in terror and ran off with several small children squealing after her. The warriors among the watchers put their hands on their weapons without drawing them and stood back in wonder, convinced that little could be done against this approaching object.

In a somber voice a shaman began a vocalization of the story that seemed to be materializing before their astonished eyes, for it first appeared that the *Horn* was coming right in to shore.

But Fair Beard was only following the bow of the current. His intention was to take her on down to the junction, where he planned to head back on the Ohio eventually, to move upstream on the Shawnee to Meadows-of-Mint on the east side of the Land Between Two Rivers, an afternoon's walk overland from this place.

The current pressed the ship away from shore.

Madoc as master and Fair Beard as pilot expected the swifter Ohio to come racing in on their starboard bow not far downriver from this bight, at which point they must modify the sheet to catch the prevailing westerly that should by all reports be strong enough to send them up the Ohio to its junction not far northeast with the Shawnee.

That was the plan; now they felt the quickening westerly current pulling them past the Shawnee camp with its onlook-

ers staring at the ship. Very shortly the river turned directly
into the sunset, and the pilot sang out the orders to hurry
getting the sail up and ready for the upcoming junction of the
two rivers and the right moment to jibe.

Madoc, as the eye of the ship up on the mast, called out a
monosyllable to the pilot down on the tiller starboard that he
was seeing small whitecaps whisked by the wind off to the
northeast. This was a good indication that their wind was
picking up again. He saw, but did not yet report, more
evidence of debris swept ashore. So far the mainstream
appeared clear of snags, though he did see from time to time
smaller branches with fresh green leaves scudding by.

In the distance he saw a team of red men working a net
sparkling with their catch. There was a momentary vision of a
wide purse drawing shut on brilliantly shimmering golden
coins as the fish leapt into the slanting sunlight. But the ship
was moving faster now, and the image floated past. His angle
changed suddenly; the miracle vanished.

Madoc could not look straight without being blinded by the
sun, grown huge between two silver-bottomed thunderheads.
He watched the shore and its littoral of waving reeds.

Downstream from the Shawnee fishermen, Madoc looked
back over his shoulder to see that they had turned as a group,
shielding their eyes to watch what was to them a legendary
wing flying into the golden light.

A nation renowned for story and song, the oldest Shawnee
story concerned a magician who stole a jewel from the head of
a water dragon. Even little children knew that old story was
true, because the shamans had found the bones of similar
creatures in cliffs all along the rivers of the homeland. There
once, long ago, before this world hardened into its present
shape, dragons and other magic animals were alive in this
country, as alive as bears, buffalo, humans, or hummingbirds.
It was believed the water snake had since ascended to the
higher world of stars, but remained the essence of all rivers in
shape and in spirit, glorified in legends for a thousand
generations, painted in varying forms on cliffs beside the river
and on many a shaman's shield in hunting lodges throughout
the Land Between Two Rivers.

And now here was something that looked like those painted
dragons, with one wing furling, full of strangers magically
appearing, moving swiftly by and going on down the river.

Every Shawnee believed in the Uktena, but this was the first time anyone had actually seen one moving by, so fast it could not be apprehended.

It was even more amazing that this awesome object was followed by a fleet of round canoes unlike any made by red nations but full of Shawnee faces, some of them familiar because they were distant relatives to those on the riverbank.

When her prow resumed the direction of the main flow, and it was obvious the *Horn* was not going to make a landing, canoemen on shore were scrambling for their craft, righting them in teams and pushing off to follow the big ship.

The fleet of coracles had come into view and aimed toward the shore, where already several called out to the paddlers, some of whom were recognizable as family members. Suddenly the shallows swarmed with these overburdened round wicker-and-hide canoes unlike any the Shawnee had ever crafted—they preferred the long, low bark canoes to the southern hollow log racers like those of the Natchez left behind on Bear Island.

Mary's two boys and Father Brian were the only ones of the white people to be among the Shawnee and coracle paddlers.

Brian, one of his baby sons in a cradleboard on his back, brought his coracle in beside that of his wife, a Mabilan woman who was likewise burdened with their other. He left Matthew with his mother and went looking for Lily, also among this small-craft contingent.

Together they searched for a face familiar to her among the chiefs who knotted behind the shamans at their chants, someone specific she could relay a message to from Winnowed Rice. But the only face she recognized belonged to one of the rice harvesters, a tall middle-aged woman just approaching from the trace behind the village, hanks of twine precut and hanging from her belt, a wide conical piece of headgear, woven like a basket, tied with a twine under her chin and shadowing her twinkling, laughing eyes.

After a warm greeting from her great-aunt Sky, whom she had not seen for three seasons since the Whippoorwills last visited the home country, Lily introduced the white shaman and then answered a burst of questions from the elder. This conversation drew others who wanted to hear everything about the amazing thing they were witnessing, and who watched Father Brian with shy curiosity.

Brian graciously withstood curious touches as the Shawnee children and some of the women handled him, his strange woven clothing all of one piece and unlike anything red men ever wore or red woman could ever weave on the hand-loom, the pale, freckled skin of his hands blister-scarred from a fire he had walked through last year.

Brian had been among several of the Hundred captured and taken back to an Alabaman village where he met and married Hayati. His captors had partially scalped him and a couple of other white shamans they took prisoner, so that now Father Brian had a permanent tonsure, a healed scalping that had removed the clerically shaven spot on the top of his head and the reddish brown hair around it. This was a strange thing to the red people; several who were tall enough rubbed his pate.

Likewise it was a strangely wonderful thing to the whites, who mostly agreed with Brian that this was God's permission for him to continue as a priest despite his having taken a wife. Wyn had opposed him, saying he had broken his vows. But Father John outranked the abbot in age if not position; he reminded Brother Wyn, who was a monk but not a priest, that Brian was their only priest besides himself, an old man. That permanent tonsure given him by the scalpers had sealed his argument.

The red people among the Hundred respected him, too; they had no prejudice against a shaman being married. Chastity struck them as one of the oddest among many odd behaviors of their white brothers.

Brian smiled and let the new red people handle him, Hayati at his side telling them in trade Muskogean about her foreign husband. He tried to watch the river where the ship was diminishing in the distance.

Some of the shore contingent continued running along the beach to watch the big canoe for as long as possible, but already it appeared as small as a toy, farther and farther away on its inevitable journey toward the Ohio. Others took off behind it in Shawnee canoes, calling to sisters or cousins who passed them in the incoming coracles.

Lily trotted with Sky to approach one of the elder counselors, who asked incredulously if the strangers in the big canoe were actually going to try to take the thing upstream at the junction.

When Lily nodded, he laughed out loud, wrinkles corrugating deeper in his leathery brow. "Then we will see something terrible over there," the old man said, grabbing the arms of one of his younger relatives, a canoeman heading out to follow the others in the wake of the ship. He did not want to miss anything and so hobbled along with the young men and boarded the canoe.

Lily stood there biting her lip, watching with her great aunt as the ship became a silhouette in the bright western sunlight, the current with it but the wind against it, her single square sail positioned to windward to take that contrary breeze and use it to move her even faster in the long zigs and zags of windward sailing.

"My sister tried to tell the tangletongue," she said morosely. They watched for a while longer, then went back to the landing to help bring in the coracles and loosen the cargo, talking all the while about the significance of the strangers and the happenings upriver in the past few days.

Sky listened raptly, asking questions here and there, but for the most part letting the young woman speak. It was a long and amazing story she told, recounting how the Shawnee women and children unloading coracles around them had survived a battle with Cherokee.

Sky was sobered by the recitation of the destruction of the men of the Whippoorwills at the hands of the Cherokee, but she did not interrupt Lily's story: ". . . then our women picked up the men's weapons."

Everyone listening gasped at this shocking report, for a woman's touch was supposed to pollute a man's knife.

But Lily continued. "This astonished Fox and his warriors so much, they let us go." She finished with a brief account of how the Whippoorwills met and allied with the whites under Weather Eyes, who later faced the Cherokee in battle, lost, and fled downriver.

By prearrangement, those in the coracles would take their cargo by dog-pull overland to Meadows-of-Mint, and Lily set about organizing her red sisters to that effort. Sky called in the ricers, who had hauled their day's harvest in baskets to the council lodge; quickly they had the cargo train ready to head east after a short rest and stretch and a meal of trail food.

This was all accomplished amid the most friendly greetings and embraces, because all of these red people knew each other. The homeland wanted to hear everything about these strangers and their big canoe, now out of sight and headed downriver for certain disaster.

"Do not fret," Sky said to Lily. "They will see in time that the Oyo is high and dangerous."

By then the Shawnee dogs had caught up to the fleet of coracles and were trotting in a pack into the village, where local hounds snarled and barked. Several of the Whippoorwills' animals kept on moving through the town toward the curve of the river, among them the almost grown pups of Winnowed Rice's yellow bitch, intent on following their mother on the ship.

The permanent camp was returning to something like its normal late-afternoon activity. Trading and councils, both interrupted with the excitement, were over for the day. The last of the harvesters trailed in with their baskets of rice. The fishermen brought in their catch and were already smoking it on racks near the downwind perimeter of the village. Cooking fires were being lit in the many temporary lodges set around the shallow valley that touched the river.

Gamblers were already making bets about what would happen to the big canoe. Odds definitely favored destruction, perhaps on the island sandbars of Paducah just below the confluence of the Tennessee with the Oyo. Everyone waited with underlying tension to hear the first reports when the canoemen returned, which they surely must soon from the downriver adventure.

Lily could not help worrying as she helped Sky prepare to set off at the head of the train, leading the Shawnee on yet another foot journey. If they hurried, they could be home by nightfall.

But Brian convinced her and the others to wait and see what happened to their white brothers and sisters, so they did not harness up the dogs. They rested their cargo in line and set up a temporary camp in a section of the village reserved for overnight visitors.

Even Sky agreed that tomorrow would be soon enough to make the journey over the ancient trace to the village of Meadow-of-Mint on the Shawnee River.

While their jerked meat was stewing along with corn and onions in cooking baskets, the aromas of their suppers adding to the others already on the breeze, Sky and Lily threw tobacco on the fire and said some magic to the wind, which everyone knew was a special friend to women and inclined to listen to female petitions, which that night consisted of prayers for beneficial breezes to be good to the big canoe.

The shamans thought the events of the day so important that they set up a dance circle around a communal fire in the center of the village. Long past midnight they sang and acted out the legend of the Uktena. The old men argued over the significance of the appearance this afternoon, and masked and feathered young men laid out intricate patterns of dance under the lowering sky.

The canoemen came back with incredible tales that inspired more dancing. The big canoe had made it, they said, having seen it with their own eyes.

"I last saw its one wing leaning under the wind, moving upstream on the Oyo faster than you can imagine," said the wrinkled counselor who had gone with the canoemen. "You should have been there, Sky." He tossed a full pinch of nipowoc onto the fire, causing a long blue flame to leap up momentarily and die down slowly as he leaned over to inhale the rich fumes. The Shawnee, unlike most other nations, did not smoke tobacco but burned it as an incense directly on live coals. "To see such a thing yourself," he continued, his voice distorted as he held the smoke and let it out in a long, lazy curl, unrolling with his words, "something to tell your grandchildren!"

His report was the stuff of more stories, so the singers made up a new song that would be sung for many generations about the triumphant return of the great snake to local waters.

Chapter 8

Sometimes when the wind was perfectly pitched to speed his vessel along, when the ship was riding high and dry with a fine crew working as smoothly as the organs of a great body, Madoc experienced a giddy feeling of being in greater hands than his own, of having won a free ride from the elements that were more often contrary than cooperative.

He felt like that now atop the mast as the *Horn* sped north of east up the yellowish Ohio with the compliant southwestern coming in behind them like a mother hen wing-guiding her chicks to the safety of the nest. The Ohio was made a bitch by upriver rain in the northern country. It was a thick, rude flow in comparison to the mild Tennessee, full of mud and twisted tree trunks and yellowish gray water that snatched the clear, languid Tennessee from its mouth and rushed on down, kicking and screaming, to the Great River Road waiting below.

On his perch atop the mast, Madoc let himself think for just a moment of that great river. By all reports it was but a few leagues to the west of the Tennessee's junction with the Ohio in this heartland of rivers, a vast arterial system if one could have a bird's-eye view of it, a map's-eye that must look as complex and intertwined as the veins in his wrists. That river was waiting for him. He could feel it in his bones even as he sped up this other river. The Mech-a-sip-i would be waiting whenever he was ready to take it south to the saltwater and the ocean that would take him home so that he could collect the remnants of his huge torn family and perhaps save them—he knew at least a dozen captains who might throw their ships and fortunes into such a western venture when they heard his report of this rich country.

Such a thought added to his feeling of well-being high above

111

his splendid ship running up the current that was flowing in the opposite direction.

The gusty wind was a blessing, holding as it was out of a brilliant sunset so expansive it filled every quarter of the sky with streaks of cloud and flushed, fleshy color. Fair Beard had Ari in charge of the oarsmen running it loosely—all the passengers were below. Now, driven directly ahead of the wind, they were making good time up the stream. According to Winnowed Rice they would make it to the Shawnee home village before nightfall, though less than an hour of light was left.

Benignly the clouds further parted behind them, giving full range to the setting sun painting the water road ahead a brilliant orange.

Madoc sat harnessed onto a small rail on the mast above the yard, with the first good feelings he had felt in days, his bare feet dangling, the wind that smelled of rain coming from behind parting the hair at the nape of his neck.

He saw they were approaching the islands as the river angled more northerly, true to Winnowed Rice's warning, and called this information down to the pilot, who gave an order for the linemen to get ready to move the sail accordingly. As he continued to watch the shore, he saw a long, low sandy isle with scruffy trees along its narrow spine, and tucked below this, nestled into the southern shore, a bay formed by the water's rush against a low clay shelf behind a wide gravel beach strewn with trees, with naked roots an echo of their twisted branches.

Madoc thought about the option of putting in now and finishing the run up the Ohio to the Shawnee in the morning.

It was an inviting little harbor on the lee side of a long wooded island and several smaller companions in the stream, made all the more so by the coming darkness. Landward beyond the long beach stretched the unbroken ribbon of autumn-colored bank that seemed to be moving past them. Flecks of dark green cedar riddled the orange and yellow foliage with a narrow strip of low verge cut by a creek. The water looked still over there in comparison to the flow running below their bow hard enough to fling back stringy ropes of spray that glazed the deck. A haze lingered around the ship, giving the air a damp, fishy smell.

The pilot called out a chant that said they were running well.

As Madoc watched from above, Einion approached Fair Beard with a water skin. One hand on the tiller, the pilot took it with the other, tipped it back, and drank long.

The low island slipped by, followed, it seemed, by another snoozing in the stream, this one treeless and all a slim, sandy beach that probably came and went with high water.

Unseen in the hold the monks began a vespers song that seemed appropriate, and Madoc let the little bay slide by them, the master's prerogative, without communicating its possibilities to anyone below. He made readjustments in the line crossing his tunic so that the securing knot did not press his breastbone or bruise his tender side. Behind him he was pleased to feel the mast securely communicating the vibrations of the ship in the water against his spine and behind his bare heels dangling five fathoms above the deck.

Ahead he could see a change in color and a snaggle of isles that signaled the mouth of the Shawnee River. He called this information to the pilot below, who sang out a command that prepared the riggers to change the sail's position so the ship would make the starboard turn following the Shawnee's main-stream.

Still fluky, the wind was blowing almost directly from behind, a favorable wind for speed; Snorrison called out a minor adjustment that kept them full to windward.

As though it heard his order, the wind ordered itself into a single, long, excellent exhalation that brought them to the long approach of the Shawnee, detectable by clearer, greener water to starboard than the murky Ohio to port. It was a strange vision to witness from on high; the ship seemed to cleave the stream into two strands, the thicker one a mile wide on the left, and the slim green stream on the right.

Suddenly below him the billowing sail cracked ominously and as though kicked, sagged limp and rattling against the mast.

As it sometimes will, the fickle wind died.

Fair Beard heard it, too, and called out to Ari sitting at the drum in the far prow, who in turn picked up the rhythm and sang out encouragement to the oarsmen to put their backs into it. The men on the lines worked to keep the sail steady to catch the wind when it sprang up again, as it surely would. The rain smell was palpable, with the southern quarter a slate gray darkening to charcoal. The skirts of several squalls could be

seen sweeping the far southern skyline—the river along this
stretch flowed almost directly north by east.

The oars bit the slatey water so that they corrected the port
yaw, which the current insistently provoked and which would
cause them to approach the Shawnee with too wide an angle.
The oarsmen took up Fair Beard's modulating chant in time
with Ari's drumbeat, a hauling song in unison, and for a while
they held their own but made no headway against the current.

Madoc saw that where the two rivers merged, the current
grew more urgent against the prow. No longer was the ship
cutting the river; the river was now in control, and not for the
first time in a life on water, he prayed for wind. But the hair at
the back of his neck remained unparted, and the sail rapped
impotently below his toes.

When it suddenly gusted, he felt brief hope that was dashed
within that breath; the approaching storm had fluked the air.
The wind would be undependable from now on. A pale gust
burst against his ears as though to prove his assumption, and
the oarsmen pulled on below. Even from his height he could
hear them beginning to huff with expelled chant. Someone
called to those passengers below who were strong enough to
come out and help manipulate the oars.

Madoc's gut clutched when he shifted his attention to the
river; thicker it seemed and darker with floating objects, tree
boughs, tangles of roots and river-grass, a small dead animal.
He glanced toward the rudder, where Fair Beard now had
help from Huw. Together the two big men shared the labor of
keeping it steady so that the *Horn* aimed toward the Shawnee.
But without wind the current was quickly gaining against them
despite heroic effort.

Among the oarsmen Madoc saw one of the men—it was
Wil—drop away from the task, his place taken by a cassocked
monk while he gasped for breath and took a drink of water
offered by the cabin boy, who either had been told by one of
the sailors or had decided for himself that these sweating,
groaning men needed water to keep going.

Madoc blessed the child and the hauling hands, but despaired to see the ship's head leaning farther to port. Fair
Beard and Huw strained to keep the rudder straight—he
heard the Norseman swear an oath against the stream.

Still the wind stalled; the sheet flapped, sagging under its
own weight in the renewed gusty puffs.

He heard someone yell forward. The current had snatched an oar. It angled parallel for a moment, then was caught in its socket by the stream and snapped like a twig and whirled away. The two men it had thrown struggled to get to their feet amid the legs of the others at the paddles and of the line crew working on the rigging.

Madoc thought he saw a flash of blood there, but was too far away to be sure.

"There is a bay back there," he called.

Fair Beard was standing with straining arms braced against the tiller while Huw pulled against it from the opposite side. It was vibrating up into both men's bones, rattling the Norseman's teeth as he strained to hold it in a position that gave some resistance to the current and kept the stern in line with the prow. But it was finally too much for the two men on the rudder, who were nearly thrown overboard when the thing surrendered to the press of the river and slammed in a half turn in its pintle against the ship's waterline, flapping like a leaf and completely useless.

Dreamlike, Madoc felt them haul around so that for a sickening moment they seemed about to go broadside downstream, with the odd vision of the muddy Ohio to port and the clearer Shawnee to starboard, the oars tangled, the rigging loose, and the sail tilted with linemen and passengers thrown into confusion and slipping on the washed deck.

The ship's sleek, unresisting shape prevented them from broadsiding; but they were careening fully out of control downstream and backwards, any chance of making the mouth of the Shawnee lost, the sail hanging without wind askew like a broken wing, the rigging slipped under the hands of the linemen, while the beam crew had miraculously managed to stack the yard in its forward cradle. At least a gust would not sweep it around to do horrible mischief.

Helpless to do anything except witness, Madoc was sickened to see someone thrown overboard, close to the ship but moving swiftly away as the stream toyed indifferently with different pieces of flotsam.

The various coils of flow collided midstream to yield a frothing brew that sucked at the ship fore and aft and side to side so that she jerked along, a heavily laden cork in the unremitting grip of the stream.

The man in the brink waved a long pink arm and shouted

something the moving water drowned out while Wyn and a sailor at the closest rail tried to send him a line, too late. Madoc saw that it was young Brother Andrew, and in the fraction of a second before the undertow took him down and out of sight, his buffalo-brown cassock flashed by and was gone.

The sky perceptibly darkened as clouds squeezed off the ball of orange sun just touching the western horizon, forging narrow rays and beams to lance the purple thunderheads.

They must have hit a deeper channel that their passage upstream had avoided, because the river flattened out, her current no less but her surface more glassy; this had the effect of spinning the ship in a long, almost lazy, circle. On deck something had happened between the oarsmen. He could not see from this angle, but it looked as though another monk were facedown with Mary bending over him, looking back and calling for help.

Caradoc, who had been pulling in another oar with one of the seamen, held on to tangled line and other people as he made his way to the woman to help her turn the fallen monk over.

It was Father John.

The useless tiller abandoned, Fair Beard was making his way forward to help get the sail righted because now the wind had sprung suddenly alive again from the southwest. If they could just catch it, they could at least get to the nearest shore, the gravel beach down at the bend, for that was what appeared to be their best chance coming up very fast behind them.

But they must escape being thrown onto one of the long sandy islands, so the only hope was to use the sail to guide them, a tricky task under any circumstances and too close for a captain's comfort under those prevailing: oarless, rudderless, and approaching darkness.

Through cupped hands Madoc called to the pilot their distance to the first low island, which he could now see by twisting around to peer over his shoulder. Fair Beard called back an affirmative without looking upward as he grabbed a halyard to help the men get the sail up from the canted position into which it had slipped. Growing fat under the wind, the heavy patchwork leather sail groaned up below Madoc's position, cutting off his view of the deck, where Wyn left the rail and hurried across the deck to drop to his knees beside John.

The wind in the sail slowed their breakneck run sideways and backwards, and as the crew hauled on the sheet and the oars, the ship came around to point toward the beach ahead, well away from the pull of the first island. But here they must do a delicate thing. They must come not so close to the second, yet be ready to make for the harbor, praying for a channel between the tail of the second island and the cup of land below it.

There was still a strong current close to shore, a current that would be against them, suddenly pouring as it did from around the island and scooting with cutting speed as the worn bank testified.

Thirty feet up, Madoc swayed with one hand on the king knot in his harness as the wind action brought them briefly but directly across the current, Fair Beard hanging onto the sheet now to keep them in line with the landing, controlling her totally with the sail.

They would be positioned to make the turn with the island still a good three ship lengths to port; very shortly they would be in the calmer bay that fronted the beach, stretching for several furlongs along a headland where a wide, brisk stream poured itself into the greater Ohio water.

It looked like the ship could overcome all obstacles under the effort of her crew and passengers with the help of the wind, despite the current that pressed them landward.

The water was stirred, and the light was not good, but it seemed that they were not in shallows—no indication that the island had laid a treacherous sand trap for them.

At that moment they felt and heard a terrible low crunching sound belowdeck.

Madoc felt the jolt vibrate up through the mast. This could not be sand, he was thinking.

Someone screamed, and moments later people poured up out of the hold and onto the already crowded deck, where the crew was slipping around trying to let out the lines against the billowing sheet amid the rhythmic movements of the straining oarsmen.

There was not enough light for Madoc to see into the hold to make out what the damage might be. But he recognized that awful sound of wood violently split, surely an oak strake or two impaled on the roots of a submerged snag or an underwater protrusion of shore drawing nearer and nearer on that side of the ship.

Below him there were crew and passenger collisions and more splashes, as a few jumped purposefully, screaming that the ship was taking on water.

The wind sagged once more, but the pilot grappled with the suddenly slack line, sure that it would gust again.

Madoc watched as Fair Beard handed the halyard over to the man behind him, Dag it was, and stumbled on a sloping deck back to the hold just as Einion slipped on the wet deck and nearly tumbled him. The Norseman caught the boy, who was trying to grab hold of the decking, and pressed him close to an empty oar cradle. He whipped a coil of line off a peg around the cradle and knotted it quickly, bringing it under the child's arms, then handed him the knotted end hoping Einion would know to hold on for dear life. Snorrison then proceeded on down the peg stair to see what damage had been done below.

In the gloom Fair Beard could hear water trickling in, louder and louder as he moved aft behind cane crates and laden baskets. He had the impression of several people cringing in the shadows, staring in frozen panic in the direction of the water trickling in loudly between the strakes to starboard.

Around him the ship groaned as the current tossed it back and forth.

By feel as much as by sight he staggered through the tilted cargo, expecting to see a tree branch sticking through the ship's starboard skin, which would give them only moments before she went down. But when he saw the flow squirting between two strakes, he realized that miraculously they were not breached. They must have hit a snag, but it had only jarred loose the caulking; the clinker-built straking held.

The sickening sound of bursting wood must have been the tree trunk that rammed them.

With great affection he slapped the bulkhead above the leak and mumbled something as he calculated out loud how much time they might have until the ship began to sink. Just then, as more caulking curled in a long, soggy roll from between the boards, the water flared out in a plume that shot halfway across the hold, drenching him and everything in its path.

He could tell by the feel of the ship around him that they continued making for the shore as fast as his beleaguered crew could haul despite the bobbing swell. When he returned dripping to the deck, the fluky wind was hissing at them again; then it picked up directly from the west, filling the sail the riggers had managed to hold onto, sending them running before the wind in a staggered, current-tossed tilt.

But even Madoc up on the pinnacle could feel the drag at starboard where the leak was admitting the river into the ship's bowels, and this knowledge moved eveyone capable of it to lean harder on the oars.

High on his perch, Madoc's abdominal muscles involuntarily tensed in anticipation of impact with the rapidly advancing shore, the ship's salvation and her peril. Over his years of sailing, he had developed the sailor's gut; the ship's keel was his breastbone, and her lower oak straking his own skin. What happened to this ship happened to his flesh and bones as though the vessel were an extension of the man's physical body.

Fair Beard frozen at the rail, watching the land approaching like a living thing swimming in the water directly in their path, was feeling it, too; likewise Huw and Dag and all the sailors in varying degrees that depended generally on how long each had been at sea.

This time there was no amazed red contingent gathered on the shore to view the great ship as it glided as gracefully as a princess kneeling for her marriage vows, scooting in upon the long altar of the shallows, running aground on the bottom he could not see just below the water's opalescent surface. He felt his own innards impaled by the grinding impact, but no rocks, thank God, only the slow crying friction of wood against implacable gravel, muffled down to the thick choking gag of mud.

Madoc was in front of the mast, tied to it by knots he quickly tested, then flung his hand up and back to grab the knap of the mast behind his head. The knots would either hold or they would not, and his holding on would do nothing against the inevitable force; but he instinctively sought to brace his head and neck against the upcoming impact.

The vessel lurched into the thick grip of land.

Madoc's breath was slapped from his lungs, first in one direction as his spine slammed against the mast, and then in the other by the pressure of the ropes that held him fast to the stick, which leaned backward, then suddenly forward. It would have flung the insignificant human off its tip if he had not been securely lashed there.

His eyesight reddened out; he hung suspended, weighing in that moment, it seemed, as much as the ship herself. The long pine mast curtsied toward the beach then, as the ship righted herself like a cork in a tub, but at an angle that favored their starboard toward shore. White spots whipped across Madoc's vision as the momentum of the mast seeking equilibrium whiplashed his head.

He felt the bite of the ropes crisscrossed on his chest like a brand. That would leave a bruise, he thought in an attempt to stay conscious, swimming up from the red depths.

Vision returned in a dizzying set of circles. He closed his eyes to keep the spin from the inside of his head and hung onto the pinnacle, praying for all he was worth.

The circles described by the masthead spiraled in upon themselves, getting faster and smaller until some kind of center was found by the stripped pine trunk; Fair Beard's craftmanship prevailed, and the green wood outfitted only days ago proved worthy in this calamity that could have split the mast.

Clarity came quickly back to Madoc's vision as he saw others rushing about below, many thrown down, a couple overboard, while on deck others leapt as a matter of choice.

Lightning crackled off to the south ahead, coming in this direction and darkening the sky, maybe an hour away.

The men were tossing out the anchors fore and aft, but there seemed little need; they were so far aground that the prow had plowed up a bank of mud where small fish and frogs still wiggled.

Gasping for breath, his chest on fire inside and out from rope burns that had torn his clothing, and with what he suspected was a couple of broken ribs, Madoc could not help but look down, laboring to believe they had actually made safe harbor with the ship intact.

The passengers and crew were jumping into the water from the tilting ship, dragging ashore up onto the gravelly beach, falling into shadow as the last shoulder of the sun flared and was snuffed out behind the western clouds.

Fair Beard and the crew were working with lines, anchoring

the tilting ship to big trees near the water with wet debris in their crowns that marked a much higher flood line.

It seemed in a very short time that Madoc was the only person still on board as he gingerly loosened his saving knots and crawled clinging down the mast, pain searing his chest every time he moved his arms.

The mast of the Norse-style knaar—a sailing ship built for cargo hauling in deep water—pierced the center of the square that opened to the hold, braced as it was in a thick whole oak trunk that made up part of the skeleton of the ship. Called a mast-fish because of this shape, the trunk had been adzed to a rounded slope of polished wood, which Madoc now slid down without control to the slatted bilge deck aslosh with oily water littered with bits of oakum and other debris. Small loose items bobbed with the movement of the ship in the softened current.

Aft it was already up to his ankles while the forward part of the ship, where he saw shadows of human figures, was a more shallow zone.

"Who goes there?" he asked, each word a knife of fire behind his ribs as he clung to various appurtenances of the ship's internal structure and got unsteadily to his feet in the cold dark water.

At least two broken ribs, he thought, unable to stand fully upright.

Outside and above he heard the rumble of near thunder and the faint voices of the crew as they secured another line. Madoc knew that Fair Beard was using the ship's several anchors, bracing her where she stood; line whined and the ship righted a little as they heaved against her, no doubt while the Norseman himself lashed the big iron anchor, Odin's Nosehair it was called, in a grapple around a stout tree.

Madoc's attention was drawn below. He stepped over a dovecote—the pigeons inside were drowned, and another broken open, the birds gone.

"Over here," Rhys said, the baby in her sling on his chest. "Help me—she is down in the water."

He was pulling at someone slumped in the swell—Winnowed Rice, Madoc could see as he edged closer through the tumbled cargo and personal items, bedrolls, sodden pillows, clothing, baskets floating by, a child's sandal that made him wonder about Einion's fate, a wooden cup, a small chest he recognized as his own tightly sealed and bobbing like a toy ship on the little seepage sea.

He made some comforting noises for Rhys's benefit as he slogged on through the water to the poet, who was standing braced against the port bulkhead amidships holding the face of the unconscious red woman above the waterline.

She was slumped between his legs; all that kept her from slipping under was his hands under her arms while her yellow dog licked at the wound in her hair.

Madoc took the deepest breath he could and bent over into the fire of his pain to relieve the blind man of the woman's weight. A trickle of blood oozed from her scalp and across her face—it looked as though she had taken a bashing on the right temple.

Rhys eased back against the bulkhead. "Thank you, thank you," he said softly. "For coming down."

Madoc's hand on his arm brought him aright.

"Help me get her on my shoulder," Madoc whispered, unable to do more against the pain.

"You are hurt?"

"Just shaken up—I was on the mast." He gasped as Winnowed Rice's full weight was hefted up onto his left shoulder, and he sagged, momentarily unsure he could make it, but renewed after a pause.

He felt Rhys's firm hand on his shoulder.

"Are you ready?" he asked, and Rhys grunted affirmatively.

Together they set out over the slope of flooded bilge deck to the ladder, where at the first peg Madoc looked up in gratitude that almost brought him to his knees to see Brother Wyn's red face peering down like a benevolent moon above him.

He could hear Winnowed Rice moaning near his left ear, calling for Rhys, who comforted her in Shawnee words that Madoc did not understand, a complicated-sounding sentence or two, repeated.

"Let us have her," said Wyn, dear Wyn, dear Brother Wyn, as he reached a strongly muscled arm down toward Madoc.

The peg stair was in the forward port corner of the open square hatchway; another pair of strong arms reached from the other angle of the corner to lift Winnowed Rice by her leather clothing expeditiously off him, relieving him of what seemed a hundred needle points under his ribs.

He swung down into the water again and guided Rhys's

hands to find the peg and climb up, glad for a moment to rest, but it was short-lived, because he felt raindrops on his face.

He dragged himself up after the poet.

"We must get the hold covered," Madoc panted, forcing himself up from the wet deck, where he dropped in exhaustion and pain.

The other pair of helping hands belonged to Huw, who was already swinging down into the hold to retrieve the extra sail patch they used to catch drinking water and keep the hold from taking in rainwater.

Awaiting his return, Madoc sat there on the sloping deck catching his breath, watching Rhys cradling Winnowed Rice's head in his lap, holding her and crooning to her as she blinked awake. She was frightened at first and confused, holding onto his arm as fat raindrops smeared the blood on her cheek.

Huffing and panting, Huw brought up the sail remnant as though it were another unconscious body thrown across his shoulder. One corner of it was wet and heavy, but they managed to get it spread out and lashed down before the main deluge opened up the sky and dumped everything wet upon them.

The heaviest barrage lasted only a few minutes, with double-bladed lightning knives and thunder that kept the teeth on edge. The river swelled a little, and the ship settled in her muddy groove so that the deck was not as slanted.

Debris clattered and scraped against her stout straking, and the current rocked her through the night.

The wettest and most miserable of refugees, unable to light any fires for the minimum of comfort, each few found what shelter they might, huddled together on land or on board. Madoc would not leave the ship but dragged out the watch tents stored and miraculously dry up in the belowdeck rafters. He found his spot at the stern, where he could keep an eye on the river beyond the rail and be close to the anchor lines.

Fair Beard set his tent up at the tiller and went to sleep, sitting in the folding bench built into the top strake.

Yngvild slept with others who would have nothing to do with the rattling ship, including Mary and the red women who had been aboard the *Horn* instead of in the coracles. Brian's and Ari's families occupied the cut of dripping clay, carved by the curling action of the water over many seasons, to get in out of the downpour. Others—crew and passengers, found whatever shelter they might while Brother Wyn would not stop praying beside the stiffening body of old John, who had surely had a heart attack back there pulling on the oars at a younger man's labor. Wyn in his mourning was alone in the rain beside the dead man.

And he mourned for more than the old friend the river had taken from him. It seemed that all their failure was on his shoulders, perhaps because he had let himself be distracted by Madoc's bright plans instead of fulfilling his own spiritual vow to go on crusade and help win the Holy Land from the infidel.

"Just tell me what I must do," he whispered to God, ready to take any command. "Just give me a sign, give me a sign."

Ari's plump mother-in-law, who always smiled no matter what was happening, ventured out after him into the deluge. "Come, come," she urged softly as if to a puppy or a child, "come in out of the rain," and pulled the rattling priest into the relative shelter of the underridge. He went to sleep missing one sandal, still mumbling his prayers in dreams, "Just give me a sign," without realizing he had put his head down into the comfort of a woman's lap.

By then Winnowed Rice's dogs had come slinking onto the beach closest to the ship, where they stood still and dripping for a while, then set up a low, mournful howl quickly answered by their dam, who as nurse to Cari had stayed on board.

Through some kind of canine wisdom, the dogs, all exact copies of the buckskin bitch, turned from the water and crowded in with the people pressing themselves close to the undercut, trying to keep warm.

The rain slacked off to a drizzle and was slowly replaced over the long cold night by a clinging fog that stole up the long river before sunrise and gave everything a strange light with a moon degrading to quarter somewhere behind the haze.

Spent rain dripped everywhere; the river had a sparkling sound as the flow peaked and leveled off, lapping at the sides of the ship and ringing hollowly up through the capped hold.

Madoc took that watch because he was unable to sleep. He went over the day's events one by one, judging his actions and seeing his mistakes, weighing the choices he had made and wondering at alternatives. Despair was not one of these, but he was brought low by their situation.

Rhys leaned against the soggy bales, Winnowed Rice sleeping peacefully with her head in his lap, the dog with her head on his knees, and the baby asleep on her own and the dog's stomach in a nest made by the warm bodies. They had not been able to find the harp in its case, but Rhys sang anyway, some fair old airs and stately songs about the sea.

Now he was fully awake as he stirred and stretched.

Madoc, crouching at the tent opening, watched the fog thicken above the effervescent river.

Rhys was also reading the river, listening to its music against the ship.

From somewhere landward, a low croaking sound had him puzzled. It sounded like some kind of animal, not crickets, perhaps tree frogs, though it was late for such, this early November. It almost sounded as though it were coming directly from the water. He remarked the vast low humming to Madoc, who had been focused on the wider expanse of the river.

"Maybe the water is tumbling over underground caverns," Madoc said after listening for a while, though that suggestion sounded lame.

"I think it is alive," Rhys replied, realizing that to Madoc it would seem he was admitting red superstitions, that the river was a living being. "I mean," he amended, "that the sound is something alive we cannot see, perhaps a species of frog or such."

It was a puzzle about which there was little else to say, so they talked about other things, the likelihood of some of their people showing up in the morning, perhaps with Shawnee allies. Then their conversation wandered to the damage done the ship, how it would be necessary to bring her up into dry dock, perhaps dismantle her as Fair Beard had done before.

Fair Beard, sleeping lightly at his post, awoke and strolled over to join their quiet conversation. "I will say this, that when we dry-dock, I wish to put the dragon head on her prow."

"And become a viking ship?" Madoc asked as Fair Beard hunkered down beside him.

"These people are all scared of the kraken," the Norseman replied, referring to the man-eating sea monster of Scandinavian mythology. "Why not use their fear—it has saved us more than once on this trip so far." He punched Madoc's sword arm.

"It certainly saved all our hides at Muscle Shoals," Madoc agreed, adding what he could not say often enough, "and I thank you for salvaging the *Horn*." But he shook his head slowly, "I still cannot fathom why Fox let us go—he had us." He made a fist. "But he let us go."

It was something Rhys had wondered at more than once, and now he was certain that there was more to the story. But he agreed with Brother Wyn and did not want to trouble Madoc with those implications, so he said, "Quite a coincidence that these people have a mythological beast almost identical to the ones in our own old stories."

"Perhaps our only luck is this ship," Madoc said, taking Fair Beard's side.

"And what if we run into the Celts of Vitromannaland?" Rhys asked. "They are reputed to first hang anyone landing from a dragon ship and then hold the trial."

"We are far west of their territory, which is just south of Vinland," the Norseman said, gesturing toward the northeast sector of night. "Besides, that country has long been overrun by Dublin Norse fleeing the blessings of Christianity—last I heard of that place, they changed its name to Greater Ireland, so many Norsemen emigrated there rather than take up the cross on King Olaf's invitation." He uttered a low, dry, humorless laugh. In his own Icelandic family were stories of baptisms in boiling oil for those reluctant to accept the Christ.

He and Madoc discussed the ship's condition, scaffolding and log rollers to bring her up out of the water before inevitably seasonable weather set in, and how to appoint the men to get her repaired.

This looked like a good camp, and since it was where they found themselves, they agreed that fate had assigned them winter quarters. They would stay here at least through the season—it was near enough to their allies that they felt confident of a neighborly reception. Winnowed Rice had told them of much game in the surrounding forest, wide-open meadows that would do for planting, and metal in upriver creeks, at least copper and gold.

Having bolstered their sagging confidence with colloquy, Snorrison finally stood just outside the tent and stretched mightily, tendons popping in his arms and back. He returned to starboard, where presently they heard him snoring, sitting at the tiller, his favorite pillow.

But not an hour into the watch, a voice of alarm awakened everybody.

From the murky darkness downriver Brother Andrew came

calling in his piping Saxon accent, "Hallo the ship," stumbling in like a drowned rat, Wyn could not stop repeating in delirious joy. He accepted this as the answer to his prayer, a sign from God, the young monk coming suddenly upon the company from the damp, foggy west, wet but otherwise unharmed, no bones broken and burdened with something wonderful.

"Look, Domme," Andrew exclaimed, turning out his pockets full of what felt like mere slime. For a fleeting moment Wyn thought that his good brother, like the Norseman's wife, had gone mad from his ordeal; then he leaned closer in the darkness, unable to see clearly but quite able to smell.

"My God," Wyn whispered.

"Praise to God!" Andrew cried, his teeth chattering.

"What?" Madoc demanded, stumbling in the dripping darkness from the coracle he had taken to shore when he heard the commotion.

"Iron hat!" Wyn told him, holding some of the muck out for him to smell and smearing his mustaches with it.

Madoc gave an involuntary little shout of triumph that brought the dogs out, sniffing with curious growls.

The crumbling limonite was pungent with the smell of sulfur and the metallic perfume of rich rust, a sure sign that the right minerals were precipitating from streams feeding the swamp, where bog iron formed in peaty, rotting vegetation. With it a soft metal could be smelted, and with Wyn's smithy skills and charcoal, a fine enduring sword steel could be manufactured.

"Not a half a league downriver, Captain," Andrew said, shivering as Wyn bear-hugged him and laid a blessing upon his forehead. "A huge swamp—I do not know how far inland it goes, for darkness fell, but you could smell it easily enough now if the wind was right."

"You bring a wonderful gift, good brother," Madoc said with a rough embrace to Andrew, who was suddenly shy under the attention.

"You shall have your bloomery after all," Madoc shouted, slapping Wyn's stout shoulder.

"And I will forge you a new Durendal," Wyn pledged, knowing how Madoc mourned the loss of the great French sword; but to himself, the abbot silently renewed his promise to God that he would take the cross of crusade against the Turks to save the Holy Land, which surely must lie only a little way west of this place—now that he had his sign from the west, he was sure a few days travel in that direction would bring him to the desert and the spice lanes of the Orient, which would lead right up to the eastern gate of Jerusalem.

After soggy embraces all around, and Wyn's public blessing, everyone stumbled off to various makeshift shelters, the clergy muttering prayers to the clay bank behind the ship's few tilted coracles, with the others, sailors and red women, remarking the significance of it all.

Madoc made his way back to the ship, where Fair Beard and Rhys agreed with heady excitement that the clay had the right smell. Revolting as it might be to the nose, to a man who knew what to do with it, the muck was rich ambrosia.

They talked awhile about what they would forge first— replacement swords, axes, saws, hoes, plowshares, and skillets; what would do for their own use and what they would need for trade. From what he had seen of the upland before sunset, Madoc liked the look of the oak forest turning yellow mixed with evergreens. He hoped for a species of hardwood that would cook into a charcoal suitable for maturing iron.

For a second time Snorrison bade them good night.

Frogs, or whatever was making that humming sound, started up a drone in the slackening rain, and the long night took on a chill glow as Madoc and Rhys veered their conversation into reminiscence of their good old days as young soldiers in Owen's military; these two shared good times and bad long before their present circumstance, and had talked through many a downpour while others slept around them.

As it often does, their dialogue grew philosophical after midnight, when in a low, private voice, though they were the only two awake, Madoc confessed how strongly he felt compelled to head as soon as possible down the Great River Road to the saltwater and a return trip to Britain.

Not at all surprised, Rhys replied, "And I shall stay."

Madoc regarded the poet with his family asleep around him. In the spill he had lost the scarf. Madoc discerned the face paint through the fuzzy darkness and asked him, "You are not homesick?"

"I shall never return, my friend. But you will."

"You are a shaman now, I suppose, who can read futurity with magic." This was as close as he had come to commenting on Rhys's painted face.

The poet knew the red women considered him a powerful shaman because of his face as much as his music. It seemed to give them comfort and insured their cooperation in difficult endeavors.

"They have a tradition about the broken, bent, blind, and brainless," Rhys said in a tone of light self-deprecation that was almost made into song by the alliteration he knew would provoke Madoc to grin. "The idea being that we best know how to deal with all manner of trouble, including the hereafter. It puts us to almost as useful work as hunting or hoeing."

Madoc was intrigued. "What do they expect, then, that you heal them by the laying on of hands?" he asked with a suggestive little laugh. In the back of his mind was the question of exactly how Rhys went about satisfying the red women's spiritual needs.

Rhys uttered a grunt of denial and shook his head. Some of the red women who came to him for counsel asked for dream interpretation or advice with troubling personal problems such as rancor between friends. Some asked to buy sexual secrets. "Lily made new moccasins for me in exchange for a love-poem to ensnare the soul of a certain man."

"Poor Evan."

"She did not say whom. Very discreet." He cleared his throat—he had been singing all evening. "It was apparently a very good poem," he said around a yawn. "They might ask such a favor involving another, but to them I am much like a priest back home."

"Some shamans tell the future with magic, I hear," Madoc said with playful sarcasm.

Rhys leaned closer. "I do not need magic to know you will go back. You will settle the score with your brother. You will settle more than one score—you will accomplish whatever you wish."

Madoc expressed a cynical but pleased growl to have such a sanguine confirmation of his own expectations. He settled back to await firstlight, his mood only somewhat lightened, his mind still laboring with schemes and worries.

As Rhys drifted toward sleep, he thought about what Madoc said regarding magic. Poets in his native land were the only survivors of the Druids, who once in pagan times took the public roles of lawyer, judge, musician, and priest, as well as magician, in an elaboration of the old Greek nature religion that was also the loose structure of Celtic tribal government based on tribute to a chieftanship.

The red people seemed closer to that style than any other, and it gave Rhys comfort to find it so because of echoes in his own tradition. Back home he had been secretary to Madoc's father, who administered a third of what would become known as Wales, about the size of a county, each region with its princely head descended from a human stew of Roman military, Norse freebooters, and Celtic warlords who bodaciously claimed descent from the losers of the Battle of Troy.

Rhys ab Meredydd had sung court poetry celebrating that ancestry and praising the princely deeds of the local chief. He composed letters to foreign kings and neighboring princes variously allied with Gwynedd in opposition to the Saxon English, who were bent on making their king Prince of Wales and unifying all of the British Isles under one monarch. It was an old dream of Arthur's, another Welsh prince who used the services of a Druidic bard and magician named Merlin.

While Rhys contemplated these things in keeping with his profession, Madoc in keeping with his own gazed off into nothing, thinking already of an expedition as soon as they repaired the *Horn* to go search for those iron deposits.

And sitting there feeling the heaviness surrounding his master moodily perusing this foreign river in the midst of their dire circumstances, Rhys wanted to make the man smile, to lighten his load if he could even a little and, helping their chief, thereby help them all. So he began humming a song he had been working on about Madoc's youthful exploits with a certain Icelander pirate, then started singing the lyric, which Madoc had not heard before.

It was about a journey marked not on any chart but in the songs of men's voices, oral maps and oral stories sung about the numbers of days from place to place, bounding over the Western Ocean, following the time-honored Norse island-hopping path from the Faroes to Iceland and thence to Gunnibiorn's Skerries—vanished now under ice—to Greenland south of the icebergs past the great fog bank and round to the warm southern current that would take a ship to Vinland the Good, an island of unknown immensity with abundant cranberries that made good wine. There they took timber, vast rolling forests the Norse were eager to jack having lumbered out their own western islands long ago and needing spruce to

strake their knaar. They cut pine for masts, and so-called oak
moors naturally bent at root and branch for critical keel and
ribs. From boglands stretching to three upland horizons, the
clever Norse smiths found enough irony clay and firewood to
forge swords they baked and hammered over charcoal. Of such
things and places, as well as the journey back northward and
eastward through storm, erupting volcanic islands, pearly
icebergs, and a place where a single day lasted more than
twenty hours—of all things and more, Rhys sang in a pleasing
old melody devised for just such storytelling.

As though they had rehearsed it, but quite spontaneously, a
sailor taking the early watch put a hornpipe to it. The music
was soft and mournful in the humid night of sloshing, watery
sounds pierced now and then by the calls of shorebirds.

Rhys, who mourned the harp's misplacement, was glad to be
accompanied. He felt Madoc listening intently—*he likes it, I
can tell he likes it*—and with any poet's great relief and
satisfaction at a good response to his poetry, thought, *Where
we once had magic, we now make do with song.*

PART TWO

Teach us to number our days
that we may get us a heart of wisdom.

—Psalms 90:12

Chapter 9

The drumfish always sang after a rain.

Their low musical thrumming vibrated the still air of predawn, where light expanded like a fragrant pink sigh, where there were as yet no shadows, an indistinct region of possibilities where anything might happen.

Into this pale zone spilled the sound of the deep-noted drumfish singing each individual fish-note but blending into a single great music. It came from the direction of a low artificial lake where ragged cattails harbored tame mergansers, glittering carp, and the duller drumfish with insistent song fracturing the water's surface into a visible pattern like hammered silver.

High up on the pyramid called God's Hill, Chief Speaker Mickanac M'kin Mah'kina, Turtle-in-the-Sun, cast his keen glance in that direction. The gardeners were shoveling insects picked off the crops by the hands of little boys, tossing them by the basketful into the still water. The royal fish sang most wet mornings as would the speaker, soon, to bring up the sun, but generous feeding increased the drone.

Around this big pyramid ranged more than a hundred others, arrayed like triangular game pieces on the checkered board of the flat floodplain of the Great River Road, the Mech-a-sip-i.

Just below his eastern perspective from the top, the steeply sloped, baked clay sides of God's Hill dropped off to the near bank of Sky Blood Creek, which ran nearly north-south parallel to that face of the pyramid, but snaked off chaotically so that it eventually wound around in both directions toward the river to the west. The creek was in fact a fluid arm of the Great River Road, making of the city and its nether western villages a big island between the two separate streams of identical water.

135

The jetties down there were silent now, and empty. The
slow current was not visible from here. Several long canoes—
hollowed logs, skin-and-bark varieties—sat the water like slim
ducks. Dozens of others nested upended in neat rows against
the bank behind the staging area.

A new orchard lay slightly south of the wharf, just this side
of a wet line of cattails and willows hugging the bank farther
on.

Immediately below, the breakfast fires of Oldtown already
stained a layer of air above two lower grassy pyramids, both of
which were crowned with thatch buildings much like the one
behind the miko on top of the highest pyramid. Smaller
crowded high-pointed thatch houses clustered around the
fire-blackened, red-clay skirt of God's Hill's southeastern face,
goslings around a goose.

Somewhere off in that direction, more than a hundred feet
below, a dog barked faintly in the crystalline air.

A kingfisher angled out over the southwestern array of low
truncated mounds, each crowned with its own thatch temple
with fluttering ribbons and narrow columns of smoke flattened
at a certain height above the absolutely flat ground.

To the west a scattering of smaller grass-covered mounds
were interspersed between distinct village precincts where
nothing stirred except smoke. Beyond these, about a quarter
mile away, was set a huge circle of tall shaved posts with a
single taller center pole capped by a small platform.

Turtle knew that the daykeeper crouching there in his high
seat was, like himself, waiting with sacred pegs and a raven-
ous, youthful eye yearning to see the sun. The predictions of
a long line of ancestors hung on this moment every morning;
would the great orb rise at the spot along the horizon predicted
by generations of daykeepers?

Or would the mightiest being in the known world keep
rolling down over the southern edge? It was warmer down
there, of that the miko and his timekeepers were certain. The
ancestors of ten fathers back had come from those benign
climes where, legend had it, the sun shone directly above in
the sky to mark each Day of Equals—the two yearly
equinoxes—casting shadows dead center one's own feet,
downward with no angle and no decline. If the noble ancestors
could wander here from their own country of the sun, thereby
bringing civilization to these barbaric places, then the sun,

too, might wander to other lands unless men kept him reminded of his duty to his devoted children.

These thoughts sobered Turtle as he stared at the circle of poles in the far western plaza.

What if it really happened one day that Lord Sun ignored the pleas of this devout nation?

There would be no more light here, only the twilight of a winter morning, perhaps forever. The eldest stories said this was the age of the fifth sun, that there had been four others before it, each inhabited by a species of men who were deemed by the lords of creation under God to be inadequate. The underworld was where those other earths with other humans had been cast down under the western horizon of this present middleworld.

Might not this earth, too, become a somber badland when a new age began a little farther on in the sun's celestial wanderings?

Sobered down to his bones, Turtle-in-the-Sun shivered in the mild, breezeless moments before dawn and shifted his glance.

Farther toward the western reach, the sky was still densely purple with night slinking toward the underworld like one of those underworld humans who sometimes through magic stole across the borderlands and delved into this world as a thief.

Between west and south, scattered among the only groves of trees left standing in the city's precincts, were a string of shallow lakes where the drumfish sang.

To the south, below a long unseen flight of peeled-log steps, stretched a swept clay plaza that the lower stepped terraces of God's Hill cut off from the miko's immediate view. But beyond the edge of this terrace, he could see the top of a low rectangular mound, the Little Mountain of a Thousand Souls. Turtle did not know how many ancestors were buried there—it was not their number, but the nobility of their significant deaths, that named the little pyramid. The grass was kept clipped there, a token of esteem. Prayer ribbons fluttered on slim sticks.

Beyond that sacred zone of the ancient dead, another dense village of twelve hundred households waited hushed in shadow between its tilled fields that would transform, when the seasons turned, the now-bare soil into kitchen gardens.

In all his expansive view, there was no human activity

except for the curl of his own bare toes, as brown as the earth, as brown as the finest pottery made down on the devotion platforms by the hands of uncounted women.

In each temple and house lingered the people—men, women, and children—who would hunt and build, dig the earth, pick the bugs, grind the corn, pinch the clay, man the docks, knap the flint, haul the bundles, sew and hammer and bead and flake, making the city sing with their labor.

But they all waited for their miko to accomplish his own unique task before time could begin again and daily human life was free from the bonds of the underworld to resume. The city had paused like this each morning for more than 170 years, since the ancient fathers from the Land of the Sun taught the children of Ix to know the true belief.

Ixtulan, the city north of north, abided the moment of the lord.

Turtle-in-the-Sun sighed heavily at the significance of it all. Naked and oiled for the ceremony to come, squinting at the eastern horizon, Turtle made himself more comfortable on the pile of pillows supporting him on the dais.

Before him on the top log of a stair that led up to the dais, another bowed motionlessly, dressed in sooty black leather and crow feathers. This other was so dark that he appeared through the miko's squint to be merely a shadow. Panther, his name was, but none used that name anymore except the speaker.

Panther had been bowing that way for some time, a lean, aging man whose hair was tied off and singed into various significant bundles and knotted hanks. Other than the tonsure and a plain shell plug through his left earlobe, there was no decoration on this one, who now felt the miko's left foot touch his neck. Slowly, like smoke from a new fire, he lifted his forehead from the dust at the miko's feet and leaned back on bare ankles ready to wait all day if necessary for his master's regard.

Presently the miko looked down and acknowledged his high priest, who looked up at him through sooty face paint and said, "The fire be must be fed."

Panther hoarsely whispered the formal ritual phrase as he revealed, under a napkin, a mat-covered tray. On it sat a pile of whitened human knucklebones, among several other items. The high priest took up the knobby bones and rattled them in his palms, then threw them out. He called out several numbers and cast another throw.

He looked around at his master, who spoke a number, the first that came into his mind: "Ten and two."

The high priest cast the bones again, separating them according to an ancient tradition, mumbling a series of multiples until he had arrived at some calculation that required his leaning back on his heels and closing his eyes.

"The number for the day is five tens and two," he pronounced solemnly, and further revealed upon his tray a small bowl adorned with a river-polished white stone weighing down a stack of pale, narrow material—mottled cane-bark paper—and a thin object he reverently unwrapped from a decorated strip of leather.

"Hello, old friend," the miko whispered, not to the high priest, whom he had known most of his life, but to the object, a giant eyeless needle with a narrow groove carved along its length, fully as long as a grown man's finger.

Looking away, Turtle held out the palm of one hand, revealing an intricate small tattoo at the base of his thumb at the point where a blue artery laid throbbing across bone.

Quick as light, the high priest pricked the wrist dead center on the tattooed target. "Blood of the sun, blood of the sun," he murmured as the brilliant crimson drop expanded.

Inured, Turtle did not react in the slightest way to the ritual stab or to further ministrations as the whispering priest drew a narrow line of blood by tapping the sea-urchine spine, catching several drops of the precious stuff on a sheet of the grayish paper. The miko's lidded eyes gazed far into the distance, penetrating the intervening swamp mist clear to the eastern horizon where the expected arrival would soon occur.

The crisp paper sagged, saturated with red.

Chanting the phrase, the robed shadow recovered the tray. He stood and backed off, holding it with both hands as he retreated down the several steps to the top terrace of the pyramid.

Turtle straightened his back and adjusted his cross-legged position on the mat while continuing his perusal of the depthless sky, forcing down the slightly sickened stomach he felt every morning when he fed the sun with his blood.

Overhead the sky hovered behind a veil of purple haze.

Below, the priest laid the saturated paper onto coals crackling in a raised firepit. Flames briefly flared. A puff of black smoke was sucked upward and dispersed on the prevailing westerly. It still smelled this morning like cold rain.

"Blood of the sun," the priest repeated until the soggy paper burned and the smoke thinned out to blue again.

Suddenly a blaze of light seared the far ridge of flat eastern land.

Hand still sticky with its own juice, the miko stood up from the pillows and cane matting on the little rise at the northeast corner of his high domain, and with arms outstretched began a low chant that grew in intensity as the splinter of light revealed itself to be the sun's molten shoulder.

Turtle-in-the-Sun began this slow song:

"Sky Father of all, you know everything and you alone can make everything known in the world of heaven or the middle world or even the underworld, where you must travel each night. You feed us by giving life to all. Everything stands beneath you. Take this food we offer you. Because you see everything, see into our hearts, forgive our failures like any good father. It will be your way and on your day."

Behind him, the priest raised to his lips an incised conch shell from saltwater he knew only as a legend and blew a long, mournful note that echoed over the tops of the lower pyramids and houses.

To peasant farmers in dark hives at the farthest forking paths outlying the city, the bugle note came floating over all on the still, damp air like a smell for the ears. Thousands of lips repeated the phrase of devotion, *blood of the sun*, underscoring like a heartbeat their miko's sacrifice on behalf of them all.

It was the signal for old men to light up the first pipe of the day. Women no longer tried to silence their first rising, fire-stirring motions or the crockery voices of their cooking pots. Men threw back the painted hides from their sturdy little house doorways and stretched their arms, intoning prayers and smelling the air just the way Lord Sun supposedly did to start each of his days.

This morning's work for Turtle-in-the-Sun was done, but he lingered in his devotions, stretching muscles in his arms and back, letting the sunlight permeate his body while he crooned his long, melodious chant, waiting, longing for a visitation.

Some mornings it would happen quite suddenly—he would glimpse the familiar strong-faced warrior standing in the new light, and sometimes, though more rarely, the Lord would speak. A word, a phrase, a chant, an ancient reference to the ancestors who brought enlightenment from southern places where God was more dependable. Sometimes Lord Sun's utterances suggested to Turtle a name for a newly initiated priest or newborn, for naming was his duty as chief speaker, or there might be other technical enlightenments that aided the miko in his never-ending decision-making process. Turtle hesitated, eyes slightly cracked so that the brilliant gash on the horizon blurred into a cross within a circle.

Eyes stinging, he finally blinked. Wetness under his eyelids made prisms, slivers of rainbows under his eyelids. Beyond those he hoped to witness the divine.

Silently, without formal recitation, he thought thoughts at God, things that he would have said if he were standing face-to-face: *Do hear the voice of your son, Father. The land is troubled. The corn is not as plentiful as it once was. The people are whispering. The nobles are angry, and the old women have dark visions. Guide this son of yours as to how he can increase the food to feed all our people.*

The sun guttered like a round flame behind the overcast.

"Say what must be done," he whispered, feeling the rosy glow on his face and outstretched palms. "Tell this man as you told his father and all the fathers and the grandfathers before him who came from your own country."

He leaned into the expanding light, calling in his mind.

But there was no answer.

Turtle sighed and fell into the formulas again, ending the long song, which he muttered low in his throat; none would hear it, not even someone sitting in the audience area, a three-tiered baked clay riser about ten paces behind him. The slightly curved structure set comfortably under a thatch pavilion against any weather, demarcating that end of the terrace.

Beyond it rose the clay-covered upright log walls of the temple with its high crown of pointed thatch, a feather of smoke poking upwards from perpetual fires within.

It appeared that the Lord was not going to manifest in more than his mundane appearance today. Still, it was a magnificent, shimmering, golden-edged circle that profoundly hefted up that part of the sky.

Turtle-in-the-Sun lowered his arms and licked his wrist

where the skin was pitted and hardened from daily surgeries. It was up to him to choose which part of his anatomy would be offered daily. He tried to keep a circle going round his body in the path of the sun, so that no part would be abused. Years ago he had commissioned Butterfly Man to tattoo the seven points that experience had taught him produced the quickest spurt.

The blood was salty. His thirst flared. Just as he turned to step down the stair, he heard a strong male voice say from behind him, "The fire must be fed."

He whirled around, facing the sun again.

What he had just heard was a powerful phrase that always signaled bloodletting. He had never heard it pronounced in any other context. So at first he thought it was his high priest heretically inserting the phrase in a rigid protocol, though for him to do so was unprecedented in the many years the two men had been performing these rites together.

But Panther was several paces away, down on the clay surface of the terrace tending the sacral fire, his back to the dais where the miko stood on the top stair, hesitating.

There was none other nearby who could have spoken.

Turtle regarded the sun, now too bright to look at directly. He squinted and asked, *Is that you, Lord?*

But all he heard was the call of the kingfisher on the other side of the creek, making wing with a full beak.

Turtle continued down the stair, still watching the growing day. When he left the last step, a mumbling acolyte with bowed head was immediately at hand holding a beaker of water, which the miko quaffed in one long swallow.

"Blood of the sun," the acolyte whispered.

Turtle looked down at him. Could it have been this youngster? The student's single quoit hung over his left ear, the singed blunt end tied and glued, the rest of his head hair close-cropped. Panther's favorite novice would not dare commit such an out-of-sequence prayer that only the highest officers—the miko and the priest—ever uttered. Besides, he did not yet have his man's voice.

The novice backed away as self-effacingly as a shadow, having never made eye contact with the miko.

No, thought Turtle, this boy's was not that voice.

He stood there watching the molten orb groan up from the horizon. It seemed to be straining this morning, bloated and held back by the forces of the underworld. He intoned a

. continuation of the prayer for as long as he could watch the shimmering circle. A low cloud layer seemed to seize the crown of the sun and struggle briefly with the underworld for possession of it.

The image of so dire a conflict made Turtle hold his breath. What if it slipped? The lords of the underworld were strong.

There were old stories. . . .

The air trembled as the light passed behind it, darker-stained, then re-emerged above the inversion layer a brighter, stronger copper color as it continued pulling up from darkness.

A new day had begun.

Because of the almost unbroken expanse of cleared fields from here to the flat horizon, streamers of golden light could already be seen stealing through the forest to the east, casting a long line of shadow at the verge of the cleared city precincts and illuminating dusty paths between houses and pyramids that cast their mirror shadows long across the ground.

As though summoned by the light, a sudden breeze came up from the east. It bent the smoke columns down below Turtle's position and rattled the long streamers of feathers and mussel shells hanging on temple poles behind his dais.

He glanced downward to see here and there between the houses and out on the plazas, people already moving about. Potters and flint knappers were strolling to work on the low, wide platform pyramids, where they would put the blessing work on their crafts.

Some had baskets or other burdens on their heads. Very far off, just on the edge of hearing, a baby squalled for a few seconds, them stopped abruptly.

Seeming to emerge from the ground itself, a knot of workers was forming beyond the southwest villages. There, another barrow lake was being scooped out, basketful by basketful.

Soon, from that direction a line of bearers would be trudging this way, their back bent with loads of dirt balanced by trumplines that scored their foreheads. They would climb the long southern flight of stair, which the miko could not see at this moment, and deposit the soil where the engineering priests were completing a small mound on the third terrace of this pyramid.

That conical rise would be finished in a few days. It marked the point where the daykeepers had predicted the sun would rise at his most southern limit at the winter solstice less than two moons from now.

The daykeepers were never wrong.

This morning's observation would verify that Lord Sun was moving in that direction, rising a little more to the south each morning until that day when he would dance on the horizon above the point of that mound, hesitating, perhaps deciding whether or not to abandon this cold winter place or keep moving into warmer regions forever.

Below, to the miko's left as he walked, near the base of that side of God's Hill, a team of workers was already making a fire to repair the pyramid's clay sheathing. Each rain smeared some of the fragile clay skin. It was a never-ending labor that kept four Oldtown teams busy year-round.

A deferential middle-aged woman was beside Turtle without his bidding, holding out a buffalo hide marked with winter-sky star symbols. Rubbing his bruised wrist, the miko let the woman slip the fur side over his bare shoulders—the salutation to Lord Sun was always committed in the nude. It was a strange mild winter with no frost in the air as yet, but he had been sitting out on the dais for some time, and now his skin was chilled. As he hugged the robe around himself, the woman bent to place low moccasins on his feet.

"Blood of the sun," he heard her reverently whisper, his auntie, who was also his body servant. She bowed her head at the sight of a drop of blood drying on the puncture wound at his wrist. He could clearly read the tattoo clan signs that snaked around her neck and down her bare back—her mother was from a proud old family who had ancestors back before the illustrious old ones claimed by the miko. She was one of the children of the old miko just as Turtle was, by a different mother.

Still, she was called Auntie because of her position in the miko's household, one of several senior women who inherited their positions, served until they were married, and often returned later as had this one after she was widowed some years ago. She was older by a generation than Turtle; they never acknowledged their relationship—there were at least thirty-five of the old miko's other children walking around the city, each with his or her own family and duties all connected to the miko's temporal and spiritual households.

Behind her scurried another, aiding the auntie in the

presentation of the water, holding a larger flask with which to refill the cup should the miko need more. He could not see her face because she had cast her eyes downward with the deference expected of all who stood in the miko's presence. But through a long veil of her loose dark hair he caught a flash of a bright glance; she was young. Her cheek was firm and plum-colored, and she was flirting with him, using the strands of hair to peek through and catch his eye with the glistening white of her own.

Turtle-in-the-Sun purposefully looked away from her.

When he licked his blood off, he saw the injured vein swollen under the toughened flesh. He rubbed it tingling and stepped into the slippers beaded with rare blue stones from the far west.

He continued walking toward the tall thatch building already glowing gold in the light of the sun now free of the horizon and climbing.

As the servants hurried to precede him toward his private quarters, Turtle noticed that only a handful of spectators attended today. During high ceremonials as many as five hundred nobles, called suns for their aristocratic lineage, would crowd in their finery onto those three steps to watch the miko shed blood. Those he saw on this ordinary morning were old men, several of them priests themselves, of lower or technical rank. Turtle had never thought of the people watching, but it occurred to him now that fewer and fewer nobles occupied their places for the daily sun calling.

The ones who had witnessed it today were drifting off to duties. A knot of them, mostly older men with clan markings from the various villages clustered around God's Hill, formed up and moved purposefully as a group to the far side of the big temple, where servants would have their mats rolled out and their breakfasts waiting. There, in the grand hall where the ancestor's bones for six generations back rested in respected order, they would expect to meet their miko in council.

Turtle-in-the-Sun, host of that daily meal, watched them with a curl of disdain on his lip as he approached another smaller entrance in this end of the temple. *Let them wait*, he thought.

From behind, the high priest caught up with him and held back an elaborate woven cane screen so the miko could enter.

Turtle knew the council of elders would be waiting for him

inside, expecting to discuss this year's crop now gathered from all the far-flung fields in this domain. He could already smell the pipe they were passing around in a sectioned-off part of the cavernous central chamber of the temple. They knew by now it had been another short fall. They would be demanding satisfaction from the miko and his daykeepers—what was being done to bring back the abundance the miko had promised?

Turtle's long brow furrowed with these thoughts as he threw one last glance over his shoulder. A line of bearers was already snaking this way, each man or woman bent with reverence as they gave their labor to God.

He could hear the first strains of the hymns they sang along the way, songs so sacred they were chanted only once a year, this long moon of ceremony that climaxed with the upcoming winter solstice marking Lord Sun's southernmost point on the horizon. Its turning would be the beginning of another solar cycle. By the solstice the daykeepers could predict when spring would commence and when it was safe to plant Mother Maize back into the ground again.

The laborers' song never failed to please Turtle. The breeze picked it up and broadcast it louder as he stood hesitating at the temple door. The forwardmost of the bearers was coming up the steps now, approaching this precinct of the upper terraces. Turtle-in-the-Sun could tell by the sound of their song how close they were. He wondered if his brother was among them this morning; then he knew that, of course, he was. Afternoon Moon was always at the labor.

Turtle-in-the-Sun glanced down in that direction but could not tell from this distance which of the workers was dumping a basketful onto the growing pile of earth.

The high priest cleared his throat to hurry the miko along in his busy schedule.

Without catching the priest's eye, the miko ducked inside.

Panther followed. A turn to the right would take them into a long room where daykeepers worked at carving or knotting while they memorized ritual and song.

To the left lay the miko's private apartments.

Making for the left, the miko whispered softly so that none of the nearby students or servants scurrying along after them could hear: "Your single claw grows dull, Panther."

He uncurled his hand from behind the robe to reveal the blue swelling on his wrist.

Panther, with his head down, did not speak until they were inside an alcove behind woven mats hung to permit privacy. Beyond this cell and communicating with it by way of a long dark hallway was the room of the big mat. The grand chamber was so called because it was where the chief speaker conducted the few indoor rituals of the faith, met foreign guests of sufficient rank to merit it, passed judgments, and convened his councils.

Once they were alone, Panther fell on his knees before the miko, who found his most comfortable position against a buffalo-hide draped backrest and sat down with his legs crossed. While Turtle adjusted his robe, the priest produced a small flint knife and without ceremony of any sort sliced his own palm from little finger to thumb, while whispering, "I beg my miko's forgiveness for causing him pain."

Turtle nodded, watching Panther as he bound the wound with a dark sash from around his waist and said in a more normal voice, "Perforator will be sharpened immediately."

The truth was, the priest revered this sacred object imported long ago from the southern saltwater that the ancestors were supposed to have crossed. It had been handled over the past six generations of high priests so that it was black with finger oil. Honing had whittled it down noticeably just in Panther's tenure, and he hated to further whet away its sacred substance.

Noiseless servants—all women—scurried about laying before the miko and the high priest a ritual breakfast of blue-corn cakes and late plums, which the two men proceeded to nibble as they talked.

". . . and the father of the young priest we caught selling seedcorn is among them," Panther was saying, reeling off the topics that the council expected to discuss at the miko's pleasure.

Turtle snorted a chortle as he munched a fritter.

"And his maternal uncle, Buffalo Eagle . . ."

No response from the chief was forthcoming.

". . . ready to pay tribute for clemency."

Turtle shrugged and wiped his hands on a steaming rag of mulberry-bark cloth.

"Then there is the matter of the crops."

"This is not the day of reckoning," Turtle snapped. Not all the tallies were in; Panther's accountants were still measuring and itemizing with their knots and notches the miko's vast treasury. This was done once each year just before the solstice, which marked the time for disbursements.

Now it was the priest's turn to shrug, but he did not speak.

The miko was silently staring into nothing as the high priest consumed the last morsel of a plum. He sucked the pit and placed it delicately on the tray before them—it would be a tree again someday, since it was traditional to plant all seeds and throw none away that might feed the future.

The room was still as Panther wiped his fingers and waited for his master to speak.

Through various cane draperies they could hear the staccato chant of the women grinding corn in the big plaza on the other side of the council chamber.

A fly buzzed between the miko and the high priest and presently settled upon the plum pit.

Still the miko did not speak.

Panther watched him watching the fly feast on the wet, pink seed pulp.

The miko muttered something.

Panther wondered if the sacrifice this morning had affected the miko's mind. Most mornings Turtle endured the rite without a flicker of response. He had given blood so many times that it was the body's habit to shed its juice without any emotion. Panther himself had trained Turtle to be a warrior against the pain at a very young age.

His own palm throbbing, Panther doubted that Turtle even felt Perforator, so usually quick and efficient was he at the high priest's office.

But sometimes, after the rite, Turtle would be tranced all day. The high priest was unnerved by those times when the miko was just a little crazy, or open to the wind, as the priests among themselves called the holy inebriation. He leaned closer and politely asked the miko to speak up.

When Turtle did so, the tone of his words gave the leathery priest a thrill up his spine as though he had heard an owl speak his name—an ancient harbinger of death.

Turtle's large black eyes were shimmering wetly, and he spoke in a hoarse whisper:

"Tell them that we will perform the butterfly dance on the solstice."

"Lord," Panther said obediently, himself excited by this announcement because of its high drama with the spilling of the miko's blood in a beautiful, dramatic dance.

"That will appease them, no doubt," Turtle-in-the-Sun said.

Panther thought he detected a flash of defeat or something kin to it in his master, who rarely showed any emotion, especially a negative one.

"They love to see my blood."

Panther could only nod, so unused to seeing this mood in the miko, who never referred to his own royal sacrifice in so personal a manner. Usually he was as cool as jade.

"Ah, well," Turtle said, lighter, it seemed. "The fire must be fed." He beamed a smile so innocent that he looked like a child.

"Yes," he said, thrill turned to chill because he had never heard Turtle recite the ritual bloodletting prayer outside the sacrament. As far as he could remember, he himself had never uttered the phrase except in the ritual context so that he felt a new emotion, a mixture of fear and daring when he repeated the words, "Yes, lord, the fire must be fed."

Chapter 10

In a changed voice Turtle said, "No council today."

Panther looked up in surprise, interrupting his concentration upon the miko's mood. He was also the miko's chief steward who saw to it that the man stayed on a schedule arranged around small ceremonies scattered throughout the day. These ceremonies all had to do with watching the sun's progress and must be committed in private. The council convened every fifth morning, and this morning was it—four or five times during any one moon because the number twenty and its divisibles were held sacred by the ancestors.

The miko continued. "The next council will be held on the day of the solstice—we will meet on the dance ground."

Panther nodded.

"Get the chief of protocol working on the procedure." Turtle-in-the-Sun could not remember the details of the butterfly dance, so long ago had he performed it. "We will let the thieving priest have the greatest honor."

"Master," Panther said reverently.

It was an unusual thing for the miko to do, announcing the heart sacrifice so near its performance. Such ceremonies were extraordinary, usually saved for a solstice or equinox, or certain alignments of Bright Snake as the morning or evening star, or the inauguration of a new miko. But they were always planned long in advance. The high priest knew without asking that his master was preparing to seek a special vision.

It was an entirely appropriate reason for canceling an ordinary council. Turtle-in-the-Sun was good at this kind of dignified kingly gesture. This particular method passed judgment on the thief, whose relatives were out there ready to pay the miko large tribute for mercy. This would be their answer. They would have no grounds for complaint, since their nephew

would have the highest honor his miko could bestow upon him
as his punishment.

"Still," Panther said, "it is a shame to lose the tribute. . . ."

"The only thing the treasury is short of, Panther, is corn.
Everything else they might offer does not fulfill our immediate
need." This was true. As host of the miko's eventual funeral,
the high priest was vexed with a duty to constantly amass grave
gifts. In better seasons the outlying dependent villages had
contributed highly worked and crafted objects of leather, flint,
baskets, beads, and featherwork, plus the labor-intensive fruit
of the hunt or gathering, such as dried meat, herbs, grains, and
nuts. The miko's treasury was bulging with these commodities,
traded for corn in past abundant seasons. He had fifteen years
of goods from places far away—mica, virgin arrowheads,
pearls, various found metals, in addition to bales of feathers
and fabulous oddities for which nobody had names.

But for the miko to announce a great feast so suddenly—this
was a remarkable change in the order of service, and the high
priest availed himself of the opportunity to question Turtle-in-
the-Sun about it.

Before answering, the miko set out the makings of a long,
slim reed pipe with a bowl in the shape of a stylized raptor
carved in bright red stone. "This is not an ordinary year. In
these lean times we cannot take a chance on an ordinary
sacrifice." He shook his head, his long coal-dark hair loose and
shining upon his shoulders, blue highlights standing out in the
firelight.

He was the only man who ever wore it that way, like a
maiden or a small child. Everyone else from high priest down
to the lowest bearer on the line wore some sort of tied-off,
plucked, braided, or bluntly bound and singed pattern to their
black locks. Panther watched in admiration as his master filled
the pipe from a simple leather pouch and prepared it for
lighting as he continued speaking softly. "Heart blood will
make our medicine more powerful, Panther, to insure that
Our Lord will be able to hear."

Panther nodded and leaned over a small smokeless flame
burning in a firepit to his right.

Using a blackened deer antler, he tonged out a coal,
thinking that a heart sacrifice would be powerful, surely
enough to get the Lord's attention in these extraordinary
circumstances. And it would be a wonderful diversion for the

restless council and the people. He immediately thought of several elaborately costumed dances that would enhance the ritual for which he held special reverence.

To himself, who had the intricate daily patterns of the faith to set, the most sublime was the rarest ceremony central to his beliefs. There was a purity about it—its symbolism of the deified heart was the essence of the whole system. He loved the technical perfection its performance demanded of him over the years. It was not given for the chief priest to have visions, but once Panther had seen something. It was during this ceremony, and only that once in all the years of assisting the chief speaker to play that sacred role. It happened during the tenure of the previous miko, when Panther was young.

Each time he served the great feast, he hoped he might have another vision.

The councillors all loved the rite, too, the holiest memorial in their cycles of years. They counted time from such events— the season of so-and-so's heart sacrifice, for example. Still, those uncles out there would go away dissatisfied, despite the fact that their miko was saying that he was going to take drastic measures to deal with the problems they all faced—namely that there was not enough gathered crop to fulfill all the labor contracts it took to grow it.

"Give the eldest councillors ten daysticks, each with a yellow bead." It was ten days until the solstice. The gift was the equivalent of ten jugs of the finest cornmeal, since each bundle of daysticks took hours for the squad of daykeepers to carve from cedar. It was a generous tender of disbursement, since each daystick could be redeemed for the cornmeal when all the days had passed, marked by the breaking of a stick each dawn. The broken sticks were burnt as incense, so their manufacture made a kind of sacred currency that flowed between the faithful and the priesthood.

The councillors would surely be appeased by this generous gift, their feathers smoothed by the promise of grand entertainment.

Panther got to his knees and put his forehead down upon Turtle's left toes, then stood gracefully and backed out of the alcove.

Turtle sighed and warmed his hands over the flames. The heat rose up full of cedar incense, delicious and cleansing to the nostrils and throat.

His wrist still hurt. With his other thumb he rubbed the vein just this side of the bulging bruise as he stood and walked toward his private quarters.

Four of Turtle's aunts lived in the stucco apartments that shared walls with the temple on the northeast corner of God's Hill. They kept house for him in the larger of two fine lodges on the fourth terrace. They sewed and repaired his nonceremonial clothing, cooked for him and his visitors, and generally took care of his household. This included providing, depending on ceremonial schedule, girls from proper households of surrounding villages.

The miko did not take a wife, but was expected to impregnate as many as he found to his liking.

The time right after a royal bloodletting was considered the most auspicious for ripening royal progeny, and many girls vied for the privilege. The idea was to have many potential mikos out in the villages; most of these children did not ever meet their father. But their mothers held high esteem in their home clans, daughters as well as sons. The mothers received generous gifts upon the births of their royal children and always took good marriages. The boys usually grew to fill out the lower echelons of the local priesthood, or if talented, earned respect as leaders of war and hunting parties. Once in a while one of them would go live in the temple with older half brothers to be trained to succeed the miko. Panther had a small flock of boys under his present tutelage.

The four aunts were least busy during extended ceremonial times such as this, just before the sun's return from the south. So they did their handwork together around the firepit in one end of the structure, weaving the hours into their bead patterns and stitches while they gossiped and plotted.

Two of Turtle's aunties were elderly sisters; one was wife to a chief war-planner, and the last was the youngest living sister of the old miko, Turtle's favorite blood relative, Burning Rose.

It was Burning Rose who came to him now. She was several times a grandmother but still straight-backed, greeting him with hot mulberry cloths to bathe his hands, stinging red tea, and fruit if he wanted it.

He growled that he was not hungry as he shed the star-robe along the way from the woven cane screens across the swept clay floor to an opening in the south wall that led to a small garden where they grew the household herbs. By way of a simple stone path, the enclosed garden communicated with a low log structure half-buried in the ground and from which a plume of heat rose, ruffling the air. The faintest evidence of smoke blew off in the breeze, which stirred the door flap of the miko's private sweatbath.

He crawled inside without speaking to One Reed, the leathery gardener who cultivated the herbs and tended the sweatlodge. The old man crouched to one side on sinewy haunches, nothing on but a breechclout and a multitude of clan tattoos. He grunted the morning prayer to himself—identical to the words the miko offered to the sun, who made equals of all men—and snugged the flap across the sweathouse door.

"Sky Father of all . . ."

Still crouched, he fed small cedar boughs to the fire as he intoned the prayer, and with a fire-hardened elk-pelvis hoe shoved the coals under the lip of stone that led to the firepit inside. Presently he heard the sizzle of steam that reported the miko had sprinkled the coals. ". . . your way and on your day," One Reed mumbled, leaning back in his favorite sitting spot against the warm logs, watching the sun climb as he lit his pipe between yellowed teeth.

The women had queued up, each with some item for the miko's pleasure.

One Reed squinted at them, hating them with their heads all bowed, their braids all tightly cabled and curving down across snug bosoms. They descended in rank and age from the crone, Simple Greenbrier, holding her jug of oil. The miko would pause with her inside the sweatlodge, where with still-strong hands she would pummel and grease him, loosening muscles in his back and arms, and in the calves where cramps lodged after the strenuous fasting and postures of ritual.

Turtle would make more steam to sweat off the oil, then he would depart the sweathouse.

Behind Simple Greenbrier stood Morning Owl with tea, and the other sister with fruit. Burning Rose was next with the same huge clipped buffalo robe warming near the fire, its strange star designs on the outside picturing a different sky, said to be that above the southern land of the ancestors. She would toss this over the miko's shoulders and help him buff dry. The huge robe was ratty and heavy with its own obscure meanings and the shape of the big man who loved it before all others; it had belonged to the old miko, and Turtle would not suffer it copied and destroyed before it rotted from his shoulders.

After his drying, Burning Rose, chief speaker of women, would walk with him to the eating lodge, where he would take whatever informal meal he desired. She was the highest-ranking woman of the female lodge that matched the men's tradition passed down from the ancient grandfathers.

One Reed noticed a fifth auntie standing beyond the others this morning, a new one, the girl with the loosened hair. She lingered in the shadows around Burning Rose, a relative on her mother's side not related to the miko but from a high-ranking Oldtown family.

The gardener watched the girl, her sweet little breasts touched by the rosy eastern light, shielded by the mature women. She was a blossom, he thought. The lucky miko would have her tonight, if he wanted her. After tonight he would begin the days of abstinence that always preceded the solstice.

One Reed growled a chortle and spoke to Burning Rose. "You waste your time with our lord," he whispered.

She growled back at him, but her manner encouraged him to continue. She, too, knew the details of the miko's sacral responsibilities.

"He will take no woman—remember my words."

She lifted an eyebrow to inquire further.

"I tell you that great things are about to happen," One Reed said with some self-importance.

"What?"

He shrugged and waddled in his crouch closer to the fire, where he cracked a cedar twig lengthwise before sliding both aromatic slivers into the coals.

"You must wait and see."

The fire snapped up the juicy cedar sprigs, filling the air with pleasant aromas.

"You know nothing, you crazy old man."

He smiled to himself. "What you do not know, woman, would fill the miko's war canoe."

"You know nothing."

"I know he will not crack that sweet nut over there." He wiggled his lean, sinewy hindquarters and spread his bent knees to expose his intentions. "Let me have her, instead."

The girl, who had just finished her first blood, shrank back behind her mother's relative, who was calculating the last time the miko had been with a woman, far too long, more than three moons, back in the late summer when he couched a girl from Burning Rose's own fireside.

There were two considerations: It did not take. That girl was not pregnant as she should have been. And it was not good for a man to go so long. Not good for the bones, not good for the mind. Not only was it bad for himself. His last child born to the clan of Burning Rose had reached manhood ceremonies. There should be more royal progeny in the city.

One Reed stood, almost squeaking as he unfolded his spidery appendages.

Burning Rose turned boldly. Before he had time to react, she grabbed his member, holding it with knowledgeable gentleness, and inquired close to his face, "Do you have a problem?"

He backed off, slipping easily from her grasp.

"I will be happy to help you," she said mildly, dusting off her hands in the cedar smoke, a blunt cleansing gesture that indicated some degree of implied pollution.

"What you do not know would fill your own bottomless hole," he retaliated out of her reach.

"Anytime," she said, taking another step toward him.

He hurried around to the rear of the sweatlodge, where the supply of cedar boughs was getting low. Cursing the workers who were lax in fulfilling their duties, he grabbed an armload so that his manhood was covered when he walked back around to the blackened clay pit to feed the fire.

Ignoring him, Burning Rose had turned with a smile of victory on her face to finish arranging a tray of sweetmeats—smoked rodents and herbal pestos, steamed mushrooms and mussels on-the-halfshell, quail eggs, fried cornmeal mush, pecans, and crisply broiled caterpillars in maple syrup traded from faraway eastern tribes.

The miko's hand appeared at the flap, waving with two fingers for his oiling down. Simple Greenbrier scrambled inside with speed and grace that belied her years.

One Reed glared at Burning Rose, one generation his junior.

But she continued to ignore him until the miko came out with sweat glistening on his body. Morning Owl enfolded him in the buffalo fleece that held the permanent shape of his shoulders, its weight dragging the ground as he made his wordless way toward his quarters.

Burning Rose hurried with her tray behind him, his wide shoulders draped with an image of the sky somewhere, all star-marked against blue-clay background—the skin side of the great buffalo pelt, Sky Father himself in a bad mood from the woman's point of view.

Above the hum of the unseen corn-grinders, he heard someone speaking in a voice of oratory from the council chamber beyond this patio, but he did not stop to hear what was being said.

The voice faded behind the miko as he hurried on to places where he did not have to listen to the rattling of old bones.

From across the plaza, a little boy of about six, child of one of the feather mistresses, darted toward him.

The boy's mother scurried after him and caught him up but not before he handed the miko a clay jug with a fitted lip stylized like a small person with head thrown back in deep slumber. The miko held the jug up to one ear without removing the lid and smiled when he heard the buzz of insects inside.

The shell disk in his stretched earlobe rattled against the container, which the child's mother had let him decorate—his small handprint was among the patterns outlined with spaced holes that let air in for the creatures to breathe.

Turtle looked down upon the child's flattened forehead. The child returned his deep regard, looking up at him with wide brown eyes.

"For Sukse-and-Sohe," the child said with unchildlike seriousness.

Red-and-Blue was the miko's two-headed king snake, which he had managed to keep alive with hand feeding since early summer—quite a feat. Though two-headed snakes were not uncommonly born, they did not survive long, because one or the other head would mistake the other for an enemy and bite it, killing the whole animal.

The miko's Red-and-Blue was an object of great curiosity and wagering, probably the most priceless possession in his vast treasury. There were many wagers among the warriors and councillors as to when the stupid thing would finally kill itself.

Turtle kept it in a tightly woven basket one of his aunts had made for him. He fed it dried beetles, crickets, and weevils diverted from the drumfish supplies. But the snakes loved live food, harder to come by in these cold moons.

"Woman!" he called, and the boy's mother hurried closer to drop on one knee before him. "This is our child," he said, making a statement, not asking a question.

She nodded, head still bowed.

Turtle reached out and lifted her chin. She was still a girl, still plump with baby fat. He tried to remember her; she was from the village of diggers and carriers to the west. But, among the many, he could not recall her name.

"His name?"

"Five-Tens-and-Two."

Turtle repeated the significant number to make sure he correctly heard her.

"He is number five-tens-and-two of my lord miko's sons."

Turtle-in-the-Sun felt the low earth-rumbling sound of destiny beneath his feet; the boy's name was an astounding revelation the same as today's number. He felt his heart pound as though it anticipated the future.

But outwardly he retained his usual calm, composed demeanor.

Together Turtle and the woman watched the boy, aware in his innocent way that he was the center of the moment. He stood sucking on two fingers, looking between them, first at his mother's, then the miko's, eyes.

"This is a wonderful gift," said Turtle as he cracked the jug lid. Sukse-and-Sohe would have a feast on the live food inside. A brown cricket aimed inquiring antlers from the jar rim.

Turtle nudged it back with his thumb, closed the lid, and said, "Come."

The child reached out for the miko's hand, slipping from his still-kneeling mother's grasp. Together the man and boy continued into the thatched house the aunties kept for the miko.

Behind them, the corn-grinders' hum droned on, and another kind of hum intensified as argument brewed in the temple where the high priest had settled himself upon the miko's mat of command, which sat a little higher than the gathered elders arguing on their own council mats.

He had just now told them that this morning's meeting was postponed; it was as though he had poked a hornet's nest.

Smoke thickened in the high rafters as each councillor took his turn to speak. They all knew their places—the lesser ranks spoke first, between discreet silences during which everyone passed the pipes and sipped their murky teas.

The outlanders were the loudest. They felt out of place in this holy building full of the nation's treasures lining the walls, bones of ancestors stacked in neat baskets, the tribal bundle full of memorabilia from generations back, and magic things such as the great sky rock. They were gawkers here in the city, and it showed. Their braided hair full of raw bear grease, their scraggy furs and crudely bound feet, gave them away: They wanted corn, and they wanted it now as they had been promised for their peltries and other trade goods.

Despite the acrimony, Panther was comfortable listening to the uncultured westerner's harangue. The high priest was where he most liked to be. He loved to assume this place in the miko's absence, and felt most at home in this high hall full of smoke and words. He let his mind drift upon the words and smoke as the meeting progressed.

Next to speak were the locals.

The eldest of the villagers enjoyed the opportunity to remind the miko's man of several grievances his people had against the royal lodge, one of which went back to an old blood feud between the noble and an Oldtown household. He finished in a rattling of spear butts and loud, gruff agreement from the men around him.

Panther, still in his dark ceremonials, sat as immobile as a stump, apparently listening with extreme politeness to each man.

They smoked a noisy round, during which the twenty or so elders, each akimbo on his personal mat coughing and grumbling, was waited upon by his boy or young warrior. Jugs of water were passed, and busy hands reamed out the stems of each pipe in turn as they were smoked, then filled them again, and lit them from coals kept in each man's small personal fire-jug, which the assistants were charged with keeping hot.

All this while the old lodge firemen tended the central pit, where four logs were kept eternally burning end on.

After a traditional time, the elder from Oldtown cleared his throat of smoke and began to speak in a slightly louder voice that gradually grew into fine oratory style and silenced all other conversations in the spacious somber hall.

". . . but still the high priest has not told us why the miko would insult his most faithful servants," he said, indicating his brothers seated around him. His mellow voice filled the hall along with the smoke; ribbons and feathers tied with dangling shells moved in the air charged by the old speaker.

Panther signaled to his young assistants, who bore bulging slings. They quickly spaced themselves throughout the chamber, and when Panther gave a quick clap of his hands, they began to hand out tied bundles of beautifully carved sticks.

"At the end of ten days, bring your broken sticks to the dancing ground and see a great feast laid before the Lord."

Behind the hanging cane curtains, musicians began to play appropriate music on flute and drum that celebrated the solstice and the return of life after the harshness of winter.

The amazed chiefs accepted their daysticks, but one among them called out, "And will the sacrifice live again after this great feast?"

The sacrifice was a young priest this moment languishing in a pit-cage on the other side of this pyramid. He had been caught not only dealing in seedcorn—the miko's exclusive privilege—but had been caught cultivating the sacred plants in a secluded field. The illegal plants had been ripped from the ground in the secret patch the young priest was tending and tied to his bare back, where they still hung, dry and tattered, tied with cords denoting his clan associations.

Panther was of a mind to have the offender brought out right now with the incriminating burden on his back, just to shame these old men who were demanding the offender's release.

Panther silenced the musicians with a loud clap of his hands and replied, "That is a valued ceremony."

"It is a valued sacrifice," the Oldtowner said, voice blurred by restrained emotion. The marked young priest was in fact son to this man's sister, and among this people, nephews were as highly regarded as sons.

"Perhaps it could be arranged," Panther said, looking into the eyes of the old man before him.

"Perhaps a tribute could be gathered," the elder said.

"Once a heart has been cut out, it takes all the miko's power to put it back so that it beats again."

"There is mighty tribute among these nations," the Oldtown

speaker said, looking around at his brother councillors, who all agreed with generous head nodding and pole rattling.

"How much tribute, Buffalo Eagle?" Panther inquired.

"Name it," the old negotiator snapped, the sweat of the deal upon his forehead. Not only was he Oldtown's spokesman, he was also the city's finest bonesetter and highly respected for that as much as for his leadership.

"Rescind all your labor contracts with the miko."

The old men gasped at such a suggestion, and the gasp swelled back like a wave through the ranks of councillors.

"Is the miko so poor that he must go back on his agreements?" called someone from the thickest knot of councillors.

"Now you insult us further," the Oldtowner said evenly, but the others rumbled around him, their ire mounting. Several well-aimed lines of spittle singed on the central coals.

"Well, then." The high priest shrugged. "This great feast will be offered solely for the Lord." Meaning, the thief would be sacrificed.

The old men's voices broke into uneasy rabble. The one who had spoken turned to his brothers and delivered some stormy words.

Panther sat there and politely listened to them, giving them all the time they needed before he spoke. "It is fitting to give away the sacrifice, because on that day our miko will confront God himself."

He had their attention.

"Our lord will perform the butterfly dance."

They liked that and agreed among themselves as Panther had known they would.

Chapter 11

Panther returned to tell the miko that his announcement was a success.

Turtle-in-the-Sun nodded, rubbing his wrist where the puncture wound still ached, dull now, but persistent with every heartbeat. He listened to his heartbeat, letting it mark the sting in his hand, but he spoke with no trace of the earlier strangeness. "That little boy, Panther."

"The cricket boy?"

"He was our crop six winters past?"

Panther nodded. "A good season, that." They had gathered so much surplus maize six years ago, he had been able to acquire thousands of arrowheads for the miko's funeral treasure.

"Bring that boy into your service and let us speak to him from time to time, if we forget."

Panther was delighted the miko was attending to this duty, which he had neglected for so long. There were only a dozen lads in training now, and none showed the slightest promise.

"Let him witness the butterfly dance. Let him have a close view, and watch him to see how he takes it."

Panther nodded compliance.

"Listen, Panther . . ." the miko commanded.

The hairs sprang up on the back of Panther's neck, grizzled hairs not often spooked; he did not like the sound in Turtle's voice as he said, "That boy's name is Five-Tens-and-Two."

Panther was as struck with the reoccurrence of today's number as the miko had been. He could not remember the timely repetition of such a large number in a long time.

"What do you think it means, master?"

It was strange to hear the miko laugh, a high, piping sound that might have come from a small child or an old woman. The sound of it made Panther wonder, *What is happening to my master?*

Then, reasonable again, Turtle asked, "What was happening in Ixtulan five-tens-and-two winters ago?"

Panther clapped his hands together three times, bringing forth from the shadows a beautiful sloe-eyed youth of about thirteen winters, one of the dozen with the noble forehead in training under the high priests' tutelage. This boy had in fact been the acolyte who assisted in this morning's sun ceremony. He leaned over, under the hand of the high priest on his back, to accept a whispered order.

The lad trotted out again, leaving the miko and the high priest alone only a few moments. Presently he returned with a gang of daykeepers who arranged themselves behind him on mats they brought with them rolled up neatly under their arms along with the other implements of their profession.

"Our miko wants to know something," Panther said presently when they had all bowed before their lord.

"What are the significances of the number five-tens-and-two?" the miko asked, sitting now with folded legs upon his meetings mat, looking refreshed and kingly and sane again, leaning over on one arm stiffened against a knee, peering down upon them all from his slightly higher pedestal. Outside the persistent song of the corn-grinders filled the air. Here inside the council chambers, cedar incense writhed around him, veiling his mood in soft light. Panther thought he looked particularly dignified this day, a beautiful man who did honor to the chief's mat.

The numberers rattled their sticks of many carved heads, each a sign for some thing, some event, or some conjunction in the sky. The elder counters threw knucklebones down onto the mats of honor, which were spread over the floor, and whispered calculations that were also prayers.

"Five-tens-and-two is one of the numbers sacred to Bright Snake, according to the ancestors."

The most vagrant of heavenly bodies, Bright Snake went through a complicated dance, apparently close to the body of Lord Sun himself. Around the sometimes dazzling star had grown mysteries and traditions of it being the sun's boon companion, part of a warrior-guard band who went out with the king of heaven.

But because of the erratic patterns Bright Snake wove in the night skies throughout the year, other darker stories circulated about the star's fickleness, about betrayal and abandonment that had once, in ancient days past, endangered the sun's own fiery body on his nightly journey into the underworld. Some of these stories even went so far as to place Bright Snake beside the Lord Himself, a dark twin who through the ages had played the evil brother in contrast to the benevolent sun.

For 236 days Bright Snake preceded Lord Sun's arrival every morning. Then the star would disappear altogether for 90 days and reappear for 250 days as the Evening Star, lighting up winter skies with brilliant crystal feathers shining so brightly on some nights as to cast shadows on the ground at the stargazers' feet. Eight nights later it would reappear, beginning the cycle all over again in the east at morning.

But the times most dramatic of all were the few hours every one hundred thirteen and one hundred thirty years, alternately, when the black disk of Bright Snake danced in front of the sun's face.

Turtle had witnessed the latest eight-year paired transit some years ago, which had been predicted by Ixtulan's daykeepers during the reign of the old miko. In his eighteenth year the brilliant star had moved to the east of the sun across the solar face, a minute black speck that began as a tadpole with a tail that seemed to adhere to the sun's edge. Then, when he was twenty-six, it moved back toward west of the sun. He had seen it briefly with his own eyes, though it was said some went blind watching the rare spectacle.

There had been vast, raging fires on the western buffalo prairies that season that had placed a pall between earth and sky, so one could gaze at the sun for some time. It had been a dull orange ball most of the day; Turtle would never forget the oppressive brown smear that veiled it and turned it into a persimmon on a gray branch, dotted with the dark little circle of Bright Snake throbbing its way across the face of God.

It was awesome to contemplate what the significance might be of such an event, which would not happen again in any living man's lifetime.

"There was an eclipse of the moon that summer," said Fire Wolf, the youngest daykeeper but the most talented in all of Ixtulan and her daughter temples, after consulting with his pattern of sticks.

"And a new star with a tail," said an elder man, who was Fire

Wolf's teacher. "It made a path across the sky from Rose Moon until Hunting Moon. Pieces of fire rained down toward the west, and was found our great sky-rock, which fell from heaven and which no weapon can dent. Many twins were born the next spring among men and animals."

"What was happening down here in the middleworld five-tens-and-two winters past?" the miko asked, looking into the faces of the men in a half circle around him.

"It was a time of drought," said the third daykeeper who had unrolled a large hide with a circular pattern of discrete designs winding outward from the center.

"A time of famine," said the last old man, a rememberer who had served the previous miko.

"Our predecessor was a young man, serving the former miko his own father," said Turtle, who had studied the symbols before.

"And that miko's name was Walks-in-the-Sun."

"Five-tens-and-two years ago he gave his heart to feed God," said Fire Wolf, looking up from a narrow carved paddle full of holes plugged with pegs carved as stylized animal heads.

The bonecaster agreed with the brilliant young daykeeper after consulting a significant passage of symbols drawn on the hide.

"And my miko's predecessor was named the new chief speaker, who was ushered in with much dancing by the warriors and the maidens."

"There was a battle that year," said the man who kept the spiral design and added to it with other large buffalo skins full of small meaningful pictures. "The warriors of Ixtulan conquered Daughter of Ix, and a new holy hill there was raised." This other pyramid center was up Sky Blood Creek a ways, situated near the point where the creek branched from the Mech-a-sip-i.

"Our temple was burned down and another built to replace it on top of the present highest level of the highest terrace."

"Walks-in-the-Sun was buried with the sacred ancestors," Panther said, indicating the low, long burial mound covered with grass and rippling with hundreds of yellow and red streamers down on the southern plaza. "He was the last to be buried in the Little Mountain of a Thousand Souls and follows the line of the first miko to give his heart to God."

Turtle's own father had lived a long life, died in his sleep, and was cremated along with his favorite wife and two of his children. Their remains had gone into the market as small bags of dust and heavy ash, said to be good medicine for the soil before planting. Mediciners also prescribed a potion mixed with other items, herbs and such, which would cure all manner of physical ailments from arthritis to chest pains.

"The first miko was named Nine-Sun," said the elder daykeeper. "And when he gave his heart to God, he had five-tens-and-two-winters on him, but he was still young and strong in the eye of Our Lord."

"Five-tens-and-two is the number of brides miko Nine-Sun took with him into the underworld," said the man with the sticks. "He was among the first of the lords from the south to come to this place to teach us the true way of God."

"And upcoming," said the elder counter, "five-tens-and-two will be the summers of our miko." He looked up with rheumy eyes, trembling slightly because of age.

"I had forgotten that," Turtle said, leaning back as though this last information pressed him. He had not considered his own age—his people did not celebrate birthdays, and he did not often ask his counters for such specific information. He thought about it—yes, he would be fifty-two in the spring.

It seemed that all bones that could be rattled had been rattled and set into their patterns, along with the counting sticks and the great wide hides with their picture spirals, the march of seasons, the names of the years and events of the nation. Everyone was still. Dust motes filled the air breathed by the counters and the high priest and the miko, all men, all breathing the ordinary air that stirred with the holy equations.

"Ahhh," was all the miko said.

He did not say much to anybody, not even to Panther, who was made anxious by his odd behavior that continued into the next week of preparations for the solstice ceremonies. The miko spent much of the time in isolation, fasting and praying, so Panther was not able to watch him as closely as he would have liked.

Panther had the servants report, but they were reticent, saying that the aunties kept him too close, and he did not speak even to them. He held his silences, even in the crowded rooms of common meetings with petitioners, elders, and various technicians preparing for the holiday.

High ranking guests from far away nations began arriving,

each to be feted inside the great hall full of the miko's hospitality. Juicy meats were roasted, whole carcasses, and laced with chili peppers. Corn forever persisted upon the air, redolent of warmer days and brighter sunlight. It was a festive season with the year's climactic ritual and feast looming over everything and everyone who came into the city's precincts.

Reports that the miko would dance the sacred butterfly drew many who had heard of the ritual but had never seen it performed. But the promise of a great feast drew even more audience than would normally be in the city during this festival when the sun would turn back to the north, when the reckoning would be made, and all markets would be open down in the main plazas.

Panther watched him, unable to fathom what he was thinking. He would have loved to ask, but it was not his place to do so. Turtle saw him staring once or twice and made that sweet, childish smile. They cast the numbers each morning, but there were no more significant repetitions—all the days remained in the small digits, less than powerful ten. Panther wondered what the miko would do if another fifty-two showed up in any of their calculations.

Turtle fasted for two days before the solstice and did not sleep. He was wide-eyed and lucid when Panther came to escort him outside for the ceremony in the still-blue darkness of the predawn. But the miko was quiet, that strange mood thrown over him like another, but invisible, star-robe.

It had turned bone-cold, though the air remained dry. The miko was stripped for the rite; but seemed to glow with an inner light that kept him warm, along with the aunties' oils, and kept his skin smooth and free of chills. The powerful medicines he had imbibed, the fasting, and lack of sleep contributed to his physical condition, all aimed at preparing him to endure what was waiting for him out on the dancing ground.

They began assembling the elaborate headdress upon his shoulders, strapping and tying him into it so that the mask did not become complete until the player stood beneath and behind it, animating the inanimate object with the breath of life.

The sky grew lighter.

Turtle-in-the-Sun felt himself floating above all of it, the black resting fields, the city, the people, the wide, rolling creek, and lakes of silver blood. He was even above the dawning light of the sun itself; he felt lines of power in his fingers that would urge up the thickened lazy circle of the sun and call it back from too long a sojourn in the south.

Everything was in place. Even the drumfish over in the sacred lakes were singing away as though they knew the significance of this morning's events.

Turtle-in-the-Sun heard Panther's whispered orders to the musicians, felt the tension in the air as the eastern light began to pool toward some kind of fuzzy center over in that direction.

He had a fleeting impression—and that only slight because his peripheral vision was limited inside the towering apparatus of tasseled wicker, feathers, shells, fur, and buffalo leather—of a packed audience, at least two hundred in ranks like stacked cedar a dozen paces to his right.

They were bored by the daily rituals, but this one was a spectacle to see.

Down on the plaza and well within the royal zone of which this high wide pyramid was the centerpiece, below its southern face gathered more people, lesser-ranked nobles in several groups of several hundred, each dressed in festive garb, many with slashed foreheads or cheeks, ashes rubbed into usually proud braids. Among this contingent were many visitors, chieftains minus any weapons from vassal nations down the river, the northernmost Chickasaw who shared borders with Ix, the southern Caddo, most of them who spoke variations of Muskogean. But there were also representatives of buffalo hunters from down west and even wandering bands of northerner dog-people, with whom Ixtulan traded hides and dried meat in exchange for tsalu.

And beyond those of rank gathered the city's common people, the craftsmen, farmers, seamstresses, pearl-borers, feather-workers, hand-loom and basket weavers; potters, shell and wood carvers; flint knappers, minor priests and shamans of every stripe; bonesetters, healers and herbalists, strong-backed bearers of corn and salt, and basket loaders, who with sweat-stained trumplines built the pyramids, as well as hundreds of others from outlying villages and places where were spoken other languages of no relation to the tongue of the people of Ixtulan.

All were silent down to the calluses on the hands of each man, woman, and child. Today the sun, living embodiment of

God above of all that breathes, would stray dangerously close to chaos. With one's own eyes he could be seen yonder on the eastern brink. Unless the speaker gave blood offering, the sun was likely to continue south on its hunting journey looking for food—this happened every turning of two seasons, resulting in the freezing up of the land.

And every year the people convinced the sun to turn around, tantalized by the way this people would feed him with their highest offering, the blood of their king. And so the speaker saved the world again.

It was so clean, so precise from Turtle's point of view, that he would have dropped to his knees to thank the One Above for the privilege of standing here as a servant of the Lord. He never failed to be deeply touched by what he was doing when he called up the sun each morning. But the duty of the ritual was such habit to him now that he often went to sleep practicing it, and still standing, proceeded.

Below, everyone down to the dogs was respectfully quiet. Some of these were the yellow pull-dogs who would carry the visitors' trade cornmeal back to their homelands. But most were the local and normally vocal half wolves. They sat with peaked ears along the edge of the wide, perfectly swept plaza, listening with the people like a great breathing mat woven not of cane but of muscle, bone, and sinew, spread out at the foot of God's Hill in the center of the city toward which every eye and all lengths of trampled path and forest trace were directed, where the four-faced prominence, at least a hundred feet high and more than a thousand long, sat majestically near Sky Blood Creek, an ancient meander of the Great River Road itself.

Between groups of village houses and to every horizon thousands of acres of fields had been scraped clear, the fodder burned and spread over the earth awaiting next season's seed. Garden patches, nut and evergreen trees between the larger fields, stood unmoving without a breeze, wet gumbo soil as dark as smoky old flints for the naked earth was the richest of bottomlands and like a ragged patched robe from this high position overlooking all, the city, plazas, flat processional surfaces, grand market, lesser markets and service zones, where a spell or a slave could be bought for a good piece of worked flint or a stack of hides. Beyond that lay the docks and warehouses, and the low, flat platform pyramids where artists most days finished the blessing work on their crafts—sharpening flint and painting pottery.

Turtle-in-the-Sun relaxed his shoulders, feeling like a cat among the rushes as he sniffed out the presence of the sun, wonderful ball hesitating just beyond the eastern horizon. Turtle whispered a prayer much older than the city or the pyramid on which he stood:

O Lord, hear your son who petitions your return for renewed life for these people below within the sound of our horns. . . .

"Turtle-in-the-Sun, are you ready to feed the fire?" Panther's voice echoed—he faced the miko but turned his head toward the musicians, whom he directed personally.

"Yes," replied the man inside the costume hung with wide bands of woven ribbons so that his lower body was hidden in the streamers, and nothing but bare toes in tall platform sandals showed that this was indeed a human being.

Then, quick as a snake, Turtle-in-the-Sun reached out and slapped the high priest on the rump, goosing him slightly with his thumb as he pulled his hand away.

Turtle was quick and nobody saw.

The high priest whirled around with a flash of real anger in his eye, but he saw his miko laughing behind the mask.

The priest eyed him keenly. Turtle sometimes made a private joke in rituals. The speaker in this aspect was the Trickster, old Coyote. The proof of God's laughter lay all around, making the deity the greatest holy clown of them all, and was it not said that a certain species of black demon could be killed only by making them laugh themselves to death?

Smiling, but nowhere near mirth, the high priest in his black-demon clothing hovered in his sooty paint for the rituals as a skull, the Lord of Death. Everyone knew a cat was lord of the underworld. As host of the ceremonial meant to feed God, he would perform the knife cuts if the sacrificer was unable to complete the act himself, and he sometimes performed a more radical ceremony.

Equal partners they were in this ceremonial dance, despite the speaker's higher rank in all else. Panther as host had final call here on this day of days, backed up of course by the master of protocol stationed on his pallet nearby and directing the chorus of acolytes, priestlings, and servants without whose complicated production mechanics the dance could not be performed.

Panther's twenty horn players sounded their hopeful conch as was done every morning since Turtle's ascension fifteen years ago. Like the drumfish the musicians each gave an individual note, and none played the same, yet all their sounds blended into one fine, concentrated harmony that poured from the apex of God's Hill and spread from that center like rings on a pond, so that a raptor lounging on a high thermal or someone standing well outside the city could have heard the sound. The musicians had timed their expellation so that it never ceased as each player stopped to take a breath while his brothers continued in a round.

It was almost time.

Turtle could feel the trembling liquid gold swell of the sun, now paused just below the lip of the underworld on the other side of day, where each morning the sun stretched on his mat and greeted his wife the moon. The air bent over in that direction. Sometimes it silently exploded a green flare, but not today. The color today was clear, pure gold like nuggets found in certain streams; the pink tinge here was caused by the river's loyal companion, the haze.

The light must climb up out of this film that stretched all the way to the edge of the underworld in the far far east. The sun then would stroll out from his lodge in the farthest land in that direction across the sky to the other side of earth, where he must each night walk down into the underworld and fight his way back to morning.

This morning Turtle knew he would not only see but earnestly confer with that splendid being. He knelt out on the sacred square under his elaborate feathers and woven basketry that strained his head upon his neck, though now, after certain medicines, he felt no discomfort. Besides, a young warrior-priest knelt at each corner ready to help him lest he falter in the demanding ritual.

But he was strong, made so by many days of fasting and purging, of sexual abstinence, and of daily sweatbaths and minor bloodlettings. He was armed with the knowledge that his sacrifice of royal blood, by tradition of the sons of the sun himself, would be rewarded with a vision, a moment in the presence of the supreme being whom he already knew personally from previous fasting and drug-induced experiences atop this pyramid, called God's Hill or high place of egress to other worlds in the old language of the ancestors.

His kneeling provoked a respectful sigh from the gallery behind him where watched many official witnesses to this event that would insure prosperity for the coming year for thousands of people living within sight of this pyramid and also within days of journeying from this place.

The intricate seat into which Turtle settled himself was made of polished interlocking cedar roots padded so that rests cuddled his knees. Assistant priests respectfully helped him fold the heavily beaded and tasseled ribbons back across well-muscled thighs kept trim by enthusiastic ballplay, exposing his sex already lying upon the small horn altar built into the wooden throne.

Panther was there immediately with the sacred blade upon its feathered pillow.

"Hello, Old Friend," Turtle addressed the knife.

When he was very small, the first time his earthly father led him to this sacrificial place where they propped him up with many pillows and his father's own rolled-up bear robe so he could reach the altar, Turtle had watched his child penis on the horn polished with sinister dark shine, as though it were a separate small being apart from himself. The penis-shaped depression had been so huge and his member so insignificant within, it had appeared lost there. But he grew to fill it over the years, little by little, so that this throne had become a yearly measuring rod for his manhood each time he took this solemn ceremony.

He was about eight years old when he and his twin, Afternoon Moon, first came to live here with the old speaker, his father now gone to live in the west with the father of all. Turtle, out of many offspring of the speaker, because every woman of every village wanted to bear such a royal child, had been chosen to be trained by the old man himself.

Now, beyond fifty cycles of seasons, he felt the familiar chill of the oiled repository taking on his body heat. It was the work of a master carver, an intaglio impression of a male member, female encasement of the male in holy symbolism intended to be erotically stimulating, the idea being that a man must greet the sacrificer, the blade, with joy, presenting the most precious flesh available for God to feast upon.

He savored that old, comforting, but brief, erotic charge as he watched the obsidian surface, a series of serrations narrowing the natural glass ever thinner to its translucent edge.

He held the knife high, facing east.

When the first sunlight glazed that edge, he would feed the sun while the priests and all the people set up pleas and music and song to urge the sun to go no farther in his hunt to the south, that his people would feed him if he only would return to grow the crops.

The first time it had been difficult to cut himself, though he sat watching the old speaker disclosing all that was needed to know on his own royal person. They had tranced the boy Turtle, tranced him with fasting, sweating, and herbs and with the graceful eye of the old speaker, a renowned magician.

But to take that blade and slice with one's own unwavering hand—for even then at eight years, it must be voluntary—if he could not perform this most central rite well, then the old speaker would not have adopted him, and he would not be here calling the sun up on yet another day as the grandfathers had done now for six generations since the ancestors' arrival from the south.

Each time he experienced a flash of that little boy's terror and each time recovered to complete swift, expert surgery. This one hurt, unlike the common daily pricking by the knife, a minor irritation compared to this.

The glass knife inscribed his penis with two parallel lines in the fleshy foreskin. He expertly avoided musculature while aiming at specific arteries of the reddest blood with the caressing blade—now it was sublime because Turtle anticipated the rush of feeling that would accompany blood loss as he was helped to quickly thread a length of thin, supple material about a hand wide and ten hands long through the parallel wounds on either side of the muscle. Once the cane paper was in place, he nicked the artery, which immediately began to bleed profusely.

A soft chant arose from the otherwise hushed gallery: "Blood of the sun, blood of the sun."

With assistants representing the four winds at each elbow and others either side, Turtle stood from the sacrificial stool. Together they walked slowly to stand formally before the high priest stationed by a low altar made of fire-hardened red clay baked black and shiny.

Panther's dark, heavy leather robes, stained with soot and

tannin and sewn with crow feathers as oily black as tar, obscured activity behind him.

Turtle gazed into the priest's eyes, blacker than usual with resolute purpose.

Panther went about the ritual, every gesture of which was well rehearsed and performed many times so that it was an old, familiar habit.

"Why do you approach God?" Panther asked, more sacred formula, while the mumbling chant from many voices continued, "Blood of the sun . . ."

Turtle focused on the beads of sweat upon the priest's corrugated face, his wide upper lip, and the bridge of his nobly bent nose. Despite the chill of the dry midwinter morning, Panther was sweating heavily enough to begin melting his face paint. Already streaks of his copper-colored cheek showed under the soot. The considerable wrinkles around his perpetually narrow eyes were draining their chalk white like tears of milk; the man was bursting through the mask.

"Your miko intends to go to the underworld to find the light of day," Turtle responded breathily with the ironic ritual phrase. Despite his great strength and hardening through austerities to these labors, he was beginning to feel the first effects of blood loss as the stiff white paper threading his member got heavier and redder.

Panther reached out his blackened hands, grabbed the speaker's slick, well-oiled shoulders, and kissed him firmly, almost an attack, squarely on the forehead. When he reached back, an attendant was immediately there with a tall pottery beaker of meaningful design and superb workmanship. Panther brought it to the funnel of Turtle's mask and poured the thick liquid down into Turtle's open mouth while softly muttering a rich old prayer.

Over in the ranks of witnesses a few women began to moan. One crone, more than a hundred summers in age, stared in stony silence, tears running down her leathery cheeks, which had been scored with sacrificial lines more than once so that she was marked with a pleasing design, the newest lines of which were still wet red turning to brown. The speaker was her beloved great grandson; she traced her lineage back several generations to her own great grandmother, whom legend said was among the original mother-fathers who brought civilization to this place from southern regions.

Enthusiastic shouts rang from the men's gallery, where other nobles who had earlier shed blood identified with the speaker. It was traditional here for a band of children to swarm out onto the packed-clay plaza tossing handfuls of pebbles around, imitating farmers sowing. But there were only three little boys this year, all the sons of a strong subchief visiting from the pyramid up the local creek and near its junction with the Great River Road.

That center, called Daughter of Ix, was almost as big as Ixtulan. Its chief, father to these children, was a first cousin to the speaker and a powerful priest in his own right. But today he and his entire family were among the spectators, and his three sons the representatives of the people in the children's dance.

Instead of performing the dance for which he had been well rehearsed, the youngest of the boys began to cry and call for his mama, who stood somewhere among the seated nobles under the pavilion. From that befeathered throng leapt their father in his own elaborate court plumage, scooped the squalling youngster under the arms, and began puppeting him through the pantomime.

Turtle glanced over at Panther, who stood apparently enraptured by the performance. Jangling bells on the great mask alerted the high priest. Turtle's eye communicated his distaste for Lord Hard Walker's display of vanity in what was supposed to be the innocence of children.

This amid flutes and drums by the musicians off to one side, who blared a sudden warning note upon the rush of a dozen outrageously feathered dancers, the clowns, great exaggerations of all aspects of reality including Mountain, Flint, the Thunder Boys, Catfish and Trickster Coyote, Lightning and the Whirlwind Thunderbird. They capered around making thunderous, bestial sounds, howls and caterwaulings that sent the children-farmers scattering in shrieks with their toy hoes dropped behind.

The monster-dancers picked up the toy tools and began to dance in imitation of the little ones. But they were soon interrupted by the four long-nosed chacs, the four winds, the friends of human farmers who threw cornhusk lightning bolts and handfuls of golden seedcorn from the speaker's treasury at the monsters. Meanwhile the drummers imitated thunder, scattering those who howled and crouched against the barrage of corn as if its mere touch burned them. The laughing children ran out to gather up the kernels and dance a little jig with the four colorful chacs, all four huge warrior priests beneath the masks.

This diverting little comedy over, the high priest pushed Turtle forcefully away from himself, sending him spinning off in dizzying circles.

The dancer began to chant while whirling around and around, the fragile absorbent paper standing out as he spun faster and faster, blood being pulled out toward either end of the sheet, which dried with his circling movements that elaborated into a formal dance.

Gradually the white paper turned stiff crimson.

Like gaudy moth wings the two sides of the paper reached saturation. The sun was just grazing the far dark hip of land that marked the eastern ridge of an ancient Mech-a-sip-i meander. The rosy light bathed Turtle and all the plaza atop God's Hill, and in that state of red splendor, he commanded the Lord Sun to continue pulling upward, though it might be difficult because he had wandered so far south.

Panther stepped aside to reveal to the packed galleries on the west side of the little ceremonial plaza what his robes had obscured, the blackened clay altar around the four corners of which were kneeling the burly dancers painted and costumed in the respective colors of the four winds—white for north, red for east, yellow for south, and black for west.

Each man held a hand or ankle of a fifth young man, buck naked and flung over the altar so that his bare breast was pressed upward. One of his wrists had recently been slit. It hung over the beaker from which Turtle had drunk. The victim was not struggling. His head was thrown back and hanging down, his wide stare and lolling tongue invisible to the gallery, where there sounded a combined voice of amazed anticipation.

Several older witnesses called out something akin to "Amen!" when the sacrifice was exposed. They all knew him because he was a native Ixtulan; his father before him had been a priest of the speaker's household.

The young man, as docile as a puppy under the trance of powerful medicines, had been led by the four masked priests to the clay altar. He was naked except for the tattered dry cornstalks still lashed to his back—he wore his crime for all to see. There were a couple of shriveled corn ears amid the brown leaves that crunched as the attendants pressed him down upon the altar.

His breath came in long drafts that vibrated the concavity of his belly. He did not protest but only stared at the warming sky, his lips moving in some unintelligible sounds that may have been a prayer.

Turtle hoped the boy would remember the sacred words so he could speak them to Lord Sun the moment after death. By taking his life at this holy moment of sunrise, his executioner was assuring him eternal companionship with the sun himself.

The miko waited for everyone in attendance to get a good, long look at the sacrifice in his last moments, then he continued the loud prayer to the east.

"It is now time to come back to the north, where your children eagerly await your visitation," Turtle implored in a formal musical phrase, but his heart was bursting with emotion at the sight of the trembling disk rising over in the east.

Arms outstretched and groaning as though engaged in heavy labor, he seemed to be physically drawing up the golden orb as he brought his trembling hands higher above his head in perfect time with the ascent. The several assistants scattered behind him in smitten awe as it appeared for yet another time that their king had this awesome power. They did not want to know how he did it, but he respected the blood-soaked relics and the sacred person on whom such wounds were inflicted so the speaker could speak for the entire people to the father of all.

It was so holy a moment that they covered their faces and moaned along with the people far below, who were screaming for the sun not to desert those who loved him most.

But others were working despite the holiness of the moment.

The high priest adjusted the cords that bound the cornstalks to the sacrifice so that nothing would impair his slice.

He raised the monolithic black flint ax with an edge as fine as a baby's eyelash, poised above the victim's chest. This was his seventy-third great sacrifice. It had never lost its splendor for him, nor would it ever if he lived to perform it a thousand times. He felt the muscles of his strong arms ripple with just the right amount of force he would need to come down in a slicing motion that would split the skin, muscles, and ribbons of veins and arteries in one motion if he aimed perfectly, opening up the chest laterally but without nicking the beating heart that the gaping crack of a wound exposed. Then with an angled motion he would isolate the heart from its network of veins and arteries, and in a stroke adz it out by scooping the blade under the organ, which would still be midbeat when he lifted it out, serving it on the flat of the flint blade without further injuring it. He would have to hold the organ with the other hand because it would be trembling vigorously and even sometimes jumping about—he learned more each time he performed the act.

If it fell on the clay ground, it would be unfit for the holocaust, and its antics would provoke nervous laughter from the gallery—a fact that was used in other ceremonies that mimicked this one.

Laughter here, however, tended to distract from the solemnity of the occasion and ruin the drama.

Panther prided himself on the fact that he had never dropped a sacred heart nor had to canter ungracefully about or sidestep to balance it jittering like a frenzied squirrel or a drop of water on a hot cooking rock.

The precise shape of the flint ax made the single stroke possible, but surgeon's skill and steadiness of hand made it perfect and beautiful butchery. He had seen others before him botch it and have to climb up on the body of the victim to release their blade from the tough gristle, vilely puncturing the heart and polluting it for other ceremonies that would follow over the next day or so, not to mention rendering it unfit for the wholly burnt feast that was supposed to be offered to God.

The young victim who had just enjoyed his seventeenth summer went sublimely; there must never be a struggle to profane the moment, and so the journeyers of the heart always took the dark liquors and smoked the medicine smoke so that they were smiling until the end, and even afterwards.

Panther observed that smile and made his cut precisely and with dignity, then lifted the quivering heart on the blade to the pottery jar, where it would be kept for a while. He took a beaker handed him by another helper and caught it quickly full of blood from the open chest of the still-quivering corpse and carried it, overflowing, to a heavy stone crucible already simmering over coals.

He poured the blood slowly.

It sizzled robustly and sent up a belch of satisfying black smoke that seemed thick enough to possess weight. The air was full of the aroma of meat cooking. The crowd gasped. Some even cried out while others prayed aloud or chanted old formulas.

Wishing the heart had displayed a little more vivacity for the fullest dramatic effect, but all in all satisfied with his performance, Panther stepped back still holding the slick ax in both hands. He lowered it and stood there momentarily relaxing, savoring the sacredness of the moment, watching the coil of oily smoke to see if he might catch a glimpse of the vision serpent. But he never did—that was reserved for the speaker alone.

Others were equally diligent at work. Several furlongs to the north a young priest had climbed the great pole in the center of the sun circle of four tens of logs and had been poised all night awaiting this moment when the sun would clear the eastern corner of the big pyramid on which Turtle was falling into trance. The young priest now sat on a small platform on a peeled tree trunk more than eight man-lengths above the ground, where a chorus of lesser priesthood swayed with an appropriate chant for bringing up the waning sun at his most southern point along the horizon.

The man atop the pole wore the paint of a daykeeper who kept the great knots of the number of the nation's and the speaker's days. He and the other daykeepers under his direction would observe their great piles of temple pyramids marking once again the timeless movement of the sun. This man's eyes were very keen, for he was trained to observe small differences in vast patterns; he would stare at the sun for as long as he was physically able.

Some of his brotherhood were blinded from this occupation. There was an old, old story of one who had his eyelids removed in sacred sacrifice so that he would better be able to observe.

Fire Wolf would not have to go so far today. A quarter mile away he saw Chief Turtle-in-the-Sun's silhouette against the growing orb that started to ooze from the far eastern horizon exactly where it was supposed to rise on this day, the shortest daylight in the year. This confirmed again all the old stories passed on for generations from grandfathers who had come from a place where men were wise about the stars and about the counting of days.

Fire Wolf sat in the hovering glow carving a small stick to commemorate this day, which he would add to his collection devoted to this year so far, while below him on the clear dancing ground a hundred men stamped out their demands for the sun to cleave to its duty and come back along the horizon toward the north. Their cries grew louder as the great disk rolled upwards. The stick collection was ranked in a circle around his seat upon the pinnacle of the pole. The circle of wood, a water-bent hickory sapling, could be moved around the posts of the platform and had been so moved so that the only empty space between the pegs was along a line that pointed to the coming sunrise.

Fire Wolf snapped off the end of the stick he had carved.

Below his position he heard the drumfish and the people blending into a single long plea to the sun, but he was concentrated on the light appearing just as it should over the shoulder of God's Hill. Still, Fire Wolf was young, and no matter how often this moment happened, he never ceased to wonder at it.

He placed the stick along his line of sight, and with a flint awl proceeded to bore a hole in the movable rail of his little platform, into which he inserted the daystick. The wood was old and heavily polished with bear grease. Still, it was silvered by the weather it had endured up on this pole for the same number of days as the pegs in its holes. It was highly satisfying to him to look around at the circle of 365 sticks, each carved with some animal's head the way he had been taught by the old daykeeper. This was Fire Wolf's third time marking the winter solstice sunrise. He removed the flat wooden slab from his robe and took the tip he had broken from the daystick, which he had been safekeeping between his teeth. He put the peg tip into a hole already bored into the grain, and by tens he counted the pegs in their neatly ranked holes.

The high priest had insisted he bore the hole and not wait for the sun's appearance this morning, which was the traditional thing to do. Fire Wolf and the other priests had obeyed Panther when preparing their personal boards. But Fire Wolf resisted putting the hole in the hickory circle until this moment. He felt somehow that the old master would not have approved such revisionism in the ritual.

Tomorrow Fire Wolf would go out and find the right two-year-old hickory to sacrifice for a new circle, which he would patiently bend and lovingly shape, drying it with the heat of his own hands and withying it around a mortise and tendon joint. The hickory circle had been the invention of the old daykeeper who had been alive when the first cycle began back in the days of the ancestors. Fire Wolf was joyous and awed that he was carrying on the tradition.

He stared at the sun.

A new great circle was begun. It was profound and simple, like the rising sun that was soon too bright. He looked away, already distracted because there was a disturbing change in the sounds coming from the people below.

Chapter 12

Fire Wolf listened to the new sound.

What had been a note of dire pleading from the assembly was turning into a more ominous communal groan as the day brightened. Now they beat small drums and rattled shell tambourines.

The combined sounds of several thousands of people swelled into a presence while in counterpoint, outside the ring of posts around this center post women and children of the city keened out in high mourning so that the human voice did not sound as this one or that one but all a single chorus of pleading children begging God not to abandon them.

Fire Wolf stared down at the throng of humming people as they surged away from his position toward the greater pyramid and the granaries on the attending mounds. Already people were pushing past the skullrack with its grim decorations, climbing the peeled log stairway of God's Hill.

The daykeeper continued his duties connected with observation but he continued to glance down to watch the crowd which was now chanting a single word—tsalu.

"Corn, corn, corn," they called, moving like something liquid across the red clay plazas.

Below his position Fire Wolf saw the priests cease their formal incantations and hurry after the human surge.

On the pinnacle of God's Hill, Turtle had completed the round dance so that the paper was totally saturated. He almost swooned as Panther in his duty as high priest drew the stiff paper through the wounds and showed it to the crippled old master of protocol, who inspected it minutely as judge of the offering, whose duty lay in making sure it was perfect with no white fiber unstained.

Heartless Singer squinted, perusing the paper with a huge

natural crystal, peering at a speck in the material, which he himself had made from cane pulp. Except for his two students, who were stationed near him as he watched the proceedings, this old man was the only one who knew the secrets of making the paper, a knowledge that came down from the ancestors. With a yellowed hoary thumbnail, he scratched at an imperfection, removing it and leaving a minute, unstained white mark on the otherwise red material.

Without comment he showed it to Panther, who was long used to the old man's rigid attention to detail.

"The maker of this paper should be whipped for imperfect workmanship," Panther commented dryly, wiping his fingers across the back of his sweating neck, the only spot on his head where he had not been painted with soot. He smudged the dampness into the dry blood so that it covered the white mark.

Heartless Singer, whose entire right side from his twisted face to his toes was contorted since birth with a withering bone sickness, made no response to Panther's jibe. His infirmity had not kept him from becoming a respected priest at Ixtulan; in fact, his physical condition lent him veneration. It would take more than the high priests' disdainful remark to disturb the old man's dignity. He held the material close to his one good eye, chewing on the inside of his withered mouth, and grudgingly but without further comment returned it delicately with crooked thumb and forefinger to Panther, who in turn laid it upon a bed of red coals. The fire was hot enough to ignite the blood-stained sheet, which evaporated in a puff of blue smoke, through which Turtle saw the sun grow more molten between his outstretched fingers.

"Blood of the sun," Heartless Singer chanted softly, joined by the whispering, respectful voices of young priests all around him.

Turtle prayed in a loud voice: "Walk with me today, Father, I beg you, as you have walked with me before."

The smoke roiled upwards, taking on a solid shape.

Panther had brought other persons' offerings: nobles, priests, warriors, who let their own blood from ears, noses, and tongues before this time on similar sheets of paper pounded for just this purpose by Heartless Singer, eldest of the speaker's clergy, who had learned the craft from the man who learned from the ancestors themselves.

Panther threw the other offerings onto the brazier. The

smoke was thickly coiled like a writhing snake. The fire made a hungry small roar.

Turtle again felt himself fainting, but the assistants were instantly at his elbows, blowing acrid smoke from the brazier into his face to keep him conscious. He felt the power of the vision serpent rising from his groin up through the houses of his spine into the zone of the heart, where the heart leapt aboard the fire serpent and dived toward the mind's eye, where he felt himself drawn like a dream sucked up through a sorcerer's straw, but awaking where there still were no shadows but where the bright disk of the sun reflected off the forehead of a handsome man from a kindred tribe dressed for the winter hunt in buckskin, his dark hair flowing loosely down his strong shoulders.

"O, Lord," Turtle cried softly when he saw this apparition.

The assistants heard Turtle utter these words while he gazed at the engrossing red sun blurred behind purple mist that hugged the river most days this winter season until noon. They peered eagerly in the direction that the miko stared but saw only the thinning coils of smoke before the smoldering disk.

It was true—only the eyes of the miko saw God, but the eyes of all others saw the miko and wondered at the conversation he carried on with someone unseen.

The handsome middle-aged warrior with sad eyes may or may not have been a chief, but he certainly was a proper man of noble lineage, who carried himself proudly and with interest directed toward the human being Mikanack M'kin Mah'kina, whose own eyes were running with sooty tears from the smoke and from devotion.

Turtle-in-the-Sun felt no pain now from the purpling wounds already closing on his much-scarred member. He had endured this rite on several principal days of his reign, often on a solstice, and on certain other occasions deemed auspicious to wandering star Bright Snake, or eclipses of the sun or moon, at least two times twenty times during his reign so that his scar tissue had the quality of glyphic script. His penis was a weighty thing as close as flesh can come to marble, indeed a venerable artifact so sculpted to display a lifetime of devotion.

And women adored him, contending among themselves for the honor of receiving seed from such a vessel. Already Turtle's sons and daughters numbered more than six tens in the several villages and Oldtown.

"Mikanack, my son," said himself whose face sometimes seemed to quiver and age; it quivered again and returned to robust manhood. He stepped from the brilliant cloud, his face shining with a sheen of sweat like an ordinary warrior who has exerted himself since rising and has the angling sun behind him, perhaps met on the trace beside the river.

"Come," the tall man said, "and tell me of the things that have happened among our people since the last time we walked together."

Turtle escorted his father the sun to the east and south on the four-tiered pyramid's highest terrace, pointing out several projects, some ongoing, some new.

Only recently they had removed the old grain sheds from where they used to stand beside the docks, where canoes from far upriver and down brought goods and laborers to contribute to this city.

Since the past few poor crops, all those unsightly, dilapidated sheds reminded everyone of the shortfall. Many neighbors had been told for the third year in a row they would get less corn than their people had worked for. Where the sheds had stood now grew a new plum orchard. The young trees stood no taller than children, bare and frail, looking too small for the surface given them with future growth in mind. Behind the fruit trees bordering Sky Blood Creek grew a tangle of blackberries like naked wire.

Closed granaries bulging with this season's corn crop drying from every rafter had been adapted closer to the miko's seat and high up on several medium-sized pyramids. Former tall cane-and-thatch temples had been used to store the corn, all of it the personal property of the miko, who would soon distribute it and other caches at other locations to all the people down on the valley floor looking up at this heightened place.

Turtle thought of the thousands of pairs of human eyes that must be watching this pinnacle. From below, the sun must be grazing the steep side. He was standing at the southeast corner so that he could not see the primary granary, which the people surrounded like a vast tide, still chanting their single cry on the other side and end of the pyramid.

The horn players slowly faded out their song that was planned to last during the entire ascension of the solar disk from first glimmer until the final lift-off from the horizon.

God stared down at the salient eastern horizon, which by a

trick of the pyramid's height did appear to be below their position, as though they were looking down from the lower reaches of heaven, through layers that divided the over from the middleworld, at the sun straining with about half his disk above the dividing line.

Turtle drew God's attention to other things, such as how there was under construction down on the next terrace a special platform to house the upcoming highest feast of the sun, the summer solstice scheduled six moons from this day.

Turtle was not surprised that Lord Sun had risen this morning, nor by the horizon point of rising, thus fulfilling the daykeepers' predictions rounding out the cycle.

"Your father shines only for his children," said Lord Sun in a humble voice, just a bent old father.

"Then what are we doing wrong?"

The sun frowned and aged a little more.

"Tell me why the corn does not grow as it used to," Turtle demanded softly.

God perused the sky. "My son North Wind grows stronger."

Turtle nodded with this information; it was his own diagnosis, that the weather itself was getting colder, the growing season milder than in his youth, odd years of too much rainfall followed by years of too little. "So," Turtle said, "there is nothing for us to do, then, but beseech your help in going to war against North Wind to change the weather."

The brilliant being, who was for now just a mortal, looked piercingly at Turtle-in-the-Sun, beaming what appeared to be love and fatherly attention upon him. "I remember you are a devout man who has offered me much—" he gestured at the brazier, where the debris of the sacrifice still smoldered.

"I have been having dreams, Lord, that I cannot interpret."

"That you cannot or will not interpret?"

Turtle felt he might pass out from the weighty stare the lordly being laid upon him.

"Yes, Lord, I am afraid," he said, casting his glance down like one of his own servants who has seen the blood of the sun. "Tell me what I must do."

"You must feed the fire," God said, his eyes ablaze, as he reached up and ripped open his shirt, then pressed his fingers against the divine flesh. The fingers mashed the skin and sunk beneath it, ripping open his chest.

"Oh, Lord . . ." Turtle felt his knees dissolving below his

thighs, the strength draining from him like sweat. When he looked up, he saw God handling a huge, throbbing red mass that glowed with a molten blue light around the edges. He did not want to look more closely at that terrible pulsing organ that God had taken from the open wound in his breast.

Turtle-in-the-Sun could see the empty cavity behind God's hands, where his great heart had been. He held it like a man holds water, with both hands, and offered it to Turtle, who almost cried out, so full of terror was his trembling body. He could see the whitish ribs and the pillow of muscle and cartilage where the heart would fit, and it, still attached to its trembling veins and arteries, glistening with the red thick essence of blood and pulsating, glowing life.

It shown so brightly that God's face was obscured.

Turtle-in-the-Sun drew himself upright, put aside the cringing he felt between his shoulder blades, and looked back into those dark eyes that were so calmly regarding him from the other side of the beating heart.

Turtle blinked, tears forming in his eyes, and God was nesting his heart back in the hollow of ribs. He tucked it neatly in the hole and patted his chest, closing the yawning cavity as though it had never been opened.

"You have already given me much, my son. Perhaps it is not for you to give more."

Hands over his own heart, pounding like a frightened animal's in the last moments of the hunt, Turtle said, "If I must, I would this moment feed my Lord."

Spontaneously, God said, "Here, my son, let me care for your wound done in my name." The holy warrior bent on one knee to wipe away a splatter of blood from Turtle's thigh. At the touch, a blend of cold and hot, Turtle felt a bolt of clean, pure pain course through his being, leaving utter relief from any unpleasant sensation. "This rod is blest and will cast many more sons upon the earth to worship my name," said God in his aspect of an ancient man resembling the old miko, then just as suddenly winked back to middle age again.

According to tradition this was supposed to be the fifth world of men created to worship God—all previous humans had been imperfect and so were destroyed or turned into stones or lower animals.

Turtle lowered his glance under heavy gratitude and thanked the supreme being for his generosity, touched by

healing grace and as grateful as a little child to its father for a
hug. "Then I will go and fight North Wind. I will meet him on
the Day of Equals. Will my father assist me or spare me that
supreme honor and let me live out the rest of the days of my
life in praise to his name?"

The father's forehead continued to glow as though he had to
work at withholding grandeur. He was silent so long that
Turtle began to get nervous and importuned an answer. "Must
I set out the great feast for you, master?"

Again the supreme being looked away, watching the gilt-
edged clouds for a while, then with loving eyes full of sadness
regarded this man, but still he did not answer.

Finally, when Turtle saw God starting to shine again, unable
as he was for long to suppress his brilliant countenance, Turtle
said, "I see that my father must leave."

"I must continue on my journey across the sky to the other
side."

"I would go with thee now, Father, and meet North Wind in
combat immediately."

God looked directly at Turtle with a faint smile.

"You must be a real man if you think you can follow me."

"Anywhere you lead, Father."

"Then you would end your days here too early, for there is
much for you to accomplish before we sit down for the grand
feast you will surely lay upon my plate."

So that is it, Turtle thought as he watched the sun stand and
stretch like a common man. That was his answer. In standing
he seemed to grow up and out until he filled all of Turtle's
wondering view and as quickly as a blink took a step that
flicked him back into heaven, his benevolently smiling young-
old face haloed by the quivering molten light at the rim of the
great disk just breaking free like a bubble of blood from the
grasp of the underworld. A knife of light already sliced it from
the dark horizon, marking the traditional end of the time of
visitation.

The gallery expelled a single long sigh as though all the
people there were connected. They had watched their miko go
about his holy conversation, pounding his chest and crying
out, walking here and there and pausing once in a while,
though none could hear what it was he said to the air or see to
whom he said it.

His wounded flesh, the headdress with a life of its own in

shivering feathers and bloody mouthpiece, his doubled, mirrored countenance, bits of copper and mica glitter and breeze-blown tassels, the coil of oily black smoke snaking up from the altar in a premeditated theatrical display of contrasting background—all illuminated in the dramatic dawn light played upon the imaginations of the witnesses; what they saw was his movement inside all the trappings of a holy dance.

Now he stood rooted but trembling like an oak, rattling the tiny copper bells sewn into his gear, staring at the sun until finally it was too bright to face any longer.

The musicians who had played through it all continued in a different rhythm as Turtle swayed against the strong arms of his helpers who sustained him. One splattered his wounds with salty water from a pottery basin depicting the sleek body of a stylized beaver diving through the water, another visual rendition of the myth of underworld adventure. This was meant to aid in healing and to close the wound more quickly.

"It was our Lord," Panther said, himself showing the victim's blood from his efficient surgery only on his hands and arms under rolled-up sleeves. He threw himself down onto the clay court, on his knees in his performance as high priest and servant before Turtle so that the miko could sit upon his back.

But Turtle did not take the human bench as he often had been forced by weakness to do in past ceremonies and instead leaned one trembling hand on Panther's shoulder, bent close to his ear and whispered hoarsely the high priest's personal name, "Yes, Istepapa, yes."

He extended his hands to be grasped by Panther, the miko's elder by a generation, so that he could rise.

Panther felt a spark between his hand and Turtle. The miko was trembling, but his eyes were clear.

Behind Panther as he stood in his sooty robes, the disk of the huge common sun, no longer any hint of that uncommon sad-eyed warrior, quivered under thick atmosphere and turned several shades lighter as it moved farther from the eastern horizon on the flat plain, the only heights of which were this pyramid and its lesser companions.

The drumfish presented their combined music even louder at the lightening of the day.

"Master . . . ?" Panther queried, disturbed by the shine in his lord's gaze.

"I know the meaning now, Panther, of five-tens-and-two."

The high priest hesitated, waiting on the miko who turned from watching the sun, and walked away from him without further explanation.

When the crimson disk paled out to a hazy, sad orange ball, broken from the horizon like a grand, slow head of thistle, Fire Wolf knew it was time to climb down from the pole with his board of pegs. He did not look down. His secret was that this was what he hated. He had been chosen for this task not only for his cleverness with numbers and remembering, but for his youthful strength. No old man could climb the high pole.

Though it was a young man's job, Fire Wolf hated it. He felt something even stronger than hate for the task of retreating down the pole upon the small slippery pegs implanted for that purpose.

What he felt was clutching fear.

Despite the rising tremble in his stomach, he took a deep breath and lowered his bare right foot to the top peg and with great care, not daring to glance at the ground so far below, began the descent.

Confident that their rituals had once again saved them from the sun's southern departure, the nobles and other guests in the gallery ambled away from their dancing ground, instruments put aside. Everyone was eager for the first meal in several days, since all had been fasting except the very old, the very young, and nursing mothers.

In traditional exuberant festivity, the city hummed below; the sky vibrated with the light and sound of renewed expectations. At least for now all appeared well in Turtle's domain, which he could feel below his position at the eastern side of the pyramid in the aftermath of the visitation as though the wide community of fields, bogs, and raised roadways were his own body, the undulations of land cut with veins and arteries of streams and branchlets; the upland forest he could just see fringing the southeast like an outflung arm reaching for something just beyond view, and the city's central precincts his own chest and abdomen, geography as anatomy with the nearer pond dug to build God's Hill vibrating love songs of drumfish like a great, puddled heart.

Turtle's heightened senses were wings on which he might soar high above his kingdom, but his mortal stomach growled. He still felt no pain at all, not even when he took a step toward one of his acolytes, who proffered a beautiful black clay cup of mint-infused water, decorated with an incised thunderbird design.

It was his first taste of water in three days, so austere was Turtle's abstinence above all the others in the city. The water ran down his neck and across his chest, where blood was drying in splotches with radiant sweat.

He drank deeply of the water, emptying the cup. He flung it back as ceremony demanded—all the pottery from this special meal would be ritually broken—killed—and saved to be buried someday with the man who turned ravenously toward the trays of food his servants had prepared for him, all thoughts of the divine absorbed by taste and smells and texture of hot corncakes, pleasantly stinging red tea, dried plums and crisp fried caterpillars.

Turtle was aware of an added hum in the drumfish song this morning, but because his head was still open to the wind, as the priests called the miko's trances, he thought that he was hearing some kind of mystic thunder.

But, strangely, Panther heard it, too; anxiety was evident on his face even through the sooty black paint and owllike white circles around his eyes when he looked back this way across the array of food and drink between them.

If any among the gallery heard the ominous thunder, none showed it as they fell upon their own meal provided by the miko's household for the two hundred guests. Servants who had finished their duties sat off to one side at their own trays and beakers; today everyone celebrated.

In isolation on his mat out on the dance field, the heartless remains having been removed from the sacrificial altar behind him, Turtle gave a long savoring glance at the beautifully prepared edibles he was about to devour.

Tradition demanded that he ravage the food to reenact an old myth about a boy who returned from a journey of ordeal through the underworld, and he was a man devoted to tradition. He began with the towering wicker-and-feather construction still on his head and shoulders, cramming corn bread down into the funnel.

Then, greasy from the fritters slightly salty from the bloody funnel, he untied, whipped off, and threw behind himself the headdress of thousands of feathers of egret, bluebird, turkey, eagle, and several kinds of duck, including the royal green-crowned mallards. That single mask was the product of hundreds of hours of gluing and sewing by the feather-workers like the mother of Five-Tens-and-Two, who had been trained since childhood for the delicate labor.

He plunged his entire head into a large stone bowl of water meant for drinking and came up sputtering, his long dark hair freed from the glued ties and encumbrances of the headdress, flying out under the shower of slung water drops, himself laughing a joyous honk of delight at being alive.

"Now—" the Turtle roared, "I want to play ball!"

A ball game was part of the ritual, but by now Panther had been informed by a scurrying relay of messengers moving a dire report from ear to tongue through the attending priests around Panther and the miko.

"Eh, master," Panther said, coughing lightly behind his fist, on his knees playing plate-servant to the miko's fast-breaking. As such he handed Turtle a steaming damp napkin on which the miko elegantly cleaned his face and fingers, though remaining nude and splattered with his own drying blood from the neck down. He would remain thus for the rest of this morning's sun ceremonies.

"Well?"

"There has been a . . . a disturbance at two of the new granaries."

"That strange sound . . ." Turtle said provocatively, cocking his head and listening as he handed the stained mulberry cloth to Panther, behind whom three assistants handed it away in a basin of warm water, and behind those six more stood waiting to whisk that away and bring on the ballplaying equipment, the padded leather stockings and belly rings, the feathered helmet of silvery moose hide, the copper-studded arm and wrist bands, all the traditional gear for the ritual game that was played down on the plaza on this day every year to celebrate an old myth about two boys who ventured into the underworld, where they outwitted the lords of darkness and saved the present fifth world for humankind.

Panther gave a subtle affirmative gesture and paused, listening along with Turtle to the crowd-buzz, the low, undulating roar of the people that combined with the drumfish song.

"Our people want their distributions before you meet with the barbarians."

Nobody had to wait until the reckoning to figure out that the crop had been short; it was well-known among the farmers and harvesters—even the barbarians knew it, and everyone speculated about how the miko would distribute the disappointing harvest.

Turtle nodded solemnly, the brightness that had earlier burned with athletic clarity in him now darkening and slowing his movements. "They know the distribution is in sacred contract." He glanced briefly at the visitor's gallery, where several chieftains from those barbarians along with several familiar others were beginning to gesture and turn toward the western precipice, where the cry of "Tsalu!" had grown louder so that even the most distanced and distracted by food and music could not miss it.

"Nevertheless, they are surrounding the granaries and demanding their first quotas of cornmeal now." He glanced toward the west, where lay the major stores beyond and below the present view. "So far the priests have not surrendered any of the caches."

The local people grew bountiful kitchen gardens of squash, beans, peppers, amaranth, various roots and tubers—everything except corn, which was for the speaker's fields alone.

Silently Turtle calculated how many men he had at each position. It did not matter, for no unit of warrior-priests could hold off a mob, though they might accomplish something with religious rhetoric or hastily crafted illusionary tricks to divert them with entertainment. The clowns might perform a pantomine of some old story that would make people laugh, or provoke a spontaneous contest or game of chance that offered an opportunity to gamble, maybe win some prize. Such performances were part of the ongoing festival and would be performed out on the plazas of the city during the next few days anyway, and the men at each site would not wait for orders to do what they must to protect the holy stores.

Thinking these things, Turtle recalled that it was the traditional time in the ritual for the reckoning.

"What do your counters say, then, Istepapa?"

The high priest shrugged and changed position; his legs were going to sleep. He picked up a prune and munched on it as he continued. "Despite the fact that we planted twice as many fields as last season, we have only a little more than last year's crop."

He did not have to remind the miko that this was the third year of deficit.

The surplus from cleared northern fields had been promised for the labor extended by a tribe of wanderers, who were only gradually taking on the way of the city. Their various proud and somewhat wild chiefs were among those the miko would host in a distributive feast after the sun turned back north—tomorrow or the next day.

The feast would openly announce the cornmeal quotas for the next twelve moons for more than fifty bands, tribes, clans, and nations within a radius of two-days travel from this city, as well as seedcorn for this principality and its vassal communities.

Panther removed one of several flat leather satchels slung over his shoulders and flipped open the flap. From inside he withdrew small tied bundles of exquisitely carved cedar sticks, all representing woodland animals and local water creatures. He laid these down in a quick alignment of groups. Some were wrapped with fine colored threads or gut line that held small beads of copper, pearl, or shell, each denoting a certain hoard of the precious edible gold. The sticks, weighted with implication and well oiled with much use, clacked with larger sounds than mere size. With these he communicated to Turtle their exact accounts of at least ten varieties of seed and trade corn—red, blue, small-eared and long, white, pop, sweet and salty, hard and soft—stored here and at three other primary centers awaiting the distribution.

In another line he laid out a different species of carved sticks, these with two heads dyed various colors, each representing a certain kind of good given in trade to the miko over his many seasons—raw or worked flint, pearls and other kinds of beads, peltries, mulled clay or firewood, salt, tobacco, fish, fungi for food and medicine and other dried perishables. There were more than a dozen sticks representing tobacco in vast quantities.

Another wealth of sticks represented huge stores of salt from three wells and a rock-salt mine that kept a hundred bearers bent under trumplines all controlled by priests of Ixtulan under the miko's name. Also represented were other more rare imports like mica from the far east, copper from the Great Lakes, and flint from the rugged southern mountains where grew the finest orange wood for bows.

Still another type of cedar carving of a miniature human hand meant labor already used or in reserve. These were the miko's debts, and there were many more of them, set out in patterns that represented various other communities, than there were sticks representing the corn crop. Looking at all those little hands with palms up as though begging, Turtle could almost hear them clapping like the people down below, clapping and stamping for their demands, louder and louder so that they could no longer be ignored as the two men conducted their cool arithmetic.

But, Panther had noticed, there were no fifty-twos lurking in these calculations. He watched the miko, thinking that was what he was looking for. *What had that number said to him?* the priest wondered.

Turtle perused the ledger in sticks on the smooth, hard clay surface of his high throne. He leaned over, mulling its myriad details, such as how many of each denomination of basket or clay jug, then with a discriminating, well-manicured forefinger parceled out the corn symbols into three unequal piles, which represented what would stay in the royal store, what would go to the local people, the principal laborers in the fields, and what would go to the trading partners whose representatives mingled with the crowd below.

When the rearrangement was complete, a detailed accounting of the season, Panther nodded and sat back stiffly like a boy presenting his recitations to his teacher. The miko's proposed distribution worsened a headache that had been nagging him all morning. It would please nobody—even the miko's share was smaller than they both had gambled, for this was the final hand in the great game they played every season—would they win enough to make their labor worth it?

Panther did not relish passing the word on down the line to all concerned. There had been loud grumblings from all the councils of elders at the various locations. These old men represented older nations who had taken on the ways of the sun-worshipers within their own lifetimes. The promise had always been that Mother Maize would give a better life to them and their children than would the traditional hunting life of nomads, low dog-people, homeless wanderers ruled by the whim of seasons and the roamings of wild, unpredictable animals.

Three poor seasons had weakened what was already a

less-than-avid faith in the ways of Ixtulan, whose promises seemed empty, and whose demands were great.

"But," said Turtle, straightening, "I will tell them."

Panther was visibly relieved, though for polity's sake he might have protested, but Turtle leapt up in a single swift athletic motion, totally belying his exposed ritual injuries.

"Come with me, old friend."

The miko almost never moved about the city like an ordinary person, so it was highly untraditional for him to walk among the people during the solstice ceremony.

However, Panther did not argue with his miko because he knew Turtle had made up his mind, and the people would love this gesture. It would placate many of the older generation and would impress the youngest hotheads. Instinctively he knew the miko's unusual presence among them would calm everyone just because of its rarity if nothing else.

Sometimes Turtle donned disguises to move around in anonymity, usually as a common laborer with his own trumpline kept just for the purpose, when he wanted to know about a particular situation happening in his domain. He liked to hunt with his favorites, going out at least once each moon to take the birds that provided feathers for his many ceremonial masks. But for the most part the king stayed up on his high seat, constantly mediating with the Lord for his people.

Panther gladly grasped Turtle's proffered hand and followed him down the wide steps.

The sun was well up above the haze now, casting firmly edged shadows as the two men—one almost naked, the other in charcoal robes, both of them in the lumbering sandals with high backs laced above the ankle—crossed the terrace, where temple construction would continue after these two or three days of festival were complete. All labor ceased during this time when the most important work was calling the sun back to his duty.

The elevating sandals enforced a certain dignity, a slow, cantering, stiff-soled stride.

As they neared the edge, they could better hear the people's roar. In it one word dominated, and that was *tsalu*—corn, corn, corn.

"Mother of all, mother of all," cried a knot of chanters made up mostly of women with very young children on their backs in cradleboards, more than a hundred of them singing the old prayer, "Mother of orphans, mother of warriors, mother of sky, mother of God, Mother Earth, who gave her body for all her children, golden Mother Tsalu." It was an old, old prayer.

The skirt of the pyramid's western face was a sheer, fire-hardened red clay flank a little darker color than human flesh, uninterrupted down to the floodplain as full of people as was possible, the great bobbing flood of them compressed between the several lesser mounds where the grain was stored. The nearest of these was less than an arrow-shot away.

They did not seem to be in panic, and their surge was orderly, almost liquid from this vantage point, a slow sunwise movement around each of the granaries so that from Turtle's point of view, it was a groaning human tide washing against his sacred places that loomed up like orderly islands in the seething stream.

Turtle, standing there arms akimbo, said after a great heave of a sigh that disclosed minutely his pain and fatigue, "Let us do well what we must do."

Chapter 13

He gave Panther a quick, decisive nod with a gesture that ordered replacement of the feathered headdress, quickly fetched and slipped on with the help of several hands.

Turtle-in-the-Sun could smell the fritters he had earlier crammed down into this funnel, which ended at his mouth. He wished he had eaten more, feeling like a hollow log so great was his hunger. He pressed his tongue against the greasy inside of the device, where a shred of tortilla clung, and nibbled at it, savoring the corn taste and silently thanking God for it.

The young attendants and even the old master of protocol, Heartless Singer of the outlander nation to the northeast, already permanently bent over on his pallet—all prostrated themselves as soon as Turtle donned the heavy helmet, because it was believed the moment he put it upon his head, he became the aspect of diety that particular headdress represented.

This one had been refurbished while he ate by three women working for today's ceremonies. It memorialized the spirit of the Morning and Evening Star, the one in two who was a companion to the sun, who brought rain, who called chacs from the four corners of the world, east, south, west, and north. Nobody would be surprised if lightning sprang from the eyes behind the mica-lined orbits. Flecks of the glittery stuff littered the helmet's surface, and strips of polished copper dangled amid the flared feathers, picking out light in bright reflections.

The helmet and its towering feathered apparatus sat upon the wearer's shoulders as a sort of shoulder-pad basket that rested uncomfortably against the shoulder and under the armpits, the supports rounded and padded with fine rabbit pelts. Attached to these bridges and lying upon the breast from clavicle to nipple was a solid sheet of copper. It was polished so brightly it reflected the narrow T-shaped slit of the glittered eye opening along the bridge of the nose, and the chin strap made from the mounted bones of two human mandibles complete with yellowed teeth so that his face appeared protectively cupped in these antique ivory relics from some long-dead ancestor's face.

Mirror-like, the mica breast ornament gave Turtle the appearance of having two faces, one above and one below, with the jawbone on the exterior, a powerful doubled image when seen frontally. The long heron feathers were arrayed like a silent explosion around the faceplate with its beaklike nose that represented lightning and its gaping mouth and widening funnel, clean now of the juices of corn and men, that broadcast the wearer's voice.

As Panther tied on the helmet at its macabre chin strap, Turtle, staring straight forward so he did not have to see his image reflected in the mica panel on his chest, said, "We must give them something to see, yes? Something that they will talk about all year." He whispered, but already the megaphone effect of the mask was working, putting chills onto Panther's arms, despite his familiarity with the performance.

Panther whispered at the ear slots a few quick words that affirmed the speaker's order for music and a procession of priests to accompany him.

Quickly Turtle described what he had in mind, the way he would approach right through the crowd, which would have to peel back to let the royal progress through.

He gestured; Panther listened and turned to the others behind him with brisk directions while Turtle continued. "And by cutting across the plaza, we will be right at the stair—it will be very grand. Bring out some flints and feathers to distribute behind us."

"But consider this, master," Panther said as he gave the disturbing, roiling crowd still shouting its single note another reconnaissance. "If you go among them, you will lose your power as the highest."

Turtle scowled behind his mask, but then he saw the point of the priest's reasoning. "Then we must bring them to us. . . ." he said as he strode toward the line of descending stair that would take him to the plaza below, which was now a solid human ocean streaming toward the granaries.

Panther was relieved by this change of plans; the security of the royal person had never been in question among his beloved people; but then the beloved people had never before stormed the royal person's granaries.

Panther ran close behind his master, speaking as he followed, getting nods of affirmation from Turtle; they kept well rehearsed in various routines for different ritual occasions. The schedule of illusions decided on the run, Panther passed this information on down the line, and the sun climbed higher, losing all its rosy hue.

For a winter morning it was mild and very bright above the haze.

"And we will produce doves, yes. We will be coming out of the sunlight you see." Turtle could feel his heart pounding with excitement, as though he were preparing for certain battle or as close as the hunter can be to the quarry before the kill.

A cadre of young priests scurried to the royal mews, where the birdmaster kept his charges ever ready and in fine condition. They would have been used in several afternoon ceremonies today, anyway.

Turtle ran through a menu of magical illusions in the speaker's mystery bag, most of which he had inherited from his father and great grandfather, and some of which produced articulated wooden snakes, sparkling confetti, smoke, and fire. That was fine for an ordinary display, but for today as it was unfolding, there needed to be a sign of sustenance, something edible, at least something that could be imbibed by all.

"Tobacco—a gift of tobacco for everyone," Turtle said, recalling that he was overstocked with the herb, one of the few surpluses of his various treasures. Another, of perfect unused black flint arrowheads, was being hoarded against the speaker's eventual funeral, for which the flints would be a grave gift. "A fist of tobacco each," he added, realizing that this would wipe out his store. But this was easy to get and not in short supply from eastern tribes like the Leni Lanape or the Iroquois, who last year gave away vast amounts of it for cornmeal.

"Get your men over to the tobacco cache and begin the distribution—take a dozen warriors to guard the bearers." All the young priests wore as belts a woven trumpline made specifically for their use.

"Among the crowd?" Panther asked, hearing in the sound a threat that pulled a chill on him.

"Have the warriors accompany the distributors, who will be assisted by the tobacco guards—a fist for each man and woman in the crowd.

"And salt," Turtle added, still light-headed but thinking rapidly. "For every family, a hawk-basket of salt."

This was also a commodity he had plenty of, since it came from his own wells, where his workers crystallized it and sold it to many nations who did not enjoy so accommodating a situation. This item would have to be distributed later since it was not stored here in bulk but would have to be sent for at the upland location.

He looked ahead to see if the horn players were ready. Panther had called for them to be gathered on the first tier of steps, and there they stood, like good soldiers, their leader looking over one shoulder to see how the speaker progressed.

Behind them ranged the guests, who had moved from the gallery to stand around the northwest side of the high terrace to look down upon things. But this was too far for some of them who ran in their feathered finery down the stairs to the second terrace and across the dusty compound still under construction. Most stationed themselves along that edge to watch the speaker's performance on the main stairway.

"And when we are finished, send out the tumblers and gymnasts and the clowns, especially the clowns, to help distribute the tobacco. Make it joyous, Panther—joyous!"

Turtle in all his splendor, the voice of wonder upon him, turned to the great living carpet spread out below his feet. It seemed to be a gigantic woven mat made up of eyes, thousands of eyes. Though he had stood before the people many times, it had never been like this, with their eyes looking back in anger and fear. It was a many-eyed beast looking back at him, and it made him tremble under his glitter.

But he remembered who he was and why they were turning their faces upward toward him, their chief speaker. He was the one voice who could still them and calm them and bring them to him like a father with unruly children.

"Blood of the sun," someone, a woman to his left, called hoarsely, when she saw his mutilated flesh.

"We are proud to give to the father of us all!" Turtle called, adding a phrase that was the title of a joyous harvest song. The master raised his hands and dropped them, unleashing sounds of moose horn and shell trumpets with their variegated notes upon the wide prospect below.

So far the crowd was making too much noise with their chanted shout for tsalu, but the nearest fringes heard the call of the horns behind them. Soon a human current curled back this way as an eddy of a river wraps around a rock.

This trump was also a round like the previous ritual, so the note was sustaining and reverberated back upon itself, claiming more and more of the crowd's attention, increasing the eddy around the base of the big pyramid and centering on the wide log ramp that started there on the west face and climbed more than a hundred steps up to the highest terrace, where the speaker stepped between two wings of horn players, his feathers fluttering in the upping breeze, his glitter shining in the polished sunlight, and the music playing tricks on the ears, eyes, and minds below.

High, fluffy clouds moving behind him gave further support to the image of him lofted upwards as though floating on the streamers of color and glint surrounding him.

As though directed by the master of protocol, the wind came up, lifting the creamy white heron feathers that denoted lightning quivering behind his head, and the musicians slaved their rhythm to his pace.

He stepped down.

He raised a rod handed him by the dark-robed receding figure of Panther, who had passed orders concerning the tobacco and now moved around Mickanac like a shadow, the perfect anonymous stage assistant, always there to hand off the next conjuring device or to relieve the speaker of a spent illusion.

And on the other side of the pyramid, a steward hurried anonymously down to pass on the speaker's orders, the tobacco priests bucking the crowd that was surging around to see the big show on the western face.

The scepter blasted a small bright sphere of heat and light—a clam shell of pine tar torched with a live coal just before Turtle took it in hand. It seeped an oily black smoke that coiled up like a living serpent, causing the nearest flank of crowd to gasp in wonder and cease their cry for corn.

The mask reflected in the copper breastplate, the clasping skeletal hands, the shimmering copper spirals hanging from the mask's elongated ears, the flecks of shimmering tears that appeared to pour from the eyes—this apparition had a strong effect on the people.

The man's body below the great mask had clearly been recent venue for autosacrifice, though the ritual wounds had completely closed and were turning purple, the splatters in an almost purposeful pattern like dark red paint on his pectorals, abdomen, and thighs.

"Blood of the sun, blood of the sun," several voices chanted, and it warmed Turtle to hear them for the recognition and respect they bespoke. He was still shaken by the field of eyes, the swamp of eyes, the army of eyes all turned imploringly to him. They were putting the blame and responsibility upon his shoulders like the awful burden of the wicker headdress and the pain of the bloody ceremonies endured over the many days of his lifetime. He wanted to cry out with the weight of it all, with the remembered loneliness of being out there in front of them, the one on whom they pinned all indictment and all hope.

He took several more steps downward as tall as a man and a half in his fist-thick platform sandals, towering above those closest in the crowd. He peered through the hole of the mask—the hole itself making the sign of the most high God, the T-shaped tree of life—making eye contact with the nearest people, three young men who looked like dockmen or perhaps carpenters or even bearers of dirt fill, who had climbed the broad steps to the second terrace, where the new temple was under construction. Such would be bolder about coming up into these sacred precincts.

Several people, including women, were sprinting farther up to be stopped by the countenance of the brilliant giant who stood at the verge above them.

Already the cry of *tsalu* had diminished, replaced by a growing stillness as more and more people turned from the granary to this new center of attention. A great calm seemed to wash over the floodplain spread out below Turtle's bare toes. He was less than twenty paces from the thickest edge of the crowd, all those eyes turned in his direction, unwavering and unblinking, watching for what the magician-king would do next.

Without looking he handed back the smoldering scepter.

Panther, as sure as a shadow in his plain dark robes and charcoal-painted face, was there to relieve him of it. He stepped back out of sight away from the edge so that nothing distracted from the spectacle of the speaker who raised his arms, a clear signal to those behind him to release the doves.

The gray wings clapped upwards, drawing another admiring groan from the people, a swaying carpet stretching from these steps westward to the granary where the crowd still surged but was turning upon itself, swinging back to partake of the fresh action around the superior pyramid.

The truth was, arms up or out was the only comfortable way to wear the headdress. And to make it even less comfortable, in throwing it last time, he had broken something so that a sharp point of fractured cane nagged him between his shoulder blades. He tried to settle the thing differently, but he was too firmly tied into it to readjust it and escape the thorn that would leave a bruise on his flesh.

Allowing his upper back muscles to experience the worst of the torment in his shoulder, Turtle-in-the-Sun stretched his arms farther out, which seemed to relieve the sore spot. He stood there letting the wind ripple through his decorations, enjoying the refreshing chill breeze through his sweat, the diminishing cry of *tsalu* giving way to a looming species of silence down below.

Forty thousand people breathed in the sunlight. Their exhalation was a rare steam, like wind or river vapor.

"Our father has heard your cry," the speaker called, amplified behind his conical mask, echoing off the sides of this and the closest pyramids.

The musicians gave a good blast from the terrace above and behind him.

"A distribution for everyone of tobacco!" he called out, and the crowd responded with a cheer.

He spun them higher when he called out, "A fist for every man and woman here—"

Their cheer rose when someone cried out that there was the distributor now, and someone else cried, "Praise the speaker!"

"And over the next three days," Turtle continued, "salt, a medium-sized basket for every household."

"But what about the corn?" a woman's voice echoed shrilly from his left.

"Corn for our hungry children," another female voice called, joined by many sisters who raised their digging sticks to identify themselves as farmers from Oldtown who grew their corn in the late-afternoon shadow of the king's own house, considered very auspicious. It was this group whose husbands kept the clay sides of the pyramid in good repair—anytime of an ordinary day or night their small fires glowed, blackening and hardening repairs in the face of the high holy temple where the speaker spoke to God.

Not wanting to stir up any more cries for corn, Turtle shouted above them with his built-in bullhorn, "We will embark on a sacred journey into the underworld, where we will find the sun and escape with him to the other side!"

This was announcement of public sacrifice, held perhaps once every three years or so and only on the most solemn occasions. Instead of a heart feast within the private inner precincts of the great pyramid, the ceremony would be held in full public view upon the ballfield tomorrow morning immediately after the sun made his turn toward the north.

"But what about the distribution?" cried discordant voices from several directions.

"We want corn!" sang the chorus.

"There will be twice as much tsalu as before," Turtle cried, using the megaphone in his mask to full effect, and repeating the phrase as he pivoted around so all the crowd could hear the word itself, which was considered magic.

"We are going to grow, we will prosper, we will take down the forest itself for golden mother corn!" Turtle sang, and the people took up his last words in a chant that swelled to vibrate the teeth in his jaw.

They went wild, cheering and stamping their feet so that the roots of God's Hill itself trembled under them. Turtle had never heard such a sound before, and privately, behind his protective mask, he felt a rush of blind, cold fear. The sound was like the roar of a single huge, unruly animal, like a wolf pack at the edge of the forest. It put a chill on his arms and brought up the hackles on the back of his neck.

"Now, tsalu now—" some younger voices chanted in counterpoint, one here and there, and soon the single cry swelled until it hurt his ears. It was as if the crowd were sucking him into itself with the shattering din, and he longed to clap his hands over his ears to keep it out of his head.

He stood there unmoving except for what the wind did through his feathers and let the crowd have its own mighty groan. Finally, confronted by his startling immobility and hypnotized by his glitter, the cry died.

And when it was as silent as a field of living humans can be, he told them, "We will play a ballgame for the honor of being the journeyer."

A cry of astonishment and delight went up, for this was considered a rare opportunity for a great game of chance, gambling being a favorite pastime in this and most red nations.

"Let me play against you!" cried one of the courtiers from the balcony above him. It was Hard Walker, miko of the pyramid center just north of this place and father of the children who danced earlier. He was a renowned ball player who had participated in the ritual many times and often played Turtle for sport.

"No—let me!" called another, known by voice to the speaker as a cousin who played a heartless game.

From the lower crowd came other cries from many warriors and workmen, all of whom enjoyed the ball and chunkee games on an equal footing. There was a game almost every day, with the fishermen the current champions.

The people who flocked to the game always brought some small items of trade, a good bunch of arrowheads or finely woven baskets, which the priests collected before the play commenced. Later the winner got some of this, and even the loser in ordinary games received a bladder of crushed corn or meal.

But this was to be no ordinary afternoon's play. The loser of this game would be sacrificed upon the clay altar at the end of the playing field when the game was over.

Whoever was the opponent, Turtle had no doubt who the winner would be.

And immediately thereafter the speaker, as brother to all men, would ritually call the priests to spare the other player, who was a good sportsman. The people would cheer because the victim was almost always a local boy, and there would be wild clown dances as the clergy ritually protested. But in the end the game was stacked, and the priest would be forced by the speaker's rhetoric to bring the dead man back to life.

The resulting theater piece never failed to draw every living man, woman, child, and dog for miles around, because that is exactly what the high priest was forced to do: revive the dead man whose heart he had just cut out in full view of everyone.

Turtle's was the promise of great and soul-shaking entertainment.

Below in the throng, a vocal group of potters all demanded to play against the speaker one by one so that they as a group might be killed and resurrected. "Kill us, kill us!" they demanded.

"No, it is our turn to live again—" screamed one of the salt bearers, signified by the bright green turban on his head.

Some of the more robust women of the group threw themselves down on the steps almost touching the speaker's toes. He stepped back lest they touch the royal person as he took a long look at the sea of faces confronting him.

Among the potters was someone who appeared out of place, tattooed and dressed as a messenger from a southern nation distantly related to this one by ancient ties that went back more than six generations.

Imala'ko of the Chickasaw cast an impressed gaze upon the high king, fell to his knees, and cried out, "Lord, use me—!"

Mickanac saw that here was a fresh youngster. Judging from his physique, he was a ballplayer. And with the clan tattoos and paint of his nation on his forehead and arms, he was identified as a distant cousin on the speaker's mother's side, and therefore notable. This one would not try to lose on purpose as would many of Turtle's jaded colleagues whom he had played so many times; they were boring opponents who only wanted to participate in the theater of the moment and were cynical from having been allowed as royal favorites to die and be born again more than once in the past.

This one would truly fight to the death, because he was a country boy who truly believed in the ultimate sacrifice and how one could rise again immediately afterwards and have a second life.

Dispatching him would be fine sport, Turtle surmised as he looked him over, sizing up the honorable opponent before the match.

"Rise," he commanded through the funnel, a hoarse stage whisper that could be heard in the second ranks.

The startled young man looked up with fear in his eyes, but the speaker himself reached out and touched his shoulder, so he got to his feet.

Turtle took his unresisting wrist and threw both their arms upward over their heads, uniting them in a sort of brotherhood and broadcasting his fine musical voice. "This is the one we will fight. The loser of the contest will take the journey to the underworld."

It had been more than five years since the great sacrifice was performed before all the people. The last time three warriors had had their hearts ripped out after a terrible flood that swept away hundreds of people in three villages and destroyed more than half that season's crop.

The crowd roared a ringing cheer as the speaker drew the bedazzled Imala'ko with him up into the sacred heights.

When he saw Panther, he caught up with him and pushed the Chickasaw into his hands, saying, "Prepare him."

Panther gestured to two warriors and briefly instructed them to deal with the young man, who appeared too dazed to move.

Panther saw Turtle striding toward his quarters and called after him, "But, lord, the council meeting—"

"They have had their council meeting," Turtle said over his shoulder, not interrupting his headlong movement toward his quarters, longing to be alone and quiet to think of all that had happened as well as the words of God. He knew now what he would do—all signs pointed to it—but wished to contemplate exactly how he would announce his great sacrifice.

"But, sir, they demand to speak with you about the distribution."

"You speak with them," Turtle said, having shed almost all the ceremonial garb. He saw the cricket boy standing to one side holding his little jug and knew he had brought an offering for Sukse-and-Sohe. The child looked older now that he had been in the high priest's service for a while. He stood very seriously, watching the miko approach.

Turtle-in-the-Sun waved to him, and the lad hurried out to walk the rest of the way with his father.

"I thought you were not going to feed them today," he said, looking up at Turtle with a squint.

"Do not frown so, child. Our Lord does not like to see us squint at the sight of his face."

"But his face is so bright."

Yes, Turtle thought, hand on the boy's shoulder. He felt him draw back when he saw Panther approach in dark swishing robes. Turtle saw fear trace the child's eyes and wondered why.

"Master, if you would only speak to them, just for a moment," the high priest was saying, ignoring the boy who was trying to stay on the other side of Turtle as they crossed the plaza that fronted the miko's quarters.

"Tell them that there will be a meeting next quarter, on schedule, when we shall make a great announcement."

"But, lord, I do not satisfy their demand—"

Turtle-in-the-Sun let himself through the doorway, hand still on Five-Tens-and-Two's shoulder, leaving Panther standing in the brilliant sunlight in frustration. He stared at the trembling door flap for a moment before turning toward the great chamber and the waiting council.

They were eating their feast, even grander today for the grand ceremony just performed, and abuzz with critique of it as Panther entered their midst, his mind distracted with what Turtle-in-the-Sun was planning; the miko had given his high priest no hint of the grand announcement. Not used to being ignorant of the miko's moves, Panther gathered his thoughts in preparation for confronting these quarrelsome old men, who were not going to be satisfied with what he must tell them.

"Priest!" Buffalo Eagle called in a friendly tone when Panther tried to slip in without being seen, hoping to sit among them to one side and judge their temperament. By the sound they seemed pleased with the sacrifice—the dead priest's relatives were conspicuously absent, all except Buffalo Eagle, who as chief councillor for Oldtown had never missed a council meeting in all the time Panther had known him, which was all of Panther's tenure as high priest.

The assembly shouted praise and slapped their hands against the floor to indicate approval of his performance today.

Panther, used to being the shadow and not the central figure in ritual, rose and bowed his head, taking their accolades modestly before assuming the speaker's position before them on the raised platform, hoping that this would force them into accepting his authority. He felt swelled up by this position, looking down upon them all: *This is my rightful place,* he heard his own voice say inside his head, but fleetingly as he suppressed the thought lest it put a suspicious mask of pleasure upon his face that these canny old men would see.

"Esteemed elders," Panther said, hand raised to quell their

applause, which had an ominous rumble to it even amid the praise. "You do me too much honor, for it is not I but Our Lord who makes the day."

"Our Lord and our lord," quipped Buffalo Eagle, and the others agreed with another cheer, but already Panther was shaking his head, and their cheer rumbled from high to low, with one or two of them asking already, Where was the miko?

"This has been a most unusual day, I am sure you will all agree—"

"Do not say that he will not share himself with his servants for a second time," the Oldtown bonesetter demanded, the hall ringing with the displeasure of the councillors.

"He is exhausted from the dance and must get ready for the ballgame tomorrow."

"No! This is not according to tradition—he must speak with us!" the Oldtowner said, the old men around him noisy in their demand.

"We can discuss anything you wish," Panther said, stiffening with dignity.

"We demand his presence!" another chieftain called from the ranks.

"You know my word is his," Panther said, but he gestured to a young runner, one of the boys he had personally trained, standing along the sidelines. The lad took off in the direction of the royal quarters.

"Why do you take the miko's place there, high priest?" asked Buffalo Eagle, matching Panther's dignity.

"Only the miko sits there!" someone yelled.

"You are not the miko," growled another.

Buffalo Eagle continued. "We would hear from his own mouth what he plans to do to insure a better crop this season."

They groaned agreement, the mob of them, and Panther knew the Oldtown speaker was right. Quarrels and animosities ran deeply between the household of the miko and Oldtown, whose ancestors went further back than the miko's, however illustrious the nobility claimed.

Panther stood, abandoning the high seat reserved for the miko, and spoke to them about alternatives.

The elders listened to him, then countered with the Old-towner's remarks repeated; it was traditional for the miko himself to announce these things. The elders all had the noble forehead, the only ones allowed it. This they shared with the miko, and they were due their honors.

Panther, beneath his ordinary nonnoble forehead, listened, catching the eye of the returned runner. A quick hand gesture told the high priest that the king was not disposed to answer to the council.

"You know," said the Oldtowner slowly, staring directly at the high priest, "there are many duties that fall only to the miko and no mere servant can fulfill."

This was a direct insult aimed at Panther. A flicker of fury lit up his eyes, but he kept it hidden by sighing, stretching his neck, and changing his position slightly.

But the old man caught it anyway and twisted it further. "In the old days, if we had so many bad years in a row, the miko would not send a boy to do his work. In such a time the miko himself would offer his chest to God."

The other councillors drew in loud breaths of shock and surprise at this comment, almost sacrilegious in its implications, and looked toward the high priest for his reaction as though watching a high-spirited ballgame.

"These are things too weighty to be discussed by mere servants," Panther said with purposeful self-deprecation, pointedly including the outspoken elder in the category. But he was furious with the bonesetter for having the presumption to make such a suggestion, however indirectly.

Panther stood upon the woven cane mat usually reserved for the miko and said, "I will go and get him myself. Wait here and enjoy his hospitality. Have more plums—they were very good this year."

The Oldtown speaker and several others surged forward.

"We will go with you," said the old speaker. The scalp tassels on his belt were old, but well numbered. This man had been a brave warrior in his glory days. Now he wore the war trophies to impress his clan, the entrenched families of Oldtown whose ancestors had been here before anyone else, even the Miko's revered noble ancestors from the south.

Panther bit back his fury at their impertinence but did not argue. His own warriors ranging around the chamber drew their ranks in closer and, at his gesture, formed an arrow pointing out of the building.

Together the council clambered from the hall through an

opening in the western wall, which the servants opened by rolling up a long cane matting.

The morning was splendid now, still hazy but bright and inviting with no trace of winter upon the breeze that persisted from the west.

One Reed the gardener was startled to see the entire council stamping along his paths. He unbent from his crouch to chastise one of the old men who tramped upon his herbal borders.

Panther turned to the council squinting with mostly old eyes in the bright light. "Let us select a few to go farther and not insult our miko's privacy."

The Oldtown speaker came up through the throng. "Let our miko come out into the light with us!" And the council raised its single voice in support of this suggestion.

They cast their long gaze toward the smaller attached wing of the temple where the miko lived with his women and his servants in the constantly benevolent westering light of the sun always upon his household.

They heard someone laughing inside, a high crystalline voice that must belong to a woman or a child.

Presently a woman—Simple Greenbrier with a tray of unguents—exited and looked up from her perpetually bent posture in angry surprise to see the invasion of her precincts by so many hardened old heels. Before she could react, someone inside, another woman it was revealed, began to roll up the wall of cane matting, letting the vast sunlight fill up the habitation beyond.

The council saw the miko and a little boy sitting on cane matting spread on the patterned clay floor, completely unaware that they were being observed. The miko's bare back was to the audience that leaned communally closer to watch him handle the prize two-headed snake.

The child beside him giggled, and because of his own angle and his interest in the animal in the miko's hands, he, too, was not disturbed by observance for some time.

The council had heard of this wonder. Some had even been permitted to view the two-headed snake, and all had marveled at how the miko kept it alive longer than any other such mutant they had seen or heard of. Now they saw his secret, and they marveled anew at the cleverness of their chief speaker.

He had constructed and cunningly attached by way of a miniature double leather harness two separate bonnets of bright scarlet and blue feathers from winter-birds and jays, one splendid fanning crown for each of the two heads. The little war bonnet was such that it produced a wall of bright feathers between the darting slender heads with their liquid tongues testing, ever testing the air for danger or food.

Five-Tens-and-Two held out a wriggling cricket, which the blue-hooded head snapped up while the miko gave another insect to the red. Something behind him, some movement beyond the miko's larger shoulder, caught the boy's eye. His laughter frozen, he stared at the wall of curious eyes within leathery faces beyond in the sunshine.

The miko saw the child's reaction and twisted back to see what had startled him.

He was still naked from his ordeal, still splattered with his own blood. He turned and walked out into the magnificent light, holding the snake in his right hand.

"Master," Panther started to say, but the miko raised his hand to silence him. The high priest recovered the huge sky-robe and draped it around his lord's shoulders.

Turtle looked around, catching individual glances among the elders. Drawn by the crowd, all the household servants ranged behind under the pavilion where the miko and the child had been playing. Two young warriors who served as guards of the royal person stepped into the light to stand just behind their master.

"His people hunger for the presence of their miko," said the elder from Oldtown with a slight bow of his head.

"And your miko is moved by your devotion, Buffalo Eagle," Turtle replied, barely biting back his fury at them for this unprecedented intrusion, even by as honored an intruder as his own personal bonesetter.

Panther saw Turtle's fury, and something else: Perhaps he was still open to the wind, made so by the ordeal of the butterfly dance; his eyes looked newly wild, narrowing. He was tensing up for something. Panther waited, not breathing, wondering how the miko would shock them.

"Do you think your miko does not love you?" Turtle demanded, the voice of command upon him.

It caused the councillors to shrink back, used to hearing his voice of declaration only during ceremonials.

Buffalo Eagle's dignity was ruffled by his protests that he did not wish to impugn the miko's actions, and only wished him to fulfill his duty to the council by convening it to speak of the disappointing crop and how to correct it next spring.

As though reading his mind, because Turtle did not let the Oldtowner speak his thoughts, the miko raised his arms in an evocative gesture. "All of you, listen!"

He already had their riveted attention; his call had brought out every servant, scribe, daykeeper, corn-grinder, student, and warrior in the vicinity. Even the sun himself seemed to bend lower to hear what the miko of Ixtulan had to say.

"I will show you how your miko loves you—"

Without speaking the miko swiftly unlaced the bonnets from the snake's twisting heads, letting the red and blue feathers drop to the ground.

There was a communal gasp from the councillors as the creature spun several times around itself. In a double hiss, it lashed out its dual strike. Both jaws closed on the neck of the other, and very shortly the priceless snake was twitching its last at the miko's feet.

He leaned over and picked it up by the tail, then purposefully walked with long, slow strides so that all of them could plainly see the destroyed treasure. He strolled to the sweathouse fire, where he dropped the snake upon the coals.

"The fire must be fed, brothers," he said, and they all murmured prayers of second voices. They were of sufficient rank to have heard the phrase in previous blood sacrifices, and it shocked them to hear it now.

"Do you think your miko has not heard your pleas?" he cried in a voice of command. He had a strong voice that could make babies cry when he chose to use it. "Do you think your miko can ignore the suffering of his people? Do you think your miko would give any less than the highest prize to speak on your behalf to Our Lord?" He ended this rhetorical tirade with his arms outstretched toward the sky, where the object of his address had grown whiter. Against it he was a human cross. This symbol had powerful connections in the oldest of their beliefs because it was the round of the sky quartered, and a common solar illusion of the cross within the circle.

"I will tell you how your miko loves you—come the first Day of Equals, I will offer my heart to God!"

There was a vacuum of electric silence as all ears absorbed

this startling information. They had been shocked by the sacrifice of the rare snake, and now all their surprise had been used up by this most sacred offering. Gradually a rumble of reaction started among them like a wildfire, then a growing cheer, with stamping of many feet upon the clay. The cheer subsided to the chant from many throats, "Blood of the sun, blood of the sun . . ." which did not stop for some minutes as Turtle stood there watching them accept his greatest gift.

The sun glowed upon his oiled body, the picture of fine warrior manhood. They were all proud to see him like that, their chief speaker, the best the nation had to offer, and they all bowed at their knees. Some cried out with passion to match his own, "Lord, we never doubted you!"

All the elders were shaking and as talkative as old women with the prospect of seeing this legendary performance, the first for many of the witnesses. Their gossip would draw people in from faraway rivers and the wide plains to the west, just to see the spectacle.

Panther was trembling with the news that he would officiate this most splendid and solemn of ceremonies. He had thought that it would never be his honor to take the heart of a miko and rejuvenate him, yet there was Turtle glowing like the sun already with his words still ringing in the air.

"It takes some kind of man to set that feast," the oldest among the councillors said in a tone of genuine respect. He was the chief speaker from a far northern nation on the Biggest Lake of All.

The high priest watched all this on their faces, how Turtle shamed them in this way so that they backed away from his presence, apologetic now that they had pressed him.

The snake was a marvelous gesture, Panther mused.

Turtle-in-the-Sun always knew the right thing to do, the high priest reflected as he watched the miko turn his star-clad back on the departing elders. He stood there confronting the consequences of his timely gesture, bent by unseen burdens, staring down at the smoldering remains of Red-and-Blue turning black on the coals.

He was generous that way.

Turtle was thinking, *Not only must I give the moments of my life and my blood on demand, but now I must give that which has the most value.* He looked back at the blackened serpent as though it were the work of another's hands, not something that his own inspiration had accomplished.

He longed to see his snake alive again. How beautiful its mirrored heads had been, how fine its scales in the morning light. Nobody had ever kept its like alive for so long, and now there it was, another scorched tribute to the fire.

"The fire must be fed," a commanding male voice said close to this ear.

Turtle whirled around to see who it was that spoke words from the heart of ceremony, but he was alone except for the watching eyes of the child and Panther, over there and there, too far away to have spoken so closely.

He stared upwards at the strengthening sun. "Lord?" he asked, trying to open his gaze against the glare, but it was too intense.

Panther saw the miko's confusion and was quickly there beside him, supporting him.

Turtle could not see for the upper brightness, but he felt Panther near, an arm he could always lean upon. He smelled the smoky garments and the soot upon the high priest's leathery jaw.

"Istepapa?"

"Master?"

"Did you hear it, Panther?"

The high priest watched him as the miko cocked his head and stared into the sun. He tried to pull the man back under the pavilion, reminding him that even this pale winter sun would hurt his eyes, but Turtle would not hear.

"Open to the wind," Panther murmured to a servant who moved in close when he saw the miko staring, stumbling in a small circle.

They helped him inside, where the women had medicine smoke burning in a firepit near his pallet.

Chapter 14

A large snapping turtle sunned itself on a mossy log.

This was an image of the earth inhabited by human beings, the middleworld between that of the sun's journey overhead and the lake bottom of the underworld below where each human being must pass or forever sink down into the oblivion of primal matter from which everything is created and recreated in endless cycles.

A glittering carp swam by, easily within the snapper's reach, but he was fat and just fed and too comfortable to move. The drumfish, by now finished with their royal breakfast of worms and beetles and insects pulled off the crops by children's fingers, had descended in a group to the murky bottoms to wait for another dawn, leaving the upper waters to smaller single feeders to dine upon water spiders, frogs, and minnows in the shallows.

A hawk's shadow fell across the log, but it did not bother the turtle, who had no fear inside his armor. Even if the hawk swooped and snatched him and carried him high, then dropped him in impatience when the shell could not be beaked open, the turtle would most likely bounce and roll. There was an old story to celebrate its power of survival, necessary to explain how this fifth world had made it so far.

This old veteran had been snatched before as his dented, chipped, scraped, and scarred shell attested. A heron had caught him by a foot last summer, though, and that foot was gone, but the turtle hardly noticed the loss when in the water where he chose to feed. The log was not for feeding but for delicious sunning.

The hawk passed on to easier pickings, leaving the turtle blinking in the light angled off the pond's still surface over which Mickanac skipped a smooth, flat pebble from the carefully tended path that veered off the main approach to God's Hill above, where he walked that afternoon with Panther.

The stone planed three, four, five times, touching the water's still surface lightly with circles of wavelets, and finally sinking near the log, washing the turtle, who slipped into the water. Turtle had always been good at the game, as he was good at ballplay; it was his skill as a stone-skipper in fact that had first drawn him to the old miko's attention. Turtle had come to the city from his native downriver hamlet to compete with hundreds of other boys in the annual skipping contest.

The two men strolled along the cane-lined bank. The air was still, breezeless, but from all quarters came the distant sounds of jubilation. The people had dispersed to their individual clan celebrations, feasts, games, and song that not only ended the long midwinter fast but enlivened each heart for the upcoming game and its promised high drama.

The central precinct was vacant. The hard-packed clay plaza between this garden and Turtle's high home had been swept clean of all the mob's tracks and litter by slaves who had retired to their various supervising clans.

Except for those in that far-off chorus, or an occasional dog bark, Turtle and Panther might have been the only two alive in the central zone.

The bare nut trees looked dead with all their fruit harvested by nimble boys who made a game of climbing. The only green was in the cedar planted along this bank of the pond.

The cattails were all blown, their tassels mere fragments stirred in the cool afternoon breeze, while overhead the sun had stepped behind a cloudy front that lent overcast to the day—not a particularly auspicious climate for the rituals in progress, since the exact point of sunset would go unnoted under haze.

It was crucial to the futurity of the solstice rites that tomorrow's sunrise be marked by Fire Wolf and his band of daykeeping technicians.

The sun at this time every year chose not only to wander far south but to pause there on the southern horizon in a stubborn hesitation step that took two, or worse, three days to begin the move back north. What if the sun kept marching south, leaving behind a wake of progressively worsening darkness? Both men had lived long enough to know the sun would return. It did so every year, but neither man had ever tested whether it would be so without their rituals and the people's calling.

Neither Turtle nor Panther bespoke the ominous lowering of the sky; each was hopefully thinking that it might rain, a good sign, because this time of year a sunset rainfall usually meant a clear, sparkling dawn and a perfect reading of tomorrow's critical sunrise point.

Panther in his renewed face paint and fresh costume of elaborate feathers was shaking his head adorned with hanks of hair tied off and chopped in at least six different hanks to indicate certain mourning rituals and brotherhood allegiances.

Turtle was dressed even less elaborately than a commoner, with no paint or feathers about his person, hair simply braided in a long quoit, and only the stitching of his mother's clan symbols in porcupine quill beads upon the collar and cuffs of his fringed elk-skin tunic, because he as king represented all the moieties and lodges of the people.

"That boy, how did he take the butterfly dance?" Turtle finally asked after they walked in silence for some time.

"He did not flinch."

"He enjoyed it?" Turtle said, disturbed that it would not do for the child to be entertained by blood sacrifice.

"Oh, no—he was horrified. But he did not look away. His mother cried and begged me not to force him, but when she saw how the child wanted to witness, she left him alone to watch."

"Good, good," Turtle said to himself.

Sniffing portents, Panther watched the miko from the corner of his eye. He had that sound in his voice again, hollow, open to the wind.

Without further introduction or civility, Turtle said softly, "Panther, we are going on a journey."

"Yes, master," Panther said solemnly, thinking that he wished to discuss the preparations for the great sacrifice he had announced. Everyone in Ixtulan was talking about it. The death and subsequent resurrection of a chief speaker was a once-in-a-lifetime event.

"Before that journey we wish to travel in this world as an ordinary man."

Lest he agree with something without knowing what it was beforehand, Panther said cautiously, "As my miko wishes."

Turtle nodded and said, "There have been complaints from the villages that the miko has not recently made a bride journey."

Every once in a while, the miko was expected to tour the dependencies and impregnate the best each had to offer to keep the royal line viable. Already Panther was thinking of the many preparations that would have to be made for the miko to embark on a tour, the ravens that would have to be sent out with the miko's intentions, and the party that must accompany such an important trip.

"We are going to do some hunting with our companions and perhaps take a look at these things the Chickasaw Imala'ko has been telling me about."

"But, master, the feast—"

"Prepare for it as you would. Until the Day of Equals approaches, we are not needed here."

"But each day the sun must be called."

Mickanac gave Panther a knowing look.

"And the daily sacrifices, master—without your noble blood Our Lord goes hungry—"

"Use your own," Turtle softly suggested.

Panther turned away to peruse the sky, distaste pursing his mouth. "I am not of the best blood, which my master knows."

Turtle squinted at him. He was well familiar with the background of his high priest, born a war slave of the wild dog-people, the Chichimechas, and sold from hand to hand until he was brought by a Chickasaw trader to Ix. Even his name denoted a wild swamp animal, and not noble lineage, which always named its children to commemorate the sun. "Well, use Moon, then. Just make sure he is drunk on pulque so he does not feel anything. And only from the earlobe, nothing more. And have women waiting as he awakens. Only in darkness, so that nobody sees him too closely."

"The aunties will know," Panther said.

"Nobody can tell us apart."

"I can tell you from him."

"Nobody else will, not if you do it properly—I plan to leave quietly, taking just a couple of canoes, our favorite warriors— let Fire Wolf join us as a reward for his excellent work."

"It is not the same."

"Moon and I have the same blood."

Panther shrugged. "If it were the same, then my master would not deceive the ladies who receive his seed."

"Moon is of the same seed as your miko."

Panther shrugged defensively, not wishing to be so impolite as to criticize his master. "Today is the darkening of moon. . . ." This was his polite way of saying that he needed to take blood. He withdrew from a sleeve of his garment the bindings of the knife. The miko did not react when he saw the sticker except to expose the palm of his right hand.

Panther was sure and quick.

Without any reaction Turtle observed the long splinter of sea-urchin spine. Panther tapped it, and the groove filled with Turtle's blood, a narrow red line as fine as a hair.

He wiped a strip of Heartless Singer's paper around the fire-hardened needle and withdrew the point from Turtle's tattooed flesh. Through all these ministrations the high priest repeated the phrase, "Blood of the sun," in a reverent whisper and kept his head down.

"Imala'ko says these white people have a big canoe that shines like the jeweled eye of Bright Snake, that they cut with metal weapons which they make by burning stones, that they burn the forests and cause streams of metal to flow from the hot earth. He says they have weapons that sing and other magic worth taking a look at."

"Burning stones?" Panther looked up and directly into his master's near gaze. The high priest knew that some of the tribes burnt black rocks from the Kantuck hills to make their hard pottery, but when he tried it once, the smoke was noxious.

"Our cousins the Natchez told him that five of their chiefs saw this with their own eyes," Turtle continued, making several fists while Panther whisked away the small sacrifice, which would be used in a ceremony connected with the rising of the star Bright Snake this evening at sunset.

Through none of this minute letting of his blood did Turtle wince or hesitate in his speech, and he continued while Panther threw himself upon the ground and kissed the miko's moccasins.

"They have white hair, and you can see through their heads to the clear sky because instead of eyes they have empty holes, and their heads are hollow, like dry gourds."

Panther stood to inspect the strand of blue beads Turtle

produced upon a strong wire of unknown grayish metal. "The
Chickasaw traded ten eagle-baskets of number-three meal for
this." The idea was that the wingspan of the bird denoted the
width and depth of the basket; the corn was coarse-grind, a
cheaper product than the fine flour half the women of Ixtulan
spent mortaring each day.

Panther's quick, methodical eye calculated there were three
tens of the astonishing blue beads, slick like polished sky from
the far, far west, and all of the consistent color of the deepest
unclouded summer. Ever in the market for suitable grave gifts
he was amassing for his master, Panther made to relieve Turtle
of them; but the miko made a fist and returned them to the
inside of his tunic by way of the loose collar.

"We will bring you more of those and the trick of making
them, because that is what the Chickasaw swears to me—these
people know how to make things. . . ."

He withdrew a knife from a hidden scabbard at his belt, a
small, sharp stiletto of bluish steel unlike anything Istepapa
had ever seen.

"Things like this."

It was a dream weapon, a thing of spirit that deserved a
personal name, so strong in medicine that it threatened to leap
from where it lay crosswise on Turtle's palm to that of
Istepapa's, wielder of knives, knower of cuts, and insatiable
collector of weapons.

Panther drew his hand back before touching the thing. This
close he could see his own reflection in his master's dark,
beautiful eyes still dilated from his earlier visionary experience, but softening now with heavier lids as he relaxed in the
cool sunlight in his private garden.

"It is unclean," Panther said, making a sign with his thumb
and forefinger that warded against the evil eye and other ill
luck, but still feeling the itch of desire to heft that weapon. He
rubbed his hands against his heavy robe made from a single
buffalo skin, slit for the head, with the fur clipped short and
facing inside against his skin.

Turtle picked up Panther's hand and placed the knife upon
it. "A solstice distribution to you, my friend."

Panther held it on his open fingers, studying the horn hilt
incised with delicate Celtic swirls of zoomorphic designs. The
single-edged blade was half again as long as his hand, but as

thin as an arrow, a sticker and slicer of awesome potential that
would pierce the thickest flesh to any heart.

"The Chickasaw tells me that the chief of these strangers also
watches the stars and counts the sun's days," Turtle said,
looking at the sky. "The Chickasaw says this man has watching
tools, an arrow that shoots the North Star."

"And I have a bag of meal from the trail where the dog ran,"
Panther commented, referring to a legend about the Milky
Way, but he was distracted by the knife. He noted as he tested
its weight that as wonderful as it appeared for meat preparation, being in fact a kitchen knife which the Chickasaw had
sharpened against a stone, it would not do for the great act
because it was so lightweight. The heart ax depended on heft
to do its job.

But beyond its possible use in his clerical duties, Panther
was thinking that more common tools might be made of such
stuff. His acres of peasants used hoes made from flint or the
buffalo pelvis. The other common farming tool was the fire-
hardened cane stick, the same as the swampmen's one- and
three-pronged arrows launched with bows or atlatls.

All these wore out, and even flint hoes dulled quickly,
though they were efficient as long as an army of flint knappers
kept at the edges.

He flipped the knife expertly into the gravelly path, embedding it to the hilt.

When he pulled it out, there was not a scratch on the blade,
and the point had not lost its prick. He was delighted to note
this as he tested it against his thumb, drawing a glimmering
drop of blood out into the sunlight.

He instantly produced a shred of Heartless Singer's precious
ceremonial paper from his costume and let it draw up the
blood. When the paper stuck to his thumb, he removed it and
placed it carefully in a small cylinder made of a hollow reed
joint, a repository for such debris, because as priest he could
not give in the grand yearly sacrifices but must weep a few
drops of blood each day for his private ceremonies.

"Tools of that metal in trade would be even more valuable
than Mother Tsalu," Turtle said softly, because it was irrever-
ent to speak of corn with any disrespect of comparison.

"Imagine the heart knife made from this metal . . ."

Panther had already done so.

"When we die," Turtle crooned in an echo of the lyrical

voice he used in sacred recitation, deep and melodious and used to giving feeling to the words spoken, "truly we die not, because we will live, we will rise, we will continue living. We will awaken. . . ."

It was traditional for Panther to join him in the last phrases, when all the congregation before a public sacrifice would recite, "We will awaken. This will make us happy."

It was the prayer they would recite after the ballgame, when the losing player gave his heart. It would be uttered by thousands of voices in unison gathered to witness the heart sacrifice, all of whom would be rewarded by seeing the young warrior resurrected before their amazed eyes.

Panther eyed the knife as if it were a snake. He whipped out a length of beaten mulberry cloth in which he wrapped the blade and stowed it away in one of his several bags and pockets. He bent and grabbed a handful of dirt from the path and, as they continued walking, rubbed his contaminated palm with it.

"Let lesser men go see what these things mean," Panther urged, but knowing that once his master made up his mind, he usually had his way. "Lord Hard Walker has been itching for a mission to accomplish. Let him go with his warriors—they will bring back these alleged whiteskins for you."

"My cousin is itching all right." Turtle snorted a chuckle. "He proved himself too ready when he stole the children's dance."

"He wants to prove himself worthy."

"Hard Walker will not be my successor, Istepapa."

The miko traditionally chose the man who would replace him. Until now the miko had played it very close and disclosed to nobody who had his blessing, and this was the first hint that Turtle opposed Panther's own favorite.

Turtle knew he had scored against Panther; now he realized why Hard Walker's children had been the only ones in the dance this morning, when there were supposed to be representative offspring of all noble contenders for the high seat.

Panther was not about to show any reaction. As high priest he was supposed to be above any influence or consideration.

"That child, Five-Tens-and-Two—did you see his tears for our beautiful Red-and-Blue?" asked Turtle. "He is just a little child, but he knew and did not cry out—he understood why we had to do it."

"Perhaps he did, but—" Panther said, doubting this, but not about to argue with Turtle in this mood.

"That child will follow me, Panther, as the next miko of Ixtulan."

Panther stood facing the miko, realizing that he was receiving hallowed orders from his lord's mouth on this casual stroll through the garden.

"You may begin his training."

"But he does not endure pain well. He is reluctant to put the knife to himself."

Turtle listened, thinking this explained why Five-Tens-and-Two was afraid of Panther. Turtle could remember fearing the high priest when he himself was a boy in the same circumstances.

"Teach him, Panther. Nobody knows better how to be miko than you—teach him all he needs to know, and use Moon's blood until the boy is ready."

"Master," Panther said obediently.

Turtle-in-the-Sun added, chuckling, "Use Lord Hard Walker's blood—he is anxious to serve as miko!"

Panther stiffened with offense.

"This is our decision, Panther. And it is our decision to make this hunting trip soon—we hear from traders that termites and ants have been seen marching in straight, long lines from the camp of these strangers."

Panther himself had heard rumors about lightning coming up out of the ground somewhere to the southeast on the banks of the Ohio.

"They say that Flint himself has come up out of the earth, where he dances about upon a smoking hill. We want to find out if this is true."

"Then send the Chickasaw—he only desires to be our servant." Panther took a step after the miko voiced each argument. "He is a distant relative and worthy of being named your ambassador. Let him take the risks of downriver travel at this dangerous time of year."

One by one Turtle tossed away the several pebbles he had picked up to skip on the water. "Your miko must see these things with his own eyes." Turtle dusted his hands. "Besides, we are traveling in our ancestor's footsteps."

His ancestors had indeed been wandering traders and exiles from other places. There was even an old word for them, *potechas,* merchant priests spreading the corn religion with a traveling show of masked dancers and legerdemain, often timed with solar or lunar eclipses to impress the gullible natives.

Panther willed any tenseness from his voice and stilled himself, continuing in an even, passionless tone. "The common people believe their miko brings up the sun each morning."

Turtle stopped their progress abruptly. "Number our days as miko, Istepapa," he commanded lightly, sending the high priest's eyes up at a calculating angle. Technically it was not his duty to have such information at hand, but the daykeeper's, and it was only in the nature of this man that he was able to do so.

"More than five hundred tens, master."

"And how many of those days did we bring up the sun?"

"Fewer, I know, but—"

"The sun brings himself."

Sometimes the high priest had substituted when the miko was traveling or hunting, or unclean from recent sex, or recuperating from infrequent injuries. Lately the miko did not often go on hunting parties and military expeditions as he had done in his youth.

"Whatever might be the benefit of letting the people have their faith, let us not forget that we only celebrate the rising of the sun, we do not bring it up, and in that a miko is no greater than any honorable man."

The old miko had been taught from birth that it was literally himself who was responsible for bringing up the sun, and he had never missed a morning from his ascension at five or so until he died in his eighties.

But this miko had come to the pyramid as a bright lad who had seen the sun come up each morning over the fields of his home village without his personal help, and his attitude about the daily ceremony was considerably less than his predecessor's. All that really mattered was that the daykeepers record the sun's progress along the horizon, using the circle of upright poles just to the west of God's Hill. All else was mere celebration.

Apparently armed with inexhaustible arguments, Panther continued. "I remind my miko that many preparations must be made before his great sacrifice."

"I will return well before the Day of Equals."

That was about two moons from today, one of the two days in the year when the sun was directly in the middle between winter's southern and summer's northern position in its horizon walk.

Panther did not have to be reminded of the urgency here, because he would be the host of the feast. It would be up to him to gather the necessary supplies, guardians, and grave gifts, not to mention the pledges from neighboring little mikos for labor to finish the sacrificial mound atop the big pyramid as well as build the burial hill. It would cost most of the fortune held in seedcorn, pearls, beaten copper, fine reflecting eastern mica, worked flint, feathers, pottery, and other treasures held by the miko in the city's granaries and storehouses.

The high priest shook his head with doubt. He would feel better if the principal player in his great drama was nearby throughout the elaborate clerical preparations.

"Along the way we will also accomplish the bride journey— my aunties have been nagging us that we are hoarding our seed."

"Yes, my master must make more sons."

"No, Panther," Turtle said steadily. "We mean to take brides to follow the miko on the long journey," Turtle said.

Until this moment Panther had assumed that Turtle was going to offer himself as the kind of sacrifice that the Chickasaw would be performing, a dramatic marvel of resurrection for the awed people. Panther expected, when he took the miko's heart on the Day of Equals, that Turtle-in-the-Sun would leap up triumphant like the young ballplayer who was even now being taught the procedures of the ritual he would undergo when he lost a sun's game to the miko.

The only one Panther expected to eviscerate was a criminal or some high-ranking captive who would provide the fresh heart for the other public ceremony. The only trip to the underworld the miko would make was the drugged trance he would assume for the dramatic dance to be performed at dawn on the Day of Equals.

"Does my miko mean that he will truly give his heart?" Panther asked, taken aback that the miko meant a real journey rather than a ritual, which would propel him into the underworld as companion to Lord Sun.

"All the signs imply it. It is the number of my years, the

number of the day, even the number of my successor."
Turtle-in-the-Sun sighed heavily and stared down at a drop
pearling where Panther had just taken blood.

Turtle did not often refer to himself in the first person; it was
strange to hear him do so in this context.

Panther experienced a rush of feeling, awe, and expectation
that brought up the hair on his neck. "Master . . ." he
whispered, trembling suddenly with the realization of what
Turtle-in-the-Sun was proposing.

"And my miko means to take five-tens-and-two women with
him?"

For an answer Turtle smiled.

Panther was chilled to see the skull beneath the skin of the
miko's cheekbones, as delighted as he was to think about
performing the highlight of his career as high priest—to take
the heart of the miko himself, not with illusion but with the
knife blade. A thrill coursed through Panther: Perhaps he
himself would have another vision in such a ceremony.

When Panther took Turtle's heart in two moons, he would
take his heart, and that would be that. He would bury his
master in a rich grave, despite his plans for distribution, and
the bearers would throw dirt upon him. He would be dead to
this world, for all his travels with the father in some other.

"It is the way of our ancestor Nine Reed," Turtle-in-the-Sun
said. The first great miko's heart sacrifice had been accompanied by such a mass wedding of death. "Would you have us do
any less?"

It was something hinterland tribes still whispered about, the
disappearance of so many of their daughters who had gone in
grand honor to wed the miko in the great city and had never
returned.

"How many girls?" Panther asked, his voice cracking with
emotion. Dared the miko to suggest more than fifty women
like those who lay down in a trench and let themselves be
covered with earth for the first miko?

"I do not wish to outdo our noble ancestor—four will be
sufficient. The Five Villages will greet us with a wide choice of
girls."

Panther nodded, calculating in his mind the implications of
the things the miko was telling him. His thoughts were
aswarm with details, a grand wedding ceremony that must

precede the great sacrifice. The Day of Equals loomed closer to him the more he contemplated his duties.

When he looked at the miko, Turtle-in-the-Sun was staring fixedly toward the eastern horizon, lost in his own thoughts about the upcoming event. "I begged our father to take me with him immediately," he said, trancelike.

Panther was embarrassed for his master, who did not seem sane, yet his insanity was producing this wonderful event, which Panther would conduct as the finest ceremony of his career. Panther looked down at the strange metallic knife in his hand. Flint and obsidian were the material of weapons for this man—metal was for bells, earspools, bracelets, and other decorations on the miko's masks.

Turtle pulled his long stare from the sky and observed his high priest handling the foreign blade as he continued speaking. "I yearn to follow him, Panther. Are you not sorry that it is I and not yourself who will have the honor?"

"Oh, master . . ." Panther said, bowing his head.

Panther's heart was pounding with excitement. There was so much to be done and so little time to do it, this already being the moon of the small snow, the Moon of the Lean Sun. Other nations called it other things, the Moon of White Moccasins, the Moon of Bones. Next was Hunger Moon, then Crow Moon—late in Crow Moon would be the Day of Equals, nine tens of days from the winter solstice they had so recently celebrated.

"And for the two or three times you will need our blood, use Afternoon Moon, as you have done in the past," Turtle said in a normal speaking voice again.

Panther drew back at this suggestion, but he made no comment on that subject other than the shift from doubtful worry to disdain upon his features. "Then there is the matter of the corn you promised the people this morning."

"We will plant the southeastern upland this spring."

Panther stopped walking and looked at Turtle, just one man to another. What the miko was proposing was to use a huge amount of labor that would have to be paid for out of the first harvest on the cleared land. First the forest would have to be removed—thousands of trees and many acres of scrub.

Turtle continued as casually as talking about a household garden. "I have in mind a use for the trees cleared from that land." He hunkered down and drew a rough sketch in the damp sand of the path, his movement startling a frog, which leapt into the pond at their right, sending a flight of ducks into the hazy air.

As he worked, the high priest framed his protest: "We already owe more than we possess, master."

Turtle-in-the-Sun might not have heard him, so engrossed was he in his work. What he was drawing was a large square to represent his pyramid with several smaller squares symbolizing the nearest companion mounds, which housed granaries or storage for other goods, about fifteen in all plus the main plaza. Around this he drew a wedge-shaped enclosure. He made the lines with swift, deep slashes that piled up sand around his finger.

If carried out, such a plan would enclose a huge open area that included the great pyramid and the entire central portion of the city.

"A wall," Panther mused.

"A wall of upright logs to protect my zone from such disturbances as we witnessed today."

Never in all the old stories told by the eldest priest or the departed miko had there been a report of the people rising up as they had this morning. On nothing but jubilation days did so many people dare approach the sacred precincts, and the experience of seeing how vulnerable the royal grounds really were had left Turtle shaken more than he wanted to disclose even to his high priest.

"That will be many tens of tens of trees."

"Yes—it is better to have two benefits than only one. We will have more cornfields and will have the material to build protection for our most precious treasures." *Not to mention the royal person,* Turtle thought to himself. He wanted to leave a protected area within Ixtulan where the future miko would not have to defend his high seat from a mob with mere rhetoric.

"This wall will cut right through Oldtown," Panther remarked. "How will we convince them to do this to their ancient homesteads?"

"We will not ask Oldtown's permission to do this, Panther." Turtle straightened over his drawing and eyed Panther, who was waiting to be told who the miko had in mind to accomplish the formidable labor.

"Lord Hard Walker will supervise this labor. You have just

told me he is itching to serve his miko. Let him supervise his men girding the trees and setting them."

Panther remarked that he wanted to see how the Old-towners took this revelation: The venerable precinct of the city had always been the traditional opponent to the men from Daughter of Ix to the north, and not only on the gaming fields. There had been traditional animosity between the two bands since the old days when the northern center had been conquered by Oldtown warriors under the leadership of the old miko.

This was a section of the city reserved for the old chiefs of the previous wandering Siouxan-speaking tribe that made up the bulk of the common people of Ixtulan. By ancient agreement they held an exclusive residential zone closest to the skirt of the big pyramid, and it was they who got the first of all distributions.

"Panther," Turtle said patiently, remembering the aggressive planter women screaming for corn as loudly as the men on the steps of the pyramid this morning, "that mess we saw today came from the Oldtown dog-lovers, and if we must do it, we will cut them in two to achieve our ends."

Panther leaned back and sighed as he studied the plan.

"Let Buffalo Eagle join us on the royal hunt," Turtle replied. "That will forestall a great deal of opposition and will answer his complaint that we do not share ourselves with him." He smiled with satisfaction at this inspiration. "He used to be quite a duck hunter in his younger days."

Panther had to admit it was a good idea, an invitation that the Oldtown chieftain could not refuse, because to be asked to hunt with the miko was the highest honor.

"We will begin burn-girding the forest immediately."

"Burn-girding?" The traditional field clearing method was to gird a circle into the bark and let the trees weaken. To wrap pine-resin-soaked twine and ignite it sped the process along so fast that the tree collapsed in a couple of days. The work required someone keeping the wrapping afire—a huge labor force for the lumbering that Turtle was suggesting.

"I want a strong wall of strong wood—not logs that have fallen into mulch."

To take so many trees so quickly would set off a lot of talk about bad fortune among the Oldtowners, who included the people's principal farmers and land supervisors. Panther remarked on this, wondering how Oldtown would react when asked to contribute the labor for such a project.

"But Istepapa . . ." Turtle whispered in a conspiratorial manner, drawing the high priest so close, Panther could smell the corn fritters on his breath and the smoke from the sacrifice in his hair, "imagine what tools made out of the blue metal could accomplish against a forest or dirt."

Panther narrowed his eyes, not surprised that his miko was thinking along the same lines as himself.

"I tell you the Chickasaw says these strangers down on the Ohio are planning to trade such blades."

But the priest was also thinking that the miko's ambitious plans would take far more corn than he possessed, for corn was the means of payment the Oldtown lumbermen would expect.

"Imagine how many forests we could remove to plant more of her grace, Mother Tsalu, if we had tools made out of this hard metal? Axes of this metal would be much faster than even burn-girding."

"But you have set the feast, master," Panther said, coming very close to stating the obvious: Turtle himself would not be around to harvest another crop, and in fact, his ashes would fertilize the planting come spring.

"Yes, and perhaps as my parting gift I can insure that neither Five-Tens-and-Two nor any other miko will ever have to set such a feast again."

"A child is not an appropriate miko. So much responsibility—"

"Our predecessor was a child miko."

"But Five-Tens-and-Two only just started the training—we do not know if he—"

Turtle put up the palm of his hand, which had the effect of silencing the high priest. "We will protect our successor."

Such foresight was disturbing to think about, so to change the subject, Panther said, "I wish that my master would reconsider letting the Chickasaw donate tomorrow—there is not enough time to prepare him."

"He is quick."

"He is an outlander who has fasted only two sunsets. He is unclean from recent sex and hunting—he has not been drinking the black drink a sufficiently long enough time for him to have a vision, and the only blood he has ever given was in warfare, a mere afterfact rather than food meant for God."

"He believes devoutly that he will die and be born again."

Panther nodded, too quiet now. He was thinking that his miko himself believed too much. He, who must deal with none of the troublesome details, had always been too involved, too eager to leap into the bliss of the dance.

"He will give me a fine fight—I wager you that blue metal knife he will last seven rounds."

"Against what?"

Turtle-in-the-Sun thought for a moment; his most precious possession—the two-headed snake—was gone. Then he remembered the etched bone and withdrew it from his belt pouch.

"This is said to have been carved by the ancestors from the south," he said, offering it for inspection.

Panther was impressed; he owned nothing so venerable.

If the Chickasaw did manage to keep the contest so close that the game could not be called, and thereby to take the miko to the seventh round, it would be the longest any player had ever stayed on the field with Turtle, who must win by three rounds at least to declare a heart sacrifice for the loser.

Panther did not want to lose the knife but could not refuse his master's wager, so reluctantly he nodded but changed the odds. "I wager he will not go nine rounds."

Turtle laughed heartily at this; he knew Panther wanted to keep that knife. The speaker would tease the high priest relentlessly about it.

Turtle leaned close and whispered, "Bring my brother to the game."

Panther looked down so Turtle would not see the disgust in his eyes. "Yes, master."

"He so loves the ballgame—it is his one joy, I think," Turtle remarked, still staring downward.

"That and hauling baskets of dirt—he was at it this morning. We had to bribe him with a girl to get him off the field," the high priest said as he looked up and back toward their trail over a low rise between the garden pond and the path that led back to God's Hill to the east and west of this position, the barrow pit where the fill dirt was being excavated one basketload at a time. Even the common carrier slaves had time off from this most menial work today, but there was Afternoon Moon going about his business as usual.

"Look—he is at it again—"

Turtle glanced in that direction where the lone figure of a naked man was walking with a saunter toward the first step of the grand stair, past a low clay platform that displayed the loaded skull rack.

Turtle squinted in the sunlight at the figure as it took the stairs two at a time, a number-two basket of dirt balanced on his head supported by his right arm.

"Such devotion," Turtle said, never failing to marvel at his brother's behavior. He had once supposed that the old miko had adopted Turtle despite the idiot twin, whom the old man took on as a dependent at the same time that Turtle came to live here. But now he knew better. The old miko liked the idiot because of this propensity for work that Moon displayed ever since he was a child unable to care for himself, never able to speak or even try to communicate. But since his first day here when he saw the dirt loaders building a pyramid, he had found his calling. Every day without rain he was out there, shoveling dirt, loading dirt, hauling dirt. In the time that his brother Turtle had been miko, Moon helped build three major pyramids and the large new platform mound where the craftsmen and women did their blessing work, the decorations on pottery and the finish work on the edges of flint.

Now he was building the small pyramid on the third terrace where the grand feast would be held on the Day of Equals.

Panther had to suppress a shudder of revulsion.

"Bring him—he deserves a treat. And Panther—" Turtle added suggestively, his long, artificially flat forehead tilted in the high priest's direction.

"Yes, master?" Panther was so solemn, his skin seemed to darken like dry dirt under rain, deepening the corrugations around his eyes and furrowing the parallel lines across his forehead like a waiting field of rich bottomland.

"Do not worry," Turtle said with more than the usual twinkle in his eye, for he felt comfortable with the laughing aspect of his own divine lord and master, "I will die for you on schedule."

His eyes glistened. In contrast to Panther's shadows, Turtle glowed. Light seemed to come from his benevolent smile.

"But," he added, still using the disturbing first person, before he turned away, "I will live, I will rise, I will continue living. I will awaken . . . and do not forget, Cat Paw, that this is supposed to make us happy."

Chapter 15

Among Turtle's most precious treasures were small items he kept in his personal quarters atop God's Hill. In a cedar box he kept things passed down from his predecessor, who told him they had belonged to their ancestors who came from the south six generations ago.

One was a series of folding panels a little larger than the hand that had pictures and signs for which even Turtle had only the haziest meanings. Turtle did not even have a word for what it was and called it simply a mystery. Opened, this amazing object was as long as four men, but he did not unfold it often because it was breaking at the edges. Some of the chalky surface of it was flaking off portions of the pictures so that they were fading and difficult to interpret anymore.

Another item in Turtle's cedar chest was a scrap of what appeared to be woven metal, said to have come from the far east where some sort of white-skinned tangletongues lived. There were other things, fragments of gold jewelry, precious stones and a long bone carved with arcane designs, a yellowed cat's jawbone three times the size of the local panthers or wildcats, and other interesting though understandable items.

But there was a thing that nobody understood, not even the old miko. It was a decaying ball wrapped in rabbit peltries and tied with wide colored cord, stored inside a capped pottery jar. When revealed inside its swathing, it was nothing but a dark mottled sphere a little larger than a human head; and in fact, where some of the dark substance had flaked away could be seen a human skull—part of the left eye orbit and jawbone hinge.

The stinking, sour stuff coating the skull and forming the ball was spongy to the touch, though Turtle refrained from touching it now because each time he did, it disintegrated more.

236

The old miko had told him that when he was a boy, more than ten tens of years ago, this ball would bounce on the playing field down below the western face of God's Hill. Back in the land of U-Cal-Petan, the ballgame was played with just such things, bouncing balls. He knew the balls had to bounce because of the legend of the Thunder Boys, who disturbed the lords of the underworld with noisy bouncing ballplay. The dark lords amid their own foul farts and vile, vaporous breath, which caused earthquakes and pestilence in the world above, invited the brothers down for a legendary game because of the disturbance caused by those balls.

But here at Ixtulan nobody knew how to make the once-bouncing substance that encrusted the skull, though many had tried. The old miko had held contests among magicians who made many attempts to duplicate the stuff that bounced the ball. For years they mixed tars and pine and the resin from many trees, clay and other minerals, but nothing they made bounced as the ancient ball was supposed to have done.

Legend had it that it was made of the sticky juice of a plant that grew only in the southern country where the sun was hotter. Other legends implied that the old balls bounced because they had been magicked by more powerful magicians than now existed.

Turtle had always longed to travel far to the south beyond the delta, where the Great River Road emptied into the salt-water called the Chichimec Sea, to go to the place called U-Cal-Petan and find plants or sorcerers or whatever it was that made bouncing balls and solve other mysteries he had inherited.

Now balls were mere copies of that allegedly bouncing orb, made out of hide stuffed with cattail fluff or some such, or made of stone smoothed and carved to roll along on an edge. Against this the players would slide sharpened cues, amassing points for various conjunctions of rod and discoidal stone.

It irritated Turtle that this was only the ghost of the game as it must have been played long ago with a ball that bounced, or perhaps was still played in the places where the ancestors were born, where he might find them living today in U-Cal-Petan.

Despite his doubt at the purity of the game, however, Turtle had become its champion. He was a methodical player, always knowing what he was going to accomplish before a game—how many points he would amass as play was launched—and he would relentlessly go after it.

But at those rare times when a heart sacrifice would be the loser's prize, he was pushed to give a good show to the people because his challengers did not want to win.

Games did not have to be thrown for him, because he was the best player in Ixtulan and all the region. Men came from far away to challenge him, and he never refused a player, so even though he was now approaching middle age, he was still the champion and everyone knew it.

He wore that confidence as he walked out under a blazing sun. Around himself and the stripped, crouching challenger, the crowd hushed, a single creature again with thousands of eyes.

The crowd stayed silent as the two men played with a copy of the ancient ball, whacking it with hickory wands. The dust rose up. The sun blurred, and Turtle again had the fleeting image of Lord Sun himself bending closer to earth to watch the game.

The young Chickasaw fought with his own kind of relentlessness, but he lost the game before he started because of his vast respect for Turtle and the sacred playing field and all the stories he had grown up on all his life—and the vaulted prize of being killed and brought to life again. To merely play the game here was enough to send honor back to his family and his entire nation.

It soured Turtle a little that the boy probably did not play as well as he must on his dusty field back home, because he was a splendid player. Turtle learned several small tricks from the youngster that day, technical perfections and finesses that indicated Imala'ko would someday develop into a champion if he stayed alive long enough and lost some of his religious awe.

In the end the Chickasaw lost to Turtle's redoubtable technique and stamina, to his goal-oriented strategies and feints—Turtle was a master of the offensive, where the Chickasaw was only a talented defender.

It also did not hurt that Turtle was destined, according to the ritual involved, to win.

The Chickasaw slumped there in the dust out in the sunlight, breathing hard and sweating, looking up at Turtle, who leaned solicitously over him in his bulky sporting equipment, the paddings and plumes that must decorate this most important game.

No longer a silent, breathing wall, the crowd around the huge plaza was screaming, the royal musicians banging on ten kinds of drums, the jugglers rattling poles of shells and cane bells, clattering, clacking, whistling, and yelling, flutists harping themselves into a sweat like a gang of puff-jawed birds.

The umpire threw the carved point-marking stones into the outfield, and the crowd incandesced.

Panther had kept his knife—it was the sixth round, and it belonged to Turtle, the third consecutive round win and the decisive stroke. Turtle had literally played the lad to the ground.

Turtle could keep the ball in dazzling play another round just for entertainment's sake, but he suddenly felt tired, utterly spent, and in need of privacy.

He gave the signal that ended the game, and the crowd informed itself like brushfire spreading out from the center. The people roared approval—they wanted the spectacle now, without drawing it out any farther.

Imala'ko took the miko's sweaty hand, pulling himself up to stand beside him as the crowd surged around them onto the field.

Turtle felt a swift bolt of fear cool his spine as the beast with many hands, the same as the beast with many eyes, caught him up, lifting him toward the sparkling sky. He had never felt afraid of the crowd before, and it took him a moment to recognize their mood and relax and let them celebrate him with this traditional gesture. They propelled him on hundreds of strong hands toward the altar set up next to the skull rack near the lower steps of the pyramid.

The sun seemed to hang closer, watching this spontaneous vote of love for their leader, which presented him to the light.

He caught a glimpse of another arm of the crowd (the same mob that yesterday threatened his granaries) cheerfully propelling the Chickasaw to the altar Panther's men had set up just below the steps, where Turtle now stood among his priests, who helped him refresh himself with beakers and basins of scented water for drinking and washing.

Others were behind him, hastily setting up a litter for him to sit upon, and a sunshade of cane boughs to keep the unseasonably strong winter sun out of his eyes.

Under his protective mask Turtle perused the screaming crowd of many faces like one red blur. His gaze stopped on one face in particular in the front line.

Whenever Turtle looked into the wide vacant face of his identical twin, he felt as if he were falling into a deep pit, a cavern. It was the reason he did not like looking into his reflected, inverted face inside the dance mask—he could see his own eyes looking back at him by staring down the base of the T-shaped opening where the mask was open over the bridge of his nose.

His brother was that reflected image, but distorted the way the mirror distorted his image. He stood to one side between two protective large young acolytes assigned to him, his well-muscled arms across his bare chest, grinning vacantly with Turtle's own face, covered with dust and grime from his occupation.

And Turtle could not help but love him, he was so like a little child, sweet and trusting and hardworking in his own baffling way.

The image nodded to itself stupidly, the mouth hanging open, drooling a little so that the only clean spot on him was below his lower lip and streaking his chin. They looked so much alike that Turtle always had a sinking feeling when he observed his twin, as though looking into placid water, or worse, looking into the mirror of his ceremonial masks. Traditionally the mothers of noble babies used devices on their cradleboards to shape their son's heads in this fashion, which was alleged to enhance intelligence as well as appearance.

So had Turtle's forehead been modified; likewise many men of certain clans and rank bore the noble forehead.

But in Afternoon Moon's case, though everything about him looked normal, something had gone wrong. His forehead above his eyebrows looked much like Turtle's, with his hair clipped short and a heavy hank hanging down the other side, obscuring his ear, tied and knotted in the fashion of the city's laborers.

The same body as Turtle's own stood with his legs spread, made a little more muscular by labor than the miko, clad only in a breechclout of rough band-woven ribbon, the same stuff that adorned the great mask Turtle had worn earlier, material that was used for all sorts of practical purposes such as the specially designed headbands that toted the burdens bearers carried on their backs.

Turtle looked away lest he make eye contact with his brother, who would wander childlike out to greet him in the middle of the ceremony if given any invitation.

Turtle looked back to see the four priests masked as the forces, or chacs who made the wind, holding the hands and ankles of the young Chickasaw, who was quivering with excitement in the shadow of the skull rack. He gave a startled little cry when he saw his erection spring upward and glanced at the miko, who towered above him like an inhuman being sparkling in the sunlight. "Forgive me, lord," cried the Chickasaw, but Turtle put a gentling hand upon his shoulder.

"It often happens, Imala'ko," he said from behind the apparatus. "Did they not tell you?"

The victim could only choke off a nervous, high laugh and let his head fall back, his chest arching up like an inviting drum, his member flailing.

"But what if I—?"

"Let it be," Turtle whispered, ready for anything.

A couple of women in the crowd shrieked, and a cheer grew, because this was a sign thought to be auspicious for fertility, and it did not happen every time—it had not happened with the thieving priest, whose heart would be put to use a second sacred time here.

Turtle shook the device on his shoulders and pulled a strap to let loose a barrage of golden corn kernels that sparkled in the sunlight as they rained down upon the thighs and stomach of the spread-out victim, covering his dancing penis, drawing a long, pleasured moan from him, and leaving him trembling and completely ready for the ceremony.

Turtle felt the weight of the apparatus he bore lift slightly as he disposed of part of the hidden burden, though there were several illusions built into the gear.

The crowd was whooping, cheering, stamping their feet upon the packed commons-ground, vibrating their chant through air and earth up through Turtle's feet and up the back of the man on the altar at the eastern side of the plaza just below the steps of God's Hill. Their chant was strong, it shook the skulls on the skull rack. From Turtle's point of view, the grinning skulls, some yellowed with age, some whiter and more recently defleshed, seemed to be chattering among themselves on their high perch—at least three dozen skulls adorned the painted poles hung with feathers, clattering shells, and long ribbons of colored banding.

Turtle began the progression around the little stage, going in the direction of the sun across heaven, singing the song that increased in rhythm with drum and flute accompaniment. As he spun, avoiding the skull rack, he caught glimpses of the victim's eyes, upside down and dilated as the man cried out for the sun to take him, now, let it be done. He begged for it, just like the old stories of the Thunder Boys in the underworld.

"Make me live again, lord, and I will serve you all of my life," the Chickasaw cried, and Turtle could tell that the young Chickasaw was truly afraid; he had heard the miko brought his victims back to life, but now, spread-eagled and tied down, the young warrior was not as sure.

Turtle stopped suddenly, the well-rehearsed musicians behind him ceasing their play so suddenly, the notes rang in the air after the music stopped.

He stared down at the sweat-glistened flesh of the young man's chest, aware of the faint traces of vein's and arteries below the skin, of the pulsating dance of the heart inside, measuring off the days of life in drumbeats.

His arms heavy with the engineered cuffs that held the secrets of his illusions, Turtle leaned over the boy and said a few loud, formal words.

The Chickasaw's belly was quivering now under the slimy semen-coated corn. "Do it, do it—let me live again!"

Turtle deployed a lever under his right armpit and flung his arms out, sending a long cane sword rocketing into the air. It was only fragile cane, but whittled to a point and fire-hardened, it was a deadly weapon.

He caught it expertly and flipped it around in a theatrical manner, turning so the nearest of the faces of the many-eyed beast could see how sharp it was. He slashed it at them, though the nearest were a good three long paces down the minor slope of the dirt platform and behind the ring of strongest warrior-priests linked arm in arm to hold back the crowd.

He flung his arms out again, and a barrage of such swords spewed outward and upward aimed directly at the richest-dressed of the spectators.

People screamed and fell back, covering babies and their

heads, but as the swords pointed down upon people's heads, they became only ribbons of corn-shuck, and the screams melted into startled laughter and a ripple of hand clapping and foot stamping.

A few warriors whooped approvingly—this was always an appreciated illusion.

With his own sticker in his hand, Turtle moved back to the altar, where the Chickasaw had descended into a muttering lament, a croon of pleading, his eyes so bleary and his voice so incoherent that Turtle knew the time was ripe for the final blow.

He swooped down upon the victim's chest to a great hushed gasp from the onlookers, a sound that rippled back from the center and included thousands who could not see what was going on but who got reports from those who could. His precise movements activated various devices under his feathers and glitter, concealed pockets and hollow canes flowing with sumac dye mixed with clay and some of the blood left over from yesterday's ceremony.

He slashed; the victim's feet trembled satisfactorily. He had been instructed to move his feet as though walking, even though his ankles would be bound. The idea was to provoke as much dramatic response in the crowd as possible, and a wiggling victim guaranteed it.

Turtle began to poke with his bare fingers around the midridge of the chest, provoking a tickled response from the victim that looked convincingly like writhing anguish from as far away as the front row.

Turtle pressed with his thumb, trying to hurt him, going for a good groan or maybe even a scream to delight the many-eyed beast. He gouged farther, staring not at the victim but down at the crowd now hysterical for blood, begging him for it.

He shook his arm bands and let loose a torrent of the crimson dye.

The audience screamed and pressed against the fence of guards linked around the altar.

He gave them more—it splashed like the Great River Road and all its tributaries down over the arched chest and over the clay altar. And when it seemed his reservoirs were dry, he yanked hard at the stubborn organ, stepping on a part of the platform under him so that the victim's chest was propelled farther upward—a dramatic effect which Turtle had perfected so that he pulled many times and each time the body under his hands would not yield its treasure.

But finally he prevailed and drew out the quivering, glistening heart with its chopped vessels like a head of snakes.

He held it up, and the crowd dissolved into sound, a many-throated roar of joyous approval. He tossed it lightly and caught it in his cupped hands streaked with the dark fluid running down his arms and across the decoration of the mask. The more the better, he thought, for the many-eyed beast, and he let loose a reserve tap of redder-than-red blood that pumped upwards when he tossed the heart.

Then he dropped it, and the crowd groaned.

Someone shrieked, and the heart wiggled. Turtle grabbed for it, but on its invisible line it leapt away from him. Panther on the sidelines made to catch it as it hopped in his direction.

The crowd cried out, catch it, catch it, and split into roaring laughter when it got away from him by jerking back toward Turtle who threw a number-one basket that just happened to be lying there over it. The basket scooted.

The crowd roared even louder as the masked dancer, with great exaggeration, crouched and leapt upon the basket, catching the heart and flinging it into a pottery jar, which he immediately capped. He turned, whirling like the Thunderbird while Panther and several other dark-robed priests surrounded the altar where the four masked chacs still held the grisly, trembling corpse spread-eagle. Turtle was momentarily distressed to see the Chickasaw raise his head in a most undeadlike manner, straining to see down his splattered chest, which was now quite blanketed with red stain.

But the crowd did not notice, or if it did, the victim's reactions might appear to be merely muscle convulsions—a man with his heart torn out would writhe a bit.

"Let him live!" some strong-voiced man called.

"Let him live," someone else joined the chant, and soon many were screaming for the Chickasaw's life, all part of the ceremony as it was performed by the ancestors.

Turtle went through a formal dance step that feinted toward the screaming spectators, who all knew the routine from past performances. Then, as though he had been convinced by their imprecations, he returned to the altar, where the four priests were trying to hold down the sacrifice.

Turtle reached out and pressed the Chickasaw's twisted face

back down, whispering all the while, "Be still!" He gestured to the right-hand chac, one of the youngest of the acolytes, but a strong, rawboned farmer's son who had never participated in public ritual before this one.

"Subdue him," the mask hissed, and the young priest grabbed Imala'ko's hair and yanked him furiously back down.

The Chickasaw was repeating something that Turtle could not make out in the din that seemed to be flowing like a flooded river over him; then he heard what sounded like, "—trick!" but by then they had his head pressed down, and all that was moving of him was his splattered torso twisting upon the altar.

Turtle was supposed to raise his arms here and turn the din into absolute silence—the crowd was rehearsed and awaited his commanding gesture for the moment they had all been waiting for. But if he did so with the Chickasaw screaming, it would do a great deal to spoil the entire effect. So instead of continuing as expected, Turtle reached down and grabbed a handful of dust from the swept border of the plaza beneath the skull rack and threw it onto the entirely too lively victim. This had the desired effect of shutting him up at least for the time required to bring him back to life.

"Keep him still!" Turtle-in-the-Sun barked at the two nearest chacs, who looked back at him with fear in their eyes—it was their duty to help the miko bring this off to the crowd's satisfaction, and if they failed, they would later pay for it. They grabbed the Chickasaw's hair. The chac on the left put his hand across the sputtering, filthy mouth and pressed as hard as possible.

Turtle turned back to his audience, which had now dissolved into a stamping, chanting, screaming animal. He threw his hands upwards, signaling them to be still, and they obeyed.

The drums rolled and the flutes on the stair blared as the miko turned back to the altar, pulling at more levers in his heavy costume, pouring several gourdfuls of water onto the sacrifice, splashing away some of the crimson paint. Ribbons sprang out from the collar of the device, yellow and red lengths of supple woven grass. He shook; he rattled, and a score of priests up on the stair began marching down with a dirgelike chant as they formed a circle around the altar.

Though not looking at it, Turtle could feel the sweating

crowd lean close behind him, trying to see more of the legendary ritual.

The marching priests stopped moving and sang out a piercing formula that called upon the sun to hear the petition of the people and give the gift of life to the miko's hands.

He brought his palms down, splat! upon the slimy tattooed flesh of the Chickasaw's chest, which knocked the breath out of him and made a dramatic sound. Turtle's aim was to hurt the fellow so badly he would stop his blasphemy.

The four chacs seemed to explode upwards—their well-rehearsed leap was as startling as the sound contrived to mark their movement.

The music clashed, and the miko turned back to the thousands of eyes all staring at him as he stepped aside, drawing the Chickasaw's hand up with his own, dragging the fellow to his feet much surprised and sputtering, feeling his chest and smearing more of the watered-down ink over his midsection.

Turtle did not relinquish the Chickasaw's hand but held him in a viselike grasp, handing him over to the priests standing nearby and whispering tightly, "Get him out of here."

They guided the Chickasaw toward the stair, his feet barely touching the hewn log of the first step.

But he was slippery with the theatrical gore and was able to wrench himself from his captors, tripping in their robes and knocking one of the chacs back to fall into the skull rack.

There was a combined gasp from the crowd as the massive structure of tied cane crumpled and crashed to the ground, sending its grim display cracking and rolling in all directions. Several skulls hit with enough force to break apart. Others tumbled all the way to the feet of the nearest spectators, pulling screams from many throats. People pushed back, trying to keep the grisly relics from touching them.

There was dust and confusion for the briefest of moments, but Panther and his well-trained guards swung into action. The high priest personally retrieved two yellowed ancestors' skulls, which careened near his feet.

"Get them back," he ordered the guards, who had broken their linked arms with the crowd's surge.

A venerable skull in each hand, Panther put his strength against a wall of flesh, pressing back at least six people who had broken through the line.

While Panther and his men wrestled with the chaos below the stair, Turtle leapt upon the steps and began singing an ancient lament, catching up voices as he went along so that soon the paean swelled with hundreds of singers.

Farther up the stair, the four chacs were still grappling with the victim. Turtle was gratified to see when he glanced back that they had him moving purposefully up to the less-public area. At the first terrace they spun him around and displayed his reddened body above the heads of the crowd, which was now throwing objects into the air—small personal items, kernels of corn, screaming, "Blood of the sun, blood of the sun!" in joyous unison.

Then quickly they dragged him off backwards toward the risers that led to the private upper terraces. The miko followed, hurrying to his aides who helped him shuck the mask.

He bolted from it, gasping for air and sweating, his body stained with the sumac juice. The man beside him had charge of the pottery jar, which held the heart from yesterday's sacrifice and had served so well for the second more public ceremony. It would now be disposed of upon the big altar up on the pinnacle.

Turtle took the steps two at a time until he caught up with the officers now dragging the Chickasaw up the stair.

Well onto the third terrace where construction was underway, the Chickasaw turned his eyes to Turtle. He was saying something that the roar of the jubilant crowd drowned out.

Turtle looked back down the steep slope of God's Hill and raised his aching arms to draw one last hurrah from his worshipers; they were satisfied. It had been one of the finest public sacrifices of his reign and would keep them talking for a long time.

But he could hear the mutters of the Chickasaw behind him and turned to confront the young man's face, twisted as it was with what he was saying, nearly spitting, "It was just a trick—you did not kill me at all—"

There was no precedent for this. Turtle had never known a victim to come away from the performance disgruntled. They left with nothing but exhilaration, many of them going on to become priests after the experience. The closest he had seen to this reaction was that of the young nobles who had gone through the ordeal too many times and developed a cynicism about it.

The priests on either of his arms yanked the Chickasaw farther along, and now Panther, who had run up the stair behind Turtle, inserted himself between them and spoke to him hoarsely.

But it did quiet up the enraged sacrifice, who was screaming now and might be heard by the noble spectators who were crowding up the final approach to the high seat.

Turtle started to speak to him again, but the Chickasaw spat, "You lied—all of you lied to the people—just a trick, a filthy, sneaking trick—"

Panther grabbed him from behind, finally silencing him. They pulled him onto the summit; from below it must look as though the man who had died was moving in his triumphant new life up into the sacred precincts with the assistance of the priests around him.

Behind them Turtle could feel the many-eyed beast down below, still watching him as he stepped more slowly upon the last step. He was unable to refrain from turning toward the crowd once more.

Below, the guards had the skull rack's treasures in a pile on the first step. Others of the burly clergy urged the crowd back beyond the immediate area surrounding the stained altar, which still others of Panther's helpers were already dismantling and hauling up the stair. Others retrieved the mask, which the mother of Five-Tens-and-Two would clean, repair, and store until another public sacrifice.

The wind came up and lifted the glittering ribbons of Turtle's remaining costume. The air smelled clean and cool, the first hint of colder weather in this warm winter season that was out of the ordinary.

Turtle was glad for the breeze; he felt he was suffocating under the device. He longed to shuck the rest of the burdening costume and take a long steambath.

He gave one last glance to the crowd, the animal of the people spread out on the plaza like a human flood, before he wearily let himself be led to his own quarters.

There he spent the rest of the day in the sweathouse, in private meditations.

PART THREE

Again, there comes an experiment with the human work . . .

—*Popul Vuh*
Maya Book of the Dawn of Life

Chapter 16

On the night of the first snow, Tumkis aborted.

She was green from days of taking in little else but the abortifacient tea harvested dry on the twig from the surrounding mintland forest, and weak from moroseness made more so by labor.

She worked at it for hours through that cold night.

Two of the men with Arrow Always Red, along with Ahoskas, had returned with his mother's body to their homeland, gone days ago by canoe with the coffin-boat in tow. In their clan there were two lodges who buried each other's dead. Green Woman's transport back to the homeland was in a high state of honor. Later her bones would rest beside those of the ancient ancestors in the temple atop his village pyramid.

In his heart he grieved for her as he knew his people would because of her healing skill. But Arrow Always Red was satisfied he had properly sent his mother off on her long journey, and that gave him comfort.

The other warriors remained as part of his war party. They threw together a quick bent-bough-and-skin lodge for themselves, so everyone on Bear Island had a snug place to wait for the Yuchi, whom they expected any moment.

Gwen, Tumkis, and Firefly were living by this time in the sweatlodge her servants had dug for Madoc. It was a warm little winter lodge, buried like a fox den into the embankment the flood had cut on Bear Island. They had depleted the cedar, hickory, and oak deadfall in the woodland that stood a day's journey back in three directions eastward from the river.

The snow covered all but the southern face of the sweatlodge where Arrow Always Red and his men had built a baffled doorway that kept out drafts and any animals who might have wandered in looking for shelter.

They subsisted on the hunt. Game was plentiful in that uninhabited country on the east bank of the Tennessee. Abundant mussels and fish kept them so well supplied they were able to smoke and jerk the surplus for the eventual northward journey they must take, perhaps in foul weather.

Arrow Always Red had known snow was headed their way out of the persistent northwest and had them working on snowshoes for days before the storm blanketed the low slopes and wide rolling valleys for miles around.

After Tumkis's long night of sorrowful labor, Arrow Always Red escorted Firefly with the small bundle of results out into the bush. He presently returned to crouch near his mistress, where he stationed himself and watched her in sleep. Firefly tried to push him out of the women's house, but he would not budge.

When Tumkis at last awoke, he turned away and wordlessly left the lodge, not returning until later when the women were all outside gathering kindling in the brilliant snow under a warm sun. The sky was a hard, cold blue marred by no cloud, no trace of storm that had dumped a dry, powdery snow above their ankles.

Munching a rolled corncake, Tumkis came outside squinting her perfect face in the harsh reflected light, placing blue footprints into the perfect whiteness.

"The One Who Breathes Above does not like for us to look at Him with that kind of face," said Arrow Always Red behind her.

Corncake poised to take another bite, the Natchez sun looked back over her shoulder, to keep from having to stare into the sun.

Arrow Always Red threw the four-point buck from his shoulders to the ground at her feet.

It was so freshly killed, the force of its landing expelled the animal's last breath, warm against her moccasin.

Using his foot, the hunter gracefully withdrew his arrow from the spot precisely behind the foreleg that marked the path to the heart. He muttered the last words of the prayer after the taking of a life, thanking the animal for its sacrifice and promising to return the favor someday when the hunter would offer his own body to the Last Embracer.

When he looked up at her, Tumkis had circled so that the sun was in his eyes.

She gave a long stare and said, "Why do you bring this fine kill to me? Take it to the fire so that Firefly can butcher it."

He placed one high moccasined foot on the deer's haunch, which still quivered with depleting life. "I am ready to take you as my wife, Lady Tumbling Water."

"I do not wish to be your wife, still, Arrow Always Red."

"It is time."

"It was not time when you first suggested it many winters ago when we were children. It remains not time now, long after we have grown up, and this will be so when we both are old and ready to walk westward."

"I say it is now time."

"This is not what I wish."

"Ah, that may well be the truth," he said with satisfaction. "But it is also the truth that it will be."

"I do not intend to take another husband," she said, drawing the big robe more closely around herself. "I intend to go home and study with my uncle to become a woman of power."

"Look," he said in a tone of respectful discussion, "when we get home, the people will hate you for losing Man Whose Weapon Sings and the tangletongue warriors who are husbands to so many Natchez wives. They will blame you for their favorite herb woman's death and laugh behind your back. Your ladyship knows this is true."

He modestly lowered his glance when he addressed her directly. "If you return without a husband, they will ridicule you and begin to doubt your power."

She stared at him.

"You know this is true, my lady," the warrior said softly and knelt before her, pressing his cheek against her moccasin. "My beautiful lady sun."

His embrace rooted her, wide-eyed and wordless. From that position he continued. "This has been true since we were children, and we both have only been waiting. You have had your wild time with the tangletongue. Now it is time for us to go home and set up a fireside together."

Still she did not reply or move.

"This is the only way for you to repair your serious mistakes and have the life that you desire." Squinting, the warrior looked up at her, the mute column of her body shrouded in the immense supple hide of the star-robe.

The fringe of wolf fur stroked her cheek in the slight but frigid breeze that rattled ice crystals on a nearby drift.

He withdrew his arms from around her and stood. His knees and moccasins were coated with a thick layer of powdery snow that his body heat pulled up from the path that bore only their footprints.

She stepped away from the hearing of her woman-servant and the white woman, with the lodge between them.

The man followed slightly behind her. "Lady Tumkis, what you have accomplished here will greatly displease your uncle, our beloved miko," he said softly behind her, pronouncing the words with formal dignity.

"You have no right to speak to me like this," she said, turning on him, bringing them both to a halt on the unmarred snowfield spiked with slender brown grasses.

He hung his head and lowered his eyes, everything about his posture bespeaking humility, a huge man hunched over to approximate her diminutive height. "I will protect you from anybody's wrath."

"Even the Unknown Woman?"

He stared at her, unable to suppress a shudder, as though he had a whiff from his own grave.

The toothed orifice of the Unknown Woman was the most obscene joke among his fellow warriors, the thing with which they insulted and frightened each other. Even pronouncing her name was unlucky. Horror stories were told to young warriors in training about the changeable nature of the old hag, who was supposed to be able to become a desirable young maiden who plotted to entice unwary men into her castrating embrace. Promises of an afterlife did not mitigate the horror of her revenges against the body which the soul must leave behind. In her ultimate manifestation, the Unknown Woman was a grave full of rotting bones hung with the tatters of a man's war jacket—meaning that even the strongest warrior would eventually succumb.

Tumkis, unsurprised by his reaction, tried to retreat more tightly into the supple cloak. She regarded the piled snow stirred by a minor whirlwind that died as suddenly as it began.

For a few seconds the forest was still, frozen under the blinding sun in a clear blue sky. Ice cracked minutely somewhere nearby. The air burned with the cold.

The river flowed on beyond them, its voice deeper in the

path it cut through the white countryside. Only a slim rind of frost clung to its banks, but the waters were thicker and sluggish with the cold.

Among the Natchez was a custom found bizarre by those who encountered this nation. There was a strict ranking of persons within each clan and village, so that a few were born aristocrats based on a genealogy that traced back to certain ancestors.

These noble suns had ultimate privilege, entry into the highest priesthoods and chieftainships, and owned wealth in slaves and resources and allegiance from all the lesser ranks. From this rank were chosen the chief speakers, but the nobles could only marry someone in a lower caste.

A male sun's children would never be suns, but only beloveds, or less, commoners.

But a female sun's children, even with the commoner husband, which tradition demanded she wed, would always be nobles of the highest degree, even though she was required to marry exclusively from the basest rank.

Arrow Always Red was an outstanding warrior of pleasing proportions and manly grace. But he was the lowest degree of commoner, not allowed to enter the sacred central zone of worship, and sometimes formally referred to as "those who do not smell pleasingly enough for the nostrils of the One Who Breathes Above."

This appellation often degenerated into simply "the stink-ards."

His parents and all of his grandparents had been commoners of the farmer class, blood unstirred by any nobility for as far back as anybody could remember in a nation that honored rememberers. He had been born in a small village not far from the Big Bend of the Tennessee River, a mountainous plateau area that stretched from that stream west to the Great River Road.

His mother had married a Natchez farmer's son, and so he grew up among the paternal family after his mother died. Because his father's village was the hometown of the district's present miko, Tumkis and he had grown up together, she as a daughter of the miko's compound, and he as the old man's servant, who was brought to his present situation as the miko's primary warrior because of his skill and luck in battle.

"I will hear no more of this talk," she said, casually spitting her last bite of corncake into the snow at his feet, as though she had bitten down on grit.

It was, however, a significant act, since any bodily fluid, especially a woman's so soon after childbirth, and especially spit, was considered unclean.

She did not look back to see the effect of this upon him, but strolled back to the lodge, carefully, because she was still sore in the pelvis and weak in the knees. She trudged with heavy boots to the snowfield, where she saw Firefly staring off into the crystalline woods full of blue shadows.

Tumkis stopped suddenly. "Where is she?" she asked, looking around for the white woman who had been testing the hickory snowshoes. Last night they had strung them with wet deer gut and left them beside the fire, but this morning they did not seem to be dry enough.

Firefly glanced nervously toward the woods, where a line of crosshatch footprints in the snow led away from camp. "I tried to stop her."

Tumkis threw a look of disdain upon Firefly and started to follow, the serving woman quick to accompany her with an excuse about how strong the white woman was.

But they were both stopped short by a raucous wild sound screeching out of the bare wood, probably a panther prowling after a night of bare pickings when the storm ran every living thing to ground.

Tumkis glared at Firefly. "I told you to make sure."

"I did—"

Tumkis raised her hand to strike but stopped when she saw Gwen coming back along the path of her single footsteps, not looking at the red women, but crooning to a small bundle held high upon her shoulder.

The thing in the bundle screamed again. It might have been what the local people called a panther, a thirty-pound wildcat that had lived among these hills longer than any red nation, and whose chilling cry sounded most human.

Tumkis and her servants all knew it was something else.

"Everything will be so fine, little one," Gwen promised, crooning to the baby, glaring at Tumkis as she pushed passed her toward the lodge.

Tumkis stared at the red, writhing, incredibly ugly infant contorting herself into a snarling cry in Gwen's arms.

The Natchez sun darkened, seething for a moment, then in

a controlled voice said to the white woman, "It was not right for you to undo what I have done."

"I did not go looking for her," Gwen said firmly, staring the Natchez woman down. "I took her to shut her up."

Tumkis bit her lip and squeezed her beautiful lips into a thin purple line against her teeth, thinking, *It should be dead by now, a mother's prerogative for the first few days of life among civilized peoples.* She had planned for its destruction within her body, aborted it, refused to name it, and ordered its immediate exposure on the snow bank.

Yet here it was, tangletongue seed still slick from birthing juices, a squealing little thing not as big as a wolf pup, small enough to be held in one hand if she were not so long, and red as a plum, a noisy, reddened, arrow-boned miniature human being with no name.

"She would not die, Tumkis. You have to accept this judgment or kill her now," Gwen said, feeling strong and inspired by things she had learned from Tumkis and other red people.

She held the naked baby out to its mother, feeling the upping of cold air from the northwest that slapped at their faces and must have stung the squalling infant still in the bloody, stiffening rabbit pelt that was meant to be her shroud.

The Natchez sun drew back. She glared at the stubborn baby clutching at the air with spindly pink arms. She had no fingernails that Tumkis could see. No eyebrows or eyelashes, not a hair on her knobby head, which appeared too long, as did all the baby's body. Long and skinny and bald.

She had never seen so ugly an infant, and that it would have the stamina to survive exposure and still be screaming was a chilling and amazing thing to think about. Momentarily Tumkis was secretly proud that a daughter of hers could be so strong, but she squelched those thoughts in herself by biting the inside of her mouth and turned away.

The warriors sworn to protect Tumkis did not share in any of this, but they watched. Though they might later make up stories about the baby who would not die, and secretly call her Fire Flint, the Survivor, they stayed on the side of their mistress in the argument.

Gwen swung by, protecting with her own body the bundle she had retrieved from the wood.

Tumkis called behind her, "You cannot do this thing."

"You cannot abandon a live child," Gwen said, turning on Tumkis. "I thought you were wise; I thought you were smart. I held you in high regard, but now I see you as you truly are."

Arrow Always Red stepped closer, but the women ignored him.

"You must not do this thing, Moon Fire. It is very bad medicine."

"How could it be good medicine to leave a baby in the snow? Look at her—she's alive—you were more than seven months pregnant, Tumkis. What did you expect?"

Again they both regarded the little spider of a creature in the tail of Gwen's robe, all bones and angles, wrinkled pink skin, with its mouth open in a born-angry scream, eyes screwed closed, ready to scream again but Gwen gave her thumb for it to suck.

The baby squirmed, trying to get her mouth on something more satisfying, and as she did, she twisted her long spine into view. Tumkis was horrified to see that she had a tail, a thick, tapering flesh splinter at the end of her backbone about as long as the last digit of her little fingers.

Feeling revulsion, for this defect alone was enough to expose a newborn, Tumkis said, "Among my people it is a mother's right for four days after a birth." Despite her personal feelings at the moment, she spoke with extreme patience, as though to a slow child. "Is this not so?" She turned a questioning stance toward her servants and asked, "How can it be that someone would interfere with a woman's duty in this?"

Firefly was nodding her head, but the soldiers just cast down their glances. It was women's business, after all. Their mistress was not often defied. They did not want Tumkis to see admiration in them for the white woman, or worse, amazement at such obstinate endurance in something so helpless.

"Barbarian," Gwen hissed in her own language, because that of Tumkis did not have a word that conveyed the same sense of judgment. The Welsh had so long ago left the nomadic lifestyle, the scruple of abandonment was unholy murder to Gwen ab Gwynedd.

"You white people have grown soft," Tumkis said, her voice gentler. "Sometimes it is necessary to not bring a child to season."

Tumkis was thinking, *These people probably do not even know how to prevent a baby—look at her, trying to save everything*. During this mentation the Natchez sun was silent, watching the white woman, who watched back, both women gazing across a chasm of differences older than time, a gap as wide or wider than the ocean Gwen had crossed to get to this place of judgment of another nation's moralities.

"You have let men make these decisions, sister. A terrible mistake," said the Natchez sun with a dire shake of her head.

"Nobody has the right to decide such a thing, not once the child is in you." Gwen hated it that tears were stinging her eyes—she could not help crying when she got angry.

The red woman only grew more still, passionless.

"Only women can decide life and death of infants. Only women must carry the children in their bodies and let them feed on the body later. Who but the mother can decide whether to carry or not, or to allow something to feed or not upon herself? If times are hard, the mother must make the decision. The good of all depends upon such serious choices."

Gwen got most of this—the words were simple enough. But the concepts behind the words were not easy for Gwen's Christian ears to hear. There was no trace of guilt or shame in Tumkis, who was acting as correctly under her scruples as Gwen was under hers.

"Look around you at the example of the animals, the leaves on the trees, which are so many the tree will sacrifice if there comes a late freeze. A mother buffalo will abandon a calf that is too weak to keep up with the herd. The rabbits will reabsorb their young if the winter is long. There are many made, but few survive, and those that do must eat other creatures to continue living."

Gwen was staring back, still clutching the debris of the Natchez sun's decisions. "Then with your own mouth you have said it—you are no better than an animal."

Tumkis looked back at her curiously, thinking, *Of course I am an animal*. What did the white woman think *she* was, a plant, a stone, or a supernatural being?

"Even the corn screams, white sister, when you tear away the kernels, which are, after all, the babies of Mother Maize herself. The oak makes many acorns, but how many grow into trees? So many babies are born, but not so many survive to take their adult names. This is the way of all things under the One Above—how can you say it should be otherwise, you who are just a puny human creature in this wide world of deep mysteries?"

"I will not abandon this baby," Gwen said, catching Tumkis's sinister calm if not all her esoteric words. Her red hair seemed to glow in the sunlight, all the more in her anger.

Tumkis held her own temples and forehead in the claws of her hands and pressed against the throbbing she felt there. "This is much more serious than the eagle, Moon Fire."

Gwen had seen no trace of her eagle since she chased it away. Involuntarily now she glanced at the hard blue sky, longing to see her orphan's wing against the light, even though Tumkis had assured her that it was good he had flown to other skies.

"A human baby is more serious than an eagle, I guess," Gwen said, taking the opposite of the Natchez woman's meaning.

Tumkis was blocking Gwen's way, shaking her head in the essence of negativity, while Arrow Always Red, the other men, and Firefly watched entranced nearby.

"I cannot let you bring her back into our fireside. You bring a curse upon us all."

Gwen looked around at the others, then at the brilliant silver woods in its coat of snow. She looked northward along the flowing of the river, and though she did not think at the moment how she would get to the mainland, she turned as though she would continue walking into the trees and water beyond. But she stopped in her tracks when Tumkis yelled after her:

"I traded this baby for your father's life."

Gwen, unsure she heard the Natchez woman's words correctly, twisted so that her body continued to protect the infant.

Tumkis continued. "I sold her to the Unknown Woman in exchange for his life." She stepped closer, closing the gap between herself and the white woman. "She was all I had to bargain with. The Unknown Woman is older than the stars— she is long barren and longs eternally to hold a little baby—she is always ready to take one that falls."

Closer still she moved.

"She does not belong to us any longer, do you understand?" A look of pain and frustration on her face, the Natchez sun was near enough to whisper, "How can I make you understand?"

Arrow Always Red was behind her, and Firefly was stepping quickly around to cut off the approach to the forest.

Near Gwen's face Tumkis said, "You must let Firefly quickly put her back so that her new mother can claim her." She could have reached out and snatched the child, but she did not.

Gwen saw that they could and would stop her. Her eyes darted between them, the red wall of flesh they each presented if Tumkis wanted it.

"I cannot let you steal this baby from the Unknown Woman, Moon Fire."

"I will meet this Unknown Woman of yours and buy this baby back."

"It cannot be undone—please—" she grabbed Gwen's arm, but the white woman spun away, making for the lodge, where heat waves warped the air above the doorway.

Arrow Always Red stepped closer, but Tumkis warned him with a look. She signaled for Firefly to continue on her snowshoes to gather wood for their fire, then she followed Gwen inside the dim, smoky lodge.

"You are wasting your time," Tumkis said when she saw Gwen over on a bedroll trying to get the baby to suck a swollen breast.

"Why?" Gwen snarled sarcastically. "Because this Unknown Woman will not allow it?"

"This must be your first baby," Tumkis said, not without gentleness. She was thinking how ignorant the white woman was.

Grudgingly Gwen nodded, settling back in a more comfortable position with the wriggling infant sharing her robe. Her breasts hurt. Now several months pregnant, she sometimes leaked a whitish fluid that was not milk, a kind of heavy tears. But at this moment, when she would put her aching nipples to work, she was dry.

"The Unknown Woman is just what we call the way we find the world: Life is very precious, Moon Fire, and must be honored. I do not take that child from you, even though I could, because I want you to see the wisdom of my words. I want you to give her back to the Unknown Woman yourself because you know I am right."

Gwen had stopped listening to the seductive, hypnotizing words in the melodic language of the Natchez. She was thinking of an old prayer by a Celtic saint: O, Mother Mary, ladder of heaven, let us not for mercy's sake be carried off by our enemies, nor let our souls be enslaved, O washer of souls, mother of orphans, mother of us all. . . .

She did not like seeing Firefly behind her mistress in the doorway, glaring at the baby as though she could harm her with a hostile look generated by evil thoughts.

"Get away," she hissed at Firefly, kicking at her with one hard-heeled moccasin.

"No, sister," Tumkis commanded softly to her servant, reaching out to touch Firefly, who scuttled around on Gwen's left with her bundle of sticks to feed the fire in the back wall of the lodge.

The sudden exquisite gentleness in the Natchez sun's manner made Gwen more leery. She hugged the grasping little mouth closer but saw there was no way she could prevail against this trio.

"You cannot make milk until you have your own baby, little sister," Tumkis said as she knelt before Gwen.

Gwen flared at her—the baby had bitten her dry, painful nipple.

Tumkis settled back on her heels, regarding Gwen dispassionately.

"Listen, white girl, we could take that baby away from you, but have it your own way. If you are crazy enough to snatch her from the old woman, then it is your responsibility. I wash my hands of you. The Unknown Woman can have you—can you hear me, Old Woman?" she called so loudly that it put chills on everyone's arms within earshot and set the baby to squalling, trying to feed at the same time on Gwen's pained flesh.

It was eerie to see Tumkis looking around, her eyes a little wild and crazy, listening to nothing but the air ringing with her own shout.

After listening to nothing for a moment, eyes rolling weirdly, she said in an exaggerated whisper, "Do you hear me? It is not I who takes back this child I traded in a fair bargain. When you come roaming up here in the middle-earth, do not vex my fireside or my mother's or the fireside of my uncle. Take out after the real thief, the kidnapper who sits before us all, there, with the evidence in her arms."

This was formal pronouncement.

Gwen could not help herself looking around to see if someone had just entered, expecting to see some bent crone scuttling in like dust. She felt the hair on her arms prickle, which had nothing to do with the draft of cold air coming in from the open lodge flap, where Arrow Always Red stood watching them with the steadiness of a rock.

Tumkis muttered some old formula that signified a tripling in the power of the words she just uttered and made other numerical attachments that were supposed to increase magical energies. Nines figured heavily in her calculations; then she gave some eights to the Unknown Woman, the ancient Filth-eater with her obscene second mouth full of ripping teeth, old Earth Devourer herself.

Tumkis shivered.

At that moment her own womb contracted in the aftermath of its exercise. The unexpected cramp doubled the Natchez sun over, and she almost lost consciousness. She felt a warm lump of afterbirth slide from between her legs and down her thighs. She quickly brushed it off and, propelling it with a quick prayer, flicked it into the flames, where it sizzled with a rich aroma.

Head between her legs, she bent over on her knees until a wave of nausea passed, leaving her faint and chill with sweat. Slowly she sat upright, clinging to sight, refusing to yield to the darkness that stole up behind her eyes, which she could feel rolling backwards.

Firefly was there, supporting her at one side. She eased her mistress down upon her bedroll and held onto her pale hand when she swooned back against the buffalo fleece. Her hands cupped her breasts, and she moaned a little with her eyes closed. Deeply in her gut she feared the Unknown Woman would eat her own body from the inside out in compensation for this stupid girl's interference.

"I will buy your milk, Tumkis."

The Natchez sun choked on a brittle laugh so that Firefly had to slap her back. Teary-eyed, she drank the water the servant offered, then, still breathless, she hissed at Gwen that she was as crazy as a snake—supposed to be the highest degree of insanity caused by sorcery.

From inside her collar Gwen took out a necklace of blue glass beads strung with her father's punched coin like a locket. The viking penny was almost pure gold, alloyed only to harden it. The light of the fire picked out the shape of the dragon of Gwynedd, Gwen's home country, whose sinuous shape was not without its significance among people like the Natchez who lived along the Mech-a-sip-i.

Bright Snake was an old legend where Tumkis came from, the morning and evening star, companion to the One Who Breathes Above himself.

"The Unknown Woman will not blame you," Gwen argued, wincing from pain. "You said it yourself. If anyone is cursed, it will be me. And your breasts hurt, admit it."

Tumkis was red in the face, still clutching her breasts as though they had rebelled against her, and her own body was her enemy.

"Think of how good it will feel to empty them," Gwen said, letting the coin and its magical beads drop onto Tumkis's lap.

Tumkis was about to say something that would have settled the matter when they heard a commotion outside. Arrow Always Red was out of the lodge but quickly reappeared, motioning to Tumkis.

Gwen was suddenly alone with the infant, who was falling asleep sucking on her fingers. Thinking about Yngvild and Snorrison's reaction to this child, Gwen pondered what she might name her since she would no doubt have to adopt this baby herself. She unwrapped the little thing and threw the stinking fur toward the exit.

Gwen was amazed to find that the infant was almost as long as a full-term baby, but not quite as bald as she first appeared. On the back of her skull there was a single tuff of dark hair.

Then she saw the little tail and touched it. It had no bone and disclosed no deformity. Other than this oddity she had no blemishes, nothing missing or wrong about her except for her odd lanky physique and brilliant color. Despite her dark hair, she was Snorrison's daughter, with big hands and feet. Even settling into sleep she looked angry.

Gwen secured the baby more closely in her clothing, using her leather apron as a kind of cradle. It was not as easy as the women back home had made it look, but she made do. She found a clean piece of rabbit fur among the women's handwork baskets and slipped it into the makeshift sling as a swaddling.

Ann was a good name, the name of her own mother long buried in the country of her fathers so far away over the shoulder of the world that Gwen doubted its continued existence.

The Hebrew form of Ann was Hannah, also a fine name, one

she had considered for her own child due in a few months should it be a girl. Hannah was the grandmother of Jesus, traditionally a Celtic woman from Brittany in France.

"Hannah?" she asked the child, who opened her eyes suddenly, very brightly, and yawned.

"So be it, then, Hannah."

Gwen stood clumsily at first, adjusting the sling so that it did not overbalance her.

So absorbed was she with the baby that Gwen did not notice when a tall red man bent over to enter. He stood with his turbaned head just brushing the ceiling of the log lodge, watching her as she fussed with the baby.

He cleared his throat when it appeared she was not going to look up and said in Cymraeg in a voice that snapped her to attention, "So, woman, you have dragged in another orphan."

Chapter 17

The charcoal mound was a perfectly circular black scar upon the pristine snowfield.

Heat waves distorted the air above the mound twice Madoc's height at its center, as big around as the big Shawnee council house over in Meadows-of-Mint, the Hundred's closest neighbors on the long, flat peninsula, called the Land Between Two Rivers, that marked the junction of the rivers Shawnee and Ohio.

About itself the mound cast a brown haze fed faithfully by an oozing miasma of thickish curdled smoke. It simmered and sighed and whistled, producing deeply guttural noises that caused the red people to avoid it scrupulously. The Shawnee shamans went so far as to circle it at a judicious distance to make verbal and signal containment sanctions against the death cries of so many trees.

Thirty cords of chestnut sticks roasted beneath the soil, and fern frond layers spread over the hump of the vaguely triangular mound, blackened now to ceramic hardness, and steaming ugly tongues of smoke issued from several vents. It was a festering, trembling thing, that charcoal mound, ready to explode into flame at any moment and destroy in one conflagration the entire store of baking charcoal. It had been cooking for two weeks but needed at least a couple more days before it was ready according to Brother Wyn, whose mound it was, though it had nearly killed him.

It was difficult not to ascribe malicious intent to it, oozing lazy sparks and stinking vapors, casting a rusty smear upon the air for many leagues up the course of the Ohio and her tributaries. As far away as the saltworks of the Siouxan-speaking Cahokia band of the Illinois up the Wabash River, the prevailing westerlies had villages talking about the smoking hill. Gossip flew with the ravens about the strange white tribe and their tree-felling activities. Runners from far-flung nations such as the Chippewa east up the Ohio, and Iroquoian-speakers even farther north and east stealthily approached the concentration of smoke, reconnoitered without announcing their presence, and returned home to verify the disturbing marvel for their chiefs.

Even buzzards came in the first day or two and circled, confusing the aromas with some kind of carrion. Now all animals and birds and even insects stayed away from the mound that smelled too much like a burning forest for any creature's comfort.

"The closest thing to hell," Wyn had coughed to Madoc last night. "Look at it crouching there, ready to suck you in, eat you up, that demon furnace."

He himself looked like some kind of hell-cooked demon. He was bleary-eyed and about to fall over, with only his hickory poking rod holding him up. Normally robust, the burly abbot was hollow-eyed, eyelashes and brows singed, lips cracked and peeling, with scabbed sores on his cheeks and on his bald tonsure where sparks bombarded him. He was a shadow, every patch of exposed skin sooty except the wrinkles around his eyes and upon his forehead where sweat washed through in pink sketches.

Last night he was forced to leap from the mound when a section of sod cracked and caved in, almost casting him into the inferno. Jumping, rolling across the muddy swath, he probably sprained an ankle. But he would not admit it and would not let Madoc have a look. He had insisted on immediately patching the yawning red hole himself, limping about like a gnome, his blackened face twisted by pain as he packed it with wet clay and thatch.

After they used up all the chestnut toppings, the Hundred's red women twice a day dragged in bales of deadfall twigs to keep the thing going. When the Shawnee learned the Hundred would soon be trading the dozens of iron knives stacked in neat piles in sand near the compound's forge and only awaiting the carbonizing process that would harden them, they also contributed many dog-pulls stacked high with the finest cedar kindling that burned intensely hot.

Stacked behind the hut was plenty of that cedar, which Wyn doled out to the fire with the more common oak and hickory.

Only after stuffing the vents at the base with fuel did he stand back and take weight off his foot.

When he started admonishing the fire with scripture, Madoc had insisted he get some sleep.

"'. . . cast them into the furnace,'" Wyn quoted, slurring his words, "'and there shall be weeping and wailing and grinding of teeth.'"

"Go to sleep, brother, before you fall over."

But Wyn insisted on mixing his New and Old Testaments:

"'Then Nebuchadnezzar jumped up and said to his counselors, Did we not cast three men bound into the midst of the furnace, and they answered yes—'"

Madoc guided Wyn limping, stumbling over his own muddy boots of various high-scraps roughly bound and tied off with rawhide. The ratty, thick things and the heavy, hooded, singed bear skin jacket gave him an even more bestial appearance. He had let his beard grow out, unbarbered for a fortnight, though he still kept the Celtic tonsure of his brotherhood, which was as much a product of baldness now as the razor. He looked back over his shoulder as he reluctantly let Madoc guide him across the clear circle of wet ground and through much-tracked snow to the three-walled hut.

"'And he saw the men walking in the fire and they were not hurt!'" He whirled on Madoc with a frightening grin, proclaiming, "'At the mouth of the burning furnace, Nebuchadnezzar shouted—Shadrach, Meshach, and Abednego, you servants of the most high God, come out of there!'"

Madoc took the bag of charcoal dust from the brother's shoulder and sat him down on the cot in the makeshift hovel thrown close enough to the mound so that the charcoal maker would not freeze while grabbing an occasional nap.

"And," Wyn continued as though describing something that only just happened before his own astonished eyes, "Shadrach, Meshach, and Abednego came out of the midst of the furnace—that heathen king proclaimed Our Lord when he saw the miracle."

"Sleep, Domme."

Staring at the mound, Wyn shook his head. "This is not the fire I am supposed to be feeding."

Madoc tried to force him to lie down, but Wyn gripped Madoc's shoulders. "I vowed to go on crusade to fight the Infidel in the kingdom of Jerusalem."

"That may be a long way off."

"Not so far, I think," Wyn said, gazing over Madoc's shoulder toward the west beyond the smoldering charcoal hill. "Come spring," he said in a tranced tone of voice, "that is where I go, and like Shadrach, Meshach, and Abednego I will proclaim the most high God before the Infidel."

"Let us first put the edge on our trade goods and replace the weapons the Cherokee took from us." Madoc sat back on his heels and forced Wyn to look at him. "I too want to take this river where it goes, Domme. I intend to find the Great River Road they say runs south into saltwater, then head home."

Wyn cocked his head. "The people will not like your leaving the Hundred."

Madoc shrugged. "I have never hidden my plans to go back. I will take as many back to Britain as we have space for aboard the *Horn*."

"If I forge your tools and weapons, do you promise to take me with you as far west as the river runs?" Wyn said in a bargain tone.

"It would be wiser for you to sail with me back to Africa, then travel by known spice routes to the Holy Land." Madoc rubbed his callused hands together; it was cold this far from the furnace. "West from here is not so sure a thing."

Wyn stared in that direction again, his eyes wild and watering from irritation and from his vision. "I know the Infidel waits for me just over that horizon. The arrow in the golden map, Madoc, that was God's sign. This time I intend to obey."

He pulled a ragged leather satchel from under the cot, unfolded the poor thing where glinted the gleam of gold. The flap fell back, revealing the shimmering object about a foot tall and a little more wide, a solid sheet of gold as thick as the little finger, like a tray from a sovereign's table, precious and pure in the humble hide pouch, and sketched with the incised lines of a map of the known world:

The clear profile of Europe with a prominent Britain above the hump of Africa, balanced across the Western Ocean with the vague outlines of what he and Madoc agreed were lands they had found here in the west, composed of Norse Vinland, legendary Celtic Vitromannaland, and this country bordered on the west by a coastline, a narrow sea, and Taprobane Island, called Ceylon by some navigators; then Cathay, then the

Mediterranean with its crown of the Holy Land. Just east of the cross marking Jerusalem was a puncture in the soft gold made by a Cherokee arrow meant for the abbot's back.

Wyn leaned over and kissed the wound in the map.

It was so tender a gesture, like the father's kiss upon his child's brow, or more, like devout lips upon scripture, that Madoc was pierced by regard for the old man. He was sorry he could not display such devotion. Madoc had never been able to show his feelings so easily, however strongly he might feel. He must express himself through action, like this moment when he could only touch the monk's shoulder.

"Soon," Wyn whispered in the voice of promise.

He did not resist when Madoc pressed him back and covered him with the buffalo fleece, muddy snowboots and all. His eyes were closed before he was down, but he sprinted up again as Madoc was walking away.

"Put on more elding only if all smoke disappears," Wyn instructed, meaning the richest mix of cedar and hickory. He tugged at Madoc's dirty sleeve. "If she gets hot, do not wait to call me."

He let himself be led back, buffalo fleece trailing in the mud. After he genuflected before a rough cross of bent twigs hanging above the cot, Madoc tucked him in again with assurances that he had watched the master closely enough to manage the flickering mound.

Now the brother was bound in deep slumber over in the lean-to, sleeping for the first full night since he lit the stack two weeks ago, finally relinquishing the fickle hill to Madoc, who kept vigil all night long for signs of a blowup.

It was the most awful, dirty, unforgiving watch Madoc had ever pulled, and he hated it with all his heart, that hell-mouth mound of sparks, stench, and overcooked sod.

But he also loved it, cherished it with all his attention, staring for hours as though it were a sleeping, troubled lover. They had the forge going over in the main compound a quarter mile away. Brother Andrew and two assistants were banging out instruments. Even now Madoc could hear their clanging as a steady beat that did not abate during daylight hours.

They kept the forge fire hot enough, under a more normal halo of bluish oak-smoke, to cook limonite into bog-iron bloom, while every able-bodied man who was not hunting or taking his shift with Fair Beard on the ship worked to furnish oak and hickory fuel for that hungry fire. Still, all they had was soft ingots and slugs not nearly hard enough for weapons, plowshares, or trade knives.

They had to have this charcoal.

Fair Beard had argued for firing several smaller mounds such as might be done on one farmstead. But Wyn wanted the quantity and quality assured by a big mound that would provide enough charcoal for six months of ironmongering.

Madoc stood close enough to the steaming heap fully twenty feet in diameter so that sweat beaded his forehead. He wiped it away with his grimy cuff, smearing salty grit into his already-irritated skin. His hair, eyebrows, and mustaches were stiff and gray with ash. He felt infinitely filthy and had only been assisting Wyn a couple of days.

Much work had been accomplished at the camp of Madoc's Hundred over the warm winter. By the second week of January, 1172 according to compromise calculations, a fair town bloomed amid the stumps of vanished oak, hickory, and dogwood. The log house that echoed his father's greathouse back in Wales was not a castle that might house a Norman prince. The narrow two-story structure was more a Norseman's timber lodge set well into a slope and heavily roofed with cedar shake. It served as headquarters, dormitory, meetinghouse, and chapel until Wyn got his chapel built come spring, as well as the main kitchen for the sailors and other white men who had not built lodges with red women.

Owing to the fact that stone was scarce in this low river valley, and none suitable for a fireplace was found for miles, they cooked outside on the east face, under a narrow pavilion of sturdy cane and thatch. Later, when the *Horn* was fully functional, they would haul in hearthstones. The Shawnee households, several with their white men, made individual clay firepits in each log and wattle-and-daub household.

Over Madoc's arguments Rhys opted for settling down with the baby and Winnowed Rice in one of these comfortable little lodges built in the manner of her people, rather than live in the drafty, crowded Big House. Cari, weaned now and almost a year old, was growing into a fat, happy toddler who still rode her dad's back in the cradleboard to keep her out of mischief.

The Big House was cold now that real winter had arrived just after Christmas. Hunters went out each day and brought in abundant game of all species from great many-pointed deer down to rabbits, so many rabbits that the children and women often hunted them with clever snares and miniature weapons. The red women had growing piles and bundles of hides tanned and fluffy. No hand was idle, fashioning warm clothing at night around the fires, while each eye watched the sky, expecting winter to come any day now in big white boots.

Madoc would lie on his bed of furs alone listening as the man and woman on the other side of the stairwell argued deep into the nights.

They had set up the broadlooms in part of the rough second landing of the Big House. Yngvild and the other women spent many hours weaving Shawnee buffalo wool into a supple, serviceable cloth for which the surrounding tribes paid dearly in dried edibles Madoc's Hundred had stored up for anticipated hard times.

The red people treasured the blue beads Brother Wyn had easily whipped up from river sand in his forge on the other side of the settlement, and they waited expectantly for the knives. But what they wanted even more was cloth. They had hand-looms and various basketry weaving and twining skills, but they had nothing like the wide, warm lengths of trade buffalo wool that almost magically rolled from Yngvild's broadloom, which Winnowed Rice and her red sisters copied. They would have to wait until spring to get in crops of their own and so were dependent on trading these goods with their allies, and hunting to keep themselves alive.

Yngvild had thrown herself into the weaving work. She often kept at it long past midnight after Madoc took his star reading. He always took the dead-watch, sharing the round with Fair Beard, Huw, Dag, and several others of the sailors.

He would come in during the dewy, deepest night, eyes stinging from unblinking gaze, neck aching from stargazing posture, his body hungry for sleep. And she would be over there pacing out the weft with her wide gait, barefoot but belaboring the boards of their common floor.

Sometimes she would hum a low tuneless song he could hear as he drifted into disturbed sleep. Sometimes her husband would admonish her from their nearby bed, urging her to join him. But she ignored him. She continued her seemingly mindless pattern, infuriating him so that his cajolery grew hoarser though whispered: "Come to bed, now, Flower," using the nickname he had taken to calling her, with an edge of insistence that sounded like an uncharacteristic whine in the big Norseman.

Madoc could seldom hear their words, but often they would jab at each other back and forth for hours like that with lengthy silences between the bursts of hot whispered words, when Fair Beard seemed to fall asleep. But then, as though out of a dream, he would set to calling her again, his voice rising in ire, her pace unbroken and her rhythm undisturbed.

Those almost nightly encounters were not heard belowstair, where the unmarried men snored in a tumbled dormitory against the south wall and behind the long table that served as a meeting chamber for the Hundred. Labor was keeping everyone so exhausted, they slept like the dead and did not even hear the boards creaking. Yngvild and her husband kept it just under audibility, so that only their chief was witness, and he most reluctantly. He would bury his head beneath the fox and mink bolsters the Shawnee women made for him, but still he could hear the occasional board squeak with the woman's tread, and the occasional growl from Snorrison.

Their unhappiness permeated Madoc's nights and increased his own loneliness in his luxuriously furred but womanless bed. He was thinking as he watched the quivering mound that he would take up quarters on the ship just to get away from them.

At first he had worried about having enough food to feed the Hundred until they could get crops in. But with their Shawnee allies they put in a good winter store as the unseasonably warm weather continued past the winter solstice and Christmas. When the inevitable cold finally hit, his midnight dreads more often concerned Gwen and her husband·and their possible fate down on the lower Tennessee. Sometimes his dreams were disturbing memories of his time with the Natchez sun. These were only half-remembered later; he tried not think of her in daylight, because it made him mindful of how he longed for her.

Full of these troubled thoughts despite himself, Madoc eyed the mound where a new vent had for several minutes been trickling thicker smoke close to the center post that stuck up like a naked limb, an eyeless stalk.

The charcoal mound was getting to him, he realized. He felt dizzy with dread and fatigue. He realized he was making a creature of the mound, a dangerous thing to do.

But at this moment, and guiltily, he wished Wyn would get up and relieve him of having to deal with this ominous sign. He longed for his own shift of sleep in a future that did not include a climb upon the cauldron.

He moved in closer, feeling uncomfortable warmth through the blackened leather clothing that had been clean day before yesterday.

At least, he thought, this duty kept him from getting frostbite, always a danger aboard ship, where nimble fingers must tie knots and grip line all weathers.

The storm moved in days ago, blanketing the peninsula and the land for leagues around. Though the sky had been clear and the sun bright in daylight hours since the blizzard, the air was blisteringly cold with an intermittently cruel northwest wind that piled the snow up in deep, treacherous drifts. None of the powder had melted in the last seven days.

In fact, the dry arctic air had grown steadily colder since the storm, especially in the last two days. Dawn had not brought any relief. Way off to the west, he discerned a lowering sky with tatters of a gray front pointed in this direction. His sailor's nose for weather told him it would snow again before this day was over.

Beyond the stumps of a chestnut grove they had leveled to build the charcoal mound, the land dropped off sharply toward the frozen Oyo River about twenty paces downslope. Out here all alone, Madoc under his soot felt as though he had fallen into an odd kind of hell—frozen, but in a pit of darkness encircled by the snowfield beginning about ten feet from the base of the mound. He stood close enough to feel the blast upon his face while his backside was numb with cold.

Suddenly the mound let off a high-pitched whine that grew in volume. Smoke from the new vent coughed out in a thickened plume that rolled up into the sparkling air. Madoc sprinted around to be upwind with the satchel of damp charcoal dust flapping on his arm.

On the west side it was not as hot, but he was close enough to feel it blister his face.

Looking up at the furnace looming over him, he felt his own stomach sink with nauseous fear. He had heard stories about men sinking slowly into the inferno of a charcoal furnace. More than anything, he dreaded having to climb up onto that dome.

But he could see that was what he was going to have to do,

to dust the rupture that was already spitting flame. If he did not do it quickly, the entire mound could go.

Clutching the satchel, he gingerly stepped in his thick-soled Shawnee moccasins up onto the hardened notches Wyn had purposefully hacked when the sod was moist. The crust was now terra-cotta, too hot to touch. He felt the whole mess shudder beneath him and made to back off before it consumed him.

But after a moment he felt the shuddering subside. Instead of jumping back to the ground, he took another step up over the dome's shoulder. Fumes yellowed by sulfur choked him and stung his eyes, though he pulled the muffler he wore around his neck up over his nose. It did no good at all, just cut off what little air there was.

All around and beneath him the thing simmered and sighed, making banshee noises. It whistled near the rupture where oily smoke streamed out in sinuous coils. It did not look like a dangerous hole, only a narrow crack. He tossed a handful of the black dust into the vent, anyway.

First there was a dire crackling from inside the hive, then it sighed mightily and heaved out more staggered hiccups that finally faded to a wheeze and a thinner, paler stream of smoke, the bluish haze it should properly cast until its final phase, when Wyn said the mound would emit a hemisphere of yellow exhaust that would signal it was time to let the fire go out.

Madoc gave it another handful and stood there trying to assay the various humors of the banked cauldron beneath the crusted mud and moose-hide soles of his boots.

He was already uncomfortably hot-footed.

But the mound felt sturdy and strong beneath him, no hint of collapse. With an exhilarating sense of satisfaction and accomplishment, he smiled grimly under the grime and straightened, ignoring the growing heat under his toes, and stood looking at the heightened vantage the twelve-foot hummock gave him.

From here he could see the pinnacle of the *Horn's* mast above the naked forest between this spot and the Hundred's compound just to the east. They had patched her, but it was a temporary job that Madoc and his pilot longed to amend by hauling her up on rollers—great generous oak, he thought, of so many uses—and replace the two strakes weakened by the underwater collision that left them here.

That work had to be postponed while every available hand finished the shelters in time for winter they had correctly anticipated. Cold weather had descended before they were able to get her out of the water, what with other more pressing labors to attend to in constructing shelter for everyone. They left her inside a viking puzzle that was supposed to keep the ice from cracking her side strakes, and would have to worry more when the ice began to break up around her.

The hunt had been good, at least, and they had dried a comforting surplus. Since cold weather set in, they had many carcasses hanging frozen in the high branches of trees left standing in the main community of about fifty lodges. Their local Shawnee friends gave them salt, which the women used to add to their winter store. Corn and other grain was in short supply, but there was plenty of fish and deer, turkeys, and smaller animals that yielded flesh and fur. The Shawnee women kept three smokehouses going, determined not to be caught with short stores.

Before the snow, the men finished the log house where Madoc, Fair Beard, Yngvild, Wil, Mary, and the bachelors battened in for the duration of cold weather.

The ship was ice-locked standing a way off from the bank around a promontory on the other side of the village. Its mast was all he could see from here. Out of his perspective was their community that fanned out from the beach. But he observed the blue haze of their breakfast fires over in that direction. He sniffed to catch the promising aromas, hoping they would not forget him and his partner, prisoners out here of the furnace, dependent on others. But all he could smell was the charcoal's sulfurous breath and his own sweat.

From this height Madoc could see the wide crystal surface of the river interrupted by the low dark humps of islands. It stretched a good half mile to the white-shrouded land of the far northern shore. He could see that the wide stream was frozen clear out to midchannel. It was blindingly bright on the eyes, a flat white slab under a heatless sun.

To the west his view was blocked by the thick silver wood hanging with a few rusty leaves left behind by the snow. Within a day's walk, they had cut all the big trees and floated them with coracles and guy lines upriver to their little town.

He was about to carefully back down the steaming dome when movement down the western blaze of solid river road caught his attention. He could not see perfectly because of the fringe of skeleton trees and the intervening fumy fog that hung all around him, but beyond the snowbank that edged the river, he saw specks growing into vague longish objects moving quickly along the ice in this direction. He could not tell at first what the shapes were as they moved out in a pack with no formation, a straggled line of ten, fifteen, twenty, and more individual objects sliding along the frozen stream.

He heard the unmistakable sound of dogs barking, far away at first but growing louder, a raucous, persistent nuisance of a sound, until he realized what it was he was witnessing; then he had to stop himself from leaping with joy atop the shivering furnace.

It was gihli-gasi, at least fifty of the hide-and-hickory pole sleds being pulled along the ice by dogs or people who came more clearly into view as they neared the river bight nearest the charcoal factory.

His eye was good—now he could make out individual faces aboard the dog-pulls or running ahead in harnesses. He could see the approaching train was moving on snowshoes, and in a while, before he was forced by the fire on the soles of his feet to descend the mound, he caught a flash of someone with brilliant red hair when the wind threw back a furred hood.

Father Brian was out felling timber with the Norsemen—or scribbling with sumac ink on squirrel-hide parchment over in a corner of the kitchen. As far as Madoc knew, only Fairbeard's man Lev and one other in all this vast country had hair that color.

He felt a joy in his chest that almost hurt and leapt from the charcoal hill, running down toward the water's edge, forgetting all about his brooding little mountain of fire. He slipped down the snowy embankment that approached the river's edge and skated out onto the icy surface, chunks of fire-hardened mud breaking from his moccasins.

It was David Iron and herself pulling the gihli-gasi in harness behind them, making fair time, though others with dogs moved faster. He was suddenly in the midst of a breaking swarm of familiar Yuchi faces and sliding dog-pulls he had to avoid as he skidded the last few feet around Gwen. She tried to help him, causing her to laugh and call out to him, but unable to stop pulling lest she cause the burden to run askew.

The Yuchi who knew him from their time on the mountain

called his name in their language, "Weather Eyes, Weather Eyes," and some slapped his back in greeting as they scooted by.

Scrambling to his feet, he tried to catch the satchel, which flew open, spilling the black dust out onto the whiteness.

"Tad, is that really you?" Gwen cried, looking over her shoulder as she and her befurred husband slowed their pace.

Madoc slipped again and nearly went down, but he caught the hickory rim of the dog-pull and kept himself aright. He saw a huge fur-wrapped bundle in the middle of the sling, and then a curious glittering eye peek out. He did not see enough to recognize the face in the blanket, but it appeared to be an old man.

Dogs growled around him in their little leather boots—a tradition to protect them on ice.

Others on the speedy little craft whizzed by, not stopping, but trying to avoid knocking down the sooty, tall, black shadow-man hauling himself up against the chief's gihli-gasi.

Gwen exclaimed amazement for her father's appearance, for she had never seen charcoal made before and thought at first he had been burned horribly or oddly painted in a way she could not have imagined.

He fell against her, hugging her in the harness, with David Iron grimacing beyond, speaking, but Madoc was not able to hear with the commotion of exalting cries and barking on his right and left.

"Gwyneth, Gwyneth," he said into her sweet-smelling hair, hugging her and giving away with his intensity that he had thought he might never see her again.

Her cheeks were slick with happy tears, and soot smeared now with his grime rubbed against her.

"What is this?" she asked, looking at the black stains on her hands from touching her father's face.

"Charcoal," he tried to explain, but there was too much noise and confusion, and explanation was too complicated.

Activity swirled around them as David Iron embraced him, then looked anxiously over the rim of the gihli-gasi to see his father's smiling, aged face coming out from under the blanket and buffalo robe. Madoc grabbed the old man's hand. Sun Caller greeted him awkwardly, his hand trembling, and Madoc saw the Yuchi chief was not well.

When he turned back to Gwen, she was pulling at the harnesses again, with David Iron urging them on. All the others had passed them by, leaving this gihli-gasi alone on the frozen river while the others hurried on toward the little town visible from this perspective about a quarter mile upriver.

Madoc stood there in their wake watching Sun Caller huddle down into his robes again, seeing his daughter's back bend to the work. The painful swell of joy and relief he felt throughout his aching body made him a little dizzy as he watched them grow smaller. When they vanished into the bare wood, and the sight of that bright hair was finally lost to his eyes, he trudged across the ice marked with dog prints and draglines. A thick bundle had rolled off one of the gihli-gasi. He retrieved it, still tied in its leather cover, remembering his duty back on the charcoal hill simmering under yellow fumes.

Wyn was up and puttering about, poking at the mound with his blackened hickory stick, muttering to himself.

"It is Gwen," Madoc said, feeling the blistering cold wind on his wet face. He trotted closer to the warmth where Wyn had climbed up onto the notched steps and was inspecting that vent still emitting a greasy plume, shaking his head and mumbling.

"You should not have left her," he admonished, not looking at Madoc as he tapped with the staff the sod near the center post.

He was not talking about Gwen, Madoc realized, but the mound.

"Wyn, the children are home, and they brought the Yuchi—looks as though all of Yellow Pheasant Village came with them."

Wyn nodded and backed off the mound.

"We are well more than a hundred now."

"When did that crack open up?"

"I was watching it, Domme. Do not worry."

Wyn nodded, not taking his eye off the mound. "She is evil personified, I tell you."

"Yes, Domme," Madoc said, feeling a little guilty.

"She is a hole into hell we have opened here. But that yellow smoke is a good thing—it means she is just about done, our fine black cake."

Still holding the package, Madoc watched Wyn fuss with kindling at a fuel hole.

Presently Ari with a food basket, and several of the sailors, came dragging in branches from a downed oak and began hacking it into kindling. Madoc spoke to them about the abbot's condition and asked a couple of them to stay to help him tend the mound, promising to return later after he had some sleep.

Madoc busted ice from the surface of the basin they kept in the hut, washed his face as best he could, and slung water from his hands to dry, then left the warmth of the charcoal hill to cross the snowfield through the chestnut stumps and the little draw of scrawny sumac, laurel, brambles, and briars that marked the frozen dribble of a branch trickling under ice into the river.

He took the dropped parcel with him and along the way noticed neat knots that might have been his own. He judged the weight of the long package, wondering what it was. Whatever, he knew Gwen had tied it.

Over in town, they were already unloading the gihli-gasi, loosening the dogs and greeting everyone who had come out of warm lodges and the log house to see what all the noise was. He saw his daughter with a Yuchi woman holding a very small squalling baby, and he approached Gwen, who drew him to her, still giving him a curious eye over his charred appearance.

This could not be Gwen's, he was thinking when he looked down upon the skinny babe in the red woman's arms—her time was not until spring. Sure enough, even in the bulky furred clothing, he could see that his daughter was still pregnant.

Shawnee and Yuchi had never been enemies, and now the old-timers were embracing the new arrivals, exclaiming over the journey between here and where they had come from. In all, Madoc was able to count about seventy-five people just arrived, which would swell their numbers to nearly two hundred.

David Iron was helping his father from the dog-pull. Now Madoc could see the old man was greatly weakened, bent in his robes with several of his kinswomen and counselors huddled around him.

"He nearly died," Gwen said when she saw her father's attention. "Oh, Tad," she whispered against him, "David Iron drew his own blood to save Sun Caller—it was terrible and wonderful at the same time.

"What is this?" she asked when she saw the parcel under his arm.

He handed it over. "You must have dropped it back there."

With a note of wonder, she said, "Tad, do you know what this is?" and hastily clawed at the knots. "How wonderful that it was you who saved it!"

She flung it outward and stepped back so that it unrolled to its full fathom of length.

Madoc caught his breath at the beauty of the tapestry, as though he were seeing it for the first time. He had not feasted his eye upon it since they fought the Cherokee at Muscle Shoals.

It was shocking for an eye used to winter grays, dull clays, and soot, to see the crimson dragon in attack position with claws extended, thrown into lifelike relief by gold thread and a black background over the brilliant snow.

"Our flag—" Gwen cried joyfully as she hugged him. "We are one nation again!"

Madoc felt embarrassed at her enthusiasm, which seemed so uncomfortably romantic and foreign a notion out here in this strange wilderness, but her beaming face gave him a rush of joy that made it seem possible.

The baby fussed, and the Yuchi woman pressed her close to her untied bodice.

Madoc stared at the baby suckling the short little Yuchi; it gave him an idea, and he looked around.

"Yes, Tad, this is *her* baby."

"Where is she?" Madoc asked, searching the throng of red men and women pulling off the dog harnesses, greeting others coming from the lodges and the Big House with shouts and embraces.

Then he saw Arrow Always Red staggering up from the river's edge carrying an unseen small human figure shrouded in the star-robe in his arms. He recognized Firefly, who followed the Natchez warrior but did not speak, while Gwen nearby told him, "Tumkis is very sick."

"Come inside where it is warm," Mary was saying at their elbows. Gwen hugged her and exchanged greetings while they stumbled toward the log house near the center of the compound.

Madoc followed Arrow Always Red into the house, where there were too many people crowding inside already. He gestured to the Natchez warrior that he should take his burden up the stair to the second floor. The big red man eyed the stairway—a thing he had never seen before inside a dwelling. The only stair he had ever seen was the one that led to the top of the pyramid in his home village.

He hesitated, but David Iron urged him on in his own language.

Madoc caught a glimpse of Tumkis's loose hair falling from the star-robe she was wrapped in. He started to climb the stair, heart pounding, and would have followed.

Gwen stopped him with a touch on his sleeve, urging him back down into the kitchen where Mary was passing around steaming cups of red tea amid a swelling chatter of voices and exclamations.

But at that moment Yngvild stood at the top of the stair, halting Arrow Always Red about halfway up. She did not speak but stared unmoving at the trailing black hair dangling from the wrapped figure in his arms.

Below him immediately was Winnowed Rice with Cari cradleboarded on her back, who entered with Rhys, bringing a blast of cold air whooshing in behind them.

"Not in this house," Yngvild said in a strained voice that silenced the thirty or so people crowding into the lower floor. They all turned their faces up to her.

"Fair Beard?" Madoc said, looking around for Snorrison, but he was no doubt where he had been for a week, working to keep the icy river from crushing the *Horn*.

"Please bring your mistress into our own fireside," Winnowed Rice said in the Natchez language, inserting herself between Natchez and Norsewoman.

Arrow Always Red did not have to be persuaded when he saw the tall Norsewoman take a step to descend, her face twisted, her mouth working on invective.

"Yngvild," Madoc said, moving up past the Natchez warrior, who was already backing down.

Madoc cut off Yngvild's further descent, close enough to her to feel her tense fury. "Go back and wait for your husband," Madoc said to her, but it was as though he were not there. He caught up her hand gripping the rail and pressed her back.

Below, the Natchez was just swinging his burden out the open door, Winnowed Rice and Rhys following.

Madoc watched, his former exhaustion changed now into

something else, elation, a tingling in his hands and feet, and wonder at his own reaction to the sight of that blue black cascade tumbling from the folds of the star-robe.

Near him Gwen was rolling up the tapestry. "There is much to tell you, Tad."

He dipped his sooty hands into a pottery water basin decorated with beautiful Shawnee patters, thinking that he most wanted to get to the sweathouse the Shawnee had built on the other side of the compound and rid himself of the grimy filth imposed by his charcoal duty.

He took the buffalo-horn cup of warm tea Mary offered. With the happy buzz of the people resumed around him, he and Gwen sought some privacy back near Brian's rough desk, where the priest was transcribing from memory the Book of Psalms to squirrel parchment.

Leaning on the makeshift scriptorium, Madoc listened to Gwen's story.

Chapter 18

As expected, it snowed that night.

But it was a light fall. Some of the old red people said it was just too cold to really snow, and Fair Beard, who, with Icelandic regard about such things, agreed.

Madoc missed Father John, who had been the wisest man about weather he ever knew. The old priest, who laid in the first grave in the plot set aside beyond the forge, would know what to make of the strange weather, so cold one day and beginning to thaw the next.

The warming was upon them, bringing new concerns.

Madoc and the pilot stood the the *Horn's* prow watching the bright solid river, each man wondering on his own about when the ice would break.

That morning was chill, but the sun was warm. Sun Caller and the elder red women, being familiar with the Snow Moon thaw, predicted that the next day the river would start to turn to slush. Madoc and the other whites from more northern regions were used to a lingering winter, which began while the leaves were still turning, lasted three or four months, then gradually warmed to a wet springtime.

"The river was frozen to midchannel," Madoc said. He had just awoken in his old quarters belowdeck where his sea chest remained stowed. Late last night after steaming, he had retreated out here and would later relieve Snorrison of the ship's watch.

"But not solid," Fair Beard remarked, squinting at a spot between here and the tip of the closest island. "Dag caught fish from a hole about twenty paces out." The fishermen were not out there today because they claimed to have heard telltale crackings deep under the ice.

Madoc regarded the sky brightening toward noon. "Sun

Caller is right about a channel opening out there if this holds up." He tilted his chin to indicate the definitely less cold wind that had been springing from the southwest.

Where Fair Beard was from, rivers would melt, refreeze, and then melt again, which caused chunks of ice in the current, so he expected something more dangerous than a slow, soggy soup.

He stepped closer to the rail and peered over. They had flung a hasty course of notched logs in a so-called viking puzzle around the ship when the snow threatened. Into the moat between that oak bolster and the ship's hull they poured rendered bear-grease, the most available oil.

As the river froze during the next forty-eight hours, they watched the ice-free zone. It, too, would eventually freeze, but their efforts slowed it. And when that water began to solidify, they hacked out the logs locked into the already-frozen outer water. In this way the ice expanded toward the path of least resistance away from the ship's skin.

Madoc had seen it work before and was confident it would work this time because the freeze had been gradual, over several days. The *Horn*'s shored-up inner strakes seemed to be holding against pressure on the outer hull.

But below the waterline it was still a gamble. Both men wished they had gotten her into dry dock. The pressure of the freezing river—especially if it happened quickly—could split the stoutest oaken strake, and the hull was already weakened.

They had loosened the withes that held her together to provide a little more give. The ship was built along Norse lines, each unique piece carved to fit the next, with very little metal fastening involved. On the open sea such a ship had a lot of leeway in the amount of twist she could withstand—as much as six feet laterally. The innovative Norse shipbuilding techniques permitted dismantling on short notice, important in the frigid northern waters of Fair Beard's homeland.

Now all they could do was wait with hooks, axes, and poles ready to control the ice breakage around the ship so that chunks finally set free by a renewed current did not ram her or pile against her boards.

Fair Beard was discussing how he thought it would happen.

They leaned against the rail in the shadow of a rough-hewn snarling dragon Fair Beard had found time to install upon her prow. Madoc's back was turned on the river, arms across his chest swathed in his favorite wolf-skin jacket, hood thrown back, enjoying the beneficent sun on his face. Still bleary-eyed and needing more sleep, he was apparently staring into space, only halfway listening to Fair Beard's technical speculations about their chances.

What Madoc was actually doing was blatantly observing the lodge of Rhys and Winnowed Rice amid the neat pattern of habitations set up by the red people between the bank and the Big House on the other side of a wide council circle with its now-dark center firepit amid ranks of log benches.

The air west of the compound was free of charcoal signature since Brother Wyn had last night declared the mound baked just right. It was cooling now. Likewise the abbot, who was steamed clean and resting back in Madoc's bed in the Big House.

Snorrison had helped Madoc bring all his things over here, where he reoccupied the *Horn* with quiet gladness. Coming back to the ship was just what he needed, in addition to more sleep. It gave him an odd sense of coming home.

He had no real fear that the thawing river would harm them any more than was already done, but let Fair Beard run through all possibilities because it gave the Norseman something to do, which is what he seemed to need.

Still not recovered from his shift on the charcoal mound, Madoc had stumbled up out of his bachelor quarters aboard the still slightly tilted *Horn* locked in her icy berth awaiting what could be disastrous freedom. Subsurface groanings and soft scrapings from the other side of the hull had brought him out of a musty sleep full of dreamed sparks and smoke.

At that moment they heard the groan and felt the shudder that could only mean a definite current moving under them. Each man tensed, touching the railing for instructive vibrations.

Just as suddenly the disturbance subsided.

They gave each other a look that disclosed their unspoken discomforts. It looked as though Fair Beard's chunks would be their fate after all. But one thing between them they did not acknowledge, was she who resided in the lodge of Rhys and Winnowed Rice.

Both had scrupulously avoided the place, as well as mention of its implications. No new word was forthcoming from there.

Winnowed Rice through Rhys reported that the Natchez sun lingered alive, but failing.

"What do you mean you do not want us to sing for your lady?" the Shawnee shaman had demanded. He stood in full regalia when he offered yesterday to cure the Natchez sun, his assistants ranged behind him ready to bury beads and do whatever magic they might to save her.

"My lady is dying and does not wish to have her peace disturbed," said young Firefly, who was sorry that her mistress had not kept Ahoskas with them for this kind of duty. But Tumkis had dismissed the old woman on purpose, because of her meddling in the sun's self-medications. To rid herself of Ahoskas's presence, she sent her back to the homeland on the pretext that her knowledge of protocol made it necessary for her to accompany the coffin-canoe.

"These white people cannot help you in such matters," argued the shaman.

"We welcome no intrusion into our sun's privacy from anyone," said Arrow Always Red, standing between the shaman and the lodge flap that hid his mistress from curious eyes. "We do not need Shawnee or white medicine and are here only because the river is frozen, and we do not want to increase our lady's misery in such cold weather. We will be leaving as soon as we can canoe out of this place."

The Shawnee medicine man stalked off in his feathers, his assistants behind him grumbling dark words aimed at the place where the stubborn Natchez sun languished. They seldom dabbled in female problems, anyway, and had offered only because of the rank of the Natchez sun, so their pride was doubly affronted.

The white physician fared no better.

"But I have specifics for childbed fever," Caradoc the mediciner insisted when he stood in the same spot a little later. Even without feathers, his pride was just as ruffled as the red men's had been.

Mary, who had accompanied him with her own bag of simples, said to Winnowed Rice, "At least let me see the girl so that I may know how to advise her."

But Winnowed Rice only repeated what Firefly had said. "I have seen her, and I tell you there is nothing anyone can do."

"Has she infection, or fever, then? It was a big child for seven months—was she torn badly?" Mary importuned, used to having the red women defer to her as the head white woman by default since there were no others around. Gwen's arrival had not displaced her, and she was unable to believe that any woman in her right mind would prefer death under such circumstances.

Winnowed Rice had worked at the weaving with this strong, stubborn white woman, and she had respect for her. She gave her a good long look and said, "It is an illness of the soul, I think, and cannot be touched by anyone's medicine."

She did not mention the Unknown Woman because she knew Mary would not understand. But she knew from events back on the island, and from the little that Firefly had hinted, that more than ordinary childbirth was involved. She hesitated to discuss this even with Rhys, who had not pressed her in matters that his own people left to women.

Elders among the red women who might have offered advice and concoctions against the ailment stayed away from the lodge that was set a little apart from the others on the knoll above the river. They knew by suspicion if not by fact what had Tumkis down. Abortion being unmentionable to any except female ears, and then only within the safety of the female lodge organizations, they were quiet about it, laconically implying that the Natchez sun should be left to the fate she had chosen.

The Natchez warriors, despite the cold, felled a huge cedar and were even now keeping a fire in it and adzing to hollow out a proper boat for a Natchez sun to go home in. It was impossible to tell if it was a coffin-boat or just a well-made dugout. Arrow Always Red spoke to nobody as he directed this work. Firefly tended her mistress, admitting only Winnowed Rice into their privacy.

A tense hush, something like the pall of smoke from so many cooking fires that surrounded the community, hung over the Hundred. Things seemed to be cooking just under the surface, still quietly as Madoc perused it from the wider vantage point of the *Horn*'s deck.

"Hallo the ship," a familiar female voice called from landward, out of sight forward on the other side of the ship. "Tad—Uncle Snorri," Gwen asked, "permission to board!"

"It is not safe," Madoc called back as he moved forward and swung down on the sidelines, landing before her where she stood with David Iron on the ice.

"If it is not safe enough for us," she said, gesturing at the baby in a cradleboard on her back, "then it is not safe for you."

Little Hannah looked quite perky, Madoc thought, as he regarded the fur-muffled little face peering curiously over his daughter's shoulder.

He was distinctly aware that Fair Beard lingered still at the rail but was watching from there as Madoc's daughter brought Snorrison's own baby girl within his purview. Madoc knew this was exactly what Gwen meant to do, because she had a sly look on her face as she glanced up from time to time at the father behind the ship's rail.

Gwen shielded her eyes with her freckled white hand as she told Madoc that the red people were planning a big fire ceremony in the council circle tomorrow night.

"They do not need my permission."

"They want to honor you as chief," David Iron said.

Madoc groaned, framing a protest that he had too much work to do to waste time on ceremonials.

"It is the eagle dance," the Yuchi continued.

"That is a great honor," Fair Beard was saying behind them as he descended the sidelines. "You must accept."

Madoc looked back at his pilot approaching, tamed and almost shy, it seemed, his glance fastened on Gwen's little rider. His hand already extended to touch her baby cheek pink as a rose now, the only reminder of that first alarming redness.

She was indeed a pretty baby inside her fur hood with a small spit of black curl across her forehead. Gwen had pulled the long lock at the back of her head to the front and tied it with a yellow string.

"So, this is Hannah," Fair Beard said softly, his coarse voice made almost liquid by parental pride.

Madoc stared at his pilot, having never seen him in this mood before.

Gwen grinned back at her father as if to say she had not expected it to be so easy.

David Iron saw it, too, and was quickly at the lacing on the cradleboard, undone in a second. He handed the fur-swaddled infant over to the Norseman, who took her instantly, already enslaved.

Gwen had not told all the complicated story to her father when they first arrived. She knew how the Hundred would react to Tumkis's attempts at abortion. If they knew she had abandoned Hannah, they would revile her and most likely throw all the Natchez out in the cold. Fair Beard might even try something that the Natchez warriors would have to confront. She and David Iron had decided together what would be best for everyone all around, at least until the weather freed the Natchez to depart.

She had not lied, but she left out some parts of the story.

As far as Snorrison or any of the white people knew, Tumkis had an early delivery, which she herself would probably not survive. Gwen said the Natchez sun, not expecting to live, had given her the child, asking her to find a suitable mother. None of the Natchez said anything to gainsay this, and their behavior around their ailing mistress seemed to support what Gwen reported.

"My first little girl," Fair Beard said brightly, looking up like a startled hound, his droopy face at odds with his grin.

The baby made noises in his huge hands, and he clucked back at her without any hesitation, completely at ease holding so small a bundle.

"What will you do with her?" Madoc asked bluntly, made uncomfortable by the man's uncharacteristic gentleness.

"Why, I shall take her to her stepmother."

Madoc chortled cynically.

"Do you know, I believe Yngvild will take her. Look at her—is she not beautiful?"

Gwen beamed as though she, too, had speculated on Yngvild's reaction.

"How can you think that, Snorrison?" Madoc laughed out loud. "That woman of yours is crazy."

Fair Beard blushed, his big ears fairly broadcasting what he would not say in front of Gwen; his wife complained nightly that her teats hurt. After all this time she was still producing milk, and her husband knew she would welcome relief.

Gwen suddenly stepped back and looked down at the ice beneath her moccasins. "I just felt something happening down there," she said, moving with David Iron toward the bank where they had tracked a muddy path.

Fair Beard holding the baby also took the path off the river, continuing to speak with Gwen as they walked together toward the Big House. "It all depends on timing," he was saying. "Can the Yuchi wet nurse help us out a little longer?"

Madoc, who had been feeling the vibrations since before he opened his still-reddened eyes, turned back to the ship where he would stand the next watch, shaking his head, but curious as to how Fair Beard would accomplish it.

He had hoped to get some more sleep, but saw that he had inadvertently taken Fair Beard's duty, since he supposed he was the only man aboard. He was surprised, as he climbed back up the sidelines, to see Einion at the rail where he had stationed himself.

He ruffled the boy's shaggy brown hair. "Why are you not at the house where it is warm?" Madoc asked, but endeared by the boy's presence.

"I was looking for you, sir," he answered, squinting up at Madoc, who could not help but hug the child closer to himself, his own little stepbrother and adopted son.

"Am I still the ship's boy?"

"Indeed you are, son."

Madoc walked with him across the slightly sloping deck, testing with each step for vibrations coming up through the ship from the river. "Are you hungry?"

He thought that maybe if he ate something, it would cure his headache that he figured was a hangover from his hours on the mound. He broke out a basket of cold corncakes, jerky, and beans, sincerely glad for the child's company as they found a place to sit forward in front of Fair Beard's tent, enjoying the sun while they ate their mess together.

The warm southern wind blew all afternoon and did not drop off until after Huw relieved Madoc of the watch he had taken early for Fair Beard. He had decided that he did not want to wait until tomorrow to begin hacking at the ice around the *Horn*. After conferring with Huw, he said he would go over to the Big House and begin rounding up every available hand to help. There was no hurry in him about this because the river surface was still hard, though grown slippery with a thin layer of melt now that the air was warmer.

It was still early. From several directions came the varied sounds of woodworking. Someone was chopping over near the forge. Also from the forge was the clanging of what sounded like Wyn's hammer on metal. Madoc guessed that the abbot was well refreshed and back to work. Three axes were biting in well-timed rhythm on a standing tree somewhere off to the south, and the softer multiple scruff of the adzes nicking on the Natchez canoe could be heard but not seen to the southeast.

He walked across the deserted council circle, where the

Shawnee were planning to hold their ceremonial. He dreaded having to play at ritual, but guessed that it would be good for everyone to have some kind of celebration. Tomorrow was a Sunday, according to Brian, who planned a Mass here. It was special for him because it was the first service to which they had invited the Yuchi and Shawnee headmen, and the dwindling clergy hoped without expressing it that they might take on some more red converts.

The circle predated the Hundred's occupation. It was demarked by a gathering of ancient oaks, planted at least a lifetime ago in a deliberate circle, which Brian used for Mass before the weather turned cold, but as yet for no other meetings. It gave Madoc mild goose bumps as he walked near the huge blackened firepit, thinking of how long the trees had stood deliberately planted in a hundred-foot circle. It was vaguely reminiscent of Druidic enclaves back home, which he had only heard of. Mistletoe hung in the skeleton crowns of these oaks just as it did in similar trees back home, a correspondence that mystified and delighted him every time he saw it.

Nobody stirred within his view, though high overhead a red hawk circled lazily on the southwestern draft.

Still walking, he turned so that he could see the ship. They had the pennant out and flying—it looked splendid snapping in the wind atop the pinnacle. He took in a circular view as he continued turning without slowing his pace, pointing himself back in the direction of the log house.

To his left about fifty paces began the Shawnee lodges arranged close by each other but at random with well-worn paths in the snow between them. Closest to the river's more southerly leaning bank was the slightly separate lodge where Rhys lived with Winnowed Rice.

Madoc stopped suddenly when he saw Firefly emerge with a water jug. She did not see him and headed without looking up toward the farther bank.

The woody echoes of axing, chopping, adzing, continued along with the metallic hammering ringing through the precinct of the little village.

The breeze stirred dry cattails behind Rhys's cottage under its blanket of loosening snow. From the river a brilliant redbird sang on the wing, carrying its song away.

When he approached on a light tread, he was stopped short

by Winnowed Rice's yellow dog, who suddenly appeared from
the sunny side of the lodge, ears perked, a low growl in her
throat.

But she trotted to greet him when she sniffed who it was and
gave him her ears to scratch.

He rubbed the dog's head and looked around again, feeling
self-conscious and ready to back off if someone approached.
But nobody did, and he took the last couple of steps that led
him to the doorway draped by a stiff deer hide. He scratched
at it, but heard no response from inside, where he could smell
aromatic herbs burning. A thin curl of blue smoke spiraled up
from the back of the house set directly into the clay bank,
where a kind of chimney had been formed in the bank itself,
which was also the lodge's farthest wall.

The dog curled up in the sunlight puddled to one side of the
doorway, regarding him with bright eyes between her paws.
She sighed and gave herself over completely to the ground,
blinking at the man standing poised with one hand raised
against the doorpost.

Long icicles dripped in different voices into rotting snow
along the south side of the house.

He dropped his hand and started to walk quickly away but
was arrested by the sudden sounds of light female voices
coming from his left. Over by the other lodges, four or five red
women were coming in with baskets laden with snow-ripened
persimmons under their arms. One of them was Lily, sister to
Winnowed Rice who was living with Evan in the next Shawnee
lodge. She saw him and waved with the others, their smiles
clearly visible as they went about their work.

Once again he was alone standing beside the doorway.

From inside he caught the whiff of the pleasant odor of
incense wafting through the loose flap.

He pushed it aside and entered.

Inside, the light was murky with a small fire on the clay
hearth in back. He must bend to keep from striking his head
as he moved into the single room. To his right were stacked
bales of what appeared to be beaver pelts, which formed casual
furniture. The harp box was hanging open on a high peg, the
instrument called Honeyvoice gone. As in all houses of the red
people, bunches of herbs and other drying things dangled in
the draft near the hearth, putting various aromatics into the

air, and baskets and pottery were stacked or hung from pegs at hand near the bench of the hardened clay firepit.

He warmed his numb fingers above the hearth and looked around, eyes adjusting to the gloom.

Hand on the beams, he inspected here and there, wondering why on earth Rhys would want to live in this hovel instead of the roomy Big House. It reminded Madoc of peasants' huts back home, wattle and daub that could be moved with the sheep to higher pastures. The poet was almost as tall as himself. Madoc wondered how Rhys kept from constantly hitting his head on the low ceiling.

Though there was not a civilized corner in the place, it was warm and cozy, made more so by beautiful Shawnee basketry, stretched pelts, and handwork hanging on the rough walls. He touched a feather fan worked with porcupine beads, a lovely thing, dangling from a thong, and moved to the right where a small loom was strung with what may have been a strap Winnowed Rice was weaving for the harp. The pattern was about a hand wide, intricate, the weave close and expert, nearly complete at little over an ell long with the fringe of warp threads only needing to be knotted.

As he peered at the work, something beyond in the shadows caught his eye. He looked up, arrested by what he saw in a nook at the far right.

She was apparently asleep, her head thrown back on the pillow of her loosened blue black hair, mouth slightly open to reveal small teeth shining like little pearls.

Closer, he could hear her breathe deeply as though unconscious or drugged.

He sat slowly, pulled down by wonder at the sight of her face, all of her that was not covered by a wide, supple robe.

In the flickering light from the small fire, the points of painted stars seemed to blink under her pale face glowing on the dark firmament of the furs and the blue black field of the star-robe. Her hair, which he had last seen hacked and matted from mourning rituals for Yngvild's lost baby, was combed out in luxurious tresses. A strand lay across her forehead, completing the startling image of her as a nearly full moon on a wide, starry field of dark sky.

He had always seen a woman in the moon.

Her eyelids quivered, but she did not stir. Her breathing remained slow and deeply regular.

Then he saw her small tattooed hand dangling from under the furred side of the star-robe. He let his own hand slip beneath hers, feeling a strange coolness in her flesh against his own. His fingers closed around hers but felt no response. His own skin felt rough and hot, scratched and scabbed from his labors, grime still embedded in the calluses.

The frail pulse of an artery said there was life in her. He imagined his heat moving into her coolness, but he could tell from the limp fingers that she was far away. His thumb caressed the thin blue tattoo lines, like bracelets around her wrist, that she had inflicted upon herself in mourning for the loss of Yngvild's baby.

Holding her hand against his deerskin-clad knee, he leaned his aching head back against a peeled-cedar support post, letting the softness of the room steal over him.

Outside the wind strengthened. The fire crackled with a draft down the clay flue.

Huw aboard the ship saw hunters come in with game over their shoulders and called them to the ship, where he hung over the rail to tell them the captain was going to start breaking up the softening ice around the ship. Hefting their burdens, they said they would return as soon as they dropped off the kills and grabbed something to eat.

Keeping their promise, they later returned with Fair Beard and began the task, setting small fires a ways from the ship and axing the ice around the waterline, then sliding the blocks farther out on the open river. By sunset they could see movement midchannel that announced the river was coming back to life.

Fair Beard decided to keep a crew working through the night, so they set bonfires on shore.

The various woodworking sounds continued as the sky grew fiery—the axmen and the Natchez canoe carvers begrudging the loss of light and determined to put every moment of it to use.

Firefly returned from her bath later with a long shadow pacing her. She entered the lodge with the sloshing jug full of water and puttered about with the dying fire for a few moments until she turned and saw Weather Eyes slumped against the lodgepole with Lady Tumbling Water's hand in his own.

It startled Firefly, but she recovered quickly when she realized the white man was almost as fast asleep as her mistress.

For a few moments, Firefly observed the two sleepers, her thoughts working in silence.

Then, just as silently, she slipped between the flap and the doorpost, walking quickly toward the Big House, where they were cooking outside, accompanied by Rhys's music.

It was so warm, they had the doors open; people were coming and going with food and talk, almost in a celebratory mood with the warm weather upon them.

Mary and Winnowed Rice were packing a basket to take over to the ship's hard-working crew when Firefly approached the Shawnee woman and whispered in her ear.

Winnowed Rice glanced at Rhys singing inside the open door of the house. Cari was asleep in her cradleboard on his back as he plucked the melody of an Irish love song, translating it into Shawnee. She decided not to interrupt, since it would have provoked comment from everyone around him about a subject even he would argue was best left private.

She took up the loaded basket and told Mary that she and Firefly would deliver the crew's dinner. Mary at work over the kitchen fire wiped her forehead with the back of her hand and nodded absentmindedly as she spooned out stew for her boys offering empty bowls.

Firefly spoke softly as they walked quickly back to the little house, explaining briefly what she had found there.

Nothing had changed inside except that now the fire was almost dead, a glowing red in that direction. Winnowed Rice saw Weather Eyes with Tumkis's hand still under his own, both of them lost in their separate slumber.

She watched them for a moment until Firefly's worried glance caught her. Firefly looked at the doorway; they could hear the sounds of the crew working out on the ice, yelling good-naturedly at each other amid cracks and hacking sounds.

They heard the dog outside making greeting noises at someone they could hear approaching across the snow. The man's reply to the dog revealed that Arrow Always Red had returned.

Firefly gasped.

Winnowed Rice quickly snatched up a basin of water sitting on the hearth and stepped out into the twilight.

Arrow Always Red was standing there with his hand on the

dog's head. He looked up mildly when the tall Shawnee woman exited his mistress's presence, holding what was probably a washing basin, which is what she hoped he would think.

His eyes asked the question he did not voice.

She shook her head. "No change."

He nodded, accepting, and gently made to go inside.

"We are bathing her."

Again he nodded and backed off, accepting. Remembering suddenly, he took two rabbit carcasses from his belt and casually tossed them beside the doorway just as Firefly pushed the flap aside with the big star-robe draping her arms and shoulders. To keep it from dragging in the tracked mud outside the doorway, she held it high, which hid the anxiety on her features as she turned to shake it at the spot where the big warrior hesitated.

Her movement forced him to move farther back, awkward and shy, his face etched with grief and worry. He had smeared soot in significant patches on his cheeks, as though he were already mourning.

As she drew the robe into a manageable bundle, Firefly shot a glance a Winnowed Rice that was quivering with worry. To cover it, Winnowed Rice tossed the water from the basin and turned back to enter the lodge. As she did so, she took some of the weight of the huge robe off the little Natchez's arms.

"Firefly, would you please take the basket down to the ship, and I will stay with your mistress until you return."

"I will watch over my wife," Arrow Always Red eagerly offered.

"You must be starving," Firefly said quickly, and with one hand pressed him away from the house, while handing off the star-robe to Winnowed Rice with the other. "They have wonderful food over at the Big House. Please, Arrow Always Red, refresh yourself from you hard work on our canoe. Take the sweathouse and come back later to sit with her."

He hesitated, but she urged him, and he accepted as she would have it, made docile by the circumstances. But he did not relent so far as to accept the white people's food. Instead he angled away toward the sweatlodge. He and his men had their own small camp fire going near the long canoe, which was nearly finished—it would be ready when the river was.

When he was well away and trudging in his big winter

moccasins across the council circle, Firefly took the basket Winnowed Rice had retrieved from inside.

"What did he mean, his wife?" she asked as she retrieved the rabbits tied tail-to-tail from the snow and hung them on a skinning peg to the right of the doorpost.

Firefly shrugged, let the heavy basket down to grip it more firmly with both hands, and replied by way of vague explanation, "They were children together."

"But she is the tangletongue's wife."

"She divorced him."

Winnowed Rice knew that a Natchez sun had a great deal of prerogative in such matters, but this seemed too sudden even for that nation's bizarre customs. "Did she accept Arrow Always Red?"

"He formally asked her."

"And she accepted with cooked corn?"

Firefly looked down. "She said she was going to die, anyway, so it did not matter."

One of the men on the ship called out to another.

"You must get Weather Eyes out of there," Firefly said, turning with the basket.

Winnowed Rice longed to know more, but agreed that other things should take priority over a long discussion, so she nodded. Firefly went off to feed the workers, and Winnowed Rice went back inside, where Madoc had opened his eyes, staring at the unconscious woman's still face.

She was far too pale to be healthy. On a red person this effect was ashen, a yellow tone of gray.

"What is wrong with her?" he asked in his language, and she understood a word or two, by the sound of it.

"The baby came too early," she answered in simple Cymraeg. "She was not strong enough."

Madoc leaned forward, elbows on his knees, still holding the limp hand in one of his own. He observed it now as some kind of object that might contain signs for him to read and understand. He traced the lifeline on her palm with his rough finger.

Winnowed Rice watched him the way a hunter might watch prey, seeing and understanding more than she had before in his posture and in the way he handled the little fingers of the Natchez sun.

Still in profound sleep, Tumkis made a small sound and

. swallowed. Her lips were dry—she had been breathing with her mouth open.

Winnowed Rice took a small water skin from a peg and knelt beside the bed. She dribbled water onto her fingers and slid them across the bluish lips of the Natchez sun, whose pink tongue reached for the moisture.

She realized then that Tumkis was under some kind of strong medication, which she had not known before.

"Weather Eyes," she said softly, "it is better for you to leave now."

He continued observing Tumkis, but he nodded and placed r hand down onto the starry blanket.

"If you wish," Winnowed Rice said as he was about to leave, "come back tomorrow afternoon, and I will try to explain what has happened."

He took this in, made a small gesture of weary compliance, and stepped out into the night.

Chapter 19

The wind increased, raged all night, and in the morning subsided under a fine blue sky slapped absolutely cloudless by a lingering breeze.

The warm sun had the river grinding and groaning and turning to stew.

It was the sixth day of January according to Wyn, whose dates were based on his keeping of the church ritual calendar and counting his sunrise prayers.

Madoc, who based his dates on the stars and marking midnights on his charts, still believed the brother was off in his calculations. But he was silent about it, according to their agreement, and did not gainsay the abbot that it was Epiphany, a day of celebration.

"It will not be quite the same without candles," said Andrew as he assisted Wyn and Brian getting things ready for the Mass. They decided to hold the traditional candlelight ceremony that evening just before the red ceremonial in the council circle.

Behind them, David Iron was hammering at the trade knives as Wyn had taught him, hardening them with the charcoal. His rhythmic clangs were a punctuation to the clergy's conversation.

"And no wine," added Wyn, who had taken time from his hammer and forge to get things ready for the ritual. They had run out of wine long ago and had no idea what might do to make more. The grapes they had seen were scrawny and bitter—the Shawnee did not eat them but used them as medicine or as a dye.

"Maybe we will have a miracle, and the water will be turned into wine," said Andrew, remembering one of the traditions about Epiphany, the feast of the magi.

"We have had our miracle," Wyn muttered. "We are still alive."

"I think Hayati has a good idea about replacing the candles," Brian said, hands caressing the linen stole, embroidered in some Irish nunnery on the other side of the world, the last sacred vestment they owned. In fact, all they had for the ceremony was pine knots in pottery dishes, plain water for wine, and thin corncakes for the host. None of this was proper, none of it conforming to church canon. The bread was not wheat, there was no precious metal in the candlesticks, and here was their priest proclaiming pride in his bride's suggestion about candle replacements.

Still favoring the ankle, Wyn folded the rough buffalo-wool vestments. "It is the spirit of the Mass that counts," he said, remembering Father John once saying the same thing.

Wyn knew it was true. But it troubled him that they had no wine. Everything else he could live with—concubinage was tolerated among the priesthood back home; silver in the candlesticks and wheat in the host were legal prescriptions.

But wine seemed an essential ingredient, literally the ritual's lifeblood.

Wyn wanted to experiment with those muscadine grapes, or perhaps the cranberries that grew in bogs farther up into Chippewa country. He heard that the Scandinavians made a serviceable wine from them. Perhaps, he privately mused, Fair Beard would know about it.

They placed all the religious items in Shawnee baskets and set them to one side in the lean-to that was both a rectory and shelter for the forge, a simple oven in the long bank of clay that used to be an ancient edge of the river.

Bidding them good-bye, Brian left to go to the council circle, where David Iron's Yuchi brothers were erecting a cross.

Wyn hobbled over to the forge, where David Iron stood ready with the hammer to bludgeon a trade knife turning red, then white-hot, on the bed of charcoal.

Behind him and a little beyond the forge stood two Shawnee warriors—the local people were always respectfully in attendance, watching as Andrew and Wyn pounded out trade knives. They would come and stand there, unspeaking, unmoving, sometimes one or two or three, often little boys or old men, but always a sort of monitor as the white men worked the metal from glowing, cheesy bloom to finished products await-ing the charcoaling process.

Now that work, too, was almost complete, with their store of blades stacked neatly in a sand bed near the oven to keep them from rusting.

"Domme, you surely do not intend to work—"

"A small sin I am willing to take upon my soul for a larger purpose." They had all been forced by circumstances to violate the Sabbath so many times, he could not count the Sundays.

"No—your foot," Andrew insisted as he hovered near Wyn, who grumbled good-naturedly back at his assistant in all things metallic and religious.

Picking up the item he was near finishing, Wyn said, "You know it must be finished by tonight," and scowled back at him. "Besides, I do not intend to hammer with my foot, Brother Andrew."

His anvil was long gone, but he had commandeered a head of granite ballast stone from the bowels of the ship that made a serviceable surface.

He watched David Iron watching the knife on the coals; the apprentice looked up at Wyn, who nodded—the knife ap-peared ready.

The Yuchi tonged the blade from the glow and began beating it with the hammer while the master looked on approvingly.

"You should be watching them raise the cross," David Iron said.

Wyn nodded, appraising how well his apprentice had taken instruction in the hardening process.

"Next, we build the prayer lodge," said the tall Yuchi, who was Wyn's first convert in this country, and, except for a handful of the red women who married into the Hundred, he was the only one so far.

Wyn nodded, but a trace of frown shadowed his eyes that David Iron did not miss.

"What do you call it, church—is that the word?"

"Perhaps you will build the chapel, David Iron." He flipped the blade over to redden evenly.

"I have it in mind to travel west, to go to the city of God and take it from . . ." He almost said *Infidel*, but knew that would be hard to explain. ". . . from unbelievers."

"City is a lodge of prayer?"

Wyn looked at him, realizing that this red man was probably standing in the largest human community he had ever seen or could imagine. "Not a single lodge, but many, together." How to explain a city to someone who had never seen one? "A big village, you know?"

"Ah, like Mabila?"

Wyn had not seen Hayati's hometown, the big Muskogean village where Father Brian and Ari were held captive until this man helped rescue them, but he heard reports that more than two thousand people lived there. "Yes, only larger."

David Iron chewed on this for a moment. "And this city is in heaven?"

"No, it lies west of here."

David Iron shook his head and used handsign to say, "No, there is nothing like that in the west, only an edge where the sun drops off into the underworld." He stared at the priest. "Only hell lies in that direction, Father Folded Hands." He was proud that he was learning the white names of things.

"But on this side of the edge, there must be this city. We know it exists—Our Lord died there." He gestured vaguely in the direction of the unseen council circle, where David Iron's friends were putting up the hewn cedar post, "On a cross."

The symbol of the cross was also part of the Yuchi tradition. It meant, however, the cardinal directions and not a single geographical location. David Iron replied that he knew of only one place that matched what Wyn was describing.

"It is up in Illinois country, a place of many people, west and north of us, on the Great River Road." David Iron gave the knife a couple more whacks and went on to explain. "I have heard of it, but people say evil is done there, and stay away. The Shawnee hold it taboo and will not even speak of this place."

He gestured at two taciturn Shawnee observing without a blink the two men sweating over their labor.

Wyn was excited by this and wanted to know more. "Go ahead, ask them—ask them now."

David Iron spoke briefly to the elder of the two Shawnee witnesses, who nodded with a jerk and looked piercingly at Wyn.

"He is saying, yes?" Wyn asked expectantly, momentarily catching a glimpse in the glow of his work of the holy city in all its splendor.

"He says that I am correct when I say there are unspeakable places."

"Why is this place unspeakable?"

David Iron asked, received a terse answer, which he translated. "He says, What place?"

Wyn shrugged, a little embarrassed as though he were being made fun of and expecting some joke, but the Shawnee's face remained serious and impassive.

"Does this place have a name?" Wyn asked David Iron.

"I have heard from the Chickasaw that it is called Most North, and that it has a high holy mountain where men are killed and brought back to life, but I have never been there and do not know anyone who has."

"Resurrection," Wyn whispered, his mind racing with recalled scripture, including a verse out of the Book of Daniel, *O Lord, let your wrath be turned away from your city Jerusalem, your holy mountain. . . .*

"I, myself," continued David Iron in a mixture of his own language, Cymraeg, and handsign, "believe that the Chickasaw are braggers who claim this illustrious place as their ancestors' country to make themselves appear larger, more important. They are little, ugly swamp people who have to find something to be proud of, so they make up this legend."

"And you are sure it is on a river?" Wyn asked.

"The Mech-a-sip-i, the Great River Road."

Wyn knew by reading, if not by experience, that Jerusalem is not a river city, but is situated in mountains, miles from the nearest river, the Jordan to the east. "Then it cannot be what I seek."

"You will find nothing like it farther west, where it is too hot for human people to live."

"Jerusalem is in a desert—"

David Iron quenched the knife, while Wyn hefted the longer blade he had been working on before he set off the charcoal mound. The Yuchi tossed the new knife into the sand with the others.

"I will go see how they need my help with the cross," he offered, and Wyn nodded, distracted by the things the Yuchi had said.

David Iron walked to the council circle where several of his Yuchi brothers were ready to raise the thirty-foot cross they had fashioned from the ancient cedar just felled. It was lying in the tramped snow amid a blanket of its hacked aromatic branches, with Father Brian fitting the crossbar just adzed to mate a cantilevered niche in the main post.

Evergreen perfume permeated the air ringing with the blows of an iron pommel Brian used to hammer three long, flat spikes into the stubborn green wood.

David Iron watched from the sidelines with a handful of curious red people, mostly children and women.

Then, after testing the strength of the join, Brian gestured that his assistants should help him raise the post in its sloped step-hole. They stood beneath it, stretching their arms to support it as high as possible while others further pushed it upward with long, forked hickory poles blackened by heat for hardness.

Meanwhile, Evan and Lev and others hauled on ropes guyed around two of the widely spaced council oaks.

David Iron trotted out to lend his back to this labor, and before long the tree was groaning upward, sliding into the socket about a fathom deep in the clay bottom-soil.

The men on the ship joined in the cheer all around as the cross rocked into its bed.

They maneuvered it aright and hammered in support posts around the base. The women rushed in to dump baskets of clay into the socket, then many stamped down the footing with joyous shouts and laughter.

Brian, the laborer, straightened and looked up at the cross with a chill on his arms that had nothing to do with the weather. Behind him, Evan and several other Christians blessed themselves, and someone on the ship whistled a striking note of triumph.

Father Brian, the priest, seized the moment and laid the blessing of the Trinity upon the tree and the laborers, murmuring the sacred words and a quick prayer heavily laden with communal amens.

David Iron pulled at Brian's sleeve, saying to him, "How can we stop Father Folded Hands from going into dangerous western places?"

Brian shrugged. "It would be difficult to change his mind—he has taken a vow to find souls to save."

"But," said David Iron gesturing at his Yuchi relatives and the Shawnee onlookers, "he has many souls to save here—why go elsewhere?"

Brian could not answer, but he said he would pray about the matter.

The Christians continued joyful at the so-called Little Christmas, for which Mary and Gwen prepared a big feast of fowl, cornbread pudding, and maple syrup to take the place of honey for basting. People came and went all afternoon to the piled table the women kept supplied with baked and broiled squash, nuts, dried fruit, and every other kind of edible found within a hundred miles. The red women joined with pots of their own specialties, and the men sampled every dish between shared pipes of tobacco.

Taking short shifts so they got their turns at table, the sailors and every other available hand worked at the ship, where Madoc and Fair Beard were dealing with the effects of melting ice. Most of it was cleared from around the waterline, but new leaks were sprung by the freeze and sudden thaw, so they had pine-tar boiling and were busy caulking with buffalo wool soaked in the stuff.

Their repairs appeared to be satisfactory. Fair Beard proclaimed that it was his opinion that they did not need to pull her up on rollers and replace the straking scraped on their initial landing at this place.

"But to be safe . . ." Madoc was saying, standing ankle-deep in the cold, sloshing water of the bilge deck. It was so good to feel the ship cradled on the water again.

Fair Beard, astride the temporary crossbeam they had installed laterally to shore the questionable hull sections, used a thickly coated stick to smear the last gobs of pine tar on the new caulking.

Their hands were gluey with the nasty concoction as they assayed their day's handiwork.

"It will hold," the Norseman determined, though Madoc crouched to peer at it again.

He slapped the shoring beam and straightened. All his staring had not proved that the straking was structurally damaged; it was his gut that said there was still trouble.

"You are mothering it, my friend," Snorrison said, kicking at the bulkhead. The sole of his wrinkled almost-blue foot slapped resoundingly against the strake lumbered and fitted from an Irish forest specifically to be that particular part of this ship. "Look at that."

With his heel he punched the four-inch-thick board, producing a satisfying, stout music from the ringing wood. "Now let us go defrost our toes and get over to the kitchen before all of Mary's pudding is gone."

They moved amidships, where they cleaned their hands as best they could, dried their numb and wrinkled feet, and with great comfort slipped on dry fleece-lined moccasins, then with their tools—mallets, adz, crowbar, and froe—climbed the peg stair to the deck, where Huw and two others were working on lines and patching sail.

Leaving several sailors to haul bilge water from the hold, the two men crossed the compound, cutting through the council circle below the cross, where Shawnee shamans were placing four logs with ends pointed toward the firepit, the traditional manner of building a ritual fire.

The people greeted the two chiefs, Weather Eyes and Man Whose Weapon Sings, who waved back and called out to various individuals, but kept walking toward the big lodge, where they could smell Mary's Little Christmas feast upon the breeze.

They walked in silence, crunching over the crusts of snow and avoiding mud as they skirted the enclave of small lodges to their right. Neither man looked toward the little habitation nearer the eastern bank, though Madoc tried to see out of the corner of his eye if there was any activity in the direction of the house set apart.

Fair Beard may have glanced there, too, but was discreet about it.

Inside the Big House the feast was on the boards, with all the Christians and Norsemen making their way through the food. Several red women were in attendance, wandering in and out with each other or their men, listening or joining in spontaneous songs that mixed the Algonquin and Yuchi languages with Christian hymns. Madoc saw the clergy across the room as greasy with turkey juices as everyone else.

But later, after they stuffed themselves, the red women stayed outside to enjoy the sun and divide up the leftovers. The white men sat around the table picking at the scraps, talking about home, voicing amazement that they had come this far and survived—their second year in this far western country whose existence was proved only by their arrival.

Several of the Norsemen, including Fair Beard, were

smoking tobacco, passing around small undecorated terra-cotta pipes in the manner of red men in casual congress.

Two of the Norse sailors were discussing the relative value of their red women as compared to white women they had known.

Ulf shook his saltwater blond hair, which he now wore in the red braid down his back, arguing that his Shawnee bride was better than any woman back home. "She works twice as hard and talks half as much." He had lost a brother to the first red nation encountered, but had no prejudice against red people generally and had been one of the first of the Norsemen to take a wife from among the local people.

Huw, who had just come in from the ship and was still working his way through a heaping plate of food, had been silent, but Ulf's comments provoked him to comment from the other side of the table.

"I will never love any of these cruel red people," he said flatly, setting down his plate and causing his companions with red wives to look at him sharply across the trestle table still green from the ax and the adz. Huw ab Tewdr and his wife of many years had joined this expedition together, but she had not survived landfall.

"I beg your pardon," Huw said, "but that is the truth, and I must say it."

"You do not have a Christian heart," Brian replied, shaking his head, picking at a stained splinter in the tabletop. "I have no means of comparison, but I have never known a more tender heart than my Hayati."

Huw scowled and chewed at a slab of meat dripping juices.

"You do not know until you try one," said Gurd, who had just taken up with a Yuchi woman he first met last year.

Brian did not say anything else but stood with his arms folded across his chest and a big grin on his face that bespoke his love for his own Hayati and their sons.

"I, too, love my beautiful wife," said Ari. "She is a wonderful woman, the answer to all my dreams." He looked over at Fair Beard, who sat in silence a little apart from the others, staring into the piles of food still on the table.

"I think my bride journey has been fulfilled, Captain Snorrison!"

The younger Norsemen laughed with Ari and slapped him on the shoulders.

Unreadably steeped in silence back in the shadows at the far end of the table, Fair Beard sniffed a chortle to show that he was a good sport, but his heart did not seem to be in the banter.

"It is good to know that I do not have to go to Constantinople to get you a wife, blamen," Fair Beard answered.

"They are beautiful," Madoc agreed, "but as Huw says, they have cruel ways."

This surprised several of the men, and they voiced it. Madoc had lost two women on this expedition. Both had been white, and he had not seemed interested in any of the Shawnee or Yuchi maidens, though several had given him an opening. It worried those of his crew who leaned in the direction of caring, for it was considered by some not to be a good thing for the leader to be womanless.

Even Wyn had hinted that Madoc would be happier if he would choose among the beautiful young women available in the ranks of their allies, but Madoc showed no interest.

Ari shook his head as though giving up on him.

Madoc shrugged, not wanting to confront any of the men who were so sure of their red wives, and wishing they could get onto another subject. He avoided catching Fair Beard's glance but was aware that the Norseman had to be provoked to take part in this unsettling discussion.

"Will *you* ever love one of them?" asked Huw, who was sitting next to Madoc.

"What about your own grandchild your daughter carries, Captain?" Gurd inquired before Madoc could answer Huw.

This put Madoc off; he did not want to continue this conversation and hoped his silence would shut them up.

"You do not trust them either, then?" Huw queried morosely, licking his blunt fingers and wiping them on his tunic.

Madoc said, "Not at all. I have great respect for my son-in-law and his father, and Winnowed Rice," he added quickly for Rhys's benefit, but a glance around told him the poet was not here.

"Do you not bear at least some Christian brotherly love toward she who saved your life?" said Snorrison with a sarcastic twist to the word Christian.

Madoc stood so quickly, he upset a pottery flagon of water that ran down through a crack in the table and dripped onto the packed clay floor.

Each man in the shadowed windowless room froze as Fair
Beard started to rise to what appeared to be Madoc's challenge. These two men had never fought, never so much as
raised their voices against each other in the memory of anyone
present. Their partnership had endured all heartbreak, sepa-
ration, and catastrophe. Their brotherhood was the keel on
which the whole enterprise depended. Yet here they were
eyeball to eyeball with a woman between them. It was
something none had imagined seeing, so strange as to be
unnerving.

Whatever might have happened was interrupted by Yngvild's rough laugh above them all from the second-story
railing. She was silhouetted by a glow coming from a clam-
shell lamp burning in the room behind her, where the looms
were strung.

She had slimmed down. Only at her breasts did the softness
of motherhood remain on her. Her neck and clavicle were
sharp under her bodice where could be seen the milk stains
her stubborn body produced against her will, though she had
tried for two months to starve herself dry to no avail. Her
bosom was fulsome and soft, the only part of her that was so.
The new angular boniness about her was accentuated by her
devotion to pacing labor, for by this time she spent from dawn
to well past midnight at the loom. She ate sparingly, and only
what was brought to her. When she was not weaving, she
slept, but lightly and only until the firstlight, when she would
wrap herself in a dark, rough cloak with a wide helmet that
could be drawn closed. During the pale time before sunup,
she would walk along the river and watch the reeds and the
high patterns of geese and ducks plowing their slow way
southward, but she never left the loft for any other reason.

So far she had not come down for the feast this afternoon.

Everyone, red and white, eyed her with suspicion when
they saw her, wondering if she had finally gone completely
mad. She spoke to nobody and rarely acknowledged anyone
except her husband, or Mary, who brought up food and
buffalo-wool thread the red women had taken to spindling and
dyeing out in their bustling compound.

The red women avoided her as bad medicine, but they
gossiped. All the Hundred's men were unnerved by her.

"Whoresons, both of you," she snarled. "All of you will go

sniffing after them, you filth, you love it and you cannot keep away. Dogs sniffing bitches."

Madoc was already out the door.

Fair Beard pushed away from the table and strode toward the stairs, where he glared at her still at the rail.

Gwen moving about outside with Hannah in her cradleboard caught his eye, and instead of sprinting up the stair, he darted out the door to speak privately to her. She nodded and wanted to know where Madoc was off to in such a hurry, but Fair Beard did not reply as he worked at the lacing to free Hannah.

When he came back inside with his baby on his long arm, he did not speak to anyone but took the stairs two at a time, following Yngvild, who had stepped away from the rail.

Presently the men around the table were embarrassed to hear their muted exchange in Scandinavian up there in the alcove behind the looms.

"—but you said that before, Snorrison—get away from me—"

"Just look at her, mother," he said with a soft voice.

Hannah made a cute sound.

"Look, Flower. She is just a little baby who does not know anything about the mess she has fallen into."

Yngvild was adamant, crossing her arms tightly even though it hurt. "The captain's daughter will take her."

"She has her own to worry about—besides," he said, mustaches dangling down to provoke what could have been Hannah's first smile, which Fair Beard did not miss, "I like this little girl."

Yngvild hugged herself, a wall against them both.

"Those priests down there are going to baptize my baby a Christian," he said behind her, near her ear, "if someone does not stop them."

"You stop them, then." She slapped him away, keeping her back to him.

"How can I, if a Christian woman adopts her?"

He lifted his long arm up and brought his hand full of baby down in front of her, then drew that arm close to her so that Hannah's face pressed against her tenderest spot.

Yngvild moaned and tried to step back, but he was there blocking her with his own body, hugging her between himself and Hannah, who looked up with large dark eyes, the only thing about her reminiscent of her mother. That dark scruff of hair in this light was not black at all, but wavy mink brown, the little bow Gwen had tied there coming undone. Yuchi milk had plumped out her wrinkled leanness—all that remained of her premature redness was a rosy glow—and the food and attention given her by Gwen and the Yuchi had mellowed the baby's first temperament.

Her fingernails had grown in. One long-boned little hand clutched at the fabric of Yngvild's tunic, brushing her nipple, which began leaking on cue.

The baby smelled the milk and reached for the teat it promised.

Yngvild groaned, closing her eyes and leaning against her husband, who took her weight. "My body is my enemy," she hissed through clenched teeth. "Please, Snorrison, take this child back to her mother."

"But she has no mother," he said, pivoting Yngvild around with his free hand, encouraged that he found so little resistance.

"Do you mean to deny—?" she started to fume, gesturing stiffly in the direction of the red enclave, where they both knew this child's mother was ensconced.

"The river is freeing up," he said, stroking Yngvild's cheek. He still held the baby, but his wife's left hand had involuntarily come up beneath the little swaddled weight as he continued. "Very soon those filthy Skraelings will be leaving, and we will never see them again."

"You said that once before."

"Do I control the weather?" he asked, bending in an accommodating way at the knee to seek her glance, which had dropped against her will to the baby with her searching wet lips.

Even that light touch hurt. Yngvild felt her nipple contract, already itching furiously. She was dying to rip away the cloth, just to get relief.

"Damn you, son of Snorri."

The baby made invigorated smacking noises, salivating against the soaked cloth. Yngvild could feel milk erupt and run down inside her clothing in a hot, sticky stream. Now the other nipple was letting loose its sympathetic flood. She wanted to scream with the discomfort, but she forced herself instead to look directly into her husband's eyes as he continued speaking:

"Do you know what she did? That Skraeling bitch tried to kill this child, my child, Flower, my first baby girl."

Yngvild stared at him.

"Ask any of the red women. Just threw her out in the snow, leaving her for the wolves."

The baby had his big scarred thumb in her delicate hand, trying to get from it the milk she smelled.

"But," he continued, as much to the child wrestling vigorously with his finger as to his wife, "what she did not know was that you cannot kill a Norse baby that way, huh, little one? Baby Norsewomen thrive in snow!"

He leaned the finger against her leaking nipple, causing her to cry out in true pain.

"No," she cried, trying to get away from him, clutching her breasts with her hands as though that could stop their pumping. "No—this is *my* baby's milk!"

She turned, sobbing without sounds, mourning for the little boy for the first time. "Oh, Snorri, I keep dreaming of him among these short red people, being so different, not understanding who he is, growing to manhood and never knowing—I cannot bear it—it will kill me!"

He let her lean on him, the baby fussing between them, Yngvild spilling out the sorrow she had kept to herself all these weeks.

"Our Bjorn is dead, Yngvild, taken by the river," Snorrison said in a crooning tone of voice while he stroked her hair. "But, look, this is my baby, alive and needing you."

"But it is not knowing that is so bad, not knowing for sure if he is alive or dead."

"He is gone, Yngvild. That is all we need to know."

She drew in a long liquid breath, still not accepting the full weight of the baby. But he could feel that something in her had relented even before she said, "Promise me the Skraeling will go away."

"I promise." His voice was unhesitating.

"And you will not follow her. Swear it."

He looked down, then slyly regarded her from beneath his droopy eyelids, a definite negotiating posture. "Do you promise me to keep and love this child as our own?"

She nodded.

"Then I promise not to follow the Natchez."

"And you will never leave me, never again, no matter what?"

"I will never again leave you, Flower."

"Swear it on the Kisser."

He looked up at the wall, where hung the horned battle-ax forged with filigree holes in its blade that gave it a unique screaming song when he whirled it above his head. Leaving Hannah in the crook of her arm, he stepped over to stand below the weapon. He did not remove it from its peg but laid his ham of a hand upon its flat face and pronounced his vow.

"By Odin, by Thor, by the edge of this blade, and upon my life, I swear."

He walked back to where she stood, milk oozing from her fountain. Fair Beard Snorrison knew the sky and sea and ships; he had more than passing understanding of weapons and the metalwork that produced them. But he also knew some things about living creatures, having hunted his share of fur-bearing animals. He knew that mother creatures—even the fiercest of the wildcats, even polar bears and wolves—would claim what suckled.

The baby was sucking air as he pressed her little back closer to Yngvild, who made another cry, this time of pleasure instead of pain as the baby's lips locked on and began sucking through the cloth.

Yngvild tore at the broach holding up that side of her dress—she had refused to wear clothes cut in the red fashion. With a sigh she felt the stream welling like an unbroken, hot, bright wire from its source deep within the pit of her pouring into the little mouth.

She took a step backwards, almost fainting with the sensation as the wet stain widened on the other side of her tunic.

Snorrison helped her sit upon their bed and stayed there with her while the baby fed.

Across the compound, Winnowed Rice was applying sunbeams to her husband's face, while Cari in her cradleboard hanging from a peg cooed and played with her own fat fingers.

Rhys sat on his heels in the light of the hearth fire while Winnowed Rice laid a precise golden ray up across his right eyebrow.

Concentrating on her work, she was nevertheless aware of Firefly shadowing the doorway.

"Thank you for the new strap," Rhys said, moving as little of his face as possible to give her a steady surface.

Winnowed Rice grunted an acceptance. But from the corner of her eye, she could see beyond the open doorway where the hide flap had been tied back to let in fresh air.

One of the young tangletongues lingered a respectful distance away, but obviously attending to this lodge.

She was aware that Firefly was also watching him.

"Do you wish to attend the round meeting?" Winnowed Rice asked Firefly, at the same time giving Rhys a little pinch on the thigh where Firefly could not see it, to tell him something interesting was happening.

The young Natchez woman rolled a telling glance at the man with reddish blond hair watching this cabin, holding a trenchor of food in his hands.

"I will stay with your mistress," Winnowed Rice volunteered. "You go and enjoy the feast."

Firefly bit her lip, thinking, her eye still caught up in the man's glance. He smiled and gestured with the food.

"I cannot," Firefly said, still watching her suitor. "Soon I must make her swallow the medicine."

"What is it?"

"I do not know everything she mixed, but it has maidenhair fern and some root she dug up on the island. She would not tell me. . . ."

Winnowed Rice nodded, thinking about what she would use if she wanted to pass out and stay that way for several days. There were at least a couple of alternatives, depending on whether she wanted deep, dreamless sleep or colorful visions.

The Natchez sun was not dreaming, Winnowed Rice noted, because her eyes were not moving in their dream dance beneath the lids.

"I will make sure she takes the medicine."

Firefly was silent a long moment, then she said, "My lady Tumkis instructed me to feed her a pinch of this steeped in boiling water twice a day." Her decision made, Firefly handed over a small drawstring pouch marked with significations.

Winnowed Rice took the dense, potent little bag.

"I will not be long," Firefly said. "I will take some of the feast, so the whites do not think us rude."

Firefly left the house and walked purposefully toward Lev, who held out the plate as she approached. Together they continued on toward the bright circle, where many people had already gathered, even though it was not yet sunset and time for the ceremonies to begin.

Rhys began tuning the harp, and Cari made little sounds with him.

From the firepit coals Winnowed Rice tonged out a knot of terra-cotta, which she tossed into a tightly woven basket, bringing the water there to a quick boil. Meanwhile she set inside a covered basket the pouch Firefly had given her and took another of her own from a capped jug on the clay bench that made up her hearth.

"What mischief are you up to?" Rhys asked in a playful voice.

"Hmmph," she answered, putting a pinch of her own medicine into a wooden beaker, then dipping a gourdful of hot water from the basket. It frothed to the rim of the cup, turning the powder into a pungent greenish tea that subsided under steam. When the infusion smelled just right, she brought it over to the platform where Tumkis slept.

Winnowed Rice supported her neck while the tea dribbled down her chin and into her mouth, enough to provoke a small coughing fit that subsided when the limp head settled back onto the cushions. But her thirsty little tongue had accepted some of the concoction.

"Is she going to die?"

Madoc's voice at the doorway did not startle Winnowed Rice, who forced more of the tea into Tumkis's mouth, then set aside the cup and replied, "No," and inclined her head in a gesture that told him to come on in.

Rhys made a sound on the harp, a shred of percussion and string twang that drew Madoc's attention from Tumkis, whose eyelids were fluttering.

Winnowed Rice returned to her husband, who, resting the harp beside him, leaned farther upon his knees in her direction.

For the next few minutes Madoc watched her finish painting the poet's face. Beneath her sure hand the yellow, red, and black suns grew as the a cappella hymn outside increased in tempo.

He admired the expert sureness, the economy of her movements. Rhys had lost the sash some time ago and had not replaced it except with this design. The face painting had become the couple's daily ritual. Now, seeing her at work, the effect upon his friend's face did not seem as strange to Madoc as before.

While she worked, Rhys hummed the Latin hymn along with the congregation outside, and she caught his beat, painting in time with it, each movement a small dance accompanied by his tune.

Madoc was a fascinated audience, but his eye was drawn to the couch of furs where the moon was coming out from behind a cloud.

She took in the tableau of the woman and man kneeling face-to-face with her quick movements and his song between them, and in a widening glance she perused the lodge from the cooing, dangling baby snug in her wrappings this side of the fireplace to the woven hangings at the end of the bed, her gaze landing on the nearby empty wooden cup with its ring of greenish scum.

Only then did she look up and lock eyes with the white man softly staring at her across the star-robe, then found her spine and struggled to straighten against the cushions.

Madoc resisted helping her, letting her find her own strength.

From a new height she regarded him steadily holding her in his gray-eyed gaze.

Fingers lightly touching his work-roughened hand on top of the heavenly patterns, she whispered as though they were entirely alone, "This is the hand that pulled me back."

Out in the council circle, the Christians began to sing a hymn that announced the beginning of the Mass.

Yuchi and Shawnee headmen, sitting in places of honor in the front rank of log benches, straightened in attention and leaned slightly forward to better see what the white people were going to do.

Andrew, swinging a pottery censer steaming out a cloud of thick aromatics, walked down the slight slope of the natural bowl to the cross near the blazing fire. Brian in his makeshift vestments followed slowly while the voices unrolled the hymn out into the chilly air.

The red chiefs watched, entranced, awaiting some amazing thing, having been promised that these white shamans would turn bread into flesh and water into blood. David Iron had been preparing his father and the other old men for days, explaining the ceremony.

When the faithful straggled down to the rough altar draped with a piece of cane matting and set with the pine-knot candles, the elders of the red men accompanied them, standing, with airs of deep and serious study, close to the kneelers to observe exactly what Brian was doing.

It appeared to be simply that he was feeding them flakes of corncake, while Andrew followed behind with a jug of water. The priest and his helper made their way along the line, which included David Iron genuflecting beside Gwen.

Sun Caller exchanged a meaningful glance with one of his counselors as the elder returned to his seat of honor draped with buffalo hides. Red men did not kneel in prayer or otherwise. Women knelt to do their work over children, food, or water, but warriors did not kneel in public. The red men exchanged meaningful looks that said what they saw here might be untraditional, but it was nothing remarkable.

Wyn gave them a rousing sermon on the necessity of bringing the word of God to the Infidel at the gates of the city, which David Iron had trouble translating. Brian's words this afternoon helped him interpret what Wyn was saying, however, provoking looks of curiosity from the headmen he knew would ask questions later.

But the singing was enjoyed by all as the red people began to join, first the ones who were learning from the white people; then, as the sky grew darker and the fire at the points of the four logs grew hotter, the red people took over the beat.

The women started a circle around the fire, hands joined, their pattern syncopated with enthusiastic grunts and hollers from men who stood from the bleachers and rattled shells and hollow sticks in time with the rising female voices.

Back in the lodge Rhys heard the change in patterns. He gathered up the harp, slinging the new strap across his shoulder. Winnowed Rice used the tuffed stick to make a final small adjustment in her handiwork, then with her little finger filled in the design above his eyebrow.

She spoke softly to him. He returned the remark in Algonquin, then turned to Madoc and said in Cymraeg, "So, Weather Eyes, are you ready to become an eagle warrior?"

Madoc answered with some embarrassment, yes, he supposed he was as ready as he ever would be. He looked back at

Tumkis without words, though something transpired between them that did not go unnoticed by Winnowed Rice and perhaps even Rhys, who cocked his head and smiled in her direction.

She touched his sleeve and handed him the staff, sending him out of the lodge after Madoc.

Out among the celebrants special food was being offered on trays, passed down the lines of happy people. Madoc sat with Sun Caller, healthier looking now that he had settled his people among friends with his son and daughter-in-law nearby. The man was very old—David Iron said maybe as much as ten eights—a rare degree among the red people and held in high regard. Madoc was glad to see him improved in these new circumstances.

When a plate of suspicious morsels was passed to him, Madoc whispered in Gwen's ear, privately begging her not to tell him what they were eating for fear it would be snakes or bugs or something even more revolting; but everything tasted delicious.

Everyone was laughing, singing, or talking together. All the red people, and a few of the white men, too, had painted faces and fancy beaded shirts upon their backs.

In the middle of the council circle the fire roared, casting high flames and shooting sparks up into the starry heavens. The moon set early, and now the sky was stretched densely black.

Accompanied by drums, bells, and old Honeyvoice, the young men from Meadows-of-Mint placed their patterns before the assembled chiefs and the people.

Back in the lodge Winnowed Rice asked the Natchez sun in Muskogean, "Do you want to watch the ceremony?"

"I am going to throw up."

Winnowed Rice set a wide-mouthed jug directly beneath Tumkis, who eyed her curiously before taking advantage of the receptacle.

"Your medicine has undone my work, Dog-Woman," Tumkis finally said, gasping, cold sweat breaking out on her lip.

Winnowed Rice calmly offered her a wipe and a beaker of clear water, which Tumkis took gratefully, pulling herself farther upright.

"It was sad work, Lady Tumbling Water."

"I seem to be able to accomplish little else," said the Natchez sun in a dispirited slow voice.

She was little more than a girl, Winnowed Rice reflected as she watched Tumkis swab her own face with the mulberry-cloth rag. It was hard not to feel sorry for her.

"Everything I have done has turned to coal and ashes."

She appeared faint again, dejected and drawn down so that momentarily she did not look like a young woman but a wizened crone, her eyes rolling in shadowed sockets, her trembling hand sinking down with the wet cloth on the covers.

Winnowed Rice relieved her of it and said, "One can use coals and ashes to start a new fire."

Despite Tumkis's misery she shared a pure, revelatory glance with Winnowed Rice before a cheer from the council circle drew their attention toward the doorway.

"What are they doing?" Tumkis wanted to know, brightening a little.

Winnowed Rice considered that curiosity a good sign.

The Natchez sun leaned forward, trying to see around the doorpost.

"Father Folded Hands has made a new long knife for Weather Eyes," she said, reporting what she could see from where she sat and what she knew had been planned. "He told me that it has a name."

"How strange."

"Yes."

"What do they call this knife that deserves a name like a person?"

"They call it Never Gives Up."

Chapter 20

W hile the Hundred cheered, Madoc held the sword Wyn
had made for him.

Pride and delight swelled in his chest as he heard the people
and hefted the weapon, still warm from work upon it, not as
fancy as the first Durendal finished with inlaid silver and gold
in a French king's armory, but a finely balanced double-edged
blade of dull blue steel with an unadorned crescent hilt, a
weapon fit for a king who intended to do serious battle.

He looked up at the joyous faces surrounding him, red and
white faces, men and women and children cheering, clapping,
and stamping their feet on the packed ground of the council
circle almost as old as the wide, rolling land and endless river
beyond.

He was unable to speak for a moment. Feelings clutched his
throat as Wyn formally blessed him and the sword, several
hands slapped his back, and Fair Beard over there grinned
with Yngvild at his side, holding what Madoc knew must be
Hannah in her swaddling blanket.

He fleetingly wondered how Snorrison accomplished it.

But he was swept up by the sound of the community's
lengthy cheer and moved by the sight of Gwen's sweet face
with David Iron beside her, and Rhys behind his sunbursts,
and Wyn rejoining the brothers in a clutch to one side, their
rough-spun brown robes the color of the raw earth around the
cross, where they lingered as though fearing to venture farther
into secular jubilation.

It was all around Madoc, and he the center of it, holding the
warm sword with both hands because, like its predecessor, it
was almost too heavy to lift with one alone.

There seemed to be far more feeling swirling around him
than called for by the moment. Then he realized that they

were celebrating something that had been stored inside them, something that survived through all their travails and tribulations to be brought forth at this time and place and laid at his feet.

He felt bent by it, as though he did not deserve to be the focus of so much pride. More than anything he did not want anyone to see that these feelings misted his eyes and muted his voice so that all he could do was grin back at them and hope they did not expect him to deliver a speech.

Where they might have, the red elders had other plans. Imperceptibly, they took over the ceremony. The music developed a more energetic beat with their tambourines, drums, and flutes. Madoc lay the sword in its leather wrapping before him so that it was displayed in the firelight and returned to his seat beside Sun Caller.

Rhys retired the harp and returned with the others as audience to the log benches while a flock of painted and feathered Shawnee braves darted out of the dark trees, converging on the fire in the center of the circle.

They danced the eagle for Madoc and for other heroes in the Hundred, and when it was over, the women, young local girls and the normally shy wives of the Hundred, rushed to form a vigorous circle pattern they took as fast as their feet would go.

The old red men passed around a pipe after that, and Sun Caller got up to speak. Translated by David Iron, his speech was mostly honorifics and formulas that were rituals of the men's lodge organization of which he was the highest-ranking officer present.

Using the name he had given the Hundred last year, which meant blue-eyed snakes, Sun Caller said that the kanegmati and the Yuchi with their Shawnee friends were founding a new nation under the white chief. The snake, far from being a derogatory reference, was a respected animal represented by the big serpentine canoe the pale-eyed white people had ridden into this country.

He enumerated Madoc's triumphs—David Iron and his father had rehearsed this part. The list of accomplishments went on for some time, and each was greeted with a cheer from the warrior-dancers, who kept up a low chant punctuated by in-place steps punched onto the hard ground.

The old men pushed the four logs deeper into the firepit;

flames screamed upwards, shooting sparks that rivaled stars into the wind-cleared sky.

Sun Caller offered the pipe to the Shawnee headman from Meadows-of-Mint. He was a venerable grandfather, even older than the Yuchi chief, who rose with great dignity and delivered his slow, formal address honoring others of the Hundred.

"And to Father Folded Hands, the split feather means a wound taken in the ankle from the smoking mountain." He looked around for Wyn, who hobbled into the inner ring to accept the feather.

The old Shawnee would have jabbed it into Wyn's quoit, but the abbot had allowed Caradoc to shave and barber him after his charcoal duty and had no locks to braid. So the Shawnee elder tucked the feather behind the brother's ear, causing him to blush and hurry back to the shadow of the cross, where he immediately removed the feather. He twirled it between his thumb and finger as Brian affectionately slapped his back.

The abbot looked sheepishly at Andrew, who had earlier challenged Madoc not to participate in any heathen practices.

The young brother started to reply but heard his own name being called—the red women had nicknamed him Swimming Upstream, and it was for the same triumph they awarded him an eagle feather now. "For defeating the Oyo River, who tasted you and would have eaten you without your good luck!"

"I could not have made it without the help of Our Lord Jesus Christ," Andrew said defiantly, but he accepted the feather Sun Caller placed behind his ear so that he returned to the huddle of clerics beaming, despite himself.

"I suppose it cannot hurt," Wyn whispered ironically to him. "It is just a feather." Now it was Andrew's turn to blush with some measure of pride and look sheepishly down at the heathen tribute in his own fingers.

The elder presented an eagle feather to all the white men on some pretext or other. Usually this was a battle decoration, but the circumstances provided him with many other kinds of triumphs to remark.

David Iron translated each honorific, and the pipe contin-ued hand to hand.

Finally only Madoc awaited the feather ceremony.

Sun Caller took over as speaker again, but it was David Iron who placed the huge eagle bonnet on Madoc's head. It was a veritable crown of plumes, at least fifty arrayed across his brow in a beaded leather headband lined with buffalo fluff. Long plumy wings from egrets, turkeys, and redbirds trailed on either side of his face and down his back, with hair tassels and beads as a fringe the wind tossed magnificently.

The dancers swarmed out into the circle again while the fire-tenders placed new logs beside the old ones burned to stubs, so that the fire was renewed and doubled.

The women kept the tempo, swaying in a wider circle around the male dancers, who broke their circle and began to snake their way among the seated audience that numbered well more than two hundred.

But then what Madoc dreaded was finally at hand; Sun Caller made a gesture that they wanted the chief to speak, with David Iron translating the handsign lest there was any doubt: "Esteemed sir, do not withhold your words from us."

"Must I?" Madoc asked his son-in-law, who assured him that he must.

Madoc gestured to Wyn. They spoke head-to-head while the people took this opportunity to stretch as the cheering subsided into various conversations, and the Shawnee hostesses passed around drinking water and small cakes of precious cornmeal and walnuts in maple syrup for everyone.

Wyn nodded in agreement with whatever Madoc was asking and called Andrew to join them. After listening to what his abbot instructed, he, too, nodded and trotted off toward the dark forge, the fires of which had been banked, signaling to Evan and Ari on the way that they should accompany him.

"These are wonderful gifts our Shawnee and Yuchi friends have given," Madoc began, bringing the people to a sort of attention. Licking their fingers, they took their seats on the smoothly hewn logs and leaned expectantly forward while flames glowed behind him and wind strummed the bare trees.

To one side, Rhys picked up his cue and began to play Honeyvoice in a mood that was traditional accompaniment to extemporary speeches.

Stalling for time so the men could fetch what he had ordered, Madoc retold their adventures so far: their initial confrontations with red people, their long foot journey across the hills and into the valleys of the Tennessee, their alliance with the Yuchi, the arrival of the brave Shawnee women, the Chickasaw attack and subsequent battle with the Cherokee at

Muscle Shoals, their journey upriver, the weather, the shipwreck, deaths, and other tribulations encountered and triumphed over with the help of loyal friends and allies.

"We came here as strangers with our hands and mouths open," he said. "Our red friends have fed us and helped us build shelters. We have gifts, too, for these true friends."

He timed his words to conclude when he saw approaching the three men lugging two heavy cane baskets between them. They brought their burdens right up to Madoc, still under the feather crown, and dumped them clattering at his feet on the wide skin spread out to cushion the new Durendal.

The blue steel knife blades rang with separate clamorous voices, bringing cries of awe from the red warriors to see such a wealth of the marvelous weapons in one pile.

Without a lot of ceremony, Madoc quickly began distributing these to each of the red men around the fire. Andrew and others learning metallurgy had been working to finish at least a hundred blades, which they planned to begin trading when warm weather returned.

Instinct now informed Madoc that these first products of their forge were much better spent as gifts. They could always make more.

Each red warrior had been coveting one of these blue knives on display at the bloomery, expecting to have to trade. Now they were excited and incredulous that they were being given the prize for free.

Madoc himself placed one of the weapons on Sun Caller's palm. It was a moment of triumph for the old man, who had suffered such loss of face when he was forced to give up his first iron knife and so much more to the Cherokee.

Madoc turned to heft a knife for the Shawnee elder but instead found himself confronting another red man whom he did not expect.

Rippling conversation among the jubilant people came to a halt in a diminishing wave of human sounds, so that it was gradually quieter as all attention fastened upon the two men standing eye-to-eye in the ruddy light.

The roaring fire whipped by the wind accompanied Rhys's quickly fading music when the poet heard the sudden vacuum of silence that seemed to draw everyone in attendance to Madoc at its center.

There were whispers, but finally even those were silenced.

Madoc had not yet handed the knife to Arrow Always Red, but the Natchez was waiting, hand out, for his trophy.

"Do you have gifts for the Natchez, too?" the tattooed red man asked in a firm voice, pronouncing each word so that those far back in the audience could hear.

"David Iron!" Madoc called, "please come put the words of our friend into my language."

His son-in-law was already there at hand. But instead of relaying the Natchez's remark, which was obvious from his outstretched palm, David Iron said evenly to Madoc, "Do not do it."

Voice growing very calm, Madoc answered, "Now, David Iron, we have gifts for all our friends," and without hesitation laid onto the tattooed hand the pommel left bare to be bound with a grip of cord or bone according to the owner's taste.

The Natchez let his fingers close one by one around the weapon, saying, with David Iron dutifully translating, "Are you sure you want to arm me with this blue metal, Weather Eyes?"

"Are you not our friend?"

"I am going to cut out your tongue with this gift, white man."

The red people gasped before David Iron had a chance to relay this, he with his hand on his knife, ready to step between his father-in-law and the Natchez warrior, who was dropping into an attack crouch.

Translation was not necessary to understand what the Natchez was saying.

"Then" Arrow Always Red continued, grinning now, "I am going to remove your balls."

David Iron did not render this remark into Cymraeg either; the Natchez made an expert swipe at Madoc that said it all too eloquently.

Madoc stepped effortlessly back and put his hand on David Iron's shoulder at the same time, to prevent him from interfering. His movement took him nearer to Durendal, but he did not go farther toward engagement.

The people had split into two streams of shock, pressing in close as they watched the empty-handed Weather Eyes confronting the challenger.

David Iron's quick lodge brothers had the Natchez enclosed before he could make another move. David Iron was himself in a good position to disarm Arrow Always Red, but Madoc's glance stayed his hand.

With a gesture, Madoc signaled to them all that they were to stay out of it. At the same time he was aware of the other Natchez warriors standing loose but attentive on either side of their war leader.

Madoc straightened, not taking his eyes off the other. "Is it not better to wait until another time—daylight, perhaps—for sport?" he asked with equanimity, and David Iron put this into Natchez for the benefit of Arrow Always Red, who replied, "You have not waited for your sport."

This ignited a crackle of comment among the spectators, which the Natchez ignored. "Do you think you have not been seen coming and going from my wife's lodging?"

"You do not have a wife," said another incongruous voice from the right-hand darkness.

Every eye turned toward Tumkis walking into the light of the bonfire with the robe drooping on her shoulders, stars on the outside, the wool side of it sweeping the ground behind her like a queen's train.

"Go back in your fireside, wife," Arrow Always Red replied coolly.

"You do not have a wife, Arrow Always Red," she repeated in a surprisingly strong voice for a woman reported near death. She stopped a pace to Madoc's right, facing the Natchez, who was sworn to protect her. So far she had not looked at Weather Eyes but kept her gaze steady on her erstwhile protector.

David Iron had some time ago backed from between the principals; things were moving too swiftly now for general translation. But he was near enough to Madoc to lend a private, rough approximation of the Natchez's exchange.

All the speakers of Muskogean gasped again when Arrow Always Red told Tumkis, "Hide your face in shame before I slice off your nose right here in front of all these witnesses to mark you for what you are."

Red women whispered this exchange for their white partners, who passed it around while Arrow Always Red continued speaking to one of the onlookers he was sure could understand him.

"She sold that half-white child to Lady Death," he said to Hayati standing near Fair Beard and Yngvild.

Brian's wife looked embarrassed as her husband pushed

through the crowd to stand, with his fists knotted, between her and the Natchez, who made no move to advance.

Behind Brian, Hayati told him what the Natchez warrior accused: "He says she put the child out to die."

Behind her Wyn and Andrew heard, and flung cold stares at Tumkis while crossing themselves to ward off evil.

Tumkis appeared to ignore them all, concentrating all her attention on Arrow Always Red, to whom she commanded in rapid Muskogean, "Leave us immediately and go back to my uncle, the miko of the Village of Black Cherries, and tell him that I have sent you and will return shortly."

"When I was your servant, Lady Tumbling Water, you could summon me. Now that I am your husband, you will do as I say."

Around them many people were discussing the charge against her, while the Natchez couple continued their conversation alone in the midst of the many.

Madoc strained to watch Tumkis as though merely by watching her closely, he could follow her reply and understand what her truth was.

"Is she your wife or not?" David Iron demanded, which many around him were wondering, then translated the reply to any who wanted to listen: "He says he gave her meat, and in return she gave him corn."

"You know I did not," she said firmly.

Madoc liked the way she was standing up to him as though their relative height and strength were unimportant, but still he watched the warrior's hand that held the iron knife, poised though evidently targetless.

"Firefly!" Arrow Always Red called into the crowd.

She came forward slowly, not looking up as was the normal manner of a red woman to a red man, lingering near her mistress, who grabbed the initiative from the warrior by demanding to Firefly, "Tell us all what you saw between this misguided warrior and myself that morning."

"My lady did not accept his fresh kill. She told him to bring the deer carcass to this humble one for butchering."

"Tell them about the corncake," Arrow Always Red ordered with equal confidence.

Firefly shrank back, eyeing Tumkis nearby, then glancing fearfully back at the warrior.

"Go ahead," Tumkis said crisply, "but be careful to tell exactly what you saw."

Looking stricken with the order, the girl whispered hoarsely, "But my lady, you did have a corncake. You did put it on the ground at his feet."

"I spit it at him in contempt."

Firefly shrugged as though by compacting herself into a smaller mass, she could disappear and avoid this terrible witness.

"She admits she did offer me corn," Arrow Always Red announced in a wide voice to everyone around him.

"Then they are married," someone said in the crowd, and a buzz of agreement circulated through the red people.

There were not a few curses exclaimed by male members of the Hundred in Tumkis's direction; she did not understand much of their language, but she knew the muttered words of derision by tone if not by actual meaning, the sound of disgust in a man's voice for the behavior of a particular woman.

For the first time she looked swayed, deflated, curling the huge robe more tightly around herself as though that could give her protection.

"Well," Wyn put in from the direction of the cross, "if this is a marital dispute . . ."

Andrew muttered something beneath his breath about the abomination of murdering children, which several of the white men seconded with their own judgments of such a woman.

"If what I say were not so, why would she give up her child to this other woman, her hated rival?" Arrow Always Red asked those nearest him when he saw Firefly shaking her head and moving closer beside Tumkis.

Everyone looked at Tumkis's baby fussing in the Norse-woman's arms.

Firefly said defensively, "All of you saw my lady Tumbling Water give this child to Yellow Flowers to atone for one that was lost." She looked around for vindication, but memories were short. Most of the whites had never understood what went on in that confusing time on Bear Island, now blurred further by more recent events.

"Gwen," Fair Beard said, "you were there—did Tumkis abandon this baby in the snow?" He looked right at his Natchez sweetheart and asked, "Could you have done that to our child?"

Yngvild beside him seemed to glow in his shadow when he directed this invective. She clutched Hannah closer to herself as though confirming something unspoken.

Gwen hesitated a moment too long to answer, and then she could not without bringing it all down on the Natchez sun or lying, so she said, "It is not our place to judge her."

Another sizzling buzz ran through the crowd, which had formed a sort of ring around Tumkis, who stood alone in their midst, aloof, wrapped in the star-robe and her self-containment.

"A woman like that is not fit to stay among decent people," Mary announced from the other side of the audience.

Several of the Hundred's white men agreed out loud with her, while someone translated the remark into Muskogean.

An ugly sound rippled anonymously among them.

During all this Madoc had slipped the distracting feathers from his head and was moving one step at a time toward his weapon lying back on the leather pallet. He had it now as he got into position for what he was going to have to do.

Arrow Always Red did not miss his movement through the crowd but was not disturbed by it, knowing Madoc was placing himself to his best advantage, from which position the white man said, "If this woman says she is not this man's wife, then I for one believe her." He stepped toward her as a way of expressing his intent.

The eyes of the crowd followed like verbal ballplay, turning to the Natchez for his response.

Arrow Always Red regarded the other for a long moment, still holding the knife as though ready to attack. Then, after a protracted moment, he slowly relaxed and stood aright from the battle position. He tossed the knife from hand to hand, its blade flashing dramatically in the firelight, and Madoc steadied himself for tricky aggression.

Within a pace of the two men, everyone backed off.

The air took on a texture of roughened excitement as expectations for a good fight grew among the onlookers.

A few of the red men signaled silent bets to each other. Madoc and the Natchez were evenly matched opponents; their confrontation should give quite a show.

But it was not to be.

Arrow Always Red flipped the knife expertly and slid it in a swift movement into a scabbard he had waiting empty on his belt.

Madoc knew when he saw the ready scabbard that the red man had planned this, being outnumbered and wishing only to save face and take revenge by bringing shame to Tumkis and himself.

Arrow Always Red's smile was totally devoid of any goodwill as he said to Madoc, "She is not worth fighting for, Weather Eyes, and far more trouble than any woman is worth." He regarded the people, enjoying the expressions of those he had succeeded in turning against her, then continued to Madoc: "I give the bitch to you."

He punctuated this with a well-aimed arrow of spit that hit Tumkis on the cheek—Firefly was there to wipe the spittle away, but Tumkis made no action in response to him. She just stood there with her back straight and her eyes staring holes into him.

With that he turned, signaling to his men, who trotted after him toward the canoe they had been building on the other riverbank.

He passed beside Firefly, to whom he uttered sharp inquiry. She shook her head.

Lev was there beside her, unspeaking, and Arrow Always Red narrowed his eyes at the Norseman. With a single expletive in his own language, he turned and continued with his men toward the canoe, leaving everyone staring at Madoc and Tumkis back near the fire.

The couple stood their ground in the middle of the people. Whispering, the Hundred backed away from the two of them as a dilating circle, leaving the man and woman standing isolated on the ring of muddy earth. He and she could not help taking a step toward each other, pushed together by the silent wind of all those loud glares.

Never in his combative life had Madoc felt more a target, though none but his own weapon was in sight. The hundreds of eyes had points, all directed toward the two of them alone in the center.

Behind him he heard Wyn say, "By the savior's blood, sir, you cannot be serious—"

Fair Beard was scowling at him; Yngvild's look was a mirror of her husband's but with an added triumphant glow as she hefted Hannah up on her shoulder with one hand the way

Madoc had seen warriors lift and affectionately carry their swords after successful battle.

The red women were staring blatantly between Madoc and Tumkis as he turned to assay their response. Tumkis saw it, too, and stiffened inside her robe, then said to him, "Weather Eyes, will you take me in the big canoe back to my uncle to answer the charges that warrior will surely lodge against me?"

He nodded yes, impressed by her coolness with all those judgment eyes upon her.

He had to admit to himself that they unnerved him. He saw the sword in his own hand as though just discovering it for the first time and let it relax, point down. He was not wearing a scabbard, so he slid it behind his belt, adjusting its weight while asking, "Who wants to go with me?" a familiar question most of those gathered around had heard him ask before.

There was a shuffling of stances, and men glanced at other men with the question in their eyes.

Madoc did not try for any joviality, but it was with level optimism that he said, "You must be getting cabin fever by now, Snorrison. Will you pilot?"

Yngvild's face went rigid as she darted a glance at her husband, who was already shaking his head, enclosing her and the baby in his long arm.

Madoc's face felt hot with a volatile mixture of emotions. Now he knew how Snorrison had accomplished his little family.

"It is not a good time to travel, friend," the Norseman said, casting his gaze upon the absolutely clear heavens. "The weather is bound to turn colder before true spring, and the current is too much for our boards."

Several of his men behind him were nodding firm agreement when he shook his head emphatically and concluded, "The ship needs more work."

Madoc did not remind him that only this morning he declared otherwise, but turned with burning disgust and growing embarrassment to Huw, who was standing in a locked, pillar-hard posture, arms folded across his chest, with Einion beside him anxiously watching the adults and chewing his nails.

Wyn and Brian ranked beyond like a bastion of brown buffalo wool and reddened, stern flesh. Near them was Caradoc the mediciner with a plump Shawnee woman beside him, which said all that needed to be spoken about his adjustment to their new circumstances. Evan stood with the sailors between the clergy and Fair Beard's Norsemen, all made brothers by their frowning, disapproving stares.

As Madoc caught each man's glance, the bolder ones just stared back, while others looked away from him at their own feet or at their neighbor.

Every face Madoc saw as he continued pivoting had the identical flat expression, except Gwen's, which Madoc could not see buried in David Iron's shirt while the Yuchi stared into the distance over Madoc's shoulder.

Sun Caller gave him back a frown, chin thrust out, lips drawn into a narrow, judgmental line.

Giving up on them all, Madoc regarded Tumkis, who for some time had not been looking at anyone else but him. Her look sent a chill along his arms and thighs, and he thought, I let them once keep me from a woman I loved, but not this time.

He stood so closely to her, she did not have to move anything except her arm to include him and make them one under the sky-robe. Bound in its shelter and without further futile words, he and she walked out of the crowd's heart toward the *Horn* bobbing down on the river.

The crowd parted for them. Nobody spoke or even whispered as the couple left the Hundred around its fire to knot closer together and heal the break their passing had put into the ranks.

Nobody spoke, but they did not seem ready to disburse.

Wind spanked the flames.

Someone coughed, and Fair Beard seized the moment, saying it for them, good night.

"We need to sort this out," Wyn said.

"In the morning we will see clearer," Snorrison insisted, and walked away with his family.

They broke up then, following his lead, which was significant, and David Iron saw the feather crown Madoc had dropped now trampled in the mud under many moccasins but could not bring himself to touch it.

Chapter 21

$$\rule{3in}{0.4pt}$$

The bowl of yellow moon like a ship without a mast rode the horizon, and the air was nothing if not balmy.

"So," Rhys said late that next afternoon after Madoc watched the shore where he saw the people gathering in the council circle.

"So?" Madoc asked.

"They impeached you."

Madoc said, "Ah," and settled back against the coil of line where he was taking a break.

"And named Snorrison chief."

Madoc nodded—that was no surprise. The white men would deal with the situation as though on shipboard, where loose verbal polls might replace a dead or incapacitated commander. The red men, it seemed, had a similar method of straw-voting a war leader. "They are better served."

Tumkis set a jug of water between them out on deck under the already-starry sky turning peach, then plum, then deepest blue above them.

"And so am I," he added, looking into her eyes, coaxing a smile from her with his glance: She had very little of his language.

Below them in the hold they had loaded all the bales of buffalo fleece that Winnowed Rice and Rhys had accumulated in trade, plus their hastily gathered household, for shortly after the council meeting, the poet and his family showed up bobbing in a coracle at the sidelines asking for permission to board.

And they were not the only ones.

Einion had climbed back aboard on his own in the night without letting anyone know. Huw was there at dawn. It was he who found Einion asleep among coils of line. Now Huw was below with William the Saxon setting up an armory of knives and arrows, many of Shawnee manufacture.

And they could hear Wyn down there at this moment, directing the stowage of metal slugs and charcoal. When he asked to come aboard after the gathering at the council circle broke up, Madoc had bargained with him:

"I thought you repudiated me," Madoc shouted from the rail, surprised to see the abbot standing down there with his small bundle of belongings, his hammer, and other smithy tools.

"Someone must go along to see you do not lose your soul—" He was too polite to say, ". . . to that Natchez witch." "Besides, I made that vow to head for Jerusalem, and you appear the only available passage west."

"Not until I get my ballast," Madoc replied.

And so Wyn had Andrew, David Iron, and his Yuchi comrades help him drag the makeshift anvil back to the riverside. They also brought aboard the ax head, knife slugs, and a few ingots along with charcoal to pass Wyn's time not spent as chaplain.

Madoc figured they would make a lucrative trip of it by trading with whatever nations they might encounter downstream. His Shawnee informants advised him to get as much seedcorn as he could find. It had been a bad season locally, and people were hungry for it—everyone knew that too much meat was not good.

There was much speculation as to why the crops had been so bad.

Some said it was a harbinger, even a warning, about these white people with their devastating wonders. Not all the local Shawnee looked happily on the white settlement. That charcoal mound still had some people frowning. Three clans held funeral services where people keenly mourned all those trees. But these stayed away from the Hundred, and the friends chose not to express any negative thoughts, because their eyes were full of the sight of those blue trade knives.

David Iron and Gwen had decided not to make the journey. She pleaded her advancing pregnancy, though she despaired that she would never see her father again and begged him not to go.

"Just exploring," Madoc promised, moved by her plea, and

with an ache in himself to be parted from her again. "I must see this Great River Road."

"Promise me that you will return to the Hundred before going back home," she begged.

"Of course," he assured her, but it did not seem to comfort her that he planned to go only to the lower Mech-a-sip-i to see if it did indeed empty into the salt gulf. "This is just a little trip—we will be back in a fortnight."

She nodded but clearly wanted him to stay.

"Tumkis wants to set things straight with her tad—"

"Her uncle," Gwen corrected him.

"Her chief, I guess. She thinks about a hundred of Wyn's knives might do it."

"I wish we had not lost the pigeons," she said. "At least you might have kept in touch with us."

"Do not mourn what is gone," he heard himself say, sounding old and patriarchal to himself, and it made his ears burn that he would be mouthing platitudes he had no patience hearing as a younger man.

David Iron would not go against her, though Madoc thought he could detect reluctance in the stoic Yuchi, and he privately wished for the man's company going into unknown territory.

But two of his Yuchi brothers took David Iron's place, one a tracker and hunter, and the other younger brother to the first.

A little later Firefly stood down on the bank for some time until Lev beside her whistled, catching Madoc's attention. The Natchez girl would not come aboard but called for Tumkis, who joined Madoc at the rail.

"I will come with you if you order it," Firefly called up to her mistress, "but I do not want to return to the Village of Black Cherries."

"Do as you wish," Tumkis called down. "But you are welcome if you choose to join us."

The girl stepped closer to the young Norseman.

"There I am a stinkard," Firefly said. "To this man I am important."

"I could use another hand," Madoc said to Lev, who blushed and looked at his big moccasined feet as he replied, "I have been with Snorrison since I was a boy."

Throughout that afternoon the volunteers straggled down to the waterline—higher now with the swifter river—so that by the time he and Rhys sat on the deck at sunset, Madoc had a crew of nine, two-thirds of whom were expert sailors, including himself, in addition to Rhys, Einion, and the two women.

Wyn and the sailors were troubled by the mathematics this made of their party. It was an old superstition, thirteen being the number that attended Christ's Last Supper, but Madoc disdained their superstition. They were not amused when he offered to take along Winnowed Rice's yellow bitch to even out their numbers.

But Rhys reminded them that Cari would be along, making them fourteen.

Madoc waited, hoping for Snorrison to appear, but he did not, and it was Rhys's opinion that he would not for Yngvild's sake.

Tumkis and Winnowed Rice agreed as they quartermastered belowdeck, organizing berths and supplies around Wyn's trade goods in wicker baskets. In the crossbeams they found old pegs that the Hundred's white women had used earlier for a hanging loom. They transferred one of the looms from Yngvild's loft to the ship, complete with huge beads of shale warp-weights, along with enough baled buffalo wool for many trade blankets.

Probably because of Madoc's gift knives, the Shawnee were generous with stores—amaranth, wild rice, and several other varieties of seed; dried meat, nuts, and fungi; tubers, squash, and beans, and three medium baskets of precious cracked corn.

What daylight hours Madoc did not spend with the men, finishing the last repair work on line and sail, he spent in the hold mothering the caulk. He and Wyn, who like many a smith was a fair carpenter, set two more crossbeams to shore up the strakes, though he saw no evidence of weakness and no leaks in the patchwork he and Snorrison had accomplished earlier.

Now there was nothing to do but depart, which the captain planned for next dawn. He had hoped that Wil or one of the other most experienced of his own crew would relent and join, but as darkness fell, he knew he had his number. He let others take that watch but stayed up late talking with Rhys on deck, then took the midnight star reading.

When he returned to his charts in the flickering light of a clam-shell lamp, Rhys was there, ready to talk if Madoc wished to, and they did so until early morning.

Rhys finally said good night to join Winnowed Rice below, leaving Madoc and the watch alone on deck.

He planned to be his own pilot, so he walked across the boards, studying the dark land where fire had been extinguished in the council circle. He longed to talk with Fair Beard and caught himself just before he swung over the side to go to him.

One leg over the rail, he heard his voice whisper Fair Beard's own admonition, "Let go," then looked around self-consciously to see if the watch had heard him talking to himself.

He could not see the big house in the thick, cool darkness as he held his lamp above the pilot's bench. He tested it, making sure everything was ready. The rudder had been damaged in the last landfall, but Snorrison fixed it first among many small repairs during the last few weeks.

He slapped the worn sprucewood in its socket; it was sound.

The ship creaked in the current; water lapped in the near darkness to his right. The wind, which had earlier died, threatened to rise again but so far had not maintained more than a whisper.

It would be a fine morning, he could feel it in his bones. This mild weather had no trace of the smell of snow or even rain. His wrist moved fluidly with no pain, so he knew the weather was going to be clear for at least the next day or so. The breeze had dried everything out so that now there was no lingering remnant of the white blanket that had so recently covered the January land.

He unfolded and refolded and unfolded again the built-in bench that had for so long been Snorrison's station. Sitting there in the Norseman's place, he wished again that his pilot was going along.

Madoc had sailed many times without the man and could do so again. But descending the Great River Road, which Snorrison knew from his Natchez sojourn, would be a more inviting prospect with him as guide.

The breeze blew out his lamp.

With its smolder coiling up into his nostrils, Madoc stood in the dark and refolded the pilot's bench so that morning dew would not dampen it. Just as he turned to cross the deck, go below, and make a futile try at sleep, he heard a silvery human whistle close landward.

He could see nothing, but he recognized that whistle. By feel alone he handed himself along the rail until he heard the signal again, as casual as a birdcall.

Madoc returned the note and heard the splash of a paddle below, then the muted rustlings of Fair Beard scurrying up the sidelines, as blind as himself but knowing those knots like his own bed linen.

"Permission to board," the Norseman muttered the ancient ritual, unable with his gruff voice to achieve a true whisper, but softly.

"Permission," Madoc said, a thrill in him that Snorrison would join the crew after all.

Across the blinding night they shook hands, and somehow in the grip Madoc read the truth that Fair Beard did not have to say; he was sneaking out here to say good-bye, and that was all.

He did not actually swing aboard but sat there astraddle the rail, one leg on this side, the other with toes curled in the sidelines to steady his perch.

Gradually Madoc's night vision gave him some perception. He could see vaguely the Norseman's light facial hair and long quoit, and feel his heat. The rest of him was only a voice.

"I come to give you this," the voice said, and Madoc felt something cold slide into his palm. His fingers told him instantly that it was Snorrison's Iceland eye, so white an opaque crystal that it too was a vague blur in the dimness. With it the sun could be detected in heavy fog, a priceless tool for him to give away.

"I cannot stay—she sleeps so lightly, and Hannah will wake soon to be fed."

The chain rattled against the metal setting of the disk as Madoc slipped it around his neck, wordless with gratitude and wishing he had something to give in return to his old friend and partner.

"If you make it back to Dublin, find the three captains I mentioned to you," Fair Beard said. "They will throw in their ships, I am sure, for our colony."

"But Fair Beard—" Madoc tried to say, his throat tight with feelings he was unable to express.

"We will be waiting for your return," the Icelander croaked, "with ten ships full of healthy Welshfolk ready to build another Cymru, and a couple of Norsemen, I hope, and pigs, and bees, for I sorely miss clear mead."

"I have no intention of crossing that sea without you," Madoc said flatly.

The Norseman absorbed this new information.

"But I thought—"

Madoc explained as he had to Gwen. "I go south to find that salt gulf we first entered, do some looking around, a little trading, and then I will come back and get you, and we will make that crossing together."

"Ah," Snorrison said, his sigh full of relief, "this is good, so good. I have been dreaming of the open water."

Madoc could feel Snorrison turn his face toward the Great House lost in the landward night. "I can bring her around, I know I can—this is good news you give me."

"For what you have given me."

"Wear it on the outside of your tunic—that Iceland eye will be magic to the Natchez—Tumkis's old man will be more impressed with that than a sword."

"Thank you, brother," Madoc said, clutching up again but damned if he would let Snorrison know it.

Both men were quiet for a time. It was Snorrison who broke their loud silence. "I am glad, you know," he said, and hit Madoc's shoulder softly. "I want you to take care of her."

"Well . . ."

"There is something she does—a little trill she hums while her tongue—"

Madoc felt himself blush in the cloaking darkness. He still could not believe that the woman was his, that it had been so right between them, and he knew what Snorrison was talking about.

"Ahh—" Fair Beard growled. "She is a princess, just a little girl, and I used her—I knew Flower would never accept her. I hurt her. She deserves someone who will not."

Madoc could feel his old friend leaning toward the land.

"Good sailing, Madoc ab Gwynedd."

"Luck to you, Fair Beard Snorrison."

They shook hands again; Fair Beard was anxious to leave, but half on the rail and half off, he clumsily embraced Madoc.

Then he was gone.

Madoc stood there a moment, listening to the soft sounds of the Norseman's descent, the slippery coracle with its liquid noises beneath the foot, the slap of soles when he jumped to the wet bank, then just the river's murmur, and somewhere off to landward, a true bird's stationary call.

Madoc closed his hot hand around the cool disk and went below, hoping Tumkis was still awake so she would put the throbbing chant into his ear again and he could lose himself inside her. But she was deeply asleep, as was everyone except the watch up on deck. Through three-inch-thick boards, he faintly heard pacing overhead.

Madoc always found it difficult to sleep before a journey. But this time, lying there under the great robe, the warm woman curled at his side and the cool Iceland eye clutched in his fist, he was overcome by exhaustion he had denied for days and slept the sleep of innocents.

In the pearly morning Tumkis woke him with her kisses exclaiming over the beautiful thing around his neck, which she did not ask him to remove while they dived into the little heaven of the star-robe several times before the watch called down that the sun was sitting on the horizon, the river was high, and there was a fine breeze from the southwest they could use to speed their way downstream.

Madoc threw on his clothes, woke Rhys and Winnowed Rice and the others lost in their bedrolls at the far end of the hold, then climbed out into the misty morning. Ascending the peg stair to the open deck, he felt so full of confidence that he called out to everyone, good morning.

Winnowed Rice had hot water turning into sassafras tea on the brazier—the smell was invigorating to Madoc's nostrils as he questioned the watch about various small issues concerned with launch.

Just before it was time—he would know the right moment in his gut—Madoc heard a male voice call from shore.

It was Dag with his bedroll, the only one of Fair Beard's men to show up, and with no explanation. Dag was the ablest of the old Norse crew. And though he had courted several of the Shawnee, he had not taken up with any one of them, whereas all the other men had red wives who might keep them from taking a journey. It was generally considered bad luck to travel from December through Crow Moon—March.

Madoc was long in his gratitude and tried to thank the brown-haired Norseman, but Dag would not respond. Madoc knew by that he was there on Snorrison's command and might have wished otherwise. Madoc was so shorthanded, he did not relieve Dag of the duty, though he would rather have had him as a volunteer and willing.

A good product of this last addition to the crew was in the mathematics of the situation. Madoc took pleasure in remarking to Wyn within hearing of the sailors that Dag brought them to fourteen ambulant souls, which should break any evil charm.

After securing loose ends and talking over his plans for pulling away from the berth they had held her in for three months, he took his position and ordered all hands to find their own.

He called for the sail to be hoisted, then anchors up.

His crew obeyed, and the sheet puffed out, speaking to the wind in mild argument. Nothing could go wrong, not this morning, he realized, as they eased away from the land. The current was there and with the wind; they turned the sail so that very soon they were moving along in fine form with the river.

He called out orders, and the men were right there, even the less experienced of them and the red men who were so new they did not yet have their sea legs. They held on, looking anxious but ready to learn, each beside an experienced crewman.

He saw Tumkis forward as far as she could stand leaning against the ship's high neck and under Snorrison's dragonhead, square to the wind, her black hair lifted in the draft. She gripped the rail-strake and put her face directly into their forward passage; it gave him a feeling of immense good luck to have her there with him.

All that happened before this moment seemed an obscure dream, and his heart leapt the way it always did to be on the water again with a ship beneath him and wind in the sails.

William the Saxon was harnessed up on the mast watching the river. Madoc's plan was not to let the current have them but to use the wind to tack across and back, controlling their passage down the main channel. The water was roiling so soon after the melt, though not so much as to worry him. It was not a flood, just speedy flow both he and the ship herself seemed to want to enter.

He caught a glimpse of the Hundred gathered along the shore. They appeared to be far more than their numbers spread out the way they were, a long audience on the bank up to the cleared line, but piling up where the underbrush began beyond the dilapidated charcoal mound.

But he was on the wrong side of the ship and would not divert his attention for a glance long enough to make out individual faces. They appeared as one long line of waving crowd, almost a single organism now falling rapidly behind him as the ship move gracefully along farther away from land.

He looked back over his shoulder, pleased with the thought that he did see Gwen because of her signal hair. But before he could be sure it was not someone wearing a scarf or feathers, or just a trick of the heightening sunlight coming from that eastern quadrant, the river had them thoroughly in its grasp.

The shore declined like a gray memory as the wide, tossing silvery road of the Oyo swept them westward.

He yelled an order that brought the sail around a little and retarded their forward motion. The line whined, and the sail stretched, pulling against the timbers. He could feel the ship responding below him; the rudder read the current and translated it back up into the bones of his hand.

All the rivers in that country are really one river.

Just as a human bloodstream is the branching of many streams, so is the Valley of the Mech-a-sip-i and its tributaries a tree of rivers with a single root.

But the main line is something to see, that Great River Road. If this great river system was seen as a human being's, the Mech-a-sip-i would have to be the big arteries and veins that empty and feed the heart, the heartland of something immense and living.

More quickly than seemed possible, they sped past the mouth of the Tennessee to larboard flowing into this stream and still more swiftly were approaching this river's mating with the Great River Road.

A string of small islands seemed to drift by, then to starboard, a long, low spit of what must be meandering sandbar with its tongue stuck far into the swifter, larger stream. Madoc glanced back at the sword of land that separated the grey Oyo's last wet plunge into the Mech-a-sip-i's thicker, swifter, browner flow.

He called for the slight turnabout that would point them downstream, but the crew was not fast enough. Very soon she was describing a wide arc out onto the greater river under a fist of the sou'wester roaring across the immensity of water. Madoc could see the western shore far, far on the other side of the huge, brown, watery plain.

Now they were in position for the sou'wester to propel them upstream for a short distance, against the current, but still making time. He called orders that would bring them carefully about, but his heart was pounding with the excitement of being on the strange water bigger than any river he could imagine. He made a spur-of-the-moment decision to put in near what was now the larboard bank.

He called to a man who had just come up from the hold—how was the shoring holding, and the caulking?

The crewman called that everything was tight, they had taken on only a minimum of seepage, what might be expected and no more. That was good news, better than he expected, but the shuddering he felt increased. He assured himself it was just the ship adjusting herself to the flow, the comforting communication of wood with moving water.

But he wanted to make sure, to have a look for himself at how those beams were holding out. The river would roll on forever; they had all the time in the world to aim themselves downstream.

His plan had been to pull in just above the Ohio's junction with the Great River Road, for security's sake, and that was exactly what he intended to do.

They had been moving on the water little more than two hours. Full daylight had etched away the slight dawn mist, leaving the sky a sheet of mystic blue.

A steady front of fluffy clouds marched in formation from the southwest, which might signal a weather change, as they brought the ship alongside and about three furlongs away from that extremely oblique angle of river-washed soil that had piled up at the northern lip of the Ohio.

They found a nick in the strand where the Mech-a-sip-i had thrown up a scattering of debris against treeless sand. To the east the almost glassy water stretched farther than they could see into swampland. Here they brought the ship in, Madoc's call to lower the sail instantly obeyed as she slid into a spot of water that did not have as tossed a surface as the main channel.

After ordering the anchor dropped, and a sounding thrown out to test the depth, Madoc without preliminary began his inspection, descending into the hold to scan the shoring.

The report had been accurate. They were not shipping any

more water than Huw had left sloshing around down there, and that was negligible.

Running his hand along the bulkhead, Madoc paced the entire ship's length and back again.

He did not detect a single drop of river coming through the new caulking, and the old was as tight as it had been the day she was launched.

Madoc leaned back, staring up at the radiant square of sky that showed beyond the hold.

Crew and passengers observed him going about this inspection, standing back with their arms folded across their chests ready for him to issue some order, but he found nothing to remedy.

Rhys on deck had begun to pluck from Honeyvoice a love song he sang in the language of home. A couple of the crew and Wyn joined him as Madoc stepped around the mast-fish, the great block of curved carved oak into which the mast was stepped.

His circuit complete, Madoc laid his hands on the pine mast, which Fair Beard had hewn from the Alabama forest. When Madoc put his nose to it, the wood smelled beautiful, still green from the blade.

Hands embracing the thick log, he threw back his head and stared upward to its pinnacle stabbing into the pristine blue morning. He was already barefoot, the only way he ever sailed, and quickly began to ascend the mast against the notches put there for that purpose.

Far above the deck he climbed, putting his face directly into the benevolent wind, observing their position in the bare landscape and brown stream.

The far western shore appeared to be more than a league away, though he would not have wagered the exact distance. Truly a mighty river, he thought, having never seen one so wide. Surely it must drain the entire heart of this vast country into the saltwater that communicated with the great ocean he had traveled to get here a little more than a year ago.

Buoyed by the feelings of optimism this sight put into him, he descended the mast, asking loudly if anybody was hungry.

Their brief sail having awakened appetites they had not taken time to appease with breakfast, they broke out the victuals of a small feast they ate while sitting in the hazy sunlight discussing the bulkhead, the lines, and the ship's general performance so far.

"This is some river, boys," Madoc said generally, and everyone had a comment about it, gesturing so that Laughing Dog made a comment in Yuchi in which the word *Uktena* figured heavily.

The shy Yuchi warriors could speak little Cymraeg. But the elder of the two handsigned a suggestion that Weather Eyes observe the incoming clouds.

Madoc nodded and asked Winnowed Rice what the Yuchi thought it meant.

"He says that the Uktena sucks moisture from the sky," she translated. "And by midafternoon there will be mist all along this stretch."

Madoc wanted to keep moving and said so with handsign.

The Yuchi, who had been among the laborers who raised the cross, shook his head. Already Wyn knew the man was curious about the faith—that was why he had come along at David Iron's suggestion, and the abbot was thrilled to have a potential convert to work upon.

"Laughing Dog says he would not remain on the Great River Road in any kind of bad weather, even a soft fog," Winnowed Rice said after the sober, slow-speaking Yuchi made his judgment. Madoc had never met a man named so opposite his nature as this reserved, steady-gazed red man.

It gave Madoc a private chill when the warrior cast his dour glance at the graying sky, and it seemed ill advised to ignore the warning, especially since the wind was dying.

So they anchored the *Horn* for permanent berth that night, planning to continue downstream tomorrow.

Dag threw out fishing line, while Rhys gave them all the long version of the Song of Roland, which told the story of the hero who once owned the sword Madoc had brought with him across the ocean.

Wyn did not want to fire up his little furnace set out in sand on the afterdeck for so short a stay, so he surprised everyone by joining the women who brought out their spindles. All that afternoon they worked on hanks of thread with which they would begin their first weavings. As he worked, his motive became clear—he sang hymns in time with the work, trying to get the women and the two Yuchi nearby to learn the words.

They leaned on the rail smoking their pipes, too dignified to sing with women.

It was a pleasant afternoon that turned even warmer as the day progressed. A thickening mist gradually veiled the sun, just as Laughing Dog had predicted—Madoc nodded to him to let him know he appreciated wise counsel.

That evening around a little supper fire they enjoyed Dag's abundant catch of fat, scaleless fish with long, fleshy whiskers, and Rhys played songs most of the company joined in singing. Wyn told a story or two out of scripture with an eye for the Yuchi's response, while Winnowed Rice relayed the message into handsign.

During the third watch Rhys confessed that he had a whiff of a wood fire on the breeze.

"Yes," Madoc concurred, "Laughing Dog has been staring into the mist for an hour."

Dag confirmed it. "I saw the glow of some kind of fire."

Madoc did not know what to make of that, so he ventured, "Chickasaw?"

"On this side of the river, I do not know," Dag replied.

Winnowed Rice said that Chickasaw usually confined themselves to the south bank of the Oyo and the east bank of the Great River below the Oyo. "This bank is the territory of various bands of the Caddo on the western shore and Illinois on the east."

Madoc strained to see in the gathering darkness, but could discern nothing. Dag's observation made Madoc nervous enough to station William the Saxon as security with his crossbow at the ready.

But there was no other sign that they shared the riverine wilderness with any but an occasional egret or a high-flying raptor. Calls echoed from shore, and fish plopped throughout the night, all of which made Madoc restless, especially as he continued to feel the mist thicken into full-blown fog by dull, sunless morning.

Midmorning he was on the mast but could not see the far shore of the Mech-a-sip-i. He cursed under his breath, itching to be off. The river's current had slackened, but he could still hear mild scrapings and bumps as debris from upstream rattled against them in the opaque stream that had turned from thick gray to slow blackish mud.

Suddenly to starboard in the faster, deeper river, he

glimpsed a dead tree careening along in the flow. He watched as an eddy near their stern caught it, drawing it toward them, then called out for specific crew to grab oars to pole the snag away from their straking.

Three men complied and were doing well to obey. But Madoc saw how it could be done better and began to descend to do it.

Halfway down the mast he let himself drop, anxious to get to that side of the ship more quickly. Impatient of easing himself down into the hold, which would have meant a climb back up the peg stair, he took his aim on the decking and leapt about ten feet—not even a broad jump—to hit the boards exactly where he aimed.

But the ship on the ruffled water danced a minute yaw, imperceptible to the eye, just enough to throw him off so that he came down badly instead of gracefully, twisting his left leg but not losing his balance. He was still standing when he continued the forward motion of the leap by taking another step toward the rail.

Instant shooting pain informed him without any doubt that he could not put weight on the leg again. Clamping his bite down on the pain, he hopped one-footed to the place where an oar-wielding crewman leaned on the rail poking at the snag in the water.

Madoc peered over the side, mindlessly ignoring the pain, which had not slackened since he hit the boards, still the only one aware of his misstep.

The pain subsided until he almost did not feel it, but sweat broke out on his face.

He took a careful step farther aft and regretted it, crumpling into a fire of agony, thereby announcing his trouble to the rest of the company.

He looked at the leg for the first time since he jumped.

Several hands were there, but he snapped at them when they tried to help and gestured that they should be worrying about that waterline snag.

They left him to comply, but he was not alone. Tumkis had found her way to him from her point position. Even her gentle fingers on the bent shin were like fire; he could not help crying out.

She looked up at him with a grim expression on her beautiful face that said what he wanted to deny, but he nodded, "Yes, damn it, I know it is broken," as she crouched under his arm to help him rise against the rail.

Wyn was there and Winnowed Rice, staring when they saw the unnatural angle of his leg already turning an unhealthy color.

"Well what are you staring at?" he demanded, angry now, and ready to take it out on someone.

Wyn on the other side lent him his shoulder to lean on, but was muttering to himself as he did so, and in Madoc's direction.

"What is that you say, Domme?"

"Why did you do that, jumping about like a boy?"

They got him to the spot he wanted, where he sat down while trying not to move the leg that was now throbbing with each heartbeat. When he looked, he could see it swelling, turning red beneath the skin all along the shin.

Wyn touched his foot.

"Agh—"

"Man, I must set it," Wyn insisted, but he knew Madoc knew he had never set a bone in all his fifty years of life.

"Like hell you will."

"Weather Eyes," Tumkis said, her voice almost lost in gentleness, "it must be done."

She was already undoing a long thong of leather she had twisted around her waist. It was beaded at each end, a strong piece of supple stuff, which he saw drawn between her hands to loop around his ankle.

"No!" he barked, preventing her from touching his leg at any point below the knee.

She sat back on her heels, the thong stretched between both her small fists, looking at his face and then the leg that continued swelling even as they watched.

"I will do it," he said, knowing the only way was to allow himself to be suspended at the end of such a thong, and let his weight pull the ends of broken bone apart. Then, if the procedure was well-done, they would knit back in place. He snatched the thong from her and leaned over to catch his ankle, but the effort shot new needles up his leg.

About to pass out, he leaned over his own length, forcing himself to breathe slowly, fighting against the nausea and red blackness rising behind his eyes. The cord was looped over his bare toes but was not secured around his ankle.

"Only one thing to do," he heard himself say, the words coming out slurred. "Got to go back—let Caradoc have it—I cannot, you do not know how, I cannot stand it—"

Above him they looked at each other, wide-eyed and unable to move. They heard the scraping of the snag against their side, and two of them ran to the dropped oars and pushed the flotsam away.

Wyn looked back down at Madoc and then at the two nearest sailors. "Can you get her back up the Oyo?"

"I can pilot," Madoc insisted.

They spoke together and agreed that they could do it if the sou'wester returned, but upstream against the current and with almost no wind, it was impossible.

"We can do it—I said I can pilot," Madoc insisted.

Wyn cast his gaze upon the heavens somewhere beyond the fog, folded his hands, and began to loudly invoke assistance.

Madoc gripped the abbot's sleeve. "Please, Domme," he hissed through clamped teeth, "not now."

Behind them, Tumkis gestured to the two Yuchi. Handsign was eloquent for this sort of practical conspiracy. It said, *Help me hold him while we draw the cord—that piece of wood there—* She pointed to a peg in the mast.

They moved their eyes to say they understood. Winnowed Rice, in on the silent exchange, moved in with Tumkis with a pottery basin of water and a large piece of wet rawhide.

The Natchez sun knelt beside Madoc and let him rest his head upon her lap. She bathed his hot face with the rag of leather, keeping his attention on her face while the Yuchi moved in. Very quickly they grabbed his two feet and drew the broken leg upright under the stretched thong.

Laughing Dog gave the line a good jerk, stretching the cord a little more.

Madoc screamed, but Winnowed Rice and Tumkis held his arms.

Laughing Dog knotted the line on the peg, then palpated the leg to see if the adjustment had worked.

His glance at Tumkis struggling with Madoc's right arm said that the bone felt all right to him.

"Let me see," Madoc said. "It does not feel straight."

She tossed the wet rawhide with which the Yuchi began to bind the leg from ankle to knee.

Winnowed Rice found her satchel, where she kept one of

Wyn's iron needles always threaded, and quickly began to stitch up the dripping sides of leather, which would shrink as they dried into a hardened splint.

Madoc cursed and thrashed, but his movements were already weakened. The worst of the pain had been reached and leveled off. Somewhere deep inside him, he was aware that the broken parts were back in place, or at least nearly so. The wet rawhide felt cool under Winnowed Rice's hands, covering the low, brown pain in soothing snugness.

Tumkis handsigned the names of certain herbs, and Winnowed Rice nodded, pawing around in her kit again, coming up with two small drawstring pouches. Into her own drinking cup she poured water from a bladder hanging nearby on another peg—the crew's drinking pouch. She mixed several pinches from each purse into the water, stirred it with her finger, and handed the concoction to Tumkis, who in turn put the cup to Madoc's lips. He was aware of the rows of thin tattoo bracelets on her delicate wrists as he had never been before— they appeared to wave, to undulate like blue snakes.

"What swamp poison is that?" he sputtered, but he took it, giving in to trust, watching her eyes above him.

She smiled back and leaned closer, her hair cool, black, silky water tumbling around their faces close together. "Sleep, Weather Eyes," she whispered, and kissed him.

Behind them Rhys found a melody in the harp strings while Wyn muttered his prayer, but softly.

PART FOUR

When we die, truly we die not,
because we will live,
we will rise,
we will continue living,
we will awaken.
This will make us happy.

—Ancient Mexican song

Chapter 22

Turtle-in-the-Sun had the shimmering green head of the mallard clearly targeted in the eye of his arrow.

The mist that early morning hung low on the backwater, obscuring the duck blind of reed and cattails Turtle's men had made of his canoe.

The miko stood braced on the wickerwork of the blind, poised and ready to let the arrow loose. He was dressed for serious hunting, in heavy, unadorned buckskin and high, supple moccasins lined with cattail fluff to keep his feet warm out on the cold water. His face was fringed with the full russet head of a coyote, skull, snout, and snarl intact, ears perked, fangs polished. This helmet of coyote carcass continued on down his shoulders in a fine lining of rabbit pelt. The cuffs folded to make mittens against the worse cold, but these were rolled back despite the chill this morning, so he could use the short bow and arrow designed for launch from a canoe.

Over all this costume was draped the camouflage of a woven cane cloak that left his arms free to aim. This hit would bring this morning's bag of the royal ducks to more than thirty. The iridescent green feathers of the species were prized for ceremonial masks and robes, and for that reason, within the dependencies of Ixtulan, were proscribed for any except the miko himself or his commissioned hunters. Anyone else caught killing a mallard, or in possession of the precious emerald feathers, was without appeal a volunteer for twelve moons on the earth-moving detail.

The duck bobbed its royal head beneath the water, its curly rear scooting around amid a fountain of bubbles. Turtle poised, ready to let go a split second before the bird emerged.

At that moment, just as Turtle let fly, a human shout tore the swampy silence and spooked the duck, which lifted out well

355

above the shot. The several other birds sitting the still backwater followed their leader upward in a rattle of pale wings.

Buffalo Eagle in the other canoe as disguised as this one let go his shot but also missed the huge duck on the wing toward the greater river.

Furious at losing his prize, Turtle flung his glance around the muted, misty perspective, able to see nothing that informed him about the male shout he had heard.

The fading human sound echoed over the lapping water already showing glitters as the climbing sun riddled the mist.

Turtle exchanged handsign with Buffalo Eagle about the incongruous shout that seemed to have come from the direction of the larger Mech-a-sip-i water.

It could only be intruders.

This stretch of lowland was set aside as the hunting preserve of the Fifth Village, the last in a string of Ixtulan's dependent communities along the eastern shore of the Great River Road below the city. None others were allowed to be here, much less hunt in this zone set aside for the exclusive harvesting of feathers for royal headgear.

Turtle knew that the hunters from the Fifth Village in the area today were acting as guides for the royal party, which had been billeted in the town for the past two days and nights amid great festival as he selected three new wives from more than twenty tens of young women.

Suddenly a second shout broke the stillness, the unmistakable single-noted cry in any language of a successful hunter.

Shortly thereafter Turtle heard the plop of a duck upon the water unseen in the direction of the shout.

He ordered in brusque handsign for the lead canoeman, who happened to be the Chickasaw Imala'ko, to bring them closer in the direction of the poachers who dared to hunt here.

It was difficult if not impossible for the paddlers to move with the wicker blind in place, so they loosened and tipped it off as Turtle-in-the-Sun shucked his own cane drapery.

Buffalo Eagle in the second canoe directed his people to do the same. At one point in the procedure, Turtle paused abruptly, held up a hand for silence. Head cocked, he listened to the river where he thought he heard several voices from the same direction as the first.

They continued on cautiously, the miko hoping to catch the poachers in the act.

The mist was thinning, but the glare of the sun behind it turned the world into a vast, blinding glow as the two canoes edged soundlessly around the lip of swampy backwater marked by a pile of river-washed debris. The haze hung about a man's height above the water, which was rising, louder in its murmur now that they approached the greater flow.

A kingfisher shrieked back in the swamp, and a frog or fish plopped in the nearer stream.

There were definite human voices coming from the western wall of fog shredding under the sun's assault.

Turtle touched Imala'ko's shoulder, bringing his movements to a halt as the miko listened along with his men to the voices speaking no language they knew.

Distance is hard to determine in the fog and on water; Turtle-in-the-Sun determined that his thieves were right over there, perhaps three canoe lengths off his bow, but even as he watched through the rising mist, he saw that they were farther out than he had first thought, sitting in small, round canoes, congratulating themselves over the huge beautiful mallard that had been the target of his own arrow.

He signaled to Buffalo Eagle's canoemen to come around and approach with him as they zeroed in on the poachers, who were so engrossed in their kill they did not yet see the two longboats ten times there size stealthily bearing down upon them, each armed with three archers who had their arrows nocked and targeted.

By the simple braid of his hair, clan signs on his tunic, and his modest face paint, Turtle identified as Yuchi the man who was netting the mallard from the water.

Beyond him a second round canoe held another younger man from some other nation that Turtle-in-the-Sun could not immediately identify, but who had odd brown face paint, or perhaps it was hair on his chin and lip.

Behind himself, Turtle-in-the-Sun heard the Chickasaw suck air and make a sound of surprise.

Frowning in the glare, Turtle-in-the-Sun looked back at Imala'ko to see what startled him, but something beyond the strange canoes pulled his attention in that direction instead.

Rays of sunlight cut the mist, revealing like a rising veil the ruffled shallows of the Mech-a-sip-i water and what sat upon it, bobbing in the current like the great spirit, the manitou of mallards and all long-necked mysterious creatures of both air and water.

Turtle heard himself gasp at the sight of the biggest canoe he had ever seen, long and high in the water, its prow more than three man-heights forming a sleek point that ended with the head of legendary Uktena, the river serpent that put a massive shadow onto the river below.

It was almost impossible to look at it with the sun behind the silhouette of legendary form and size.

If it had turned and roared at him, he would have fallen down upon his knees like anyone in the presence of terrible magic, but this serpent was not alive. For all its size he knew at once that it was made of wood that displayed expert workmanship of human hands.

Imala'ko whispered hoarsely, "The kanegmati—in the Uktena canoe—see, as big as I said—"

Turtle-in-the-Sun put his hand on the Chickasaw to quiet him without taking his eyes from the monstrous vessel nodding its tree-high mast up into the sunshine. The sail was reefed, but the dragon pennant was flapping up there, bright red and dangerous looking against the glare.

At the rail hung several men from the strange unpainted, bewhiskered tribe who were calling out to the others in the smaller craft. Then one among them, a big brown-haired, white-skinned man who still held the crossbow that had brought down the duck, caught sight of the two slinking canoes and called out, "Laughing Dog—watch!"

Imala'ko whispered to Turtle, "That one is Weather Eyes."

Around this man's neck was hung a brilliant white disk that caught the sun's light and flung it back into the miko's eyes. Turtle-in-the-Sun did not need to be told; he had already intuited who was the chief here.

The Yuchi followed where the shouter pointed, straightening on his knees in the little boat, the limp duck in his hands with the heart-shot arrow still implanted.

The snarling cedar dragon with its bulging steel-rivet eyes was pure wonder that Turtle could not help staring at now and again. Around him his men were all crouching beneath the thing. Someone whispered a sacred word connected with Bright Snake, sometimes the morning star, sometimes the evening star.

"It is just a big canoe," Turtle reminded them coolly.

Everyone in both parties was frozen in the moment, staring at each other across the water.

The archers in the canoes still poised to attack. The men along the ship's rail saw the arrows pointing at them and began to slide down behind the thick bulkhead, all except the bowman, who had not moved.

Even Turtle was startled when a headman from the Fifth Village, acting as chief guide in Buffalo Eagle's canoe, demanded across the water, "Who are you to be shooting royalheads in the territory of the miko of Ixtulan?"

The Yuchi, the only one on that side who came close to understanding what was being asked, dropped the mallard beside his feet and stared down the shouter, who was within an arm span of catching hold of his little boat. The Yuchi grabbed an oar and backpaddled expertly, taking himself and his craft out of reach.

The nearest archer pivoted to keep him in sight, but Turtle-in-the-Sun stopped him from letting go with a brisk order.

The Yuchi made quickly for the blue shadow of the great canoe, scrambled up the roping draped on its side, and crawled with the duck over the rail with the help of one of the light-skinned strangers who had brown hair, a furry chin, and startling blue eyes.

"Closer," Turtle ordered Imala'ko, who complied while the other canoe held back, weapons still aimed.

Now others aboard the big canoe were hauling in the little round boat, which Turtle could not help but witness with curiosity since it looked so much like the Great Turtle, far larger than any ordinary animal.

Closer, he saw the turtle-boats were not a wonder at all, but just round skiffs of buffalo hide stretched over wicker. Some outland people made longer, sleeker canoes of the same oiled material, or birch bark.

The Chickasaw's strokes brought him directly beneath the bowman, who leaned with both hands against the rail and looked down at the miko, who had never been in such a position before. He was used to being the one looking down, and it unnerved him more than he wanted to show to have to crane his head back and up into the sunlight at someone else.

"Is that Imala'ko the Chickasaw I see down there?" called

another white man with very little hair on his head who moved beside the other, and the question was duly translated by the Yuchi.

The Chickasaw recognized the kanegmati shaman the Shawnee called Father Folded Hands.

"You people have done it this time—you have broken the law of the chief speaker of Ixtulan."

The bald one spoke with agitation, moving his hands in what appeared to be meaningless, agitated handsign. The white chief nodded without taking his eyes from the water below. At his other hand there appeared a beautiful Natchez woman of the highest rank, her loose black hair sparkling in the light, who turned her unmasked stare down upon the miko's person.

"Tell him," Turtle instructed succinctly, "that if we had known it was himself, another chief in the company of a noble sun from our cousins, the Natchez, we would not forbid him to take the royalhead."

When the Chickasaw relayed this, and it was translated, the white chief yelled down that in that case the chief of Ixtulan was invited to come aboard and share the duck with him for breakfast.

By now Turtle-in-the-Sun had it in his mind that he must board the marvelous vessel, so the invitation was immediately accepted, even though several of his councillors warned him not to put himself in danger from the bad medicine of the great canoe.

"Imagine eating a royalhead," muttered the Fifth Village chieftain to Turtle. "How revolting."

"It is evil, lord," grumbled Buffalo Eagle, whose boat was alongside the miko's own. "At least it is unclean, and I will not put my foot upon it."

"Yes, you will," the miko replied, reaching for the sidelines. "And you will appear overjoyed to do so."

Meanwhile on the ship, Winnowed Rice grabbed Madoc's sleeve and begged him not to bring these people on board. Rhys beside her conveyed her warning and asked her why.

"They are unspeakable evil—my people have been at war with them for the time of six grandfathers," she whispered, backing off when the first of the red men swung over the rail and clambered onto the deck, looking around with their mouths open in childlike wonder, their eyes wide at the marvel of the ship.

"Winnowed Rice, I have never seen you like this," her husband pleaded.

"They seem friendly enough," Madoc commented, hanging onto the rail to support himself, the broken leg stiff in the splint and too tender to put any weight on. He had not slept well and was jittery and feverish this morning, glad to be in the chill air, which felt refreshing on his hot face. He avoided looking down at his foot, which seemed the color of salt. It had ceased to throb, however, under Natchez potions, and he was glad to ignore it.

Winnowed Rice, with Cari on her back, was already moving away from the red contingent, not waiting to hear any more arguments. She flung a glare in the direction of the guests and made her way quickly down the peg stair out of sight in the hold.

"I do not know what is wrong with her," Rhys said apologetically.

"I need her translation," Madoc said, peeved that she would pick this time for unreasonable temperament. But he said it out of the side of his mouth while smiling at the dozen guests now on his deck shaking cattail stuff out of buffalo robes and kicking the creases from their trews.

Turtle handed himself up the admirably knotted netting. He disdained the offer of a hand by the brown-bearded stranger, who led Turtle across the boards.

Imala'ko felt keenly his position as go-between and formally introduced the two chiefs. Rhys beside Madoc did the best he could with the Yuchi's help in relaying the conversation, and handsign helped.

Turtle-in-the-Sun approached Weather Eyes, who leaned the crossbow against the bulkhead.

As the Yuchi handed over the kill, he spoke soft words to the chief sitting on the pilot's bench and awkwardly dealing with the splint on his left leg.

Turtle then saw a light-haired man standing on the other side of the chief. This one had face paint in the form of two sunbursts. Turtle thought that this one was wearing a fine mask of crow and yellow warbler feathers. He had a similar costume under repair by the mother of Five-Tens-and-Two back on God's Hill.

"Who wants to know about my breakfast?" Weather Eyes asked as he accepted the duck. When he turned, the sun glanced arrows and needles off the white disk and its metal setting, catching Turtle's eye and dazzling him.

The star Bright Snake was said to be a single brilliant eye in the forehead of a dragon that could blind any who looked into it. *A legend,* Turtle thought. He blinked and looked away lest the ray harm him or enter into his head through his eye. But his diverted glance landed upon the face of the man with painted suns for eyes, as equally unnerving as the crystal's reflected glare.

Turtle had already brought up the sun that morning, but the illusion of its second rising upon Madoc's chest made the miko feel he should say the dawn prayer again.

He resisted the impulse, however, and shared a look with Imala'ko, who confirmed what the miko already knew.

"The one with the arrow that shoots the north star?" Turtle-in-the-Sun inquired.

The Chickasaw nodded.

"This place is forbidden to all—" the Fifth Village headman was winding up to announce, though definitely impressed by the big canoe as he climbed over the rail.

Turtle-in-the-Sun handsigned for him to shut up and signaled for the other archers out in the second boat to rest their weapons.

Turtle could see that Weather Eye's face was florid. Sweat coated his lip and forehead, and his eyes did not look good, but were a little wild and bloodshot.

But Turtle-in-the-Sun was compelled to observe more closely the true nature of the face paint on the man standing behind the chief.

The Natchez sun placed a tray of various familiar edibles on a block of wood and sat herself down on the boards at the chief's feet, watching Turtle with knowing intensity and no expression on her face.

Behind him, the bearded warrior brought up a small bench, which, when he sat, placed Turtle slightly less than eye level with Weather Eyes. He was not sure what he would do if these outlanders actually offered him the flesh of the royalhead, which was always offered as food for God. He figured it was too soon to have plucked and prepared the kill. And he was right, since the tray contained dried sweetmeats, nuts, smoked mussles, fresh watercress, and cattail root.

Weather Eyes took a morsel and ate it.

Turtle-in-the-Sun likewise took a bite and ate it slowly.

His councillors standing behind him made sounds of discomfort, but since all but the woman near Weather Eyes remained standing, Turtle let his people do the same.

As guest Turtle-in-the-Sun was obliged to be silent until the host made a comment. He was glad of this moment to collect his thoughts and closely observe the white chief and the magic-faced councillor murmuring behind him, whom Turtle had nicknamed immediately, Sun Eyes. The sun doubled was too powerful a symbol for him to ignore.

In his mind were whirling plans for somehow getting this magnificent canoe back to the city, of riding it down Sky Blood Creek and across the approach to the dock below God's Hill. It would pull all the people from their labor; they would line the banks to see their miko commanding the Uktena himself and cheer and whistle to see such a sight. The question was how to accomplish it.

His councillors were making their own small-voiced comments.

Buffalo Eagle said softly nearby, "Lord, that bone is not properly set."

Turtle observed without appearing to stare.

"See how the foot is bent in, and the toes are pale?"

Turtle saw. But when he did not respond, Buffalo Eagle took it as an order to be silent, which was exactly what the miko intended.

When it became clear that the white chief was not going to eat any more, Turtle signaled for Buffalo Eagle as his highest-ranking companion to bring out the makings of a pipe.

Weather Eyes, familiar with this habit among the red men before they got down to business, leaned back with a sigh and tried to place his leg more comfortably. Laughing Dog and Rhys conferred behind him, after which Rhys said, "He says these people value colorful feathers over all else, and we have violated some rule by taking the green-headed ducks."

The Yuchi said something to Imala'ko, who responded tersely, "He says these birds are sacred to the chief speaker."

"Then," Madoc said, "tell the chief speaker that I ask his forgiveness and give him the kill." He picked up the royalhead from where he had dropped it, handing it over by gripping the arrow.

Turtle-in-the-Sun saw that the oblique hit, while exact, had not been placed to avoid damaging the shimmering green feathers, which were mashed and stained with blood, polluted far beyond ritual use. But he accepted the gift so as not to offend, nodding to the Chickasaw to take it and thank the white chief.

In Imala'ko's hands he saw the reason for the damage, a metal arrow point emerging from the bird's throat that was far too large for taking duck. His people used bird-points as small as the little fingernail, exquisitely fine tips of translucent flint from the mountains south of here and west of the Great River.

Still, he longed to examine more closely that metal arrowhead and instructed Buffalo Eagle to see that it was purified and returned to him for later inspection.

The Oldtowner was tamping down the bowl of his long stonehead pipe but had no fire.

The Yuchi said to Madoc, "We need a coal," and Rhys relayed it so that Madoc gestured for Wyn to use the coals in the brazier he had set up in sand aft, where he had planned to so some blade finishing when the charcoal got hot enough. He had brought along a bar of iron he had forged to be his portable anvil.

He brought a coal in an iron tong to the old red man, who leaned with severe dignity to hand the pipe to Turtle-in-the-Sun, who accepted it ceremoniously and took a long draw, sending up a coil of fine blue smoke.

He handed the pipe to Madoc, who took a modest puff—any more, and he would lapse into the coughing fit this stuff always gave him.

Knowing by now the red people's deference to age, he handed the pipe to Buffalo Eagle, which was the right thing to do. Turtle was thinking that this white man was not such a barbarian after all, and he waited expectantly for him to begin to speak, as was the custom for a host to do.

But Weather Eyes did not look comfortable or in a mood to have a conversation. His leg was hurting, Turtle knew, and on inspiration he broke the tradition of letting the host set the opening of a meeting.

"I could not help but notice a change in the weather that seems to be approaching," he said politely.

"I thought I smelled rain," the white chief responded, rubbing at his wrist. Turtle himself often felt weather changes in his bones, counting it a gift.

"Indeed, it may sleet tonight."

"That is quite a change."

"The way of the river, which is a snake who sips from the sky."

"This is a good thing for me to know," Weather Eyes said, glancing at Dag and another sailor who would be responsible for battening down the hatch cover, two wide oiled buffalo hides stitched together.

"I also cannot help but notice," Turtle added politely, speaking slowly to allow for the elaborate relay translation, "that Weather Eyes has broken his leg."

"Hurts like hell."

Turtle indicated Buffalo Eagle. "Here we have the finest bonesetter in my nation."

The old man blinked.

The Yuchi said, "His tattoos and jacket bead pattern indicate he is of the first rank. The lines on his sleeve say he has set bones numbering twenty tens times ten."

"What do you think, Rhys?"

"Two thousand is a fair number of mended bones."

"Domme?"

"I hate to admit it, son, but the leg does not look good."

"God, I wager this is going to hurt," Madoc sighed. He touched the shoulder of Tumkis and felt her shiver. "What say you, Tumbling Water?"

"All broken bones look bad for a while. It will turn black, then blue, then green, and soon will fade to healthy flesh. And I have medicine to keep out the pain."

Madoc was surprised at her reaction, knowing that these strangers were from a cousin nation to her own. He said directly to Turtle-in-the-Sun, "I respect my friend Laughing Dog, and I know it is unusual for a woman to join in men's discussion, but I want Lady Tumbling Water to translate through this man for me."

He indicated Rhys.

Tumkis stood, leaning against Weather Eyes as she relayed this.

Laughing Dog, Buffalo Eagle, Imala'ko, and all the red men reacted with reactionary frowns, but the miko answered, "I honor the lady sun from the Natchez."

The other red men had no choice but to simmer in their

displeasure at such untraditional protocol. Laughing Dog stepped back with no loss of dignity.

"And I honor Sun Eyes," the miko added. He had the pipe again, filled it from a small pouch on his own belt, and sucked new life into it before handing it to Laughing Dog.

Rhys smiled when he heard this and told Madoc he liked the nickname.

"What if he puts the evil eye on me?" Madoc said half-jokingly.

"Does he look like he has the evil eye?"

"No, but I think he thinks you do."

"Winnowed Rice said they would be impressed." Rhys chuckled again. In another tone he asked, "How does it feel?"

"Not so good, I think, all due respects to Laughing Dog's work." Madoc nodded thanks to the Yuchi, who handed him the noxious pipe, upon which he only pretended to take a drag.

Speaking directly to Buffalo Eagle, Madoc offered him the pipe, wishing he understood her reticence as Tumkis translated into Muskogean what Rhys put into Shawnee: "Have a look at it, then."

Chapter 23

Madoc awoke feeling refreshed and unfevered, but with a dull rhythmic clanging he first thought was the pulse inside his head.

He remembered nothing after a brief pipe ceremony conducted by Buffalo Eagle, during which Madoc drank a cup of tea handed him by Tumkis. He remembered his leg, but was a bit fuzzy on details leading up to that pipe—some strange red people on board, something about a green-headed duck.

He realized that the clanging was not in his head, but up on deck.

However misty his thinking, he felt physically well enough to pull himself from under the covers of his and Tumkis's bed and take a look at the leg. He had been put to sleep with trews on, the pant leg slit up to the thigh. In the soft daylight coming from the open hold he saw it was newly splinted, straight, and mildly throbbing, toes pink and movable with specific pain back along the splinted shin.

Light-headed and tingling, he drew on his tunic and hopped over to the mast-fish, grabbed the mast to steady himself, and cast his gaze into the knobby gray sky.

He thought he had heard some form of red medicine chanting, having listened to enough of that music by now, but just before he called out, the upping wind brought him Wyn's voice in sermon tone between clanks of hammer on metal.

A female voice was softly translating his passionate words into Muskogean, verbally running along after him with the meaning.

Madoc listened for a while, finding odd comfort in the preaching from good old Brother Wyn. He has found his Turks at last, Madoc thought, hoping this would cool the abbot's ardor to seek infidels farther west.

Another male voice put a question to Wyn, though the female intonations were spoken too softly for Madoc to hear. When the same male voice asked something further, Madoc recognized the sound of the strange chief's voice—Turtle, yes that was his name.

The woman relayed his question, and though Madoc could not hear her words, he plainly heard Wyn answer, "Because through Our Lord Jesus Christ we have everlasting life!" and punctuated his remark with a stout blow to iron.

"Amen!" shouted one of the sailors in a different part of the ship.

Madoc realized Wyn was up there preaching while he hammered the carbonized slugs, putting the edge on them that made them steel knives. And that it was Winnowed Rice relaying his message.

He looked around for Tumkis, for anyone who might be sharing the hold with him, but he appeared to be alone. Madoc realized that Wyn had a captive congregation—everyone on board, which evidently still included the duck hunters from Shetland, or whatever their tribe's name. Another red tribe, he thought. More red people in this land he had erroneously thought was sparsely inhabited. None of the Norse sagas he could remember mentioned such a variety of human beings in Vinland or Vitromannaland or any of the named places that were supposed to lie in this western region. Yet here he found as diverse a people involved in as much contention and feuding as between different factions back home.

Madoc thought that the good brother was enjoying this far too much to be interrupted. Suddenly chill in the cool, damp air, he took it on one foot and, holding on where he could get purchase, worked his way back to the warm bed, which still smelled of Tumkis when he buried his face in the covers.

Later he woke again, surprised that he had slept, but feeling even better than before. Light coming from the hold was grayer now—it must be a couple of hours past noon, with an overcast sky, he thought, stretching until his bones popped beneath the furry warm star-robe.

Again he clumsily made his way to the mast and looked up to confirm his suspicions—there was a weather sky out there. The air was colder. He wondered how long he had been out.

He listened for the hammer and the sermon, but both of

Wyn's labors seemed to be idle, and he called out, "Anybody up there?"

Dag's face appeared first at the edge of the opening, then several others.

"Did you save me breakfast?"

"It is a day later, sir," said the Norseman, "and past breakfast time."

"There is a storm on the way from the west," said a woman whom he could not see, and a moment later Winnowed Rice peered down into the gloom.

The two Yuchi warriors joined her, then Wyn moved up to the edge where he said, "Chief Turtle says we are in for a good one."

"Our duck hunter, yes," Madoc replied just as the chief stepped into view. Madoc thought he was certainly odd looking with the long, flat forehead of the nobles of some red tribes.

Tumkis was scrambling down the peg stair, surprise on her face that he was up and about so soon.

"Can we move this big canoe?" Turtle-in-the-Sun hand-signed, crouching down at the top of the stair, and Madoc was pleased to find himself understanding without translation.

"With some difficulty, yes," Madoc replied in words and handsign as he leaned upon Tumkis so that he could get to the bottom peg.

"It would be best do so before nightfall."

"Ask him what harbor would be safer." Madoc said to Winnowed Rice as he pulled himself up carefully on the first step.

She threw a sidelong glance at Turtle, hugging herself, but before she could speak, Rhys—behind her with the baby on his back—called down, "She will not speak to them." But he repeated the query about a safe harbor to Tumkis, who called it up to the miko.

"I thought I heard her translating Wyn into Muskogean for them."

"For the Yuchi."

Madoc knew they all used Muskogean, the language of trade throughout this vast river valley.

With no language except that of the eyes, Turtle-in-the-Sun put his long, muscular arm down, hand out for Madoc to grab.

Madoc hesitated; could the red chief heft his weight while leaning with no leverage over an opening?

"Take it," the red man plainly said, and began to haul Madoc up on his unimpaired foot rung by rung until he rolled out onto the deck, then let Turtle pull him upright. He grabbed the rail, wincing when the splint scraped the boards. But he covered his discomfort by looking around, pleased to see everyone smiling back at him just before they broke into a cheer for his good arrival back up in the sunshine however dull it was and short-lived.

"Thank you, all of you," he said, then in handsign said directly to Turtle-in-the-Sun, "Thanks for the hand up," and took the gourd of water someone gave him, then made it along the rail to the pilot's crib, where he was glad to finally be seated. But the ominous, corrugated sky above them was not a restful sight. All its dire lines of moving cloud were pointing from the northwest.

Turtle-in-the-Sun said in handsign and through the translators, "Less than half a day's canoeing from here, there is a safe harbor."

"How deep a channel?" Madoc handsigned, feeling more confident of himself than ever before with the signals.

Turtle turned an inquiring gaze in the direction of Buffalo Eagle, who was seated upon an oar block while Fire Wolf dipped pigment out of a clam shell and applied it with a stick to the elder's sleeve.

Accepting the cold corncake Tumkis offered, Madoc saw that the younger man was adding another hash mark to the many already denoting the record of bones set.

The old man shrugged and spoke to Fire Wolf, who looked up dreamy-eyed, as though his thoughts had been far away.

"Sky Blood Creek—how deep is it?" the old man asked impatiently.

"Three man-heights," the daykeeper rattled off by rote, being the official rememberer, a walking textbook of a mass of small details about the city of Ixtulan.

Tumkis waited for Turtle-in-the-Sun to say it before she said it in Shawnee to Rhys, who told Madoc, "Sounds like three fathoms, more or less."

"And how wide?"

Fire Wolf got Madoc's handsign immediately and answered in kind: "An arrow shot."

Which might be interpreted differently, depending on the bowman's power, but Madoc was satisfied that the water would be wide enough to accommodate the *Horn*.

His eye was on the clouds. It was cold enough for the wolf-skin jacket, which he asked Tumkis to find below.

He asked Dag if he thought the crew could do the tricky line work and tacking to keep her with the wind abeam, coming as it did from slightly north of west, while the route indicated by Turtle was almost due north.

Dag sniffed the wind, calculating for himself its speed and direction relative to the current against which they would be moving.

"Well, girls, what do you say to the man?" Dag asked them, he being first mate to this scruffy crew, which gave him back a rough cheer. Even the two Yuchi nodded enthusiastically and joined the chorus, though they may not have understood what was being asked. Dag had to admit they had quickly learned the several signal calls among the crew.

Tumkis helped Madoc put on the jacket. His ears were cold, so he found his woven buffalo-wool cap and pulled it down over his head, again a member of the crew by this action because all of them were wearing the traditional sailor's headgear, which kept the head warm and would not blow off in the worse gale.

"And," Madoc said to Turtle, knowing there had to be a price, "how much will it cost me to put my ship in your safe harbor?"

Turtle-in-the-Sun shrugged. "You are welcome to stay as long as you like for free, Weather Eyes. But Lady Tumbling Water tells me you want to buy corn. I will trade you one hawk-basket of corn for each of these you have." He produced a new ax head in a clean handle, no doubt the one Wyn had been hammering earlier.

"I gave him and his bonesetter one each for the work on your leg," Wyn said, and Madoc knew that Wyn had been using the wonder of the metal that glowed like the sun to set his preaching. It had worked with David Iron; all the red people were awed that Wyn captured the sun's glow in the hard metal.

"They did a fair job," Madoc said, gesturing at the splint. He caught Buffalo Eagle's eye and made the sign for good. "How big is a hawk-basket?"

Rhys and Tumkis conferred about the exchange. She finally made a gesture with both arms that indicated a medium-sized basket—about a bushel.

"These are fine blades," Madoc said, shaking his head. "There is nothing like them in all this country."

Turtle-in-the-Sun conferred with Buffalo Eagle when he saw Weather Eyes was negotiating. "An eagle-basket for each blade."

Tumkis rounded her arms, not letting the hands touch— bigger than a bushel.

With a grin Madoc held his hand out to be shaken by Turtle, who stared back at him, understanding the deal was made, but not familiar with the handshake as a seal to the bargain.

"One ax head for each bushel of corn—we have a bargain," Madoc reiterated, making the sign for trade. "Trade."

Turtle-in-the-Sun nodded with excitement, setting down his ax and giving his hand to Madoc's, letting him shake it rigorously. Taken by the gesture, he went to each of the white men, grabbing up their hands and shaking them vigorously, repeating the white man's word, "Trade, trade."

"I want to stay just this side of midchannel," Madoc said to Dag, ever nervous about lurking sandbars and snags this close to land that was mostly swamp toward the east. "You take the pinnacle."

Dag made to climb the mast, which Turtle-in-the-Sun had seen him do at least once while Madoc slept.

"Let me offer the services of my daykeeper—" the chief said enthusiastically. "Fire Wolf, climb the big pole to watch the river for Weather Eyes."

The young daykeeper eyed the slick, naked mast and gave his miko back a disdainful look.

"Fire Wolf, I understand," Turtle said in mock sympathy. "You fear to climb this tree so far above a moving canoe."

Fire Wolf did not like to be told he feared anything, but he did not want to go up there, and his look said so. "Bright Snake is heavy medicine, my lord."

"Companion to the sun," Turtle whispered, and Fire Wolf looked down, about to drop his knees to do proper homage to his miko, who was reminding the daykeeper that he himself was scheduled for exactly that service.

"Do not kneel, son," the miko ordered, "to keep secret what

is sacred," and in another public voice called out, "Then, let me watch the river, Weather Eyes," in speech and handsign.

"Are you sure?" Madoc asked. "It will be cold up there, and she will try to shake you off."

"I will do it," Turtle said, looking up.

"Translators?"

Rhys and Tumkis nodded to Madoc across the boards.

"Here, then," Madoc said to Turtle, "this will keep your ears warm," and gave the chief his own woolly cap, which Turtle pulled down over the coyote-head helmet—an odd thing to see, a coyote wearing a sailor's cap. And Madoc could not help smiling at it.

Turtle-in-the-Sun took it as encouragement, and, disdaining the safe approach by way of the peg stair, leapt unexpectedly out over the gaping hold and adhered to the mast like a cat up a pine tree.

Madoc was surprised he did not shuck his shoes for better traction, but scrambled up in the supple moccasins as though he had done it all his life. He was amazingly strong and agile from a lifetime of ballplay and other athletics. Because he had watched when Dag earlier sat the harness, he slipped into the sling without hesitation.

Perched securely, Turtle-in-the-Sun peered below his feet when Madoc called them out to haul up the sail and hoist anchors. Very soon Turtle felt, more than everyone else, the ship leaning down into the current, picking up speed in the stiffening stream.

The elders huddled together with the wind flapping their heavy braids, saying their prayers against any evil that might come from riding in this big canoe, eyeing their miko from time to time up there not appearing to worry at all.

Several orders, and the ship gradually began describing a wide arc upon the rattling water. The crew obeyed the captain's calls, and the sail found the right angle with which to reach into the wind.

Before long they were making fair time upstream under the northwest wind.

They saw on the eastern shore a line of people waving and running along, following the ship. The shore widened into the plaza of a fair-sized town with a small pyramid about forty feet high, where smoldered a coil of smoke from a tall temple roof.

Turtle watched the shore whiz by, laughing, calling back to

Buffalo Eagle trembling under prayer-formulas amidships, "The elders of Fifth Village will wonder forever which of their girls is the prettiest and argue for generations over which of the finalists I would have chosen tonight!"

"It is truly an event that will be sung for many generations, my lord," replied Buffalo Eagle dryly.

Turtle-in-the-Sun had already chosen three girls from the other villages. These were invited to visit Ixtulan for their wedding ceremony on the Day of Equals, considered highly auspicious.

Tumkis and Rhys explained to Madoc what the red chiefs were discussing.

Wyn thought it scandalous, a man taking so many wives. He quoted scripture in their direction about leaders of men having only one wife each and digressed into a small sermon in Madoc's direction about yielding to sins of the flesh.

"Scripture says it is better to marry than to burn," Wyn reminded him, "and when God made Eve, he said it is not good for a man to be alone. But he should marry her," he paraphrased the Book of Hebrews. "Marriage is honorable in all and the bed undefiled, but whoremongers and adulterers like these barbaric savages, God will judge."

Nobody translated this lest it offend their guests, but the message got across anyway.

"Why does your sachem think negative thoughts in our direction, Weather Eyes?" Turtle-in-the-Sun asked.

"Domme, you are disturbing our guests—say a prayer for them so that they do not think we wish them magical harm."

Wyn growled but did as Madoc bid, seeing that it did not seem to mollify them—the old men ceased mumbling the chants Wyn's captious words had provoked in them.

Very soon after the Fifth Village, they passed wide, dark, empty fields between it and the Fourth and Third, situated even closer to the water and sharing a small pyramid in the middle of a huge cleared plaza that ran all the way down to a wharf area. People were gathering in the plaza as the ship sailed speedily by, and they ran along the beach for some way before they piled up, staring as a group as the *Horn* passed.

Second Village was so far back from the water that only a small dock showed its location. Several canoemen bringing in nets full of drumfish paused in their labor and watched with their mouths open in wonder at the great winged beast gliding by.

First Village owned two fine little grass-covered pyramids with twin thatched temples on their tops.

Just north of the First Village was the outflow of a smaller river, about an arrow shot in width, which emptied lazily into this greater stream.

When Madoc asked if this was where they hauled to starboard, Turtle called down a complex no. The translators told Madoc that this was the tail of the snake and advised him to continue on up the Mech-a-sip-i a short distance to the beginning of Sky Blood Creek, which fed a huge lake, once the river's main channel. It was traditional for all incoming vessels to take the creek in that direction and go with the flow, which Madoc honored.

A slow fen of thick trees and impenetrable tangled undergrowth appeared to slide past their starboard, capped on the northern flank by a pink sandy beach.

Here Madoc saw a clear junction with another smaller stream, which Turtle-in-the-Sun immediately identified as the bight of Sky Blood Creek.

He ordered the oars brought off their blocks and slipped into their sockets, and the sail reefed. However deep it may be, the channel was narrow when compared to the broad river, and Madoc felt safer taking it slowly.

Turtle-in-the-Sun was disappointed that the great snake's wing had to be folded, thinking that the ship made a much more dramatic presentation with it up and showing.

Madoc tried to explain; Rhys and Tumkis did their best, but Turtle did not understand.

But the oaks themselves were something to see in motion. Soon Dag was calling the strokes for the eight oarsmen; the ship glided on.

Shortly, beyond low, flat land that showed no trace of trees or stumps, Madoc saw on the smaller water's north bank the pyramid towers of Daughter of Ix, which Turtle explained was the port of entry to Ixtulan.

Madoc was amazed to see no guard, no sign of military activity. People on the shore gathered to watch the slowed passage of the *Horn,* and even cheered when they realized the miko was on board.

Madoc asked Turtle to use his authority against any who might challenge their progress.

"Nobody will challenge this Uktena canoe, Weather Eyes," said Turtle-in-the-Sun. "The medicine is too great."

Thinking the chief complacent in his security, Madoc kept his own council.

The stream called Sky Blood Creek angled off fairly wide— more than two ship lengths, to Madoc's eye. It looked safe enough to enter, but he decided that they would proceed slowly behind thorough sounding, and he ordered Dag to drop the weighted lines to test the bottom.

A good flow moved below their skin, and the crew pulled on to bring them around to move with the current.

The first sounding brought up fine sand at a little over four fathoms, but as they moved on toward the long lake in the northern precincts of Ixtulan, the bottom grew more shallow, weedy, and full of dark sediment. They traversed the long lake and under Turtle's direction made for the southern banks, where outflow continued on toward the big pyramid.

The white men were now all staring at what lay ahead.

Each bank of the creek was lined with open, empty fields of rich floodplain dirt awaiting next spring's seed. All of last season's debris, down to a single shred of corn-shuck, had been cleared and used or burned to be turned back into the soil. There were no trees within the eye's reach, though a long, low horizon looked to be the beginning of a modest upland fringed with lacy bare hardwood crowns spotted here and there with dark evergreens.

Madoc swore a small, shocked curse of disbelief as he gazed for the first time upon God's Hill putting its arrowhead up into the chill clouds bearing down under a steadily increasing wind from the northwest.

Pyramids he had seen all over the Muskogean nations so far encountered, but nothing like this massive, geometrically perfect triangle sheared on the north face in terraces, looming up ahead to starboard—his side of the ship—as they approached upon the creek, which flowed within ten paces of the highest, eastern face of the mound. Its sides of more than a thousand feet appeared to be of blackened clay, a hard dark red silhouette thrusting fully a hundred feet up into the lowering sky.

The wind bent the several columns of smoke rising from tall

pointed roofs up on the top terrace and rang small bells and clattered strings of shells dangling on the eaves of the temple buildings.

There were no steps on this face of the pyramid, so it was not possible to see a line of darkly robed priests rapidly descending the stair on the southern face, all hurrying out to the docks to welcome their miko, who had sent the second canoe back here to tell them to expect his arrival. But he told the warriors in that canoe not to give a hint of the big canoe or the white people in it, as even then Turtle planned to somehow get the ship to the city for its awesome display.

Tumkis's hands on his shoulders, Madoc called for him to come on down and watched as he did so as gracefully as he had climbed, easily taking the leap Madoc earlier misstepped.

He ended the jump in an easy trot to the rail, where he stood waving and smiling benevolently toward the crowd of laborers gathering this side of the pyramid. He imagined what the great ship looked like from their perspective, its huge wing full of wind, the dragon pennant snapping on the mast, the Uktena snarling down from the long neck, an image from story and song.

One of his own dances featured a mask that represented Bright Snake with the shining eye, achieved with shimmering mica from a far-off eastern place. Perhaps, he thought, he would perform that one soon to commemorate the ship's arrival.

He was delighted to see that the gathering crowd was awed beyond expectations at the sight of this marvel, which seemed from their point of view to be under the command of their all-powerful miko riding the dragon's shoulder.

Madoc was still staring at the immense pyramid, calculating how much earth it must contain, for he had been told briefly that was how they were made, piled up a basketful at a time. But presently his attention was drawn to the men standing forward and larboard with Buffalo Eagle. They, too, were staring out at their city, not in delight but in shock.

Lost in the sheer size of the colossal structure, Madoc had missed an area of large activity below the southeast side. There it appeared laborers were rolling in trees from the farther southeast directly through Oldtown. His eyes followed their path backward where the log-rolling had plowed through houses, some of which partially stood. Garden were cut in half, and dust hung heavy in that direction as yet another crew foot-rolled yet another forty-foot log over the ground.

Another crew was at work raising the logs in sinkholes similar to the one used back at the Hundred's camp for the cross. Already a long line of raw, peeled, implanted shafts stuck up close together in a straight line pointing back beyond his view. Their line had interrupted a small enclave of larger thatch houses, cutting some in two, with several fractured households in pieces beyond the wall. Farther down the line still others were troweling thick clay onto the logs so that a solid wall was formed. A stretch of about a hundred trees was already finished in this manner—persons in dark robes walked along that stretch handling blazing torches against the drier stucco, turning it blackish brown.

As the ship came into position parallel but some way off from a long, fairly well-made jetty, Madoc thought he felt the telltale low grinding of the ship scraping bottom, but it was soft-edged and slow. Probably a fathom of mud, he thought, ordering still another sounding.

Once again a huge amazed red contingent gathered on the shore to view the great ship. Its men dropped anchor after Dag twice sounded the bottom, closer to the dock each time, until Madoc called it too close for the comfort of his gut. They would have to shuttle from ship to shore. Already several canoes of gaily singing people were upon the water, headed in this direction.

Madoc called for the oars to be shipped.

Turtle-in-the-Sun showed great interest in all these operations, but his companions were at the forward rail watching the laborers who had interrupted their work for the excitement of the ship's arrival. Supervisors in dark priestly robes were directing them back to the line of peeled logs, pointing at the sky and shaking long cane sticks decorated with a fluff of white feathers.

Finally Turtle could ignore Buffalo Eagle no longer and spoke to him while watching Dag wind the line that lowered the sail.

"This is an outrage that you would have a wall built right through our homes," the old man said, staring at the shore, keeping his voice low and private. He could see that indeed his own household was one of those cut off by the wall. The pen where he raised red puppies was broken, and no sign remained of the dogs or his wife and servants. The pavilion attached to his house, where he saw patients' broken or disjointed bones, was collapsed and ruined in the path of the rolling logs, another of which was maneuvered into place even as he watched.

"Where are you getting those trees—they look burngirded," Buffalo Eagle demanded.

"You have keen eyesight for a man so advanced in the seasons, Buffalo Eagle."

"This is why you would not meet us in council."

"Momentous events are shaping up that are often out of our control."

"This is an insult to Oldtown."

"That crowd on solstice day—that was an insult to your miko, bonesetter. This wall will insure that your miko will never again be threatened by his people."

The old man's eyes narrowed, but he said nothing else. Nobody translated for Madoc, who wondered at the quiet intense conversation between the two red men while his own people hung on the edge of the ship ogling the incredible city spread out before them, crying out to the pretty girls in the painted canoes bobbing below their bow.

Hundreds of people were gathering below the big pyramid, many dressed in noble clothing, and cheering when they saw their miko onboard.

Four long canoes pulled up below the stern, where the crew dropped Odin's nosehair to hold them in place and pointing downstream on the mild current of Sky Blood Creek.

Turtle waved down to his welcomers, shouting out phrases they expected of him, the number of duck he bagged, and how many new wives he had taken. Despite his attempt at secrecy, the word had made it back to Ixtulan that the miko was ajourneying, and these good-natured shouts were traditional between the miko and his people.

By now the line of priests who had descended the steps was approaching in an orderly file to flank the approach to the dock where they expected the miko to disembark. A squad of the biggest guardsmen had hauled up an open palanquin pilled with duck-down pillows in which Burning Rose was seated with a jug of water in her hand and a sour expression on her face.

"Will Weather Eyes join me up on God's Hill?" Turtle-in-the-Sun asked Madoc.

When Rhys translated the name of the pyramid, Wyn sucked air in a tone of high offense.

"This makes me clumsy getting about," Madoc said, gesturing at the splint.

"You are welcome to stay here as long as you like—consider yourself my honored guest."

"I want to climb your amazing pyramid, Chief Turtle-in-the-Sun—I have never seen anything like it."

This seemed to amaze Turtle-in-the-Sun, who remarked, "This is what a true man—a chief—does, build pyramids to worship God. Is it not so in your nation?"

Madoc listened to this translation and did not know what to answer. He had seen great churches in London and Paris, and they were certainly splendid enough, and often built by a king's donation. But this high pyramid was an order of a different magnitude.

Turtle started to walk to the rail, then thought of something that drew him back. "The Chickasaw tell me that you shoot the North Star with an arrow each night. Does this ceremony have to be performed in private?"

Tumkis and Rhys struggled with it, but Madoc had it first from Turtle's handsign.

"You are welcome to return as soon as the overcast clears and watch me shoot the North Star."

"And you are invited to watch the dawn with me up on God's Hill as soon as you are able to climb the stair. Thank you for the gift," he said, hefting the ax. "I have need of cutting many trees right now."

Madoc saw Wyn grinding his teeth.

"My men will teach yours how to use the axes we have traded for the corn you promised." Madoc did not see any reason not to remind the chief of their bargain. "How many axes are ready, Domme?"

"Fifteen have their edge, sir, but may I object to this blasphemy—"

"That is what they call it, God's Hill," Rhys protested. "I am translating faithfully."

"Good sirs, let us settle this later," Madoc urged. "Domme, give Chief Turtle-in-the-Sun the sharpened axes. Dag—take two men in the morning and teach his men to chop whatever Chief Turtle wishes."

Dag growled an affirmative, but Wyn was still in a bad temper.

"Can we not call the pyramid something else—surely you are not implying these savages worship God?"

"Lady Tumkis says Turtle-in-the-Sun calls it God's Hill," Rhys insisted. "Call it what you will."

"It cannot be God's Hill, now can it, poet, since we are the first Christians to have the opportunity to witness to them?"

Rhys sighed patiently and said, "A great Christian teacher argued that since God is the highest being of which the human mind can conceive, the mere fact that such a conception is attainable is proof of the existence of a being corresponding to such a conception."

"But this is a primary rational argument for the existence of God," Wyn said, getting red in the face that the poet would pick this public moment to use a churchman's words to argue against him.

"It would also explain the persistent belief in God," Rhys continued mildly. "Can you gainsay their calling God the highest being they know?"

Wyn, who had been talking serious religion with the miko of Ixtulan for more than a day, knew some of what transpired up on the big pyramid. "If they worshiped the true God, they would not permit blood sacrifice," he countered, fussing with the ties of his small personal bundle.

"What about Abraham and Isaac?" Rhys was quick to retort. "Perhaps these people are about as far along as Father Abraham when he tried to sacrifice his son to prove his trust in the True God."

"I have had enough of this empty debate," Wyn fumed, "when you know well we are discussing your translation, not what they may or may not believe," and hefted the parcel.

"Where are you going, Domme?" Madoc asked.

"Chief Turtle-in-the-Sun has invited me to accompany him to that temple," the brother beamed. "He is going to let me preach to his council, perhaps even conduct a Mass." He leaned close to Madoc and whispered, "I think I have him, sir."

Rhys uttered a dry, doubtful chuckle.

"He hungers for the gospel, and I believe he will be the first of his great nation to be converted to the true religion."

"Even better than fighting the Turks in the kingdom of Jerusalem?" Madoc asked.

Wyn shrugged. "We take our opportunity to witness where we find it," and added, "I think your lady is about ready to take the cross, too, sir."

"Tumkis?" Madoc said, looking around for her. "But she wants to be a woman of power—a female priest back in her homeland."

Wyn shrugged suggestively. "She asks the right questions. Soon I think she will ask that her sins be forgiven and she be saved, praise God." He was almost shaking with excitement in his renewed mission, so agitated that he was talking with his hands.

"And Winnowed Rice, too—did you see how she was taking to heart my sermon over the iron?"

Rhys made a disbelieving sound.

Wyn glared at Rhys as though his glare could be seen. "I do not press anyone, but she will come around in her own time—she is a good woman and cannot gainsay the truth when she hears it. Likewise Chief Turtle—ah," the monk sighed with anticipation. "If he converts, the entire heathen city will become Christian—a triumph for the faith."

"So you go ashore to accomplish this work?"

"I will stay if you need me here," Wyn offered, but it was clearly mere accommodation.

"Be my eyes and ears, Domme, until I can get about."

"Of course."

"And be careful—you do not know what an insult is to them. Who knows, if you try to baptize someone, he may take it wrong."

Wyn slapped him on the shoulder and promised. "I will come back day after tomorrow, a Sunday I believe, and say Mass for you," and with that turned to join the departing red men.

Laughing Dog was on his heels.

"Are you kidnapping my crew?"

"I need Brother Paul to help me with the language."

"Brother Paul?"

Wyn put an affectionate arm around Laughing Dog's shoulders. "I baptized Paul last night."

Madoc had nothing to say to that except a gesture of good-will and farewell as Wyn and his convert climbed over the rail.

Huw came forward and asked if he, too, might not go ashore. "Einion is pestering me to climb the mountain."

Madoc turned to them and said any who wished had shore leave.

Almost to a man they hurried for their bedrolls and kits and scurried down into the waiting canoes.

"You are a woman of power," Turtle-in-the-Sun said to Tumkis. He stood near the spot where they would descend to the canoe, several steps from the Natchez, with whom he had shared a few words.

She looked away when he said this, toward the pyramid and the gathering crowd around its skirt.

"I do not know you," he continued in an even voice, following her gaze westward. "But I saw immediately that you are a woman of power."

Actually he had spoken at length with Laughing Dog, who knew the pertinent parts of her history and how she happened to be here with the white man.

Still she did not speak, but he knew she heard him.

Madoc caught a glimpse of Turtle climbing over the side, leaving Tumkis at the rail where he had been wishing her good-bye.

Presently the white men and members of Turtle's party could be seen on the water in the sleek boats, while on the little pier a flurry of priests prepared the royal litter for their returning miko. Several of the dark-robed clergy down there were rattling bells on the ends of long walking sticks, and one of them knelt to blow new life in the coals of a shell incense burner on long thongs.

Madoc could smell the aroma up here as the wind broadcast it in this direction. Some kind of emperor, he was thinking, watching the spectacle below.

Many hands helped the chief to sit the palanquin, then six strong dark-robes picked the thing up on their shoulders and began a slow, syncopated trot toward a path that led directly to the base of the pyramid.

On the other side, as his bearers ferried his chair near the work, the disheveled men and women setting logs stared over their shoulders in amazement at the ship. It was possible for Turtle to read their mood as he watched his many warrior-

priests among them, urging them to set one more log before
they lost all the light. Turtle saw Lord Hard Walker among
them supervising the depth of the next hole.

Hard Walker had kept his concentration on the work at
hand, but he glanced up from time to time watching the
spectacle out on the water and his miko's progress.

Word of the miko's presence rippled through the laborers.
One by one they began to sing, "Blood of the sun, blood of the
sun," which the white men did not understand except as a
deep respectful chant. Turtle acknowledged their reverent
gesture with a raised hand, as the miko's entourage skirted the
pyramid along a well-worn path that led around to its stair.
Someone in the crowd called out, "Thank you, lord, for
Mother Tsalu," and Turtle nodded solemnly in that direction.

The dark-robes bringing up the train of pedestrians following the chief's litter began a low, moody chant in syncopation
to the other, making a music that went right to Madoc's
marrow. He was shaken by an involuntary little chill and said
to Rhys, "God help our abbot."

"God help Turtle-in-the-Sun."

Chapter 24

Madoc handsigned the word *turtle* when he asked Tumkis why she seemed doubtful when the chief offered his bonesetter's services.

"They are strange people," she said, close to him in their starry bed. "Even their friends fear them."

He and she, Rhys and Winnowed Rice, were the only adults aboard the *Horn* the next day, and they stayed belowdeck to keep warm.

Everyone, including Einion in Huw's care, was on shore being hosted by Chief Turtle.

The night brought the promised storm with wet, huge snowflakes that came down so hard they tapped upon the stretched, scraped, slightly translucent buffalo hides covering the hold.

But the two couples stayed warm several times on the cold day that followed, so that when they felt other appetites, they shared stores in Madoc's quarters—dried fruits, nuts, and travelcakes—and drank icy stinging tea left overnight in a jug up in the cold.

Now late in an afternoon that saw no sun, they crawled back under the covers and slept or made love, dozed and made love some more, the outside world forgotten for the duration of the snow, which they hoped would last at least for several days.

Rhys was idly strumming the harp while Winnowed Rice fed Cari cornmeal and mashed hickory nuts. The baby had taken her first steps over there earlier, giggling and laughing between her parents on their pallet.

Half dozing, feeling well and happy and satisfied for the first time in longer than he could remember, Madoc said to Tumkis, "But you did not stop me from letting him reset my leg."

"I could see that Buffalo Eagle was a master."

"Hmmh," he said, nose at her neck.

"I saw you were going to do it anyway."

"What did Turtle say to you just before he left the ship?"

"He invited me to participate in the Day of Equals ceremony, as lodge-mother to his new wives."

"Do you want to do it?"

"It would be a great honor to me as a woman of power."

"You want it?"

"Perhaps, if you allow it."

"Why do you need my permission?"

But she would not or could not say; he felt her reticence and did not press her.

"Does Winnowed Rice not speak to them because she is afraid?"

"I cannot speak for her, but the miko is a very powerful man. I want to be part of his power, but I am afraid of him."

"Is that why you have been listening to Father Folded Hands?"

"He says Mother Mary is more powerful than the Unknown Woman and will protect me from her."

"He says you are going to become a Christian."

"I will if you want it." She pressed closer to him, slipping her warm, naked body over his under the star-robe. They were exhausted from lovely labor, but Madoc was renewed, as though making up for the months he had spent alone.

"This is a matter for your own heart," he said, adjusting his leg so that her weight did not burden it. "Do not do it for me."

"I am afraid, Weather Eyes," she whispered, relaxing upon him, her words breathy in his ear. "Afraid of the Unknown Woman."

Madoc had his own disturbing dreams to remember about this, though he had told nobody of his vision under this woman's medicines. In his tradition St. Brigit was the Christian version of an ancient Celtic earth mother who could appear as a young girl or as a hag. That was the personage he felt he had seen in the dream with this woman; somehow she had put the suggestion of the vision into his mind while he was suffering her cures for the Chickasaw poison in him.

"I did not make sure she got her price," Tumkis said softly. "What punishment will she take against me?"

He enfolded her in his arms and rolled with her beneath the

buffalo robe until he made her laugh. "She has given you me as punishment," he said, smothering any protest she might have made with kisses.

The overcast lingered through the next day and into the night. Sometime before dawn the sky began to get higher so that the clear disk of the sun was visible at dawn.

Late that morning the crew staggered across the snow-dotted plaza and along the dock, laughing and singing on the arms of red women, looking freshened and clean from steam-baths, dressed in feathers and newly beaded tunics, laden with food and exclamations of the wonders of Chief Turtle's hospitality. Behind them a line of bearers lugged big baskets of the promised corn and one by one transported the crew and trade goods out to the ship in long canoes.

"There is going to be a big feast with games," Einion told Madoc eating breakfast in bed, sitting on the edge of the pallet down in the hold.

"God is carrying this heavy load," the boy said with the excitement of discovery, gesturing, "not just this year but all the years of this time, and you know a year has passed because God takes another step each Day of Equals, another slow step westward because he is an old man by now."

"Did you tell Brother Wyn these things?"

"The miko is going to dance this wonderful dance in a fancy mask that shines and flashes and makes noises and smoke, and the dance means that he is walking westward with God, helping him, you know, like two knights on crusade."

The boy was transformed, steamed clean of all the grime, nails trimmed, hair slicked down with oil and braided perfectly. He wore a new suit of some soft suede, beaded lavishly and fringed with a tiny blue bead at the end of each ribbon. On his feet were moccasins of equal workmanship, finely lap-stitched and lined with rabbit fur.

"I played chunkee with the prince—look!" He took from a neat boiled leather travel satchel a painted arched hickory cane with a cord-bound handle and a peculiarly shaped head, and a perfectly smooth, round stone with a perfectly round, concave depressions in each side, a sort of huge, thick stone coin of about a palm's width.

"And the miko himself gave me these." He showed a little bow of yellow wood and a quiver of straight arrows with delicate black obsidian bird-points the size of Madoc's little fingernail but as sharp as needles, and displayed the new moccasins the miko's sister had given him.

"I stayed in his own house," the boy enthused, "with these four old ladies who kept trying to bathe me all the time, but they gave me lots of presents, and I slept in a furry bed stuffed with duck feathers."

Madoc listened to his newly polished little brother, marveling at the changes in his adopted son, who summed up his story with a declaration: "Tad, I like it here above all the places we have been."

"I missed you," Madoc said. "Without you to remind me, I forgot to read the sun last night."

"But it was cloudy last night, Tad—do you think we can stay for the Day of Equals? I want to see the sun take another step westward from the top of God's Hill—the miko says that is the best place to see it."

Madoc knew of the precession of the equinoxes but had no explanation of the phenomenon, which did not bear directly upon a mariner's needs. He had to stop and calculate how many days from now was the vernal equinox. That would be early spring, around the twentieth of March. He forgot the exact date, but it would be near Easter. "We shall see, son, we shall see."

With equal interest Madoc listened to the men, who described the miko's fabulous household full of servants; beautiful, compliant women at work over huge feathered masks; many men knapping flint; squads of older women grinding corn into meal within the temple precincts; and a huge open-air marketplace with canopied stalls where people strolled every afternoon with their baskets, using delicately carved sticks as money, or bartering handicrafts for fruits and trinkets.

"I have never seen so many priests," Dag exclaimed, "but few warriors. I tell you these people do not have to fight, they are so powerful and so feared among their neighbors."

"And rich," said Huw. "Their lowest dirt movers are paid in one bowlful of the finest cornmeal each day they labor—that is why they cheered the miko so wildly on his arrival. They do not need supervisors when they are so highly paid—they stand in line to be among the miko's laborers."

Madoc was sorry to see there was no seedcorn among the baskets, and Dag explained that Ixtulan only sold cracked, parched, or ground corn. In fact, he said that it was a serious offense for anyone but a special planter priest to even touch any viable seed.

Dag explained what he had seen: "There are many tens of women who each day sit in the miko's temple patio and grind corn on stone mortars, but even they are not allowed to touch the corn. Young boys in training under the high priest fetch it from baskets to each mortar. Special daykeepers count out the number of kernels given to each woman. And they have a simple balance scale to determine the weight of what she grinds each day, and she is punished if she is short."

"Where is Brother Wyn?" Madoc asked, looking around at his polished crew.

Dag explained that the miko had invited the abbot to lecture the many royal sons and to speak another time to his council. "He has adopted Father Folded Hands," handsigned the younger Yuchi, whose brother stayed with the abbot.

"Allowed him to watch all their secret ceremonies—" Dag added.

"And let him watch this scary priest—" Einion interrupted, "not like Father Brian at all but dressed all in black with black face paint. He is horrible; the prince hates him because he sticks the miko each morning."

"Sticks him?"

"He sticks him, you know with this long needle." The boy gestured this-wide with his hands. "He takes some of his blood."

"Did you see this?"

"No, sir, they would not permit it, but they let Brother Wyn see it, and later they let us watch the miko pray with him when the sun came up. They tried to outyell each other. It made the miko mad, but he did not blame Father Folded—I mean Brother Wyn." Einion gulped a breath. "You know what he did—?"

Madoc had never seen the child so animated.

"Instead of being mad at Brother Wyn and hitting him or something, he beat the ugly priest, and he just took it, bowed down on the floor and let the miko cane him."

Each man had other wonders to show, or a story to tell about what he had seen or how he was feted, dined, and further entertained by a series of willing, voluptuous women who showered them with gifts.

Dag finally told him that he had seen the women of the city working a very supple grade of buffalo hide that was about half as thick as the *Horn*'s present sail.

"Our sheet is patched and worn," Madoc admitted, amazed at the samples Dag had brought with him, a shirt one of the women gave him, and a priest's robe.

"Many women tend to the priest's clothing every day, all the time sewing new gowns, which are worn until they are replaced. I picked this one up from a scrap basket."

Madoc unfolded the long garment, which still had some of the shape of the man who had worn it. It was stained, but the only damage appeared to be around the tattered hem.

Madoc fingered the stuff, as fine as linen. He rubbed a little bear-grease from a nearby pot into the stuff with his thumb. If they made sails of this material, it would have to take an oiling without sagging.

The leather cloth did not seem to stretch. He tried stitching a line into it and found that it would not tear.

"We may have a use for this," Madoc said.

He had planned enough work to keep them busy as the day faired off with high, fluffy clouds marching eastward. First he had Dag and Huw construct a series of shelves on top of the forward shoring to hold their corn. Madoc expressed fear that it would mildew in the baskets and wished for pottery storage. But Winnowed Rice and Tumkis insisted that it was best left in the baskets, for it was coarse, parched, and cracked kernels. If air were allowed to circulate around the tight baskets, and it did not get wet, the corn would stay fresh.

Then he planned to replace the sail as soon as possible.

"How much will Turtle charge us for the buffalo cloth?" he asked Dag, who said it was not so dear, that dozens of women produced it for the many priests' costumes.

"Maybe a few knife blades."

They had more than a dozen in stock, already carbonized. Soon their smith must return to harden more of the trade knives.

That night Madoc had opportunity to ask Turtle-in-the-Sun about another trade.

The night was clear, the stars sparkling. A little before midnight, just before getting ready to take his midnight reading, Madoc heard someone call from a skiff on water. He limped forward and peered into the darkness riddled by reflected star-points.

"Permission to board," Wyn called up, and when he climbed up the sidelines, Madoc saw another silhouette accompanying him.

"Turtle-in-the-Sun wants to watch you take the midnight reading," Wyn said, and apologized for not returning when he promised. "I figured it was more important for me to preach over there to the heathen than to you here already saved."

"Welcome," Madoc said to the chief, who was dressed as an ordinary brave in a dark fringed tunic and trews of the supple, split buffalo leather.

They read the sun, that is, found the North Star, determining true midnight, then Madoc with a shell lamp showed the chief how he marked his charts.

"Why do you make this medicine?" Turtle wanted to know.

"To see how far north we are."

"But why?"

Madoc was frustrated as to how to explain they needed this information to determine how far they traveled each day aboard a ship at sea.

Rhys joined them up on the windy deck, willing to play awhile when Turtle requested music, asking once if he might touch the harp's base while Rhys plucked the strings.

He said he brought a small gift for Madoc and produced a gut bag full to the cork with a rich, sour liquor he called pulque, "From places over on the western edge of the world."

It was stronger than mead and quite a fair intoxicant. Madoc and Rhys had been so long without alcohol, they were eager to sample the drink until the canteen was empty.

Madoc asked how much Turtle wanted for buffalo cloth, explaining as best he could with Rhys's Muskogean what purpose he intended to put it to.

"That is many hides," Turtle said, calculating by the light of a half moon the size of the old sail.

Madoc brought out the trade knives, keeping back half of them, and finally coming to a bargain for one knife for ten hides and the rawhide cord to stitch them with. The final result of their trade was that Turtle would supply the seamstresses to do the work, plus the hides, for twenty-five hardened knives, then insisted they shake on it.

Turtle stood swaying in the moonlight, trying to find the side of the ship that led to his canoe.

"You should sleep here tonight," Madoc insisted, himself deeply in his cups.

But Turtle told him he must call up the sun at dawn, which led to a conversation at the rail between the three men on the significance of feeding God.

"Father Folded Hands tells me that God feeds you, which he insists is better than me feeding God," Turtle said, displaying more understanding of the faith than Madoc would have thought though it took some work for Rhys to translate the specific words. Several times the chief relied on handsign, finally admitting that "Father Folded Hands can be troubling, but he has made me think about these things."

Madoc felt Turtle shiver in the chill night as he slapped the rail and swung a leg over the side. "I am going to let God feed us at my Day of Equals, before I feed God," he said, slurred a bit. "That day all of us will eat—you will come to the celebration!"

Madoc promised that he would, and Turtle said again that his women would be here tomorrow early to begin work on Bright Snake's wing.

Madoc stood there in the darkness straining to watch the water where Turtle's servant plowed the canoe to the dock. The man had been sitting in the canoe all that time, awaiting his master's wish.

He relieved himself over the rail, feeling slightly guilty but unable in the darkness to find a bilge bucket. His son-in-law had burdened him with this new scruple, since none of the red men ever put bodily fluids into moving water.

But it felt a great relief, Turtle's pulque having the same effect as mead.

Rhys had gone to bed, but Madoc was aware of another on his deck whom he assumed to be the watch. His sense of time was confused, and he had to hold onto the rail to make his way back to him.

"You should not drink that vile stuff," Wyn's voice admonished from the blue darkness. "It is worse than French wine."

Overhead the clouds shredded themselves upon the moon's edge, putting a wan, flickering light on the deck.

Madoc wanted to get below and lose himself in slumber, but he found instead the crew's water bag and took a good, long drink, letting it splash on his face to revive himself.

The ship rocked in the water's gentle swell, nodding in the direction the breeze was blowing.

"I have troubling thoughts to share with you—are you sober enough to hear?"

"No, Domme."

"The chief lets a sorcerer draw blood from him each morning—a different spot each day—did you notice the tattoos here and here?" He indicated the base of his thumb.

Madoc said, "He told me you were going to perform a Mass up there in his temple on the equinox."

"It is a chance to get to them all, but that sorcerer is against it, against our being here, and wants Turtle to make us leave."

"Shortly we shall accommodate him—after we repair the sail, and my leg heals." He tapped the stiff cast against the dark decking. "It itches."

"Leave it be—it must stay on for a least four or five weeks."

Madoc drew his fingernails against the hardened rawhide in a futile motion to scratch the itch, muttering, "I must get some sleep, Domme."

They worked on the sails for three weeks, Turtle's crew of women meeting out on the open plaza below the eastern face of the pyramid each morning, cradleboards strapped to their backs. A contented buzz could be heard from that direction as they oiled and stitched the great sail in long bands that could be moved in case of weather.

Weather they had, but no more snow, just pounding rain that came upon them so suddenly they barely got the pieces of the sail rolled up and out of whatever damage the water might have done.

But finally they were finished.

Madoc's men worked for two more days to remove the old sail, which the women asked to have since they had many uses for the leather cut up and stitched into satchels, winter moccasin soles, and wood-carrying slings.

Turtle-in-the-Sun came aboard for the draping.

Madoc was not about to let the wind have the ship in the channel, but they did run the new sheet up in the late afternoon when the wind subsided, just to make sure the rigging worked.

The old sail had been thick and opaque, but the new oiled leather was a rosy translucent yellow with the sun behind it. It was a fitting golden wing for the dragon-ship, and it made

Madoc happy just to look at it. He wanted more than anything to put the *Horn* out on the water and under the wind.

The chief stayed aboard for a Mass Brother Wyn celebrated even though it was not Sunday and afterwards told Madoc that soon he would go into isolation in preparation for the big ceremony a few weeks away.

"Do you think your bonesetter might take a look at this?"

"Buffalo Eagle will be here when it is time, Weather Eyes. You must be patient," Turtle said, and left in Wyn's company.

As promised the old man let himself be ferried to the *Horn* a week later on a warm morning that was beginning to feel like spring.

He barely spoke, but inspected the cast minutely and pronounced it ready to come off, indicating that one of the assistants who accompanied him would do the job. He got up and stretched and walked forward to reboard his canoe.

"Stay, Buffalo Eagle, and take breakfast with us."

But he shrugged off Madoc's invitation and descended the sideline without saying anything more.

The assistant understood nothing of what Madoc asked, not even the handsign.

He expertly soaked the splint in warm water and cut the stitches that held it wrapped, with a fine flint blade that the light shone through, almost a crystal. Then he peeled back the rawhide to expose Madoc's pale bluish skin.

Throughout the procedure the assistant kept looking apprehensively toward the prow, at the dragonhead, and hurried away with the pieces of leather when he was finished, never having said a word to the patient.

Thereafter Madoc walked twice a day with Tumkis. He covered more ground daily, limping at first, and leaning on her, but gradually strengthening the weakened muscles.

Sometimes at night the knitted bones would ache.

She would take his leg between her warm hands and blow down through the crack made by her thumbs held closely together, putting that same sensual vibration down through her hands and into the healing bone.

For the next two weeks, she spent hours massaging it, which he did not like at first because it conjured up pain along the break. After a while the pain dropped down into a simple ache, and finally discomfort. He grew to look forward to the breathing therapy, which she explained chased away the tiny demons who had found their way inside his bone when it was broken.

"How do you know such a thing?" he asked her, forcing her to explain her way of thinking.

"Demons are in the air all around us, just waiting for a chance to enter and inhabit us. A sorcerer can send them into a body to steal the person's soul, if you do not say the formulas to keep them away."

It was the strangest explanation of a broken bone he could imagine, and his expression said so.

"It is true, Weather Eyes. I am saying formulas for you all the time and thinking right thoughts in your direction. You have to be careful."

"Why me, especially?"

"Because a powerful sorcerer hates you."

She said she must go stay in the miko's house until the Day of Equals to prepare the girls for their wedding ceremony, but when he pressed her, she would give no further explanation of the rituals or the sorcerer.

"But," she said, "you can come with me."

He decided that would be better than being without her. The ship was beginning to confine him. Now that they had the sail repaired and everything shipshape, he wanted to be away from this place. He was sorry he had promised Einion and Tumkis that they would linger here for the Day of Equals, still a couple of weeks away, however entertaining the ceremony was going to be.

Madoc set up a watch schedule with Huw so that three men would be aboard at any one time, and he left the *Horn* to them. Winnowed Rice was glad to cook for the skeleton crew. She refused to leave the ship or have anything to do with the miko's people. She would not even cook or eat the trade corn grown in Ixtulan's fields, and Rhys was disinclined to roam without her.

Neither was Huw disappointed to stay aboard. "I do not like this city, Captain. We will do well to be rid of it."

Madoc told him he agreed and added, "I think Einion should spend most of his time here."

"Yes, sir, I have him working on his knots." He cast a dire glance at the pyramid. "This place is not a good influence on any of us."

"We will shortly leave it, and gladly."

Chapter 25

Wyn was lost in the vast, gloomy temple.

Far above his head, at least two stories, the highly pitched underside of the close thatch was blue with the haze of incense burning unseen in several alcoves.

He wandered across the room of the big mat, empty now of anyone except himself and, lining the walls, shelves of bones. They were organized into various corresponding body parts— long bones of the leg and arms in one section, hundreds of neat bales of them tied with cord strung with spinal knobs. There were more than twenty shelves of finger and toe digits, all the horror stricken from the display by its cool organization.

These were mere artifacts now, with no shred of flesh remaining on the yellowed ivory.

The only grim pile was the skulls, more than a thousand he would guess, in almost as many hues of polished age.

These were stacked in several pyramids at the far end of the temple in the thickened haze.

He hurried on through the charnel room, surprised that he did not encounter one of the ubiquitous black-garbed priests scurrying about on secret missions. He had been successful at engaging none of these quiet servants of the miko. When he approached one of them, he would curl his fingers in some meaningful sign to ward off evil in Wyn's direction and hurry on without catching his eye.

He knew that he was Turtle's pet, ordered free and unencumbered by anyone's challenge, but the cold, knobby backs of those sooty, silent strangers felt more hostile than the bone room.

This afternoon, however, he saw nobody.

After watching the rituals conducted here for some weeks, he knew that few were prosecuted during midday. After the

396

miko read the sun at noon—a short prayer uttered in the nude out in one of the little atrium plazas entirely surrounded by the outer mud-smeared temple walls—there would be only occasional ceremony.

After that the miko rose long before dawn to greet the Morning Star, Bright Snake they called it.

Wyn left the large hall by way of a long side hall without any windows. All the light here came in through valances high under the cedar eaves. These rectangular openings were covered with the same material Madoc had used to replace the sail and so admitted a yellow glow like a candle through alabaster.

A dim and unpleasant tunnel was where he found himself searching for the apartment Madoc shared with Tumkis when he was not down on the ship.

The ceremony was days away.

But the interesting thing about the spring equinox was its vagueness, for whatever reason. It occured within a handful of days unevenly spaced about six months from the autumnal equinox, and the actual day must be called by careful observation of each sunrise horizon.

He turned to the left into a side hall that had no illumination. Wyn knew that the room was off a hall like this, opening into a private plaza.

He must have made a wrong turn somewhere because this one stopped in a dead end, narrow and dim. He turned to retrace his steps when he heard synchronous murmuring of voices on the side of the loose caning that made up what must be an inside wall. He put his eye to a crack between the canes and beheld on the other side a roomful of small boys.

His view was greatly limited, but he could see several rows of identically half-naked children from about six to a dozen years, all bent and muttering a monotonous chant. It sounded like numbers somehow, though he did not hear any one specifically. It was the rhythm that made it seem so.

His left eyelid was cramping from squinting it shut, so he switched, getting a slightly different angle of the room.

Light was coming from that end—he could see nothing but a glow there, but he thought the outside was exposed beyond a rolled-up cane shade, typical of the simple architecture of the place, which could produce a room from a pavilion or open a snug cubicle into a porch. They were always changing a space to fit a temporary use.

Just barely within view was a man's naked foot. He must be in repose, leaning against a post or something. Tapping, tapping near the foot was the end of a long cane, which matched the tempo of the boys droning on like a hive.

Dust motes sparkled on the air near the foot, which twitched and stretched as the man stood and began a slow circuit of the square chamber.

The light behind him made him nothing more identifiable than a silhouette, but presently as he progressed around the far side and turned back in this direction, Wyn saw it was that devil, the high priest.

The chant continued as he strolled among his students, for that was surely what they were, and this some kind of school, listening here, cocking his head there, as though listening to the individual voices. He did not pause but moved slowly, stepping between two boys, dropping a hand to hover above a head or a shoulder, but not actually touching anyone.

When he hesitated, Wyn saw the flash of white of a boy's eye glancing up at the hand with dread that was readable from here cramped behind his crack. What in God's name, he wondered, was the infraction, and what would be the punishment, because now he could see the boy's face turn upward with a look of such piercing fear it put a chill on the abbot's hairy forearms.

He must step back a moment and rest his facial muscles, but he pressed his eye again to the narrow hole, feeling emphatically the boy's apprehension. Momentarily he was a schoolboy again with a tough old cleric as a teacher who caught him napping at matins and whipped him severely with a short rod something like the one in the hand of the man on the other side of the wall.

The lad was standing now, stepping from his little rug, stumbling after the master, whose hand laid with ominous lightness upon the thin shoulder.

For the first time Wyn saw that it was Prince Fifty-Two, the one pointed out to him by Turtle as the next miko.

His head was down and therefore his face unreadable as the child quickstepped after the skirt as dark as shadow. His shoulders were hunched and his hands folded across his waist, where hung a simple breechclout, all the clothing he had on.

The rest of the class continued chanting without the slightest alteration, bent like reeds under the wind of their chant. Wyn did not see one glance stray to the open doorway, where the teacher led the singled-out student.

He strained to catch a glimpse of the room beyond but could see or hear nothing that informed him.

He walked along the wall, searching for another crack with which to spy, but the cane was tight, and there were few gaps in the woven surface. He forced a finger between two sticks to pry an opening, then stood on his toes and squinted in an uncomfortable position to be able to catch the thinnest glimpse of what was going on.

At first he could see nothing in the dim chamber, which did not open to the outside as did the classroom. Expecting to see and possibly hear the boy being admonished for some infraction in his rendition of the chant, Wyn contorted his face even further and opened his mouth to hear better.

The child was standing very still in front of the tall priest, who was totally consumed by shadow.

The child's brown back caught some light from the doorway communicating between the two rooms, the knobs of his spine a graceful arc as he leaned over and turned around so that he presented his lean back to the priest in the shadows.

Wyn gasped and stood back, denying what he saw.

He implanted his eye again, still unable to see anything except the child's bent shoulders and the top of his head; his body was undulating in a slow wavelike motion as he continued to lower his face to the floor.

Wyn heard a soft moan from the shadow, and a sharp expulsion of air as Panther fell slightly forward, putting his chopped tonsure into the light's glow. He was panting, breathing in lusty, almost painful heaves that rocked his shoulders. His hands gripped the boy's shoulders, pressing him down until the lad was on his knees with the master rocking against his backside.

Momentarily the boy looked up, pain etched on his brown face. He made a hurt sound, and the shadow admonished him with a growl to be still. The child winced and widened his mouth in a silent cry.

Wyn knew he could not be seen, but it seemed that the boy was staring directly at this secret place. He tore his offended eye from the peephole, biting on the side of his hand as he absorbed what he had seen. He closed his eyes and expelled a prayer, crossing himself once, then twice.

He did not have to look again. He could hear the high priest gasping in building small sobs, then a soft cry as though he had been dealt a blow.

Tears in his eyes, Wyn could not help looking once more.

The boy was bent over completely now with his forehead on the floor.

The high priest leaned over the boy's buttocks, one hand still gripping the frail collarbone and the other hand out as though for balance. The shadow heaved several violent thrusts, shivered, and looked down for the first time upon the head of the child, a black mop of tied-off and chopped hanks that signified ranking among all the males of Ixtulan.

Wyn must have uttered some kind of sound; he heard his own voice as though in pain, and he was thinking furiously, God help him, Lord that is it, then, I knew there was evil here, Holy Mother, Lord Jesus Christ . . .

He stumbled away from the wall, confused in his reaction to the unspeakable and unable to tell which way was out. He may have bumped the wall. The cane scraped that hand, while his other clutched the big cross tied to his cincture, which usually hung in the folds of his cassock. He pressed the cool iron to his sweating forehead, feeling fury well up where there had been horror as he tried to discreetly retrace his steps.

He turned toward the major hallway, running without control, but finally forcing himself to slow down.

He looked up just as the shadow form of the high priest stepped out into the hallway directly in his path.

Panther did not move for a moment but let Wyn's steps bring him that much closer, but Wyn stopped his own forward motion and tried, like cornered prey, to break through the seemingly fragile but very tough wall. He tried to shoulder his way against it, as though forcing a door, but knew it was hopeless as he gathered himself and turned to face the priest.

The other had taken three steps and was bearing down when Wyn whirled on him, flinging his considerable bulk against the leaner, taller figure.

Panther fell into a crouch that met the rolling attack, snarling a curse at him.

The two men crashed together with audible, breathless punches, as though two walls had collided.

Wyn had the impression of a boy's startled face staring down at him as he tumbled with the priest, their robes tangling flying feet.

But it was not only the prince who approached Wyn where he landed upon his back, the breath knocked out of him.

"Hold him," Panther ordered, rolling to his feet, stepping back from the flailing abbot, who was trying to bring his opponent down by grabbing his leg.

The bare brown foot lashed out, catching Wyn low in the chest, further denying him a gasp of air.

Panther kicked again, this time catching Wyn in the groin. He doubled up in agony as the flock of sharp little feet and hands lashed out, pummeling him, kicking him on every part of his body, falling onto him so that what little light there was, was blotted out by the avalanche of small, fierce bodies doing whatever damage they might.

Wyn found his breath, gasping through blood in his mouth, the blows still raining down upon him. With that breath he flung a curse at the high priest standing to one side adjusting his robes.

A big boy was jumping up and down on Wyn's chest, and another was still kicking Wyn's head as he felt red, slimy darkness come up behind his eyes and pull him down.

Meanwhile, outside in the sunlight, Madoc stood on the stair at the third terrace taking in the wide view from the top of the pyramid.

In the near distance, seemingly at his feet, new and busy digging was in progress at a small, long mound on the south perimeter of the huge, bare plaza.

A trench like a long back wound had been cut into the side of the grassy ridge about a dozen feet high, where sticks decorated with rippling, colorful ribbons had been thrust into the sod.

Even as he watched in the long afternoon light, and reading the weather with his bones, workers were hauling basketfuls of the loamy dirt out of the trench. He counted more than thirty laborers who carried wide baskets on their heads away from the dig, while others walked in a long, straggled line from a new pile of fill where the baskets were being dumped.

To the west a fine brilliant blue sky seemed to hang like a curtain behind smeared storm clouds coming in at a good clip.

He was sure it was going to rain because his wrist had been stiff all afternoon, and the knitting leg bone was sensitive.

Madoc's leg was almost completely healed, as strong as before with no exterior indication of fracture. But the bone was still tender, and the walk up the stair of several hundred steps was too much for him to take without a break. In the past few weeks he had used this long, high stair to build the strength back into the leg. He had worked his way to this level, and soon he knew he would be able to take the entire flight without a rest.

He looked behind himself at the final level above another raw new bit of construction, a small conical mound where the daykeepers had predicted the sun would rise as seen from the sun circle on the Day of Equals.

His ship was not visible behind this massive mound. He loved to observe her at any time, so he turned and mounted the final flight of stairs to the temple on the top.

At that moment four warrior-priests were hauling the unconscious Wyn down a shorter flight of stairs on the northern side of the pyramid, completely out of Madoc's sight.

Panther followed behind his men carrying the outlander shaman, a grim scowl on his face, his hands tucked into his long sleeves. He walked behind them as they hauled the abbot as deadweight in the sling of his cassock down that flight of steps to the northern third terrace, where several buildings huddled under their tall thatch hats.

Very shortly they disappeared into one of the buildings through a baffled doorway that hid the interior. Panther entered behind them, and when he reemerged a short time later, he was alone, but still scowling.

Inside, Wyn was knocked back into awareness when he was thrown down into a dark enclosure.

He heard the scraping of something over his head.

The first thing he saw when he blinked his eyes open was a wide cane grid sliding into place a dozen feet above him, and the foreshortened feet and legs of the man putting the cover on the cell, then walking away.

The smell was slightly moldy, loamy, with an aftersmell of urine nearby.

He struggled to sit up, feeling bruised and bleeding in more than one place. Nothing felt broken, but he was dizzy from the blows. It took several minutes before he focused in the gloaming, taking in his situation.

"Well, well, Father Folded Hands, you have come to visit me," said a familiar voice.

Someone moved in the shadows, a naked red man he did not recognize at first.

When his companion stood above him, he still did not know who it was until the other knelt, hands limp across knees. There was enough light coming from above to make out the tattoo bracelets up and down the pronounced stringy muscles of the arm, in which every bone stood out under loose flesh.

"Here," said Imala'ko the Chickasaw, handing Wyn a plain pottery bowl of tepid, musty-smelling water.

"We are in a pit," Wyn said, scripture references whirling in his dazzled brain.

The Chickasaw stifled a short, mirthless laugh and nodded.

"I thought you went home," Wyn commented, pivoting his head to spit out blood. "Why are you here?"

Imala'ko said, "They are afraid I will tell what I know," and added in handsign, *And you?*

Wyn nodded, holding his aching head. "Same, same," he moaned, remembering the little boy's face looking down at him in the hallway. As bad as it had been to see the child being sodomized by the dark priest, it was even worse to see his look of vacant disregard while Wyn was being kicked.

Wyn shook his head, but he could not shake the image of so cold a look upon an innocent face. He choked back a cry, chest aching where the children had pummeled him. Gasping, he whispered a short prayer for the boy's soul and took another drink of water.

"What is that?" he asked about the lump laying across the pit which was vaguely cylindrical, about ten feet across.

"A body."

"A dead man?"

"A woman. She was still breathing when they dropped me down here."

"Why?"

"She refused to help put up the miko's wall."

Imala'ko's eyes glittered unnaturally. "They will notice her soon."

Overwhelmed by a desire to escape the cage, Wyn cast his

glance around, eyes adjusting to the gloom. "This is a hole in the ground," he said flatly, feeling around in the dimness.

"A deep hole in God's Hill," the Chickasaw said in Muskogean and handsign.

Wyn, because of his intense preaching and subsequent translation into the Muskogean language, had become fluent in the simpler forms of Muskogean expression, though he thought he would never understand verb conjugation in the musical tongue that depended on intonation as much as pronunciation for meaning.

"Do they inspect this place?"

"They never come down. Sometimes they throw down food," said Imala'ko as he withdrew a stale tortilla from a fold in his loincloth and offered it to Wyn.

The abbot almost wretched at the smell of the morsel but forced down his gorge, closed his eyes momentarily, and gripped his cross just to have something to hang onto.

He looked at the dull metal in his hand, whispering, "Lord, help me."

He looked up at the Chickasaw, who was still sitting on his heels, watching the other curiously with no trace of emotion on his sunken face.

"What will happen?" Wyn croaked.

The Chickasaw made a loose gesture with his shoulders, stood, and stretched as he munched the foul corncake. The shafts of his powerful legs were thin, the bones starkly drawn in the overhead light. Each side of his pelvis was like a bowl, evidence of considerable weight loss, so he must have been here for some time. "I know what they plan for me, but I have no idea what they will do to you."

Wyn sighed. "And you?"

"They are going to cut my heart out so they can use it in a mock sacrifice on the Day of Equals, to make it look as if the miko is raised from the dead."

Wyn shuddered involuntarily. It was so bizarre a pronouncement, so evil in the vision it presented to the mind's eye, he found himself coughing up a shallow laugh of disbelief.

The Chickasaw eyed him steadily, his cheekbones drawn in sharpened lines of near starvation.

"Six days from now."

Imala'ko nodded.

"That is plenty of time," Wyn said, looking at the iron cross catching the overhead light.

Another derisive laugh, this one from the Chickasaw, who was a young man but looked cadaverous, staring out of sunken eyes, and all his tattoos looked like blood veins and arteries exposed on the outside of his flesh. His noble forehead was a plate of ashen flesh stretched over bone; his clavicle looked sharp enough to slice wood, and tendons in his neck stood out in high relief.

"Time for what?" he asked, Adam's apple bobbing.

"This is dirt that can be dug, Imala'ko."

"We have no tools, and the earth is too hard to dig with our hands, though I have chewed upon it a little just to put something in my stomach."

His eye followed Wyn's glance downward where the iron cross, as big as a trowel in his hand, seemed to take on a new glow.

Out on the high terrace, Madoc walked past the eastern entrance to the temple.

The cane matting had been rolled up so that three sides of the main hall were open to the breezes. Beyond, the women were grinding corn, singing the song along with the percussion of their pestles against the stone mortars.

He saw the bonesetter, Buffalo Eagle, sitting just outside the miko's audience chamber. The old man was almost naked except for a loincloth. He was painted in soot on his face and chest and sat very still facing the raised platform where the miko held meetings.

Madoc wanted to see his ship, but the old man's curious position made him wonder what was going on. He hurried to the edge of the terrace and looked down upon his ship sitting the water. The air was so clear this afternoon, he could see the faces of the men on deck finishing the new jacket that would cover the reefed sail. The sight of the *Horn* all fine and ready to move down the stream filled him with immense joy he took with him as he walked across the deserted plaza to the comfortable little apartment Turtle had given him and Tumkis.

She was standing in the doorway, waiting for him in the costume she would wear at the ceremony. It was a beautiful long-sleeved, ankle-length shift of almost pure white suede trimmed in small silver and shell beads. Her hair was loose around her shoulders, long enough to get lost in when he took her in his arms and said into her ear, "Let us go now—I have no patience to wait for this boring ritual." ·

She shook her head.

"But I hate this place," he said. "We owe these people nothing."

"We have promised," she said. "What has made you so anxious?"

He held her close. "That old man who set my leg has been sitting for days outside the miko's throne room, as though he were in mourning."

"He is petitioning for audience," she replied.

"I thought he was one of Turtle's favorites."

She shrugged.

Madoc pressed her: "Why would they humiliate him like that?"

"Perhaps the miko does not wish to speak with him."

"It gives me the creeps, seeing him like that."

"Not a good reason to insult the miko with a sudden departure," she offered.

"But if we left now, we could outrun the rain."

"It will be over soon," she crooned into his ear, making it sound like a love song, which distracted him and made him forget about anything outside this room.

Not far away, in a bare room in the temple, Turtle-in-the-Sun sat far above any mortal insult or offense to himself or anyone else, in meditation upon a simple cane mat like a student's, as naked as the day he was born. He was striding above the rain clouds, in his trance, in great white moccasins, each step hitting the earth far below, imprinting a valley of a footstep. "Closer now, Father, closer now," his dream self whispered, and he stepped out of his body as though it were a leather jerkin that crumpled raglike, dropping away.

His next step was upward.

Wyn hacked at the utterly dry earth until his hands felt sticky with more than sweat. He woke up Imala'ko to give him his turn, but could not let go of the cross to give it to his partner.

Slumped against the smooth wall of their cavity, the Chickasaw moved nothing but his eyelids, and those only once, lifting them like deer-hide door flaps to peer out at the shadowed face before him now showing a dark shadow on lip and chin. He had to pull the knife from the other's hands, which seemed to be coated with glue.

He dug a while. The light faded. When it was totally night, Imala'ko pressed the cross back into Wyn's hands, but had to wake him before the other rejoined the dig.

"We are digging the wrong way, Father Folded Hands," the Chickasaw mumbled before his eyes closed again. "In the ground. The mole digs up to reach the sky."

"We are not in the ground—are you listening? We are high up in the sky already and close to the north edge of our molehill. If you want to see the sky from here, dig sideways."

"Digging our way to heaven," Imala'ko chuckled dreamily, using an old word that meant the place of light on the other side of the underworld. "Do you have a plan when we get out?"

"Are you well enough to travel?"

"He has mountains of corn stored in the temples on top of all the big pyramids. They have held back the distribution and are giving corn only to laborers, who will take the trees and build the miko's wall."

Wyn shoveled the loosened dust from their little cave that now was big enough to hold his crouching body. "It strikes me that Sodom is ready for the fire," he said, some of the glitter in his own eyes as dirt flew between his legs.

"I think we could gather many warriors from my cousins at Paducah, who have old scores to settle with this nation."

"And the Shawnee would jump at any excuse to bring Ixtualn down."

"I never did understand why the Shawnee hate this place so badly they pretend it does not exist," Wyn said.

"Many generations ago these people killed some Shawnee women."

"Was it war?"

"These people have secret practices that are supposed to honor the One Who Breathes Above. They pretended to make them honored wives of the miko. The Shawnee have never forgotten their lost daughters, or the deception that was played upon them."

Wyn was still trying to imagine why the Shawnee women would be victimized. "You mean sacrifices, human sacrifice?"

"There is an old tradition that wives of the chief go with their husband when he follows the sun."

"Is this still done?"

Imala'ko shrugged. "There are rumors." In fact, he knew that some of his own people practiced these customs, but he did not mention this to the white man, who seemed to be highly agitated with this information.

"Someone should make sure that it never happens again."

"Man Whose Weapons Sings would lead us if I can get word to him," Imala'ko said dreamily.

"The people here are so sure of themselves," Wyn remarked, "they leave their canoes down on Sky Blood Creek without a guard."

"There are people right here in the city who have no love for the miko," commented Imala'ko with a glance toward the corpse. "She told me the high priest's men tore down her house. I do not know for sure, but I think she was Buffalo Eagle's wife."

Wyn scooped out another load of dirt, throwing it over on the dead woman. Before long she was covered.

"You know," Imala'ko said, "the high priest plans to kill your Weather Eyes—he has been doing evil magic against him since you people came here."

Wyn mumbled scripture, "'. . . put away the sodomites out of the land . . .'" the only way he could even think about what he had seen.

"And," Imala'ko said, "the miko can talk of nothing else but that Uktena canoe—he wants it even more than he wants Lady Tumbling Water."

Wyn thought the Chickasaw had drifted off into sleep, but he said after a while, "She thinks she has found someone who can teach her to be a woman of power."

"She will choose Weather Eyes," Wyn said emphatically.

"She will have no choice."

Wyn did not want to think about that, so he hummed an old hymn. He worked a little longer after finding his third or fourth wind. Later he thought he heard something beyond the wall of hardened clay.

It sounded like rain.

Chapter 26

Through pounding downpour, they made it to the *Horn* in a stolen canoe.

They scrambled aboard without asking permission, startling Huw on the watch, who went so far as to draw his knife against the intruders moving toward him across the deck.

"Put it away, son," Wyn cried when he saw Huw silhouetted by the glow coming through the hides over the hold. "Would you turn the blade on the hand that made it?"

Later, in the hold in dry clothes, while wolfing food, Wyn poured out his story to their wide-eyed stares. "I suppose the captain is over there now, on that devil's hill," he said around a mouthful.

"They will never let him return to this big canoe," Imala'ko said.

This shocked Huw, who remarked that no warrior could take the captain.

The Chickasaw pointed to Durendal hanging in its scabbard on the bulkhead above Madoc's bed. "What weapon does he have?"

Huw scowled. He knew that nobody wore a weapon in the presence of the miko.

"No warrior will honorably challenge him. They will take him through trickery when he least expects it. He will never get the chance to fight."

"The Chickasaw is telling the truth, Huw," Wyn confirmed. "Better keep a close watch—they may try to take the *Horn*."

Huw stared at Wyn, absorbing the situation, while Winnowed Rice poured the abbot more tea as he continued. "I must get to him immediately."

"How can you go back there without arousing suspicion?" Huw asked, ready to volunteer.

"You must keep the ship ready to get us all out of here," Wyn replied, neglecting to mention that he got lost every time he ventured into that maze. "If I had a disguise . . ."

"Wait," Huw said, recalling something Dag brought back from the miko's household. He found the discarded black robe and grinned at the abbot. "Think this will fit?"

Wyn could not help but chuckle with delight as he took the smelly tentlike thing. He rubbed his unbarbered head and asked Imala'ko if he could give him a haircut that would match the priests'.

Wyn winced under the blade, but the Chickasaw was fast, and soon the abbot's scruffy locks lay on the floor around him. Winnowed Rice handed Wyn a silver mirror Madoc had given her, which disclosed to the abbot his new appearance—he did not have enough hair for the elaborate tied-off hanks affected by the high-ranking priests, so his was the total baldness of the acolyte.

"Smear soot on your face and head before you go up, and nobody will challenge you."

"I am a bit old to be a novice."

When this was explained to Imala'ko, he said, "Many older men join the miko's service, not just boys. This will do, as long as you wear the black paint."

"Now," Wyn continued, "someone must get to Fair Beard."

Huw looked doubtful and remarked, "I can spare nobody—"

"I will go," said the brother of Laughing Dog. "I am the best canoeman in my nation."

"I can do it," said Imala'ko lying back on a pallet.

"But you are weak," Huw said.

"This is not much worse than a fast before a battle, and I feel stronger now that I have eaten among friends."

"We have so little time," said Huw. "It will take you a full day to get back to the Hundred."

"No," said the Chickasaw, sitting up and taking a long drink of water. "I will go now, as soon as the rain lets up."

Already it sounded less insistent against the hold cover.

"On the river at night?" Rhys asked incredulously.

The Yuchi looked wide-eyed at the Chickasaw.

"You can stay here," Imala'ko replied to the youthful red man, wiping his mouth, "but it must be done."

The Yuchi nodded, but his fear was evident. He watched the Chickasaw across the soft light from the coals on the brazier, thinking that this man's recent survival implied powerful good luck he wanted to share.

"Well," Huw said, doubtful again, "I do not know if Snorrison will trust you, our former enemy, even if the Yuchi goes along."

Winnowed Rice translated this and added that she thought he might be right.

Imala'ko considered this. "I need a token," he said, "something to prove I come in defense of Weather Eyes."

"His Iceland eye," Rhys said.

"What?" the Chickasaw asked, not understanding the poet's words.

"It must be here somewhere," Rhys said.

"In his sea chest," Huw said, but hesitating.

"Well, get it, then."

"But nobody touches the captain's gear," said Huw. "He values that above all else because Fair Beard gave it to him."

"And for that reason, the best guarantee to get Fair Beard's attention." Rhys felt his way along the bulkhead until he found Madoc's pallet. He touched the wooden box where Madoc kept his personal tools, a few pieces of jewelry, coins, and other items brought from home. "Here," he said, holding the dazzling white disk out on its chain.

Imala'ko stared with respect at the sun-painted face as he took the disk. He slipped it around his neck and under the collar of the woven tunic they had given him.

He cocked his head, listening to the rain on the stretched hide, diminished now from downpour to a splattering of drips. "Well, my Yuchi friend, are you ready?"

The young warrior swallowed, the whites of his eyes glistening in the soft light: He was afraid to go on the river in darkness. "It is only a while until morning. . . ."

"By morning we can be at Paducah," Imala'ko said with a cadaverous grin. "That is, if the Uktena does not get us."

And he laughed as he stood, all bones in the coals' red light. "I am so skinny, the river serpent would gag on me!"

"But what about me?"

"What is your name, brother?"

"Swimmer," the Yuchi replied, and everyone loved the irony of this, having a laugh that felt good under the circumstances.

"Let us hope you will not have to prove it," Imala'ko said,

slapping Swimmer's shoulder to hurry him. Together they made ready to descend the river in their stolen canoe, where their worse legends lurked under the darkened water.

Wyn shook out the leather cassock of another kind of clergy, disgusted by its smell and connotations.

"You scare me," said Winnowed Rice to him when he donned the thing over his clothes. But there was a twinkle in her eye, and Wyn knew he would be able to do it, to pass for one of them in the morning when he returned to the top of the pyramid.

"Wake me at dawn," he said, curling up on Madoc's bed.

Wyn seemed to dream, but did not remember anything when the sparkling morning was upon him, and walking up the path to the dreaded mountain, he felt he was still encased within dark visions.

It had stopped raining, and the air was washed and sweet, full of the smell of spring. Crews on their scaffolding were already out on the sides of the pyramid making repairs caused by the downpour.

Around the darkened abbot was much excitement, with many people upon the path, talking of events transpiring up on the pinnacle. He did not dare risk his shaky Muskogean to inquire what was happening as he hurried to find out for himself.

Everyone was moving toward the big pyramid, many dressed in feathers and special paint. Among the crowd he saw some of the nobles, including old Buffalo Eagle. Afraid someone might recognize him, Wyn stayed back behind others as he made his way to the broad log steps.

It appeared to be the beginnings of the ceremonies, yet there was an air of the unexpected in the talk of the people around him. He caught a word here and there, something about the Fifth Village and beautiful women, which only peaked his curiosity to know more.

He tried to overhear more gossip as he climbed the long stair on the western face and joined the stream of people moving toward the hall of the great mat, where the cane curtains had been rolled up to accommodate what appeared to be a large group of guests gathered within.

He moved closer, surprised to see across the crowd, that Panther was seated upon the high mat, playing the role of miko.

And there was Madoc, Tumkis, and Dag among the dignitaries ranged in the gallery, far out of Wyn's reach. He could only stand, watch, and listen along with everyone else, as a man in a turban and white egret feathers stood before the high priest making a statement.

"—therefore, the miko must make his choice," cried the elder of the Fifth Village.

"But I tell you," the high priest proclaimed, "our lord is fasting and cannot be disturbed."

Wyn slunk back, lest the high priest recognize him, and moved around behind the throng hoping to get closer to Madoc.

"Look at these beautiful girls," the elder commanded.

Every eye in the room, plus servants and passersby standing near the doors, followed his suggestion and observed the seventeen lovelies of high rank, sloe-eyed, plump, and fresh, not one of them more than eighteen summers.

"Lord Turtle-in-the-Sun left these girls standing there, awaiting his will. Our nation cannot bear the shame this brings to us for many generations into the future."

"But the miko has asked me to tell you that he cannot choose."

The more than a hundred voices in the chamber rattled with comment. Swelling the crowd was a squad of corn-grinders. The women were idle because the plaza where the huge stone mortars awaited their hands on the pestle stones, was too wet to process cornmeal.

They had heard the commotion and wandered over to see what was happening to disrupt the peace of the miko's morning.

Just about everyone of any rank was here, having followed the Fifth Village entourage when it arrived early this bright morning in ten canoes—the village's entire fleet.

The grandfathers and uncles in their power robes and head-feathers protectively surrounded the girls of good genealogies, assuring them that justice would be done, that the miko was a man of honor who would end the suspense surrounding the question of which was the most worthy. Never in its generations had Fifth Village failed to have at least a couple of royal brides with one or two children to maintain. It was a matter of clan pride, since the other four communities had participated in contests during the miko's hunting trip.

"He must choose, and we demand it now!" said the elder middle-aged uncle to one of the prettiest. His delegation of almost every living soul in town stamped their atlatl shafts against the hard clay floor, putting echoes up into the high rafters, where minute leaks had been dripping all morning. The water had so far to fall, it turned to a fine mist on the incense-heavy air.

"He cannot choose because each of them is as worthy as the next."

The girls tittered among themselves.

"I ask you"—the high priest offered the girls for everyone's examination—"have you ever seen a group of such perfect women?"

The audience, including Madoc, Tumkis, and Dag, buzzed with the question.

"Clever," whispered Madoc to Tumkis with a cynical chuckle.

"To prevent himself from abusing them all, our lord can choose none."

The people of the Fifth Village failed to be flattered by this announcement, in fact, were so enraged, they marched as a group from the hall without another word, herding their scorned daughters in their midst. They did not speak to any in the city but proceeded in high affront back to their beached canoes and took off downstream as fast as they could paddle.

"I told you great things were going to happen," One Reed the gardener said to Burning Rose as she walked back to the miko's quarters. She did not answer him, but she repeated significant numbers for her nephew's good luck, and for her own.

Wyn imitated the aloof mien of the temple creatures, tucking his hands into the wide sleeves as he saw other black-robes doing. Lowering his eyes, he wandered through the crowd that was leaving the hall with plenty to talk about, listening to snatches of conversation here and there while trying to spot Madoc or the Natchez woman.

The press was strong in the opposite direction. Wyn was swept up in it, finding himself out in the brightening morning. He stayed with the majority of people streaming from the great hall, avoiding others dressed like himself, while keeping a lookout for the tall white man.

Just then, emerging from the temple, he saw the objects of

his search in the company of the high priest, whose restless eyes seemed to scan the crowd like an animal's.

Lest he be spotted by the keen-eyed sorcerer, Wyn ducked around the throng and lost himself in traffic vacating the top terrace in ones and twos down the grand stair.

But at the third terrace he angled off toward the north face where the narrow log stair ran from the thatch prison back up to the backside of the main temple. If he could not reach Madoc, then he would try to find the miko isolated in his little cell. He thought as he entered the long, dim hall that he might be able to tell the miko what he had seen, arouse his anger against the high priest's treatment of the royal heir. With this in mind he spent as much uncomfortable time in the temple as he dared but was unsuccessful in his search of the labyrinth of narrow hallways, alcoves, breezeways, and plazas that like a maze protected the miko in the bowels of his architecture.

Out in the light, Panther followed the white chief and the Natchez sun as they walked toward their apartment. "Lady Tumbling Water," he said respectfully on her left side, "the miko needs a fourth bride for his holy task."

"Then why did he not choose one of those lovely girls?"

"Because he wishes to take a bride of the very highest rank, and none of these children qualifies."

"I am sure there are many candidates from this great city," Tumkis replied as she slowed her step just enough to let the two men flanking her get ahead, then she moved behind Madoc and got to his right side, leaving him between herself and the priest.

"What is he saying to you?"

"Nothing. A compliment."

"This hairy white man is not worthy of you, noble sun," Panther remarked in the same deferential soft voice. "The greatest miko in the entire Mech-a-sip-i Valley is the only man living who has the right to offer you meat."

"A long compliment," Madoc snarled, walking faster as he took up her hand and aimed them away from the priest.

"Men do not touch women in the plaza, Weather Eyes," she said, modestly letting his hand go.

He put his arm firmly around her back. "I do not care what is done and not done, Tumkis, and I doubt what he just said is complimentary."

She let him hurry her toward their quarters, Panther dropping back to let them go on alone.

When she looked, the high priest was speaking to an old man in black mourning paint and tattered loincloth. She recognized Buffalo Eagle, who seemed to be earnestly asking for something. The tall, dour priest only shook his head and hurried away, leaving Buffalo Eagle standing there in his tatters. Most of the crowd was gone. Only a few stragglers—older, slower red people—remained on the puddled plaza.

She saw Buffalo Eagle stare in the direction of the meeting hall, where several women were loosening the lines that rolled down the cane curtains. What was wrong? she wondered, but did not linger. She followed Madoc into the softened shadows of the royal residence.

Inside their apartment on the south side of the miko's household, he was waiting for her, watching the doorway as she entered.

He repeated the question: "What did he say to you?"

She looked him right in the eye and replied forthrightly, "He wants me to be the miko's wife."

"And you?"

"I want to be your wife, but I also want the greatest magician in all four parts of the world to teach me how to be a woman of power."

"Love," he said, hands on her shoulders. He ached to pick her up and forcefully remove her from this place. "You already are a woman of power."

"But I can be more if I have the right teacher. I can correct all my errors and go home in great honor if I attain the seventh degree. Turtle-in-the-Sun is the only man alive who can confer it upon me."

Madoc dropped his hands from her and began gathering up his few belongings.

"What are you doing?"

"Getting out of here."

She blocked the door, looking up at him with liquid eyes. "Please, Tumkis, please come with me now."

"Please, please," she countered, "just stay here with me and think right thoughts in my direction for a little longer, and everything will be good."

She stared back at him until he could bear no more.

He stepped around her to the doorway, where a cane mat

hung to insure privacy. He hesitated when he might have warned her that he planned to hoist anchor at dawn. She stood there unmoving, her hair full with electric life of its own. She seemed to vibrate with energy and beauty. The sight of her hurt, she was so desirable. He could smell her singular aroma and feel her heat from where he stood. He started to speak. But her stolid, stubborn silence infuriated him so, he was unable to, so he left her to go round up his men.

Not far away Wyn sidled down the same long main hallway where he had lost himself earlier, trying to find his way out. He wondered how Imala'ko was doing.

Miles to the south down on the Oyo River, Imala'ko and Swimmer listened outside the open door to the sounds of several men talking around the table in the kitchen of the Hundred's Big House.

After a hasty stopover in the friendly village of Paducah, the two red men had pulled the stolen canoe in a little downstream from the Hundred's camp. But they need not have bothered, because there was nobody out. They stealthily made their way to the big lodge beyond the council circle. This surprised Imala'ko—that the kanegmati would be as casual in their security as the miko of Ixtulan, whom Father Folded Hands had criticized.

Now they could hear men inside the lodge, talking in the kitchen.

They walked right in the open doorway, where a deer hide was tied back to let in the fresh morning spring air where the several men were smoking at the table in the windowless room. They did not smoke in the red fashion, by sharing a pipe, but each had his own, kept lit from a three-legged pottery brazier in the middle of the scorched boards.

David Iron jumped from the bench and greeted his Yuchi lodge-brother, while Imala'ko hung back, not sure of his reception.

Swimmer said, "My Chickasaw companion must speak with Man Whose Weapon Sings."

David Iron glanced up toward the second floor, where a woman's moan floated on the air like a sad song. "My wife is having her baby," he said, adding, "but the tangletoungue is toward the north end of the lodge—"

Imala'ko was up the stair before the Yuchi finished. "But—"

It was too late. Imala'ko was at the top of the landing near the low moaning sound. He passed the first alcove where the woman labored and moved on to the larger room, where there was more light coming from a shutter propped open with a stick.

He froze when he saw Man Whose Weapons Sings doggedly making the four-legged beast with his big yellow-haired woman.

The Chickasaw whipped himself back around the wall, listening with his breath held as the man and woman groaned on and on. Finally, when they seemed to be finished, Imala'ko crouched and frog-walked over to the high pallet, where the Norseman was rolling onto his back, making large, satisfied noises. The woman, unseen beyond him, made her own sounds.

Imala'ko saw one of her long pale arms rise up, stretch, then fall back down on her side of the bed.

Man Whose Weapon Sings had thrown his left foot off the edge of the bed onto the floor.

The woman sighed heavily out of Imala'ko's sight as he crawled across the floor to within an arm's reach of the bed.

Soundlessly he removed the single eagle feather from his quoit and extended it to lightly brush Fair Beard's bare toes.

The Norseman shook his foot to rid himself of the tickle, but when it persisted, he flung himself up to kill whatever bug had gotten into his bedroom.

He froze when he recognized the crouching Chickasaw warrior on the floor with his finger up to his lips in the signal for silence.

Quick handsign told the Norseman that Weather Eyes urgently needed help.

Fair Beard was shocked by the young Chickasaw's emaciated appearance but signed, *Trouble?*

"Big trouble," Imala'ko signed back, and withdrew the Iceland eye from his collar.

Fair Beard registered surprise as he stared at the flake of milky crystal that had guided him through fog and saved his life on several occasions. After glancing at his wife, who seemed to be settling in for more sleep, he rolled out of bed, reaching for his tunic and trews on a wall peg close at hand.

She muttered soft inquiry.

He answered as he drew on his clothes that he was going to take a piss.

He almost made it to the door, where he took the disk on its chain from Imala'ko, who was standing from his crouch just as Yngvild sat up suddenly in her shift hiked up around her thighs and saw, without doubt, that a vaguely familiar red man was standing there with her husband reaching for his battle-ax on the wall.

"What goes on here?" she whispered loudly in Scandinavian with a glance to her right where Hannah was sleeping.

She pulled the fur throw around her shoulders and stood on her knees, alarm on her face as she demanded to know why he needed his weapon to relieve himself.

"Go back to sleep, Flower—nothing to worry about."

"Fair Beard Snorrison—"

From the next room farther down the landing, Gwen's voice announced that she was still in the labor she had begun the night before.

"Shhh," Snorrison commanded, turning to continue out of the room.

"You promised me, Snorrison," Yngvild said, drawing herself up to fight.

"Flower, how can you deny that I must go help our chief?"

"I knew you would break your promise, I knew it."

"Flower, please, try to understand."

"Uh, Man Whose Weapon Sings—" the Chickasaw said, not understanding what exactly was going on between this man and woman, except that it was acrimonious.

"Damn you, Fair Beard—despite our agreement—you are going to go after that Skraeling whore."

"The Whip here tells me Madoc is in another mess."

"You are always running after his call," she all but yelled.

"A woman is trying to have a baby over there."

"Please," Imala'ko insisted, daring to step between them.

"You do not even know if this Skraeling tells the truth."

"He brought this, woman—" Fair Beard snapped, displaying the Iceland eye he had given to Madoc. "Do we need more proof?"

She would have said more in a rising tone of fury, but Imala'ko shouted, finally, to get Fair Beard's attention, "Hurry!"

Fair Beard glared at his wife a moment longer, then grabbed the Kisser from where it hung on the wall.

"You are going, you are going to break your promise—" she

started to scream, punching at his arm holding the great ax. He fended her off with his elbow, but she was a big, strong woman full of scorn. So he pushed her back to fall onto their pallet, which startled Hannah awake with a cry.

"Man Whose Weapons Sings—" said Imala'ko, but Fair Beard was striding toward the stair to get away from Yngvild's fury.

She yelled invective after him all the way down to the first floor, the baby's cry rising to match her own, so that now there were three females disturbing the morning with their various cries from the upper floor.

From the adjoining room could be heard Gwen's birth trill as she launched into the final phase of labor. One of the attending Shawnee women peered around the doorway and admonished the chief to keep his voice down. They did not like it that Gwen was having her baby in this house full of men, anyway, but she disdained a birthing hut.

David Iron looked up as the Norseman strode across the puncheon floor, alarmed to see the look on his face, the ax in his hand, and the scrawny, wild-eyed Chickasaw warrior behind him trying to get Fair Beard to listen to what he was saying, to no avail.

"Call a council meeting—Lev, get every able-bodied man in the camp!" Fair Beard barked.

The several men did not stop to ask why as they hurried to obey.

David Iron glanced at the stair where he heard Gwen cry out. For a moment he was torn, but Fair Beard pushed him out the door.

Before Snorrison followed, the Chickasaw laid hand upon him, speaking Muskogean words that brought the big Norseman to an abrupt halt. "Will it help to soothe your woman if I tell you that I know where your baby is?"

Fair Beard thought he was misunderstanding a dialect of the Muskogean language he learned to speak fluently while living among the Natchez. "My baby is up there screaming with her mother," he said, impatient to go out and gather as many of the Hundred, along with Shawnee and Yuchi who would go with him. Already he was calculating how many canoes they could launch. More than thirty if all the Shawnee went along. They hated Ixtulan, he knew, and would delight in an opportunity to go to battle against an old enemy.

Imala'ko shook his plucked head impassively. "Your other baby. The little white-haired boy."

Fair Beard almost dropped the ax. "Bjorn?"

"Little Bear, yes."

"Where—how?"

"He is with my mother, in my home village, but—"

"Say it again so that I know I understand you!" Fair Beard said, dropping the ax to the floor so he could shake the Chickasaw, who repeated himself.

"Flower—!" Fair Beard called, and took the steps two, three at a time back up to the landing.

"I am sorry," Imala'ko called from the foot of the stair, "for stealing your child, but we had to find out if you people were spirits or mortal human beings."

But Fair Beard did not hear him as he hit the landing where something came flying through the air at him, a pottery jug that would have gotten him in the temple if he had not ducked. The missile crashed against the wall behind him as he dashed toward her winding up to throw another piece of crockery, but his words stopped her.

"Flower—Bjorn—our little boy is alive!"

Chapter 27

The Shawnee from Meadows-of-Mint put forty boats upon the river, each capable of carrying ten or twelve men, or a full compliment of weapons and gear for six fully armed warriors who handled their own paddles.

The hasty plan was to float down the Ohio with a stop at Paducah, where Imala'ko's friends were waiting to add another fifteen canoes full of warriors with grudges against Ixtulan uppermost in their minds.

The Chickasaw warrior would not take the heavy food the Hundred tried to shovel down his throat. He was wise enough to take only broth and corncakes.

By the time they got on the river, he was already looking better, but he begged off paddling and slept curled in a buffalo robe between the rowers.

Yngvild had it in her mind that she was going to accompany the several Shawnee war-women who would go along in a supply canoe to take care of their soldiers.

She was ready to go with a travel pack at her feet and Hannah in her arms as the armada prepared for launch, but Snorrison tried to convince her that it would be better for her and the baby to stay here.

"Do not worry, Flower. I will return to you with Bjorn riding my shoulders."

But the Norsewoman was stubborn and insisted that she be allowed to accompany the army.

"I will make sure he comes home to you," David Iron promised. "You know I will come as soon as possible—please will you not stay here and help Gwen with our son?"

Snorrison was greatly relieved to see her thinking about this and for a moment thought she would take the Yuchi's wise advice.

"No, Snorrison," she insisted, tossing her bundle into the canoe of the Shawnee women, who made room for her. One of them held the baby as she climbed in and sat down. "I want to be with you when we find our son."

There was nothing he could do about it except fume. His battle-ax over his shoulder and a helmet from his homeland on his head, he stalked off to the lead canoe.

A short time later they began peeling off one by one onto the wide Ohio.

The first green blush of springtime was on the land on either side of the river as they made the easy first leg of the journey.

They camped at Paducah that afternoon, where Laughing Dog met them, sharpening their weapons and their plans.

Paducah's Chickasaw headmen and warriors unanimously voted to join the invasion of Ixtulan. They honored Imala'ko by giving him war-feathers and a champion weapon, a massive head-knocker studded with fifteen needles of rock crystal.

Imala'ko urged them to invade the city well before the ceremony, which would already be in bloody progress by dawn on the Day of Equals. Since none of the red men would go upon the river at night, a dawn raid that would nip the bud of the deadly ritual would be too close to take a chance.

Snorrison harangued the assembled red men around the council circle at Paducah about the desirability of sneaking up on Ixtulan at night. But they presented a solid red wall of resistance and would not be swayed. They were not going to fight at night, and that was that.

"What if we are killed, tangletongue?" asked Laughing Dog. "What would happen to our spirits if we died at night and are unable to follow the sun into the west?"

"But you are a Christian now and do not have to worry about that anymore. The Christian God is not so picky and will take your soul no matter what time you claim your sod."

"I may have taken the Christ," Brother Paul remarked with dignified self-possession, "but that does not mean I have gone crazy."

"You fight on the river at night if you want to, white man, but you will fight alone," said one of the war chiefs from Paducah.

So Snorrison as their strategist was left with his second choice, attack in the afternoon before the ceremony—tomorrow afternoon.

He counted three hundred armed troops in their army, with a promise by the Paducans that their southern allies were on the way to hold the city after it was taken.

"I believe Fifth Village will take our side," said Imala'ko as he munched on a turkey leg. He explained what had taken place over the fourth bride on the day of his escape from the pit. "This will be a way for them to reclaim face they lost."

The women stayed at Paducah, where the Hundred would meet after the invasion. Yngvild agreed on camping there rather than actually joining the fighting, though it was obvious she would have been happier to keep her husband in sight.

The canoe fleet moved up the east side of the Mech-a-sip-i just before noon. Imala'ko was right about the Fifth Village, where all the inhabitants were boycotting the Day of Equals ceremony after the insult to their seventeen daughters. The elders of the village, which had been a loyal dependency of Ixtulan for six generations, listened to the invasion plan and voted unanimously to throw their twenty warriors into the fray.

But a second benefit to this alliance was that the village invited the entire army to camp in their plaza that night so that they could launch the attack very close to the target, right at the back door of Ixtulan. The route upstream on Sky Blood Creek was only a short paddle, though the elders were scandalized because in the oldest man's lifetime, nobody had been so untraditional as to canoe upstream on the Creek.

Fair Beard and his planners decided that Imala'ko and a squad of Paducans would be the advance landing force. Their task would be to fire the thatch temple of God's Hill as a signal to the others, who would be following a short distance behind.

He had been trying to get an estimate from Imala'ko for two days about the size of the army Ixtulan could put into the field.

"It is not an easy thing to say, Man Whose Weapon Sings, because the miko of Ixtulan does not have any army. He has thousands of servants, everyone in the city, and hundreds of priests, who sometimes act as guards or soldiers."

Snorrison could not imagine a kingdom without soldiers to protect the king's power.

"The king's power is in his sun magic and in the golden corn," Imala'ko tried to explain. "There has never been any other nation with stronger magic to challenge them."

"They are soft," Laughing Dog said, and those who knew agreed with him. "We will take them like rabbits."

Still, Snorrison would have been happier if he had some idea of the opposition.

"Besides," said one of the Shawnee chiefs, "none of them has weapons to compare with our blue metal knives."

Everyone agreed with that and continued making their plans around the Fifth Village council fire late into the night.

Midmorning Imala'ko and his people pushed off upstream on Sky Blood Creek, and the rest of the fleet followed a short time later.

The Chickasaw had been afraid an alarm would be set off by the people of the other four villages closely allied with Ixtulan, but as the three canoes made their way north past the communities, they appeared deserted.

"Everyone is in the city for the festival," said Laughing Dog.

Nobody challenged them as they drew in on the opposite side of the dock from the *Horn*, still sedately riding the current at anchor.

Imala'ko climbed aboard at Huw's invitation and informed him and Rhys and the others that they should get ready to depart as soon as the Hundred's people were safely off the big pyramid. The white men were delighted with the military project, having heard about it from Wyn, who had found his way back to the ship; but they were unable to say where their captain might be.

"We have not seen him for days," Wyn said, but thought that was because Tumkis had to stay close to the miko for the ceremony.

Wyn described the layout of the guest apartment within the miko's quarters and offered to go ashore specifically to make sure Madoc got to safety.

"Stay on the big canoe," Imala'ko advised him, looking past the white man's shoulder at the city shimmering in the hazy light. It was so peaceful, it was difficult to imagine any contention there.

"This is going to be quick," he concluded as he secured his knife and head-knocker on his waistband. "Be ready to leave this place very fast."

He counted thirty-five thatch temples within his sight as he and his men pulled their canoes up on the little beach below the great pyramid and walked the path.

There was nothing unusual about their arrival. They might be just one of many trade groups who came and went every day in the city's marketplace.

They passed through a break in the great wall, which had now been completed on this side of God's Hill. Four post holes had been dug in positions relative to the opening, which suggested that a baffled gate was going to be installed eventually that no doubt would restrict the easy access they now had to the pyramid. The work had obviously been done in haste. No stucco was smeared on the logs here, which had not even been shaved but were jammed together so that only a crack showed between them.

Imala'ko could see far in the distance beyond the pyramid's western face, gangs working amid a pall of dust to raise more logs into their close, upright position. That explained why the city was so empty—most of the common people were over there working on the wall, which the Chickasaw could not know the miko wanted finished for the Day of Equals.

He was wondering how soon those labor crews could swing into defensive action. Probably not in the time it would take to fire the temples, since most likely they would not be armed or trained to fight.

His men fanned out, each two or three picking a pyramid with its crown of flammable temple. Finding flame would be no problem—smoke curled from vents in every one of the structures, where perpetual fires were kept burning by the old men in service to the miko.

The long noon was a traditional time for labor to cease so people could take their midday meal. So far, not one male had noticed the invaders walking in various directions toward the targets.

Two young women carrying baskets upon their heads flirted with Imala'ko from under their lashes, so he thought he must not look so unattractively hungry as before.

He climbed the great stair with his shadow moving close to his feet; the sun was at its highest point of the day. Far below to the west, the wall crews were coming to a halt in the work, pulling out baskets and sitting down in groups to take lunch.

To the south he saw the Little Mountain of a Thousand Souls with its raw, long grave against the bright spring grass, but did not yet know what it was for.

He crossed the wide plaza that led to the big temple, still unchallenged, even unnoticed, though here were more black-robes moving about on their own business.

Only one man occupied the court outside the hall. Buffalo

Eagle in rags, soot on his face as a sign of mourning, sat on a wide painted buffalo robe in a stoic posture of immense patience and meditation.

For a moment the Chickasaw hesitated, thinking that he should kill the bonesetter immediately before he sounded the alarm. But the old man's squinted gaze caught him, and Imala'ko remembered the woman who had died in the pit.

What was he doing sitting out here in the bright sun in an attitude of a beggar in the miko's courtyard?

Buffalo Eagle regarded the Chickasaw warrior, who was obviously up to no good armed and painted for battle. The old man straightened, coming out of his meditation to watch the warrior standing before him.

Imala'ko saw that the bonesetter was ritually petitioning the miko by the array of feathers and an unlit smoking pipe before him on the clipped buffalo fleece.

No word passed between the old warrior and the youth, but presently Buffalo Eagle nodded as if to say go about whatever it is that you are doing.

Still alert for trouble, Imala'ko moved past him toward the meeting chamber. Under different circumstances he would have stopped to tell the chief what he knew and ask more about the situation here. Whatever was happening, Imala'ko knew that Buffalo Eagle was making a ritual spectacle of himself sitting out here awaiting the miko's pleasure. It must mean great loss of face for the bonesetter, which would explain his lack of response to Imala'ko's suspicious presence.

Wondering about these portents, the Chickasaw entered the gloom, making immediately for Madoc's quarters, which he found empty. He did not want to fire the building until he had located Weather Eyes, however, so he wandered through the dim hallways, stepping out of sight when a priest approached. He was able to knock that one out and take his black robe as a disguise. Hanging from the unconscious priest's belt was a pottery vial that contained black face paint, which Imala'ko smeared on liberally. His own clan tattoos would give him away as a fake if anyone looked too closely, but the way he wore his hair was enough like the chopped hanks of the black-robes to disguise him.

He bound the naked priest, gagged him with his own breechclout, then continued on reconnaissance in the priestly disguise.

He came upon an alcove where several old women were sitting in a sewing circle and did not know it was the miko's sister Burning Rose who inquired archly why he was threatening the peace of the lord's brides.

Imala'ko saw four young women sleeping on pallets to one side.

"Excuse me," he said, and ducked out before the old woman got a close look at him.

It was odd that four young women would be sleeping in broad daylight under such a watch, especially when he recognized one of the sleepers as Lady Tumbling Water beneath her star-robe. Thinking about how to get her out of the temple before setting it afire, he returned to his comrades, who, after jumping the two fire-tenders, had hacked out sections of inner walls to make torches. Each of the eight men took up two rods, plunged them into the sacred fire, and used the brands to torch the walls and hanging swags of cane.

In fairly quick time the seasoned thatch was aflame at several points in the great chamber.

Smoke filled the lonesome halls. Far off he could hear someone shouting the alarm, but as he looked at his handiwork, he knew it was already too late. The temple would be a roaring inferno in a few minutes.

Carrying the torch as he made his way back to the women's alcove, he continued igniting rooms on the run.

A screaming clutch of schoolboys in breechclouts ran in the opposite direction, breaking around him like a living stream.

Fire had not yet spread to this side of the building, but he saw his friends remedying that with their torches.

Thick yellowish smoke rolled down the hallway, obscuring landmarks so that he was momentarily confused. Soon, however, he swung into the room of sleeping maidens, knowing now that they were being readied for their funeral weddings tomorrow, when they would be laid asleep forever and covered with earth in the trench dug down in the Little Mountain of a Thousand Souls.

"Get out, get out," he screamed to the hysterical old women, who clutched their sewing and crowded each other blocking the single exit, where smoke was curling around their feet and oozing through wall cracks.

He pushed through them to the four pallets where the slumbering princesses were not disturbed by noise or smoke and would no doubt stay within their drug-induced naps until they burned.

He tried to rouse them, but it appeared impossible.

"Help me save our lord's brides!" he ordered the old women, as he began to drag the pallet on which Tumkis reposed through the door. He was forced to elbow his way through the women, but a couple of them saw what he was doing and composed themselves enough to grab the ends of the other pallets to pull the sleepers outside.

Flames flickered in the hallway, which had an outside wall.

Imala'ko hacked through to smoky sunlight, hauling the pallet through the opening. He pulled until he had her far enough away so that the wall would not collapse upon her when it came crashing down.

People, mostly black-robes, were boiling out of the building through the few doorways, or tearing through the thatch where there was no mud stucco. Imala'ko saw the rest of the invaders wandering around the plaza, looking in vain for someone to fight. They would be disappointed, the Chickasaw thought. There would be very few battle trophies from this odd action.

He saw at least a dozen priests running screaming from the inferno, some with robes aflame and rolling to put them out, but still nobody acted as a defender of the citadel.

It was too easy. He did not even bother to attack any of these cowardly wretches trying to save their own skins, but the Shawnee did not share his scruple and fell upon the black-robes with terrible war cries and left them dead on the ground.

Imala'ko dashed back inside, where flames licked the gaping hole he had cut in the wall to help the women drag out the other sleepers.

"Your robe, sir!" Burning Rose screamed, and he saw that the hem of his stolen garment was stitched with flames.

He stamped at it, not wishing to reveal his clan tattoos underneath, which would give him away.

The girls were rousing somewhat from the wild slides through the burning building. Two were still lying down, blinking in the thick sunlight. One of the brides was sitting on her pallet yawning, squinting in the glare even as they yanked her out so close to the flames that her pallet caught fire.

She jumped off soon enough and sat there crying while the pallet went up in flames in a stench of roasting duck down.

The robe he wore still smoldering, Imala'ko circled the building now completely engulfed by flames roaring above the pointed roofs.

Satisfied he was alone, Imala'ko finally shucked the evil-smelling robe made of well-worn supple leather, which was not as flammable as cloth but still smoldered with fire he had failed to stamp out.

Free of its stinking folds, and to get out of the smoke bending in this direction on the prevailing westerly, he circled the long building on its east and south side. People were still running from the inferno, stumbling in their haste, bumping him, who was moving more casually looking to encounter someone bearing resemblance to a warrior so he could engage and get at least one war trophy.

None of the fleeing black-robes was a suitable foe, because none seemed to be armed. None of them even appeared to see him despite the fact that his Chickasaw insignia were now revealed, the blue metal knife Snorrison gave him was in his right hand, and his big ugly crystal-inlaid head-knocker was in full view resting upon his other shoulder.

He was dressed in the traditional Chickasaw uniform of battle—almost naked but for his many tattoos and a simple breechclout.

Wandering around, lusting for combat without finding any comers, he despaired that he would not collect one scalp for this day's work.

Then he saw a tall black-robe whose tonsure looked familiar. The fellow was walking backwards toward Imala'ko, watching the building explode and collapse in on itself, so he was not aware of Imala'ko until the Chickasaw said, "Beautiful, is it not?"

Panther the high priest whirled on the Chickasaw, surprised only for a moment that he recognized him, a man he had thrown into a pit to starve to death.

Imala'ko was pleased to see the high priest was armed with a huge flint ax. The black weapon had a splash of blood upon its edge—he had challenged someone, and from the look of it, at least one of the invaders was a casualty.

Imala'ko dropped his own head-knocker, as splendid a weapon as it was, choosing to fight instead with the lightweight steel blade.

Dropping into attack position, the high priest snarled at

Imala'ko, circling the more agile warrior, who was young enough to be Panther's grandson and was dressed for combat, while the priest stumbled in his long robe.

But Panther was lean and tough despite his sixty-odd seasons, and it was with great strength and agility that he swung the dire weapon. It whooshed past the Chickasaw's head, missing by a hair.

Imala'ko got a close look at that blade and realized it must be the infamous heart ax carved from a single block of black flint.

"Is that the blade you were going to use on my heart, dog?"

The high priest did not waste time on dialogue but took another near swipe at the Chickasaw's chest, where he would have cut if this were heart sacrifice. But Imala'ko was too quick for the older man, whatever good shape he might be in.

He caught the priest from behind as Panther followed through with the momentum of the swing, and together they rolled over on the clay surface of the plaza.

Imala'ko had decided that he must have that ax as his trophy.

Panther was as determined to keep it, as he rolled out of reach and got to his feet to turn on Imala'ko, drawing first blood on the Chickasaw's upper-arm tattoo bands. The sight of his own blood infuriated Imala'ko, who decided to stop playing and make short work of the sorcerer.

He deftly feinted with his steel blade, nicking a spark from the ax in another swipe at his abdomen.

He came up with the knife reaching into folds of the black-robe, slitting it, but missing the high priest's flesh inside the huge, loose garment.

Panther twisted from harm's way, coming out of his split cassock like a mussel popped out of the shell, stark naked and pale where he had been hiding for so many years.

A few onlookers, unhurt and not presently threatened by flames, stopped to watch at the two men squared off and began in earnest their hand-to-hand combat.

Panther was good with that deadly blade and more agile shucked of his clothes, but Imala'ko was younger and quicker. With a well-placed dropkick, he relieved Panther of the ceremonial ax, hitting his neck with a hardened moccasin at the same time, staggering him backwards. But Panther did not fall, only stumbled back gasping for air.

Imala'ko grabbed the terrible black ax and let it fly.

Chapter 28

The blade whirled, catching the high priest's left temple, neatly slicing off three hanks of hair and his left ear.

Panther seemed not to have noticed. His head was thrown back, still gasping for breath knocked out of him by Imala'ko's kick. He saw the sky that did not seem so far above him. The blow staggered him. Still he did not fall but stared upwards, mouth working to gasp for air as that side of his head turned crimson.

Imala'ko had but to walk up behind him and put his knife up under the priest's heaving ribs, scoring a direct cut to the heart.

Still staring upwards, Panther sighed and fell to his knees before Imala'ko in the same position the child had knelt before him not so long ago.

Imala'ko did not notice a first, but Wyn was watching among the onlookers, holding the hand of Five-Tens-and-Two, the one who could appreciate the irony of Panther's ending up in a kneeling position. He stared down as his teacher fell back over his own legs, and in falling, slid off the blue metal blade. The Chickasaw stepped back.

The boy had a look of unreadable surprise on his face as he stared down at the heart-blood spurting in rhythmic jerks from the open chest of the high priest bent over backwards, as though upon his own altar.

Panther stared upwards into the second vision of his lifetime somewhere in the blueness of the sky behind the thick coils of smoke. His eyes did not close, and his mouth was working. Thinking to catch some final magic, Imala'ko could not resist bending to hear the high priest's last words, repeated over and over, "Blood of the sun," until the light faded as his life juice puddled around him.

432

Wyn expected the boy to cheer. Though he dreaded further proof of corruption in him, the abbot was thinking that the lad might have the right to enjoy watching this man die.

But instead of that reaction, Five-Tens-and-Two just buried his face in Wyn's robe and sobbed with relief.

His mother, standing amid the onlookers, took up his other hand.

"You and the boy may come with us," Wyn offered, touched by her situation. What would happen to them now that their protector was gone?

The red woman stared at the Christian priest for a long moment, then shook her head. "No," she said. "We will go back to my mother's people—it is not far, just a short walk to the big river. We will be safe there."

She drew Five-Tens-and-Two to her and led him away without looking back, while Wyn watched along with everyone else as the high priest stopped twitching.

When the abbot turned to speak with one of the invaders, he saw watching the inferno of the blazing temple the old bonesetter, Buffalo Eagle, with a grimace on his leathery face.

"I am sorry we have destroyed your miko's holy place," Wyn said as he joined him.

The old man tore his gaze from the fire and regarded the foreign sachem dressed in the garb of a temple priest. Not for a minute would this puny disguise fool anyone; in fact, the sight of the outlander in sagging black leather and feathers turned the elder's grimace into a strange grin.

"So," Wyn concluded in halting Muskogean and handsign, "it was your woman in the pit."

Buffalo Eagle's laugh died as he looked away, his eyes glimmering in the light of the fire. "You have done us a great service, Father Folded Hands," the red man said, regarding the white man with no trace of the grim laughter. "That one has abused my people too long."

"What does he say?" Wyn asked Imala'ko, who was wiping blood from the great stone ax while other red warriors gathered around him admiring the monolithic weapon and congratulating the Chickasaw on his kill.

"We thank you for what you have done this day," Buffalo Eagle said to Imala'ko, who translated as the old man continued. "Tell him also that we honor great warriors here. I invite your chief to join me in the council meeting." He made an expansive gesture that included those of the invaders who had stopped to listen. "You are all welcome to bring your households to this place and join our nation."

Imala'ko dutifully passed on this invitation, while some of the white people and their red allies gathered around to discuss the chief's offer.

"Thank him and say that we will consider his invitation," Wyn said.

Buffalo Eagle nodded and moved off with some of the younger Oldtown warriors, who excitedly addressed the bonesetter as their chief. These were the men who had been conscripted to build the log wall through their own houses. Wyn was fascinated to see that they were urging a huge feathered headdress upon the old man's forehead. He seemed to be protesting, but the warriors insisted upon installing the bonnet on his brow.

But too much was going on for Wyn to follow what they were saying to Buffalo Eagle as more of the invaders gathered in the plaza of the main temple rendered into a solid wall of flame. There was very little blood on anyone, but several had singed or burned clothing, and everybody had a sooty face.

"Where is Weather Eyes?" David Iron asked.

"He missed all the fun," Snorrison answered, pulling at his helmet. He was one of the bloodied few, cut not by a weapon but by the temple flange of his own headgear.

"Good to see you boys at last," Wyn said to a new group approaching across the wide plaza. Laughing Dog and his brother joined the white men and their allies out under the smoke-filled sky.

It was less than two hours since they had begun their invasion of Ixtulan. It seemed to be over too quickly.

All around them the tops of temple pyramids were aflame with long black snake coils of smoke rising into the sky, while down on the ground-level plaza, Oldtowners and Fifth Villagers were beginning a round dance of victory that had belonged to their great, great grandfathers ·here before anyone else, including the miko's illustrious ancestors from the south.

"Having trouble with your helmet, Snorrison?" Wyn asked, able to see clearly that he was.

"The damn thing will not come off," the Norseman snarled, trying to pry the two sides of it apart.

"How were you hit without crushing your head?"

"Hard-headed Icelander," commented Dag, cleaning his knife on his tunic, and in a sour mood because the miko's slinking warrior-priests had all vanished, cheating him of more blood sport.

The center roof beam of the big temple bent behind them and collapsed in a boiling wash of flame that shot sparks far up into the blue.

"One of the bastards hit me from behind, first left then right with a black ax. Almost knocked me out so that I missed the son of a bitch, and he ran off before I could kiss him." He still held the Kisser, as clean as though it just came from the grinding wheel.

Imala'ko displayed the high priest's weapon.

"That is the weapon," Snorrison growled at it as though the monolithic ax were alive.

"Where is Madoc?" Wyn asked, looking around at the members of the Hundred seeking this center amid the boiling columns of smoke.

"Nobody has seen him," replied Ari, walking up from the lower level of the mound with two others of their party.

"Well, blacksmith, are you or are you not going to help me get out of this thing?"

Wyn regarded the big Norseman struggling to remove the helmet, while Dag tried to lend a hand.

"Watch the ear there."

"Tight as a monk's arse," Dag said for Wyn's benefit.

"Well?" Snorrison said to Wyn, ignoring the insult and the plea.

"Well, what?"

"What do you want, then?"

"Oh, you mean, what do I want to remove that bucket from your head?" Wyn peered at it from all angles. "I have removed several helmets under these circumstances, for Owen's army," he said to Dag. "See how the left ear might have to go?"

"Stop jesting, churchman."

"Perhaps in time it will just rust away." Wyn gave the helmet a stout knuckle rap.

"Odin's balls, man, what will it take to get you to cut this blasted thing off my head?"

"I am no surgeon."

Snorrison grabbed him up by the collar and growled into his face, "Name your price."

"Very well, Snorrison. My price is your soul."

"Eh?"

"Take Jesus as your lord and savior, and I will get that thing off you."

"Conniving priest!"

Someone called on the run from the direction of the stair, a small woman in a ruined white suede dress and a star-robe clutched around her shoulders. "Come, help," Tumkis cried, wind flinging her hair as she grabbed Wyn's cassock and pulled him in the direction she had come. "Weather Eyes, Weather Eyes is going to burn up!"

They ran as a group down the stairs to the third level.

"Where is he?" Imala'ko asked, and she pointed toward the prison building whose roof was just now catching flames.

"Just before he made me drink the black drink, the high priest bragged that he had made sure Weather Eyes would never return to the big canoe," Tumkis cried, coughing, but continuing to run toward the place. "I cannot loosen the trap—hurry, this way!"

Imala'ko and Wyn both realized where Madoc had to be. With Fair Beard and Dag close behind, they sprinted past the others to get inside and raise the cane grid before the entire building was consumed.

"So once again I must save your hairy hide," Fair Beard yelled down into the pit below.

Madoc had pulled himself up and was hanging onto the grid while burning debris rained down upon him. He tore at the latticework with little success and ten bloody fingers for his trouble.

Fair Beard looked up to see that the roof was going to come crashing down before Madoc got free.

"Just stand there, Snorrison," Madoc cracked as he dropped from the grid to the pit floor. "We have all day."

"How did you get into this mess?" Snorrison inquired, kneeling above the pit.

Imala'ko had the secret of how the complicated grid was secured over the hole, which had been repaired of the damage done to its wall. Three other men, all laborers of Ixtulan, were also trying to claw their way out of the pit. The Chickasaw unhitched the canework and with Snorrison's help pulled it back.

Fair Beard knelt and offered his old friend a hand up, while the other prisoners screamed for help and tried to climb the slightly concave sides, falling back unsuccessfully until Imala'ko bent to help them.

"They jumped me from behind," Madoc growled, hands red-slick so that Fair Beard had difficulty getting a grip until they grasped each other's wrists.

"You look terrible," Snorrison remarked.

Madoc had a blue chin of several day's beard, and his hair and mustaches were dusty and unkempt. Already after five days with almost no food, he was hollow-cheeked, wild-eyed, and weakened, but with Snorrison's help scrambled out as an entire section of wall behind them fell inward in a firestorm.

The freed prisoners and their rescuers sprinted from the flames, making it to the outside just as the structure collapsed.

Tumkis ran to Madoc as he staggered through the smoke. They held onto each other, speaking words only they could hear.

"Please, please forgive me, Weather Eyes."

"Forgive me for leaving you."

Beyond the reach of fire, Wyn, Dag, and several others, including David Iron, stood watching the man and woman until the wind shipped the smoke in that direction, forcing everyone to move farther westward.

Madoc walked with his arm around Tumkis toward David Iron, who congratulated him on being a grandfather.

"How is she?"

"Proud to be the mother of a fine son."

They reached the western verge just in time to see an amazing spectacle across the way on several lower pyramids. On the nearest Buffalo Eagle, clearly visible in the bright feathers, stood with his arms upraised in the direction of the sun as though speaking with The One Who Breathes Above. He called in an echoing voice a chant of thanksgiving, joined by many of the people swarming around him. Their single voice swelled into a hymn as the young men hacked at the walls of the miko's warehouse behind the praying chief.

As the Hundred watched from their vantage point on the stairway of God's Hill, a trickle, then a growing gold river of corn began to pour from the ruptured wall.

The tumbling kernels made a noise at first that sounded like rain, then swelled into something not unlike water over stones. The sound and the people's chant blended into one rumbling song as more holes were hacked into the storage bins.

Before long, corn in huge baskets and loose deluge was raining down the sides of each of the mounds, the miko's golden treasury flowing like nuggets of honey to be caught by the people waiting below with baskets and jugs. This was not meal or cracked corn, but the whole living kernels of seedcorn, the heart of miko's treasury. It was thousands of cornfields, the grandmother of corn that would be grown throughout the region for years to come.

Below, the people cheered as they harvested their distribution at last.

But the golden flow was short-lived. The people swarmed over the pinnacles, scooping up the corn and hauling it back down the steps, and soon those buildings, too, empty of treasure, were blazing.

The Hundred remnant strolled as a group down the stair and onto the dock, where they shuttled out in Ixtulan canoes.

Yngvild was there, along with the Shawnee women, who were all supposed to have remained back in Paducah until the fighting was over.

"We wanted to see this great battle for ourselves," Yngvild said sarcastically.

"Some battle," her husband muttered, still trying to escape from his hat. "Damn you, priest," he snarled, his long face distorted by the crushed helmet. "You would hold me hostage in my own bucket."

"Have it as you will," Wyn said lightly, tugging at his backpack to set it more comfortably on his shoulders.

"Domme," Madoc said, "I see that you are a man ready to do some walking."

"I understand you will pull in at the mouth of the Ohio."

Before Madoc could comment on what he did not know, Rhys said he and Winnowed Rice wanted to go back to the Hundred's village in the Land Between Two Rivers.

"I suppose you will force Fair Beard to stay, too," Madoc said to Yngvild.

"Not at all, captain," the Norsewoman replied, "I intend to get my baby back."

"Bjorn is alive?" Madoc asked incredulously.

Yngvild gestured at Imala'ko. "With the Chickasaw."

Madoc handsigned, *You know about their child?*

"In my own mother's lodge," Imala'ko replied, tucking Panther's big black ax into his waistband.

Madoc remarked congratulations to Yngvild and turned to Rhys to ask him to stay aboard the *Horn*. "Now that I have my pilot, we may just keep on sailing when we get to the mouth of the Mech-a-sip-i."

His arm around Winnowed Rice, and with Cari in her cradleboard on his back, the poet shook his head. "I told you I would never go back to Britain."

"You will be sorely missed, old friend, but I will take you to the Ohio as you wish. Anyone else?"

Huw said to Madoc, "I am with you wherever you take this ship, captain."

"I am glad to have you, Huw," Madoc replied, and looked around the crew, most of whom had red women they were anxious to get back to. "Ari?"

The black man looked at Snorrison, who owned his decision. If Snorrison returned to Britain, this man would have to go, too.

The Norseman shrugged. "You are a free man, Ari Al Ghazal O'Daliagh."

"You release me?" Ari said, unbelieving. His family had been virtual slaves to one or the other Norseman for several generations.

"I release you, I release you, I release you," Fair Beard said in the legal thrice-spoken formula of manumission.

Ari drew himself up with new pride, accepting the gift with a nod. "Thank you, Fair Beard Snorrison, but I must return the favor by leaving your service if it means going back to those cold places."

Fair Beard shook his head. "A free man makes his own choices."

Ari stepped forward and shook Madoc's hand. "Sir, I want to go home, and home for me is now the Kantuck, where I left my wife and children."

"I am the Hundred's only priest," Brian said. "Besides, I love the Kantuck and hope to spend the rest of my life there, God willing."

One by one they spoke to Madoc, most deciding to stay, and a few others deciding to make the return trip.

"I will ride a ways downstream with you," said Wyn.

"Will you listen to reason and forestall this vow of yours in favor of these people here? They need you more than the crusaders in Jerusalem."

"The Hundred has Father Brian," he said. "They do not need me."

"As smith then."

"Andrew is good with the hammer."

Madoc saw that Wyn was really serious—he had given Andrew the big forge hammer and the little anvil he had been using on deck.

"At least take Brother Andrew along."

"He wishes to stay—ask him."

When the monk blushed and looked down at his feet in fine new moccasins, Madoc knew some woman had sewn them for him. The last of the clergy had succumbed to the charms of red women. Only Wyn remained alive and chaste.

"Besides, Brother Paul is going to Jerusalem with me," Wyn said, and Laughing Dog nodded beside him.

"This is all very touching, but what about my head?" Fair Beard demanded.

"Do you accept Jesus Christ?" Wyn asked again.

"Damn you, double damn you, priest—I hope you find your Infidels over there—" Fair Beard said as he tried one last time to pry the temples of the helmet from his bloody face. But the metal held its crush, pinching him further, and drew a borrowed Natchez curse from his lips, "—and I hope they cut out your bleeding heart."

Wyn shrugged.

"Wait!" Yngvild called, striding over the boards with Hannah on her shoulder. "I will convert for both of us. Will that do?"

Wyn paused and gave her serious regard. "It can do for you and the babe if Father Brian baptizes you as soon as possible. But not for this man's lost soul lest it be voluntary."

"But if I give you two souls, mine and Hannah's, you will get the helmet off my husband's head?"

"I thought you hated Christianity even more than he does, madam."

"Do we have a bargain or not?" Yngvild insisted.

Wyn, not wanting to lose two sure souls for one as chancy as Fair Beard, nodded yes and crossed himself. Andrew and Brian shouted hearty amens, while Wyn called for the ship's crowbar and a wooden vise.

"Watch the ear!" Fair Beard said when Dag found the crow-bar in a leather tool bag.

"I have done this before, Snorrison, and have not lost a patient, or an ear yet."

And there on the deck in sunlight behind shimmering veils of brown smoke, Wyn took his own sweet time prying the helmet off Fair Beard's heathen head while praising God in the highest voice for the gift of two souls added to the faithful.

Brian hastily put together a little ceremony right there, lest Yngvild change her mind once her husband was no longer hostage to the helmet. He grabbed the crew's water bag to baptize Yngvild and Hannah, who already had a suitable name for a Christian girl. But the heathen name Yngvild would hardly do.

"What do you want your Christian name to be, daughter?" Father Brian inquired.

"I do not know any Christian names."

"How about Brigit?" Brian said, thinking of how, when she nursed two babies, the Norsewoman had looked so much like the Celtic earth goddess who was transformed into a Christian saint.

Yngvild had no objection. She only wanted the smith to hurry and free Snorrison scowling under his metal lid. So it was Brigit, though nobody but Brian would ever call her that name. Madoc was sure Wyn took longer than necessary to decant the Icelander, who whooped for joy when his head was free, throwing the distorted hat up into the air and letting it clang somewhere out on deck beyond his caring.

"At least let us ferry you across the river, Domme," Madoc offered, and Wyn thought that was a pretty good idea.

"I was working on how we might ford it, sir—quite a river eh?"

"The biggest I have ever seen, a ribbon of ocean."

They could easily make the mouth of the Ohio before nightfall, but Wyn had changed his mind about sailing south. "I want to go west as soon as possible—may we disembark at the mouth of Sky Blood Creek?"

Madoc said he would accommodate the abbot. "Are we all accounted for?" he inquired, clapping his hands together in an impatient gesture that announced his readiness to depart. While everyone was counting heads, they were all surprised to hear someone calling from the water where their many allies in various canoes were preparing to depart.

"Permission, permission," the voice called again.

They peered over the starboard rail to see whom of their party they had missed.

Treading water below was a middle-aged man of Ixtulan who looked like a laborer.

Madoc took a good, hard look at him.

"Permission?" the red man called up, using the word he had heard the sailors use.

"Who is it who wants to board?"

"I need a home—mine has been burned, you see," the man continued in Muskogean.

"My God," Madoc whispered.

"Chief Turtle-in-the-Sun!" Tumkis exclaimed in disbelief.

"No," the red man corrected with a glance toward the smoldering city. "The miko is dead."

"Then who are you?"

"I am Sunning Turtle," he replied. As the swimmer continued to tread water, there could be seen something in his hand that Madoc could not immediately identify.

"I am good with my hands," the man in the water continued, "and I can entertain with dance. I know many old stories and songs, I read the sun and stars, and I am a good climber. I will be crew."

The red man used the Cymraeg word *criw*—overhead the first time he rode this ship—as he pulled onto his wide head a rough woolen cap that matched caps worn by the sailors.

Madoc caught Fair Beard's eye. The Norseman shrugged. "Can always use good crew, captain."

Tumkis beside Madoc regarded the petitioner down below. "What do you think, woman of power? Should I?"

"Do as you wish, Weather Eyes," she said, but her voice was excited and her eyes bright with *yes* when she turned to him.

"Yn y cwch," Madoc ordered in his own language, gesturing, *Come on into the boat.*

Sunning Turtle scrambled up the sidelines and grabbed Madoc's hand, which he shook vigorously until Madoc pried it loose. "You need me to go up?" the new crewman asked eagerly, gesturing at the mast.

Madoc was not ready to test his weakened leg by climbing, so he asked, "Snorrison, have you any objections?"

"I should say not—give me my pilot's bench anytime." And he took it.

"Take your station, sailor," Madoc said, stepping to one side to watch Sunning Turtle put his wet footprints on the deck as he made for the mast.

"Let us be out of here," Madoc called. "To oars!"

They socketed the oars, and amid hustle and passenger distribution, Madoc told Dag to hoist anchors.

Dag at the winch obeyed, and on Ari's beat they began slowly to descend Sky Blood Creek in the midst of a canoe armada that scooted ahead of the larger vessel.

Children ran along the shoreline beside the new orchard, where the little trees looked alone and abandoned in all that dirt. The children were joined by young women throwing flowers into the water, and an increasing number of young warriors who shouted victory cries between their hands.

As the *Horn* rounded the bend below the orchard, those on board saw a host of red people gathering at the water's edge, waving and calling out. Not a single black-robe was among them. But in the midst of the joyous throng was Buffalo Eagle in his wide, bright feather crown, and holding a tall lance adorned with eagle plumage. Around him stood other Old-town elders, who waved at the passing riders on the ship.

Buffalo Eagle raised the lance in a high salute, unmistakable homage to those on board.

"They are cheering us!" Madoc said.

"You freed them," Tumkis said, eyes shining in Madoc's direction.

"Their children's children's children will sing songs of this big canoe," said Imala'ko.

Everyone who was not working stood at the rail and waved back at the joyous people on shore, while the *Horn* found the Creek's midchannel current.

Dag sounded for depth, but the bottom remained consistent, so that shortly they were rounding the last bend of the smaller stream and making for the long sea of the Mech-a-sip-i.

Through tricky corrections of their sail, they made a wide circle and came to the little bay at the First Village, where they dropped temporary anchor. Many of the Shawnee and Yuchi had already made it back to the town, which was all but abandoned by the people who had gone to Ixtulan for the Day of Equals.

To the northeast the air was still thick with yellow smoke bent by the western breeze, but to the south and west the air was clean and inviting, dotted with pure white clouds.

Wyn and his assistant stood at the starboard rail gazing westward.

"Taprobane Isle is known to lie in the sea east of Cathay," Madoc said to Wyn, "so even if you cross whatever unimaginable land mass lies out there, you will most likely still have to get across some body of water."

"We shall solve all those problems as they arise," Wyn said confidently, shouldering his own personal hammer with his bundle tied on the head. He had seen the island of Ceylon on several maps in his monastery's library back home.

"Still," Madoc suggested, "perhaps you had better take a coracle."

Wyn was glad to accept the offer as Madoc cut loose one of the oblong craft. It splashed in the water below, its line playing out in Madoc's hand.

"Well, it is time," the abbot said, tearing his glance from the dazzling western horizon.

Madoc nodded. Despite his many differences with the stubborn monk, he loved him and was sorry he could not dissuade him from his crusade. "Good-bye, Domme," he said hoarsely.

"Go with God, my son."

Madoc thought as he bear-hugged his friend that Wyn's voice sounded as choked up as his own.

"This is yours," Wyn said, hefting the ragged satchel into Madoc's hands.

Even if he had not recognized the rattily tied bundle, the weight of it immediately told Madoc it was the map of gold.

"Take it back with you to prove to the Lord of Lundy Isle that we have truly gone around the world to another land—he will give you ships, I am sure, because of his respect for your father."

Madoc took the wonderful gift and could only tell him, "Domme, thank you."

The two crusaders turned to the rail, where Dag handed them both a paddle and shook their hands in good-bye.

David Iron was quick to embrace Wyn, who whispered a blessing in the Yuchi's ear and very lightly touched his head. One by one the people bade the abbot farewell. He muttered the blessing of the Trinity on them all and could not resist taking the opportunity of the moment to utter a quick prayer for guidance to all concerned.

Finally, everything said, he clambered over the side with Brother Paul close behind.

Madoc tossed them the line, and presently their little boat pulled out of the ship's shadow and, under their hearty pulls, made for the western shore.

Someone suggested they anchor here for the night to get something to eat, tend wounds, and get a good night's rest for the continued downstream journey to the mouth of the Ohio, where Rhys and the others of the Hundred would take coracles back home.

"No," Madoc replied, covering the emotion he keenly felt as Wyn's fragile round boat bobbed and curtsied in the great Mech-a-sip-i, growing smaller as it was forced by the current to cut an angle south and westward. "I want to keep moving."

Then, sure the coracle was well away from the bow, he called to his crew, "Are you ready to take this Uktena downstream?"

Everyone aboard cheered, and nobody looked back.

Not the red man up on the pinnacle. Despite his soft hands Sunning Turtle did not look much different from them, with their sunburned faces and squinting eyes, capped in woolen socks that let their hair flow braided behind them.

He was thinking about dying and going through the underworld to heaven, reborn like the sun after encroaching on the immense darkness, trembling at first and frightened, because even a sun must confront that thing much larger than himself—only something divine would attempt to shine in all that darkness, or to arrogantly count the little cycles of days. Like the triumphant sun at dawn, Sunning Turtle looked eagerly forward to his new life.

Everyone on board faced the wide, promising water ahead.

Madoc far forward, with his arm around Tumkis, never looked back but only ahead as was his bent, glad to be rid of that slow bog and the rigid, morbid pyramids that had seemed to him like lost ships becalmed on the ocean of flat land. He had always been able to see beyond the moment, through whatever present circumstances, to salt water, for which fine sail he hungered like a pup anticipating sweet milk, in his dreams of return to islands that smelled like home.

Fair Beard at his tiller used his eyes like axes to sweep the forward path of shimmering river with his glare, as though expecting to do battle with it at any moment. Free of the shallower stream, he was still suspicious of sandbars and lurking, ship-eating debris, sure in his gut that ancient wisdom was absolutely correct in depicting all rivers as snakes. He did not look back, either. It was not a snake's tail that was dangerous. With his wife's sure hand on his shoulder behind him, Fair Beard Snorrison could only look forward.

Yngvild saw her son in the fluffy southern clouds, at least saw baby faces with puffy cheeks. She cuddled Hannah and hummed a Norse lullaby to rock her to sleep.

The crew likewise must certainly be concentrating on what lay before them. Sailors were forced by immediate occupation to live in the present. What was behind was as done as the watch just finished, as gone as yesterday.

Imala'ko and the Yuchi warriors were full of the thrill of victory, and the honor of being associated with this great dragon ship, which gave life to their most sacred legends.

The red women aboard the *Horn* could not help but be drawn into the promise of that forward horizon tossing below the dragonhead prow.

Tumkis, with Madoc's arm around her, could only think of going home.

Winnowed Rice stood with Rhys at the starboard rail with the wind in their faces, witnessing the Great River Road to him.

Rhys listened to his wife's voice as the sail was moved about by the crew with their practical incantations. The wind batted his long braids streaked with white, the Welsh legacy he would pass down to generations of his red daughters and sons, who would be born with light skin, hair, and eyes among red people, and cause a mystery that may never be solved to the satisfaction of those curious storytellers who question such mysteries.

Given over to the benevolent current, the ship like a clean blade slipped through elements—water and air and light.

Rhys tried to imagine what lay ahead.

He was thinking that whatever happened, the river was indifferent to the puny human beings in their little boats as fragile as bubbles spun by water spiders, arrogant human beings to believe they could confront something so powerful as a river with something so vulnerable as a coracle or even a stout ship of British oak.

Rhys felt the wind on his face and knew in his heart that despite any invention man might throw upon it, the Mech-a-sip-i was and is and always will be triumphant.

Afterword

On the ancient banks of the Mississippi just east of Saint Louis you can still climb the ten stories of God's Hill and look out over the flat, verdant floodplain.

We call it Cahokia Mounds today, giving the ancient city the name of local red people who were there when the French arrived from Canada in the mid-1600s.

When it was built in A.D. 1050, the city of forty thousand red people lived around the pyramid as long as a football field. The city's name is forgotten, but the ruins include streets, plazas, docks, warehouses, suburbs, workshops, and the stumps of more than a hundred huge platform pyramids.*

In one of the lesser mounds was found the grave of a man surrounded by four other men who had been beheaded. Beyond were found the skeletons of fifty-two young women, who apparently laid themselves peacefully down in a trench to be covered with earth, where their neat bones were found more than eight hundred years later by archaeologists salvaging the site before highway construction.

Twenty thousand Gulf-coast shells were placed like a blanket under the central skeleton buried with rich grave goods, including hundreds of perfect unused arrow points made of Ozark chert, rolls of beaten Michigan copper, and a hoard of reflective mica imported from Virginia.

The basis for Cahokia's economy was corn, a hardy variety of which was recently introduced to North America from the south. In the city's prime it took thirty thousand pounds of corn *per day* to feed the population, and apparently much more was overproduced for trade. Pottery and shell ornaments

---

Scientific American, August, 1975.

447

show a long-nosed personage who bears resemblance to the Mezoamerican rain spirit Chac, whose priests were merchants bartering corn.

It has been only since the work of University of Wisconsin anthropologist Melvin Fowler in the 1970s that the full implications of the site's chronology have been available for discussion. Intruders into the region occupied small Woodland villages from A.D. 600 to 800. These early people built low burial mounds, but there is little evidence of temple-mound building until after the tenth century, when the old Woodland culture adopted what anthropologists call the Mississippian. The next century and a half saw intense construction, including the hundred-foot-high pyramid that to this day contains twenty-two million cubic feet of dirt piled up by the basketful. The big pyramid was the centerpiece in a 125-square-mile region that included more than fifty villages networked by river to outposts as far away as the Great Lakes, the Carolinas, and the Gulf coast.

Despite many similarities, the experts are reluctant to make a direct connection between this sudden Mississippian culture and the contemporaneous Central American Maya and Toltec cultures south of the Mississippi Delta across the Gulf of Mexico. The most the experts admit is cultural influence on local elites by foreign elites.

We know from excellent stone calendars that in the tenth century the society of Maya city-states was disintegrating. Nahuatl-speaking Toltecs from Mexico invaded Mayan territory—there is a splendid record in stone, gold, and wall paintings, and on objects recovered from hundreds of Central American sites including Chichen Itza, the Toltec name for the formerly Mayan city.

But the Toltecs were only late-coming opportunists, not the cause of the Mayan collapse, which has been discussed in every discipline; the consensus is that it was caused by the hauntingly familiar combination of overpopulation, ecological devastation, and social revolution, which exiled or killed off Mayan noble families, the cultural bearers of all literacy, mathematics, astronomy, and architecture equal to or superior to anything achieved in the Old World by the same time period.

The coincidence of dates—within one human lifetime around A.D. 1000 for both the Maya collapse and the construction of Cahokia's big pyramid—suggests to the storyteller a more specific relationship between the two zones than necessarily conservative scientists will allow: There was a moment in time when new ideas, dramatic variations on an old theme, arrived in Illinois, to become ancestor legend six generations later to the intruders' principal descendant at Cahokia, Chief Turtle-in-the-Sun, the antagonist in this story.

It is striking to see on a map that Cahokia lies directly north up the Mississippi and in line with the Pole Star from the major concentration of Yucatan pyramids. Many Mayan buildings, as well as the pyramids at Cahokia and hundreds of other Mississippian sites in the American southeast, are built to exacting specifications of orientation, which requires mathematics and celestial knowledge to plot. The city at Cahokia may have been the first of many Mississippian centers planted with specific orientations to the north and built to maximize architectural opportunities to view summer and winter solstice sunrises and sunsets five hundred years before Columbus in what is now the United States.

Other intriguing correspondences between the Mississippians and Mezoamericans include the repetition of the number fifty-two, which was important in the Venus cycle. As the Morning and Evening Star, Venus was an important object in Mayan astronomy/theology because it represented the godman Feathered Serpent, a cultural hero who is closely associated with the Lord Sun and the four persons of Chac. And every fifty-two years the two Mayan calendars coincided and began a new cycle.

Then there are eccentric flint creations found at Mezoamerican sites that bear striking resemblance to similar ones found throughout the Tennessee and Mississippi valleys. Many other art objects in shell and beaten copper echo Mayan and Toltec motifs, including long-nosed figures with distinctive features such as clothing, dance regalia, jewelry, headgear, animal masks, and artificially sloped foreheads.

First-contact journals reveal customs among Mississippian descendants that were similar to Mezoamerican styles, including cradleboard deformation of noble children's heads, sophisticated trade networking, worship of nobility associated with the sun, human sacrifice and self-mutilation, ritualized ball games, building methods, a skull cult, maize cultivation, and a hierarchical social system rather than democratic, which reflects agriculture rather than nomadic hunting as the primary economic activity.

It is also interesting that Maya lords were called Mah K'ina, while Muskogeans who inherited the Mississippian culture called their chiefs *miko*. There are other linguistic similarities, as well as correspondences in legends and mythologies.

Both cultures practiced a highly ceremonial religion augmented by priestly manipulation, music, theatrical illusion with mirrors, group hypnotism and hallucinogenic substances, and autosacrifice to produce visions that evoked powerful mythology. This ethnic information comes primarily from French/Natchez confrontation in the late seventeenth century—the city at Cahokia was an uninhabited ruin by the time of European incursion. In the 1600s the exploring partnerships first of Marquette and Joliet, and later La Salle and de Tonti, missed the tree-covered big pyramid altogether, even though they canoed directly past it coming and going.

The city at Cahokia reached its apogee sometime just before A.D. 1200 and for unknown reasons just faded out after that. The crisis could have been climatic, since all over the northern hemisphere it was getting colder. That was why the Scandinavians had to abandon their Greenland and Iceland colonies and why the northwestern route to Vinland was closed to them as it would have been to Madoc after the middle of the twelfth century.

From about A.D. 1000 through the early 1300s the city (and hundreds of other pyramid centers along the Mississippi) were prominantly in the path of anyone traveling on the Great River Road. Sometime after 1150, the city's rulers ordered a hastily built stockade that used more than fifteen thousand trees the size of telephone poles, but it is not clear what they were defending against. Perhaps invaders, or perhaps their own people barred from the central complex that surrounds the great pyramid. Whatever the reasons, there is intriguing archaeological material that could mean the downfall of Cahokia was violent and preceded by popular unrest.

"In some places," says Fowler, "houses were abandoned with everything in them, pottery and flint artifacts left in place. You get the feeling that people had been living in the houses until just before the demolition work started, that they were there and then suddenly they weren't."

This is an intriguingly specific thing for an archaeologist to say, something a storyteller cannot ignore, a piece of physical information that helped me reconstruct the city that Madoc might have visited.

British tradition specifically dates Madoc ab Gwynedd's first western journey in the fall of 1170. The pertinent Cherokee legend through Tennessee's first governor John Sevier relates how several generations back that nation fought light-skinned people called Welsh at Muscle Shoals and drove them north on the Tennessee River, which communicates via the Ohio with the Mississippi and the Upper Missouri, where the artist George Catlin was sure he found Madoc's Mandan descendants in 1836. If there is truth to the Madoc legend, then he might have encountered the city in its heyday on the Mississippi River located just below the confluence with the Missouri.

These are the lines of correspondence that inspire and inform this series of novels.

For clarity I have used modern spellings that are derived from pre-Columbian languages. The Ohio we know today was known as the Oyo, or great water, to the people who lived there before Europeans. What we called the Cumberland River was some variation of Shawnee, the people who lived along its banks. Various river reclamation projects have created lakes out of the Cumberland and the Tennessee, so what this story and earlier people called the Land Between Two Rivers is now an outdoor playground called the Land Between the Lakes. The vast western region of Kentucky is still called Pennyroyal because of the abundance of wild mint growing there. Muscle Shoals was named at a time when mussels thrived and spelling was looser than today. The misnomer stuck—some old-timers said that was what the Indians called it when white settlers arrived in the early 1700s.

Tradition says Madoc made two trips over the Western Ocean. In the third book in the saga, *Songs of the Big Canoe*, Rhys leads the Hundred westward up the Missouri, where legend says their descendants became the Mandan Indians, while Madoc returns to his homeland to gather a second colony and take a little cold revenge.

PAT WINTER
The Ozarks

From a nation born of strife and christened with patriots' blood, there arose a dynasty of soldiers. They were the McQueens of America -- a clan hungry for adventure; a family whose fiery spirit would kindle the flame of a country's freedom. Keeping that flame from blazing into tyranny through the generations would take more than merely courage and determination. It would take a sacred secret: the proud legacy they called THE MEDAL.

THE MEDAL BOOK ONE: GUNS OF LIBERTY

by Kerry Newcomb

The British called it a bargain. But for Dan McQueen it was a deal made with the devil. To save his own father from the gallows, he must murder the one man fated to lead a new nation against its mother country -- General George Washington. First McQueen engages in a ruse to gain the trust of beautiful innkeeper Kate Bufkin, whose inn is the very spot where Washington will stop on the road to Philadelphia. But as the deception deepens so do other things: kinship with a brave band of patriots...and unexpected passion for a headstrong young woman.

The author of **In the Season of the Sun** and **Scalpdancers** begins with this book a multigenerational saga that will span the history of America, as seen through the lives of one family.

On sale in January wherever Bantam Domain Books are sold.

AN210 -- 2/91

TERRY C. JOHNSTON

Winner of the prestigious Western Writer's award, Terry C. Johnston brings you his award-winning saga of mountain men Josiah Paddock and Titus Bass who strive together to meet the challenges of the western wilderness in the 1830's.

☐ 25572 **CARRY THE WIND–Vol. I** $4.95

☐ 26224 **BORDERLORDS–Vol. II** $4.95

☐ 28139 **ONE-EYED DREAM–Vol. III** $4.95

The final volume in the trilogy begun with *Carry the Wind* and *Borderlords*, ONE-EYED DREAM is a rich, textured tale of an 1830's trapper and his protegé, told at the height of the American fur trade.

Following a harrowing pursuit by vengeful Arapaho warriors, mountain man Titus "Scratch" Bass and his apprentice Josiah Paddock must travel south to old Taos. But their journey is cut short when they learn they must return to St. Louis...and old enemies.

Look for these books wherever Bantam books are sold, or use this handy coupon for ordering: